Double, Double, Paws, and Trouble . . .

I looked at the cat. The cat looked at me. We both blinked.

"Shoo?" I suggested.

The gray cat yawned, displaying a curling pink tongue and a whole lot of very white teeth.

I folded my arms. "All right. What do you want?"

The cat blinked his (her?) slanting blue eyes at me again. It looked uncomfortably like he/she was waiting for me to say something sensible.

"Okay. We're gonna do this the hard way."

I lunged forward as if to make a grab. With a rolling growl of feline contempt, the cat flowed away from my hands. Victory! Or so I thought, until I realized the cat was now pressed against the pavement, under the Jeep, and right beside my front tire.

I swore. The cat hugged asphalt and put his/her ears back.

"Hey. Everything okay out here?" called a man's voice from behind me.

It was Sean the bartender. He was strolling out from the Pale Ale, wiping his hands on a side towel.

I sighed and sat back on my heels. "I seem to have a cat."

Berkley Prime Crime titles by Delia James

A FAMILIAR TAIL
BY FAMILIAR MEANS
FAMILIAR MOTIVES

A Familiar Tail

A Witch's Cat Mystery

DELIA JAMES

BERKLEY PRIME CRIME
New York

BERKLEY PRIME CRIME
Published by Berkley
An imprint of Penguin Random House LLC
375 Hudson Street, New York, New York 10014

Copyright © 2016 by Penguin Random House LLC
Penguin Random House supports copyright. Copyright fuels creativity, encourages
diverse voices, promotes free speech, and creates a vibrant culture. Thank you for buying
an authorized edition of this book and for complying with copyright laws by not
reproducing, scanning, or distributing any part of it in any form without permission.
You are supporting writers and allowing Penguin Random House to continue to
publish books for every reader.

BERKLEY is a registered trademark and BERKLEY PRIME CRIME and the B colophon
are trademarks of Penguin Random House LLC.

ISBN: 9780451476579

First Edition: February 2016

Printed in the United States of America
5 7 9 11 13 12 10 8 6

To my feline inspirations:
Buttercup, Isis, Kuzbean and most of all,
Buffy the Vermin Slayer

Acknowledgments

No piece of work is written in a vacuum. I'd like to thank my fabulous editor and my equally fabulous agent, as well as the people, cats and city of Portsmouth, New Hampshire, who inspired these mysteries. As always, I need to thank my husband, who has supported me in so many ways through the writing process, and the fabulous members of the Untitled Writer's Group who, as always, offered honest and firm advice about the writing. Thank you all.

1

❧ I WANT TO be really clear about a few things. I don't chase after stray cats, I don't break into houses and I most definitely do not steal valuable antiques from dead people.

At least, I didn't used to.

My name is Annabelle Amelia Blessingsound Britton. My well-meaning parents settled this bit of nom de overkill on me at the request of my grandmother Annabelle Mercy Blessingsound Britton back when she declared that her dying wish was to have a namesake granddaughter. I was already on the way, and it was only after they filled out the birth certificate that my folks realized Grandma B.B. wasn't departing this vale of tears anytime soon. Or ever.

Some other pertinent facts and figures about yours truly:
Age: 35.
Profession: Freelance artist and illustrator.
Relationship Status: Emphatically single.
Height: Short.
Weight: Seriously?
Skin: Exceptionally pale, except when burned lobster red.

Eyes: Goldy-browny-amberish, kinda.

Hair: Medium brown, shoulder length, with either too much curl or not enough, depending on the day.

Location: On the road with most of what I owned crammed into two jumbo-sized red suitcases tossed in the back of my Jeep Wrangler, heading up I-95 from Boston to the quaint seacoast town of Portsmouth, New Hampshire, for a couple of weeks to visit my best friend, Martine.

Technically, it's about an hour from Boston to Portsmouth, but thanks to a pileup on the interstate, it was already going on four o'clock when I eased my Wrangler off I-95 and past the car dealerships and motels that clustered near the Route 1 roundabout. The two-lane highway snaked under a railroad bridge and bent to the left, becoming Lennox Avenue, and just like that, the scenery ceased to look like an off-ramp town and became beautiful New England.

I followed shady twists and turns past old homes that ranged from stately to eclectic. Another turn, and the homes gave way to converted brick warehouses lining the banks of the Piscataqua River. I put the windows down and breathed in the late-June air filled with freshwater, seaweed and a hint of diesel fuel from the massive black-and-white tanker chugging under the huge steel-girder bridge. My shoulders, tense from the drive, too much caffeine and not enough food, finally began to relax. Portsmouth was not a place I had visited before, though I knew my grandmother had lived there for some time. But I already had a feeling I was going to like it here, and my feelings about places tended to be surprisingly accurate. Spookily accurate, in fact, but that was not something I liked to go into.

My initial destination in town was a three-story Colonial-era brick box of a building with a peaked slate roof and a sign declaring it to be THE PALE ALE INN, EST. 1768. As I turned the key to shut off the Jeep's engine, the inn's door opened and an African American woman in a scarlet chef's coat strode out.

"Martine!" I shouted.

"Anna!" My friend wrapped me in one of her patented spine-crushing embraces. Martine Devereux was almost six feet tall, with deep brown skin and arms like a major league slugger. A professional chef, as well as my best friend since forever, Martine spent her life wielding knives and fire in confined spaces, not to mention barking orders with a force and speed that would put a drill sergeant to shame. "I was starting to wonder if you'd make it!"

"Traffic," I said, and Martine groaned in deep Bostonian sympathy. She also took my arm and gestured grandly to the saltbox tavern with its weathered shutters and wood-framed windows.

"Welcome to my castle!" Martine gazed on her restaurant with open pride. She'd been over the moon when she got this job. The Pale Ale was a Portsmouth institution. The tavern had been around since before certain radicals met there over tankards of the namesake beer to plot revolution. Now it was the kind of landmark restaurant that got stars in the guides and on the Web sites. My friend had been handed the mission of modernizing the cuisine while keeping true to its New Hampshire heritage. I had no idea how she did that, but I knew Martine was up to the challenge.

"We just finished the family meal, and we open back up in about an hour, so I haven't got time to do the total girl-friend reunion right now, but I really wanted you to check the place out." She gave me a significant look and I winced. I couldn't help it.

Sometimes, some places—homes, buildings, vacant lots, doesn't matter—give me . . . call it a Vibe. Everybody else can find the place perfectly comfortable, but it will leave me cold, or even sick. Other places that might look ready to be condemned can make me instantly cheerful, even bubbly.

Thankfully, the Vibe was not a constant, or I wouldn't be able to walk into a grocery store without doubling over. In fact, I really wished I could just brush the Vibe off as part of that overactive imagination common to us artistic types. I would have, too, if it wasn't for the times I couldn't make myself walk into a place and afterward I'd find out there'd been a recent death or a divorce or some other disaster. Or maybe it was a birth or a marriage. The good impressions could be just as freaky as the bad ones.

I took a deep breath. "You know I can't control the thing, Martine."

"You will tell me if you pick up anything, though? This is important."

Martine was one of the few people I'd told about my Vibe. I didn't talk about it partly because I didn't want to give people extra reasons to think that Anna the Crazy Artist was actually, well, crazy. Partly because I had no control over when I'd get the impressions or how strong they would be. When they hit, if they hit, the feeling could be anything from a mild sensation in the back of my brain to a tidal wave that left me shaking.

Martine had held my hand through a couple of those shaky times, and if she ever thought I was crazy, she kept it to herself. The least I could do was let her know if her dream-job restaurant hit me with the karma stick. So I smiled and gave her an extra hug. "Okay. I promise."

"Great. Come on in."

Thankfully, when I crossed the Pale Ale threshold, nothing hit me except a wave of mouthwatering aromas reminding me I'd missed lunch. Servers dressed in immaculate black and white bustled around a spare but elegant dining room, lining up silverware on blue napkins and adjusting the white tablecloths. The clatter and bang of a kitchen in full swing drifted out from the swinging doors.

Martine was watching me, so I shook my head. She mimed letting out a deep breath as she steered us to a table by the windows. "Sean," she called to the man working behind the bar. "I need a plate of the brisket tacos for my friend, who is about dead of starvation."

"Yes, Chef!" he answered promptly and headed for the kitchen.

"I'm not about dead," I muttered. Okay, I was hungry, but still. Martine was a wonderful person and an amazing chef. She also had distinct mother-hen issues.

"You are. You've been up since six."

"I'm a morning person, and I ate breakfast. Pinkie-promise."

"Maybe, but you skipped lunch."

How in the heck did she always know? Her instincts about food were almost as spooky as my feelings about places.

"So, how's Portsmouth treating you, Martine?" I said, changing the subject with my usual level of subtlety.

"Practically rolled out the red carpet." She gestured around her dining room. "We've got a great staff, and there's some local farmers who have been able to supply us with heirloom ingredients and . . ."

I let Martine's talk of converting the Pale Ale to a farm-to-table restaurant wash over me and couldn't help grinning. Maybe I wasn't getting a Vibe from the building, but I got one from Martine. She'd found her place, and I was happy for her. Also a little jealous. I had been something of a drifter since I got out of college, and if I was honest with myself, it had started to get a little tiring.

Martine's talk about ramping up the restaurant's catering department and the upcoming luncheon they were putting together for some city bigwigs had faltered and I realized I hadn't been paying attention.

"And then there's this morning . . ."

"This morning? What happened this morning?"

She frowned at me. "This is what happens when you skip meals. You can't concentrate. I was telling you how the boiler in my building burst this morning."

"Ouch."

"Yeah, ouch. I tried to call to warn you, but you must

have been on the road." Since my one way-too-close call
with an eighteen-wheeler, I always turned off my phone
when I was driving. "Anyway, the building's flooded, and
they're saying no hot water until Monday. My sous chef,
Beverly, is letting me stay with her, but, well . . ."

I held up my hands. "Don't worry about it. I saw a bunch
of vacancy signs when I passed the motels by the highway."

"Actually, I got you covered." Martine pulled a business
card out of her jacket pocket. "McDermott's Bed & Breakfast, over on Summer Street. A friend of mine and her husband run the place. They're expecting you, and there's a
discount since you're a friend of the 'family,'" she added,
with air quotes. "Things should be all fixed by Monday."

"Thanks, Martine. I appreciate it." I dropped the card
into my purse without looking at it. If Martine liked the
place, it would be fine, and the food would be outstanding.
What more could a girl ask for? Yes, the budget was a little
tight right now. I hadn't been working much over the past
few months. I'd been staying with my oldest brother, Bob,
and his wife to help take care of Dad while he recovered
from his heart attack. Despite this, I could handle a few days
of B and B pampering before settling down on Martine's
couch for the remainder of my two weeks.

"Here you go, miss." Sean set a plate of fresh tacos and
a martini glass full of pale golden liquid in front of me.
"Enjoy."

Sean the bartender was very tall. He looked to be somewhere in his late twenties and wore his golden brown hair
pulled back into a ponytail that was long enough to brush
the collar of his white shirt. His beard was full and neatly
trimmed, and it worked well on his round face.

"What's this?" I lifted the glass.

"That's a Ginger Lady, the Pale Ale's latest custom 'mocktail.'" He paused to make the air quotes. "Seltzer, lime, ginger, of course, bitters and some orange blossom water for the
perfume. Seemed a little early for the hard stuff."

I sipped the drink. It was bright gold and slightly fizzy. I got spice, lime and something warm and clean, with just a tiny bit of sweet, which was perfect. I hate drinks, even soft drinks, that taste like sugar water.

"It's delicious." I sipped again.

"Glad you like it." Sean gave a little waiter bow and, catching his boss's not entirely approving stare, beat a strategic retreat back to the safety of the bar.

"New?" I guessed. "Still trying to show off for the chef?"

"Trying to show off for somebody." Martine lifted an eloquent, and not very subtle, eyebrow.

"No," I said, or rather mumbled, because my mouth was now full of a delicious and spicy brisket that had been wrapped in a fresh corn tortilla. "Family meal" was when the restaurant staff all ate together before their shift started, and Martine made sure her staff ate well. "Plus, no," I added. "I'm off men for the duration."

Martine sighed. "Anna, that thing with Truman was approximately forever ago."

"That 'thing' you're referring to was when the nineteen-year-old, exceptionally perky blond woman arrived on our doorstep at three in the morning." Sometimes what happens in Vegas just won't stay in Vegas. This was a life lesson Truman, my now very much ex, learned just a little too late. "And it wasn't forever ago. It was eight months, two weeks and six days."

"But who's counting? You need to get back on the horse."

"I'm thinking about getting a cat. Does that count?"

Martine sighed heavily. She also looked like she was about to add something, but I was spared any further assessment of my social life when the dining room door opened behind us.

"Uh-oh."

I twisted around and saw an older blond woman stride into the dining room. Her gray slacks were tailored, and her white blouse didn't show a single wrinkle. Neither did her face, come to that, even though as she got closer I could see she was old enough to be somebody's grandmother. Her hair was pale blond, cut short and perfectly coiffed, and her nails were perfectly buffed and polished. She had a designer purse across her shoulder and a matching portfolio in the crook of one arm. Taken together with the designer scarf around her throat and the pearls around her wrist, her outfit and accessories were probably worth as much as the deposit I'd put down when I bought my Jeep.

"Mrs. Maitland." Martine got to her feet, her most professional smile set firmly in place. "We weren't expecting you this afternoon."

"Chef Devereux," the woman answered coolly. "I have the changes to your proposed menu for the chamber of commerce luncheon. I thought you might want some time to look them over before we talked." She pulled a piece of paper out of her portfolio. I couldn't read it from where I sat, but I did see there were a lot of circles and crossed-out lines on it.

Martine didn't bat an eye. Well, she almost didn't. "Thank you. I'll make sure Beverly gets these and—"

"I would prefer to consult with you directly. I have another appointment now, but if you could call . . . as soon as it's quite convenient." Mrs. Maitland shot me a sideways glance.

And she froze. Her tight, polite smile faded into a deep frown.

Martine looked from me to the blond woman uneasily. "Elizabeth Maitland, this is Anna Britton, a friend of mine from Boston."

"How do you do?" I held out my hand and gave her my own special smile, the one I reserve for tricky clients and reluctant gallery owners.

She did not take my hand. Instead, she leaned forward, like she was trying to make out a blurred face in an old photograph.

"What is your full name?"

I pulled back. "Annabelle Amelia Blessingsound Britton."

"I *knew* it," Mrs. Maitland breathed. "You have that Blessingsound look. You're *her* granddaughter, aren't you?"

"Umm . . . which her?"

"Annabelle Mercy. Did she send you here?"

"You know my grandmother?" It was only Martine's slightly panicked look that kept me from asking what the heck was going on with this woman, and what business it was of hers whom I was related to. It was, however, pretty obvious that Mrs. Maitland was an important client for the restaurant, so now was not the time to pull out the Boston attitude, or too many questions. "What a nice surprise," I made myself say, very politely. "I'll be sure to tell her we talked. She's living in Sedona these days, you know."

"I did not know." Mrs. Maitland pressed her mouth into a hard, straight line, which made me think she was disappointed to hear Grandma was still aboveground, wherever that ground was. "Well, welcome to Portsmouth, Miss Blessingsound Britton. I trust you will enjoy your *brief* stay. Chef Devereux, I will be expecting to hear from you shortly."

With that, Mrs. Maitland marched out, a little faster than she'd come in. It almost looked like a retreat, except that Mrs. Maitland was clearly not the retreating kind.

Martine was staring at me. I didn't blame her. "Who in the heck was that?" I asked.

"*That* was Elizabeth Maitland, daughter of one of the oldest and richest families New Hampshire ever saw. Her son's heading up this lunch we're catering." She held up the menu, with all its circles and *X*'s. "And she's got opinions about it."

"I can tell. But is she usually that . . . pleasant?"

"No. Not that I've seen a lot of her." My friend turned the menu over in her hands. "I didn't know your grandma B.B. lived in Portsmouth. I thought her people were from Massachusetts."

"They are, or they were. But Grandma was born here." And she'd lived here until she met her husband, Charlie, the man I knew as Grandpa C. After that, they lived just about everywhere except here. "I didn't know she still had any friends left in town."

"If that's your idea of her friends, I'd hate to meet your idea of her enemies," said Martine.

"Yeah. Probably not a good idea to start that family history project with Mrs. Maitland there."

"Seriously?"

I shrugged. "Not my idea. Ginger's." Ginger was my sister-in-law and genealogy was the love of her life, after my brother Bob and their son, Bobby III. She was constantly on the hunt for new tidbits for her scrapbooks and family trees. "When she heard I was coming up to visit, she practically gave me a take-home quiz."

"And she can't just call up Grandma because . . . ?"

"Sensitive subject. Grandma's always been a little fuzzy about why they left Portsmouth and didn't come back. Dad thinks it might be because he was going to show up a little, ah, early, and they didn't want people doing too much math." But considering Mrs. Maitland's little display, I couldn't help wondering if there might be something more to that story. Like maybe Grandma stole Grandpa out from under her cosmetically straightened nose?

"Well, if you're going to get into all that, you should look up Julia Parris, too," Martine said. "She runs the Midnight Reads bookstore, and she's an expert on local history. If there's a Blessingsound branch in Portsmouth, she'll know all about it."

"Thanks. Maybe I will."

"One thing, though," said Martine hesitantly. "Julia Parris and Mrs. Maitland don't exactly get along . . ."

"Either?"

"Either. So you might want to take anything she tells you with a grain of salt."

"Listen to you, already the expert on all the local gossip."

Martine chuckled. "It's a small town, and you'd be amazed what people will say in front of their waiter. Now, I hate to shoo you out, but there's less than an hour before we open for dinner . . ."

"I'm going, I'm going." I took another swallow of my ginger mocktail and grabbed my purse.

"Call when you're settled at McDermott's, okay? The restaurant's closed Monday. We can make it a girls' day after we get your stuff moved over to my place."

Martine had one of her minions wrap up the rest of my tacos in a take-out bag, and we hugged one more time. I got myself out of everybody's way and started across the parking lot, my head full of random thoughts of friends and families and old towns and grudges, and how many things could get lost in the cracks of time. I had the taco bag in one hand and fished around in my purse for my keys to open the Jeep.

"Merow?"

Merow?

I froze. I blinked and I stared.

A cat crouched on the driver's seat and stared right back at me.

❧ "MEROW?"

The cat on my driver's seat tucked all four of its paws underneath its belly. He (or she) was a solid smoky gray color, with a surprisingly delicate face and bright blue eyes. Somebody had given him (or her) a matching blue collar with a silver bell, but I couldn't see any tags. I also couldn't see any sign that she (he?) planned to get out of my car anytime soon.

I looked back at the inn and half expected to see Martine laughing at me. After my comment about getting a cat, this had to be a joke. I mean, the Jeep's doors were locked, the windows were up and the top was on. How could a cat get inside unless somebody deliberately put her (him?) there?

But our table at the window was empty and the inn door was still closed.

I looked at the cat. The cat looked at me. We both blinked.

"Shoo?" I suggested.

The gray cat yawned, displaying a curling pink tongue and a whole lot of very white teeth.

I folded my arms. "All right. What do you want?"

The cat blinked his (her?) slanting blue eyes at me again. It looked uncomfortably like he/she was waiting for me to say something sensible.

"Okay. We're gonna do this the hard way."

I lunged forward as if to make a grab. With a rolling growl of feline contempt, the cat flowed away from my hands. Victory! Or so I thought, until I realized the cat was now pressed against the pavement, under the Jeep, and right beside my front tire.

I swore. The cat hugged asphalt and put his/her ears back.

"Hey. Everything okay out here?" called a man's voice from behind me.

It was Sean the bartender. He was strolling out from the Pale Ale, wiping his hands on a side towel.

I sighed and sat back on my heels. "I seem to have a cat."

"Yeah, you sure do." Sean bent down to peer under the Jeep. "Hey, you know what? That might be Alistair under there. Alistair?" He held out his hand and spoke in that gentle, coaxing tone used by people who were comfortable around animals. "Hello, big guy. You got half the town looking for you, you know that?"

Alistair, if that was the cat's name, was not impressed. He just pressed his belly closer to the asphalt and glowered at the impertinent human.

"Who's Alistair?"

"Oh, he's a local legend." Sean rested his elbows on his thighs. "Alistair, the ghost cat of Portsmouth."

"Seriously?" I thought about how he'd been inside my locked Jeep just a minute before and felt a small shiver creep across my neck.

"Seriously," answered Sean. "His owner died, maybe six months ago, and nobody's been able to lay hands on him since. Whenever anybody gets close, he just"—Sean made a hocus-pocus gesture—"disappears!"

"Well, I'm seeing him now, and he doesn't seem to be going anywhere. How come nobody took him to a shelter or anything when he lost his owner?" I knew, of course, that cats were famous for self-reliance. I also knew this was New England. It was only a matter of time before the weather turned too hot, or too cold, or too wet, for anybody's comfort.

"I told you, it's like he disappears." Sean straightened himself up, and it was a long way up. "But we can try. See if you can keep him here. I'll go round up a box and some towels." Sean trotted back toward the inn, leaving me to stare at the cat.

"Okay." I sighed and rubbed the back of my neck. Alistair gave another little growl and extended his claws like he meant to dig in. How was I supposed to keep him there if he decided to take off? Then I remembered my bag of tacos. I pulled one out, tore it in half, and held it toward the recalcitrant feline.

"Here, kitty." I inched forward. "Puss, puss, kitty, kitty, kitty?"

Alistair twitched his ears and shrank backward, clearly unimpressed. I reminded myself that this cat had lost home and owner. He'd been out in the cold for months. Of course he was nervous around strangers.

"Come on, Alistair." I leaned forward, bracing myself with one hand against the fender. "You're not going to turn down free food, are you? I warn you, Martine won't like it."

This time Alistair stretched his neck out to sniff my offering. He sniffed again. He took a tentative lick of taco. This was followed by a much more enthusiastic lick and a nibble. I found myself smiling. I reached out and rubbed him between his ears. As Alistair nibbled and licked at the brisket taco, I noticed the smoke and silver color of his fur, the delicacy of his face and the way it contrasted with his rounded belly and hindquarters. If I'd had to guess, I would have said he weighed in at fifteen pounds of surprisingly sleek feline, maybe more. What breed was he? And how was he keeping himself fed? He didn't have any of that ragged, desperate air of an abandoned pet.

"So what's the answer, big guy?" I held out my fingers

so he could lick off the last of the taco sauce. "Huh, Alistair? What's been keeping you out in the cold?"

Alistair lifted his face and gazed at me with those slanting baby blues.

And he vanished.

I am not being metaphorical. He really vanished, as in there one second, gone the next. There was no trace of tail or whisker left behind, just me toppling back onto the asphalt and the remaining half a taco flying away to land *splat!* on the pavement.

"Ah, shoot," said Sean, who must have come back out at some point while the cat was giving me a heart attack. He carried an empty cardboard box in one hand and a white bar towel in the other. "Did you see where he . . . hey, are you all right?"

No. No. I really was not all right. My hands were shaking and my mind was doing that running-around-in-circles thing that happens when you don't want to believe what you've just seen. So I did what anybody would do under the circumstances.

I lied.

"Yeah, sure, fine. Just . . . startled."

I don't know if Sean believed me or not, but he did put the box down so he could pull me to my feet. I needed his help way more than I cared to admit.

"Oh, well." He shrugged. "We tried, right? I'll let Chef know Alistair's hanging around the parking lot. Maybe we can call Critter Control to bring a humane trap out." He stopped and put one broad hand on my trembling shoulder. "Are you sure you're okay?"

"Yeah. Sure. Fine," I said again, and this time I tried to really mean it. "I . . . You . . . you said something about the cat, Alistair . . . being a ghost?"

Sean chuckled. "That's just something the local kids have started. They say Alistair died with his owner and now he's some kind of vengeful feline spirit."

"Vengeful? Why vengeful?" I thought about that delicate

face, the plump belly and the way he fastidiously nibbled on his taco. "Vengeful spirit" was not the description I'd have picked, even after he vanished . . .

No. I wasn't going to think about how Alistair vanished. Because that didn't happen. It was impossible. Like getting into a locked car.

Sean glanced behind him, and the good humor faded from his expression, as if he was suddenly sorry he'd said anything about Alistair's former owner, let alone tried to make a joke out of it. I, uncharacteristically, kept my mouth shut and waited.

"Alistair belonged to Dorothy Hawthorne," Sean said softly. "She was one of those fixtures a town like this gets. You know, the ones who are involved in everything and seem like they'll just live forever? When she died, there was some talk that she'd, well, maybe been helped out of the world before her time."

"You mean she might have been murdered?"

"Some people thought so, but you know." Sean shrugged. "It's a reality-show world. Nobody believes in the normal anymore." He sounded almost angry as he said it.

"Did you know her?"

"Everybody knew Miss Hawthorne, and she loved that cat. Her nephew, Frank, put the word out after the funeral that he'd gone missing, so . . ." Sean stopped and reclaimed the box. He tossed the towel into the bottom. "Listen, I've got to get back to work or I'll be the ghost bartender of Portsmouth. You sure you're okay?"

"Yeah, I'm sure," I told him, and this time I was telling the truth—mostly, anyway.

"Okay. See you around maybe?"

There was a hopeful note in his voice. I smiled back in what I hoped was a friendly but noncommittal fashion. "Maybe. It's a small town."

"That it is." Sean smiled back. "And you never know what's going to happen next."

❧ 3 ❧

🐾 YOU MIGHT THINK somebody with a Vibe like mine would be open to all sorts of . . . let's call them "alternative perspectives" when it comes to the nature of reality. That's not how it works, though. What really happens is you get very good at talking yourself out of having seen or experienced anything the least bit, well, weird.

By the time I turned the corner onto Summer Street I had pretty much managed to convince myself that Alistair the cat had not, in fact, vanished into thin air. He had just done the regular cat thing and whisked away, really fast. I'd blinked. I'd looked around. I'd missed it. That was all.

As for how he got into the Jeep in the first place . . . well, I must have left the window down and not realized it. Or maybe the top wasn't on quite right, or it had gotten jiggled when I went over a particularly impressive Boston pothole and there was a gap someplace. It didn't matter. What mattered was there would be some kind of simple explanation, and it'd show up soon. There was nothing more to think about here. Move along, Anna.

* * *

PORTSMOUTH, LIKE A lot of harbor towns, had grown
outward in rough rings from its center by the river. The
oldest buildings were the ones closest to downtown and the
Piscataqua. After that, it was like a tour through the timeline
of American architecture. I went from the 1700s and 1800s,
with their brick-and-clapboard farmhouses, into the Victorian era, with its cozy cottages or elaborate gingerbreaded
homes, to bungalows from the 1920s and ranch houses from
the 1950s, with the newest homes and the strip malls curving
like a shell between the town and the highways.

Summer Street and McDermott's Bed & Breakfast
turned out to be squarely in the 1800s ring. The B and B
was a beautiful Georgian house, doubtlessly the former residence of some prosperous sailor, merchant or smuggler. A
tangle of ivy and rambler roses climbed the orange brick
walls. As with a lot of older Portsmouth homes, there was
only a narrow strip of lawn between the front of the house
and the sidewalk. Here, the yards and gardens were mostly
at the back or sides of a home.

"Good morning!" A gate in the privacy fence swung open
and a pale woman wearing a denim skirt and loose pink
T-shirt waved as she walked down the drive. "You must be
Annabelle. Martine phoned and told us you were on your way
over. I'm Valerie McDermott. Welcome to Portsmouth."

We shook hands. Family vacations had left me with the
idea that B and Bs were all run by white-haired grand-
motherly types. Valerie McDermott, though, looked to be
about my age, maybe a little younger. The bandanna tied over
her strawberry blond hair matched her pink T-shirt, and her
heart-shaped freckled face was as cheerful as her greeting.
She also had a spherical bulge under her shirt, which sig-
naled the imminent arrival of yet another McDermott to the
Portsmouth area.

"Your room's all set." Valerie smiled as I heaved the

massive red suitcases I dubbed Thing One and Thing Two out of the Jeep.

"Ummm . . . ," she said. "Martine didn't say you needed a room for the whole summer . . ."

I laughed. "Oh, no. I'm only with you for a couple of days. I've been living out of my brother's spare bedroom for the past few months, and it just seemed easier to toss everything in the backseat instead of sorting out a third bag." Yes, I've heard of traveling light. It is one of those things that other people do.

Valerie was doing her best not to look relieved. "Well, let's go in. Normally I'd help you with those, but"—she gestured toward her belly—"Roger would throw a fit."

"When are you due?"

"September." Valerie sighed. "Really, really ready for the debutante here to make her appearance. Aching ankles and . . ." She stopped. "I am not going to start in on pregnant-woman whining while you're standing out here. Let me show you to your room."

Six months pregnant she might be, but Valerie set a brisk pace up the steps, across the pillared front porch and into the house. I had to blink hard to get my sun-dazzled eyes to adjust to the dim and narrow oak-paneled foyer. A staircase—equally dim and narrow, and also very steep—ran up along the left-hand wall. Valerie had her foot on the first stair.

"Your room's on the second floor. I hope that's all right?" She eyed my suitcases again.

"I'm good. I've had plenty of practice with these monsters."

Valerie gave one of those little shrugs people use when they don't know you well enough to say, *It's your funeral.* "Okay, then. This way."

Did I mention those stairs were steep? Two hundred years old, fainting-couch-on-the-landing steep. Wrestling Thing One and Thing Two up was indeed a challenge, but I'd met worse and we all made it safely, if a little short of breath.

The upper hallway had been done in shades of gold and cream—that is, where it wasn't dark carved paneling.

"Is this your first time in Portsmouth?" Valerie asked while politely waiting for me to stop panting.

I nodded, then added, "My dad's family is from the area, though."

"Really?" I watched her do that thing where you run through an index of names in your mind. "I don't think I know any Brittons . . ."

"It was my grandmother who lived here. She was a Blessingsound," I added, because she was going to ask anyway. Because this was New England and even the people who didn't give a darn in general about genealogy cared about the local families. It was kind of like how living in Detroit made you care about cars whether you wanted to or not.

"Wait a minute." Valerie staggered. She actually staggered. "You're a *Blessingsound*? You're not related to Annabelle Blessingsound, are you?"

"Annabelle Mercy Blessingsound is my grandma, my dad's mother." Okay, this was getting spookier than the thing with the cat. "And you know what? That's the second time her name's come up today. I didn't know there were Blessingsounds left around here."

"Not for years," Valerie said. "And you're really just visiting Martine?"

"Ummm . . . yes." Valerie was still staring and I narrowed my eyes at her. I did not like this. At all. "I hope that's not a problem?"

"No. No. Sorry. Just . . . no. Your room's at the end of the hall." Valerie turned away and started walking, leaving me and my suitcases to catch up.

Ooookaaayyy . . . first we've got the rich blond lady interrogating me; then we get a ghost cat with a dead, possibly murdered owner. Now we've got a landlady getting weirded out about the family name. Looks like I picked the wrong week to visit Lovely Portsmouth.

"Here you go!" Valerie's cheery tone was a little strained as she pushed open the door. "The Green Room."

And a very nice choice of greens it was. The color on the walls was clear and delicate, while the trim and ceiling were closer to a moss agate. Area rugs softened the dark floorboards, and simple white curtains decorated the windows. The centerpiece, though, was the four-poster bed with a white crewelwork canopy and matching coverlet. Anywhere else, that a piece of furniture would have looked like overkill, but it fit here. As a bonus, the room had its own fireplace, and the faint scent of woodsmoke told me it was in working order.

Valerie unfolded the luggage rack beside the closet so I could heave one of my suitcases onto it. The rack creaked and wobbled, but it held.

"It's all en suite." Valerie waved toward a small green-and-white bathroom. "I'll let you get settled."

"Thanks."

She smiled, and I smiled and kept on smiling until she closed the door.

Now, a normal person would have begun checking out all the details of this lovely sunny room, or at least started unpacking. Me, I folded my arms and tried to brace myself for a Vibe to shimmy through the bright summer morning and into my unwilling self. Valerie's reaction to my Blessing-sound ancestry had come too soon after the whole thing with Alistair, and the other whole thing with Mrs. Maitland. I fully expected the other shoe of weirdness to drop anytime now.

But the Vibe stayed quiet for the moment. Instead, I pulled out my cell phone, hit Grandma B.B.'s number and waited while it rang.

"Hello! This is Annabelle Britton, but I can't come to the phone right now . . ."

I rolled my eyes. Grandma B.B.'s social life was a matter of amazement for the rest of us. Wherever she lived, she was always joining some new club or other; then there were

all the church committees, not to mention the adult educa-
tion lessons and the knitting circles. The words "sit still"
were simply not in her vocabulary.

The message ended and I got the beep. "Hi, Grandma
B.B. It's your namesake. I'm in Portsmouth, New Hamp-
shire, and . . ." I hesitated. What was I going to say? *I'm in
Portsmouth and everybody here seems to think they know
you?* "And I thought I'd give you a ring," I finished lamely.
"Call me when you get this."

I hung up and let myself flop backward onto the bed and
sigh. It wasn't even dinnertime and I was already exhausted.
More than that, though, I had a twitchy, uncomfortable feeling, and I couldn't tell where it came from. It wasn't one of
my Vibes, really, but it wasn't anything else I could readily
identify. I rubbed both arms and told myself it'd be okay. It
wasn't like I had to stay here at McDermott's. I didn't even
have to stay in Portsmouth. I could figure out some excuse
for Martine, climb in the Jeep and head straight back to Boston. Maybe I could say an important client meeting had come
up. Martine understood about scrambling for work, and while
I wouldn't say my bank account was on CPR, it was definitely
not healthy enough to be left alone without trained supervi-
sion. I thought about this as I gazed at the canopy and tried
not to feel like I was a coward running away from shadows.
Then I thought about the client I really did have. She needed
poster art for a community theater production of *Hedda
Gabler*. I pictured a spill of white-patterned fabric draped
over a Victorian sofa and a dark and gloomy background. My
fingers twitched. I had pencils and a fresh drawing pad in my
suitcase (somewhere). Maybe I'd just get a quick sketch of the
crewelwork pattern. At the very least I could snap some pictures and work on it with PictureShop and DrawingPad.

I got up to push open the curtains to let in more light and
immediately stumbled backward. I think I said something
like, "Gaaah!"

Alistair sat on the windowsill, staring in at me.

❧ 4 ❧

❧ "GOOD GRIEF, CAT! You scared the life out of me!"

Alistair did not seem at all perturbed. He just put up one paw and batted at the spot over the window latch. "Mrrr-rowww?" The feline question filtered through the pane. "Mrrp?"

"No," I said, after I'd gotten my breathing back under control. "You are not coming in. There is no admittance for spooky cats, okay? Shoo." I waved my hands. "Scat!"

Alistair blinked those big blue eyes once, indicating that he was not in the least impressed by my strange human antics. Then he got calmly to his feet, walked along the sill, leapt off the edge and was gone.

After a certain amount of internal debate, I shoved up the window sash. Leaning out into the afternoon sunshine, I looked down. Ah-yup. We were still on the second floor. No, there was no visible cat below me.

Neither was there a cat when I looked to the left or to the right. I twisted my neck to see if he could have jumped onto the roof, but the overhanging eaves were too wide. Plus, those eaves were another whole story up above what I took to be the house's attic. I also couldn't help noticing that the ivy, which had been allowed to grow across the front and sides of the house, had been cleared away back here.

In short, there was no visible way up to my window from the ground, just like there was no visible way down to it from the roof.

I closed the window, latched it and pulled the curtains. Normally, my Vibe is reserved for places, but something about that cat set the back of my neck prickling, and those prickles spread quickly down my spine.

"It didn't happen," I told the universe at large. "I am not being stalked by the magical mystery cat with the murdered mistress. This is not the kind of thing that happens to Annabelle Amelia Blessingsound Britton. I declare this to be a Rule."

I don't think the universe listened.

MY VIBE FINALLY hit in McDermott's great room.

I'd spent the rest of Friday in my room. I called Grandma B.B. again and got her answering machine, again. I also called Bob and Ginger to check up on how Dad was doing. Unfortunately, he was napping, so there went that chance to quiz him for extra information about the family's Portsmouth history. I sketched the crewelwork patterns from my coverlet and canopy, caught up on e-mail, dined on leftover tacos, and had a long gossipy phone conversation with my buddy Nadia, who ran a gallery in the Hamptons.

In short, I did everything I could to avoid thinking about my spooky stalker cat. I most definitely did not do anything radical like tell Nadia about Alistair or call Martine to tell her about Alistair. I also didn't open the window again, not even when I woke up from a surprisingly deep night's sleep and saw the beautiful summer Saturday outside.

I dressed in yoga pants, a paisley T-shirt and my red

Keds. I tiptoed downstairs carefully to avoid creaking the floorboards, just in case my fellow guests were not Morning People. We are a rare and special breed.

McDermott's narrow foyer opened into an airy and beautifully restored great room with white-painted trim and pale yellow walls. The moment I stepped over the threshold, warmth bubbled up like spiritual champagne. People had been happy here, my sparkly feelings told me. People cared for this place, loved and nurtured it. A stupid grin spread across my face before I got a handle on it.

Even without the emotional booster shot, the room was beautiful. The French doors had been opened to let in the morning sun as well as the fresh breeze that blew across the garden and the broad back porch. All the furnishings were simple, sturdy and comfortable. The curving corner alcove with its built-in bookcases and deep chairs looked like the perfect place to curl up on a rainy evening. I thought longingly of the pencils and drawing pad back in my room. I particularly wanted to do a detail of the elaborate chandelier hanging from the smooth white ceiling, and a close-up of the carved mantelpiece.

"I may never leave," I said to myself.

At least, I thought it was to myself, but a laugh came from out on the porch, and Valerie appeared at the threshold, carrying a silver coffeepot. "Thank you. I'll tell Roger you said that. He's in the kitchen now, getting breakfast together. But the buffet's set and the coffee"—she hefted the carafe—"is ready. Or do you prefer tea?"

"Coffee would be great."

This turned out to be an understatement. The brew Valerie poured smelled not so much like coffee as like the anticipation of paradise normally associated with your finer chocolates.

"Aaaaahhhhh!" I sighed happily as I wrapped my hands around the warm mug.

Valerie grinned. "It's serve yourself today." She gestured

toward the buffet tables that took up one side of the porch. "Unless you'd like some eggs?"

"Thanks, but this looks perfect."

Is there a phase beyond perfect? If so, it surely comes with homemade pastry, granola, yogurt and fresh berries. Carafes of juice and milk had been set out in ice trays, alongside several pots of that wonderful coffee, not to mention a chafing dish from which rose the mouthwatering and unmistakable scent of bacon. I wouldn't need to move for a week.

Then it got better.

"Make a hole! I got grunt!"

A tall blond man backed out of a screen door carrying a cast-iron skillet in his oven-mitted hands. Valerie slapped a cork trivet onto the buffet so he could set it down. The pan was filled with golden brown biscuits floating on a dark bubbling liquid that smelled of berries and cinnamon. My nose thought it smelled divine. My stomach agreed.

"Traditional New England blackberry grunt!" announced the man, stripping off his oven mitts. His white apron had the words BACK OFF, MAN, I'M THE CHEF emblazoned on the chest. "Welcome to McDermott's! I'm Roger, and you must be Miss Britton."

"Anna." We shook hands and I beamed. I liked this guy already, and it was clear from the indulgent way Valerie brushed at the flour smear on his suntanned arm, she was soppy in love.

"Now, you have to try this," Roger said. I recognized that tone from meals with Martine and knew better than to attempt refusal. Not that it would have been a serious attempt. He scooped out one of the biscuits along with healthy spoonfuls of blackberry goodness. "It's even better if you do this." He snatched up a pitcher of cream from the coffee station and poured a circle around the biscuit. "There you go."

He watched anxiously as I dug out a spoonful of warm berries, cream and biscuit.

"Oh. My." I rolled my eyes in sensuous appreciation. Valerie and Roger slapped palms in an energetic high five.

"Umm . . . would either of you care to join me?" I mumbled, only a little awkwardly around a second mouthful.

"Why don't you sit, Val?" said Roger. "You're supposed to get off your feet more, and I've got everything under control."

I did not imagine that Valerie looked awkward. I tried to keep any possibly prejudicing eagerness off my face by eating more grunt.

"Well, all right." Valerie gave me an eye roll that said she was humoring the anxious father-to-be. "Just for a minute."

Carrying the bowl and mug, I decided to live dangerously and take a table on the brick terrace below the porch, in the full blaze of the morning sun. Valerie sank carefully into the chair across from me with a cup of peppermint tea and an audible sigh. I nodded in sympathy as I dug into my blackberry grunt. My invitation was not purely social, which was probably not going to come as a surprise to my hostess, who had already started eyeing me sideways. What she probably didn't guess, though, was that my deep ulterior motives for asking her to sit with me were not limited to her reaction to finding out who my grandmother was.

"Valerie, do you guys have a cat?" We could work around to what she knew, or thought she knew, about Blessingsounds slowly.

Valerie shook her head. "We'd like one, but so many people have allergies we decided against it. Why do you ask?"

"There was a gray cat on my sill yesterday." I waved my spoon up toward my window and kept my tone very, very casual. Because on the way downstairs I hit on the perfect explanation for what had happened. The cat who'd turned up here last night wasn't actually Alistair the Spooky Cat who had been in and under my Jeep. This was another cat entirely. It only *looked* like Alistair. Maybe they'd come from the same litter. It was a small town. It could happen.

Valerie followed my gesture with her gaze. She frowned

and my heart plummeted. "Was he a sort of solid silvery gray, by any chance? With blue eyes?"

"Yes, that's the one." *Oh, no. No. Come on, no.*

"Alistair?" Valerie breathed. "Oh, my G . . . *you* saw Alistair? Where? When?" she demanded, leaning forward over her rounded tummy. Her pink cheeks flushed bright red, and she clutched her mug so hard I was afraid the thing might break.

I have to admit, the force of her reaction startled the heck out of me. "On my windowsill yesterday, and he was hiding under my Jeep before that, if it was the same cat."

Valerie pressed her fingertips against her mouth and stared up at my window. "Could it . . . ? After all this time, I'd given up . . . Alistair? Really?"

"Alistair," I repeated gloomily. I was right. The universe had heard my declaration about no mystery cats for Annabelle, and the universe had laughed. "Sean, the bartender at the Pale Ale, recognized him and told me he'd been missing for a while."

"Yes," murmured Valerie. "Yes," she repeated more firmly, like you do when you're dragging your thoughts back from a long ways off. "Six months and more . . . since Dorothy—she was his owner . . . since she . . . died." Her voice wobbled.

"I'm sorry for your loss." This was a guess on my part, but normally a person didn't wobble for absent strangers, not to mention strangers' cats. Plus, I couldn't help noticing how Valerie was chopping her sentences to bits. This was also not normally a sign of emotional detachment.

"Sorry. It still hits me sometimes." Valerie took several rapid sips of her tea, as if trying not to talk too much, or to cry. Guilt shriveled my insides. Here I was worrying about a weird cat encounter when the woman in front of me had lost her very real friend. "I've known her since I came to Portsmouth. I had known her, that is," Valerie said. "We were neighbors." She gestured toward the back fence. "She was always in and out of here. In fact, she was the one who talked me into buying this house and setting up the business. It was after that I met Roger . . ." Val cut that sentence off too. "Anyway, very few people have seen Alistair for more than a minute since Dorothy passed. Not even us . . ." My hostess stopped yet again. "Well, cats, you know?" she went on, trying to sound casual and failing. "I guess we all assumed he'd come home when he was good and ready."

I nodded, trying to look thoughtful. At the same time, that thing old novels call "a profound sense of unease" welled up in the back of my brain, complete with the theme from *The Twilight Zone* playing in the background.

"Maybe somebody in the neighborhood took him in," I said, and it felt like a last-ditch effort. "He had a collar on, and he certainly didn't look underfed."

Val smiled, but it was weak and watery. "Alistair will eat anything that doesn't move fast enough. Once, Dorothy left a loaf of fresh zucchini bread out on the counter, and when she came in from gardening, there was Alistair burrowed into it up to his shoulders." That troubled, introspective look drifted back across her face. "You will let me know if you see him again?"

"Uh, sure." I scraped my spoon through the last of my blackberry grunt.

"It's just that we've been worried about him. Dorothy died so suddenly and . . ." Valerie studied the steam curling across the surface of her tea. "Well, it was unexpected and unsettled."

You're lying to me, I thought dazedly. *You're a nice, open, friendly person, and you're sitting here lying to me, about a cat.*

A cat and a dead woman.

"Was she, Dorothy . . . ill for very long?" I asked. I figured this was a better way to go fishing for the source of Valerie's lie than, *So, Sean the bartender says this Miss Hawthorne might have been murdered. What do you think?*

"Dorothy was healthy as a horse." Val's smile softened;

it was also real this time. "In fact, we were making plans for her eightieth birthday. We were going to hold it here. A surprise party. The whole . . . town was going to be here."

"I'm so sorry. That's hard."

"Yes. Thank you." A new expression tightened Valerie's mouth and furrowed that freckled forehead. I told myself she must be trying to hold back the tears again. Otherwise, I would have thought Valerie McDermott, my cheerful hostess and owner of a house that bubbled with good feeling, was deeply, fiercely angry.

Sean's words about how "some people" thought Dorothy Hawthorne had been murdered came echoing back. It seemed like Valerie McDermott was one of those people. That might explain why she thought there was something strange about Alistair's disappearance, not to mention his reappearance.

But just then a gray-haired couple in matching white slacks and blue polo shirts came out through the French doors. Valerie murmured a quick apology and heaved her pregnant self to her feet to go greet them.

Which put her well out of conversational range.

Well . . . shoot. I'd blown my chance to ask what, or how, Valerie knew about the Blessingsounds and what about them upset her so much. Instead, I'd let myself get distracted by the possibility of a murder connected to a spooky cat who wasn't any kind of relation at all. Ginger would have my head when she found out.

I smiled at my fellow guests as they took their seats on the shady porch, and tried to get back to giving my breakfast the attention it deserved. But the prickling had started up in the back of my neck again. This time I twisted around right away and saw Valerie staring at me from the French doors. As soon as she caught me looking, she gave a friendly wave and disappeared inside.

I rubbed my neck and contemplated my coffee. Fresh feeling flowed through me, so strong it was almost a Vibe. It told me I should close my suitcases and get out of this weirdness while the getting was good. I could figure out something to tell Martine later.

There are disadvantages associated with being the product of multiple generations of good, solid New England stock. One was a tendency to sunburn almost instantly when touched by actual daylight. Another was unreasonable amounts of bone-deep pride. If I decided I was ready to leave Portsmouth, that was one thing. But to be run out of town by bad feelings, enigmatic B and B owners and spooky cats? That was quite another. I would be gosh-darned if I was leaving until I was good and ready. Good and ready, though, would not come until I got a clear, solid look at whatever was going on around me, especially if it related to my family.

I pulled out my phone. Still no call from Grandma B.B. I'd try her again later. Maybe after breakfast I could find the Midnight Reads bookstore Martine had told me about and ask this Julia Parris if she knew about the connection between the Blessingsounds and Portsmouth.

I got up to help myself to more coffee. If I was about to start uncovering family secrets, I needed it. But as I set the pot down, motion caught my eye and a fresh shiver ran down my spine.

Away across the stretch of the McDermotts' back garden, Alistair the Spooky Cat was sitting bolt upright on the back fence. No, make that on the back gate in the back fence.

And yes, he was watching me.

❦ 5 ❧

❧ IT WAS WELL past noon before I had a chance to check out that back gate.

B and Bs tend to empty out in the middle of the day. At first, I thought luck, or weirdness, was with me and I might have the place to myself even earlier. I was on only my third cup of coffee when I overheard Valerie say to Roger that she had some errands to run and she was taking their Subaru downtown. After that, though, the white-haired couple seemed determined to spend the entire day arguing over their maps and AAA tour books. Plus, two plump middle-aged ladies camped out in the great room crocheting and chatting, seemingly prepared to wait hours for a third friend to call. Not that I was eavesdropping or lurking. And then there was Roger, who had embarked on an endless round of kitchen chores that rivaled anything Martine could have devised.

But finally, the senior couple settled on a trip to the Strawberry Banke Museum. The women's friend did call and they decided that Popovers on Market Square would be a great place to meet up, and Roger headed out with car keys and grocery list.

As soon as the sound of that last car engine faded into the distance, I grabbed my purse and headed down into the back garden. I had no idea what would happen next, if anything, and I didn't feel prepared without my purse. Gals, you all understand this.

McDermott's back garden was huge—maybe a quarter acre. A big rectangle of a kitchen garden took up much of the space, where, according to the labels on their sticks, there would soon be beans, tomatoes, beets and squash growing alongside a tangle of raspberry canes and a couple of what I recognized as blueberry bushes. A rainbow of daylilies lined the fence. It all looked summery and normal.

I glanced back at the house. No one was on the terrace or moving behind any of the windows that I could see. I put my hand on the gate and pushed.

It was locked—from the other side.

"And *that* is the end of the mystery of Anna B. and the Spooky Cat," I said to myself and anybody who might be listening.

"Merow?" came the answer from over the fence.

I yanked my hand away from the gate like I'd been burned.

The determination I'd felt at breakfast wavered. Seeing the subject of local legend was one thing. Following him on some kind of wild-goose chase into a fenced backyard with a locked gate—that was another.

"I can't do this," I said to Alistair and the universe at large. "I just can't. It's too much."

I turned my back on the fence and the cat on the other side. At that exact second, a plaintive yowl drifted out under the gate.

"No!" I said to the cat and all the emotions spiking in the back of my brain. "I am not falling for this one." Whatever was going on with Alistair was a job for Nancy Drew, or maybe Sam and Dean Winchester. I, Annabelle Amelia Blessingsound Britton, intrepid girl artist, had nothing to do with this cat or his dead owner. Or his dead owner's yard.

Alistair yowled again. The high, quavering sound ran along my spine exactly the way one of my bad Vibes did. Unfortunately, the Britton pride rose to meet it and the Blessingsound stubbornness came along for the ride. They wanted to know if I was scared of one pathetic cat. Curiosity wormed its way into the conversation—I'd come this far; why not see what was going on? Finally, empathy arrived to back them all up. What if Alistair had gotten stuck in that other yard, or hurt? It could happen, even to cats. Even to spooky cats. I couldn't just leave him. Well, I could, but I wouldn't like myself much afterward.

"I do not believe I am doing this," I muttered.

Believing it or not, I looked back toward the B and B. If anybody was still inside, I couldn't see them. In fact, the only thing watching me was a skinny little goldfinch perched in the right-hand neighbor's bird feeder.

Muttering about my own lack of common sense, I rummaged in my purse until I found my nail kit and extracted the metal file. That inquisitive goldfinch chirped once in puritanical disapproval and fluttered away. I couldn't blame it.

When my second-oldest brother, Ted, was sixteen, he had a girlfriend of whom Mom and Dad did not approve. Considering that my parents' first meeting involved nudity and motorcycles, this was quite an accomplishment. It also meant that in order to avoid detection when going to meet his personal Juliet, Ted started sneaking out through the mudroom window. This worked just fine, until the night I was lying awake because I'd made the mistake of watching *The Exorcist* on cable. What followed was some light sibling blackmail to get him to teach me how to jimmy the various locks and latches around our house.

I slid the nail file through the crack between the gate and the fence and wriggled it back and forth. The gate didn't budge.

Alistair let out another heart-rending yowl.

"Okay, okay, I'm coming!" I jerked the file up. There was a rattle as the latch flipped back. The gate came open, and quicker than you could say "breaking and entering" I was on the other side.

The other side of the fence was shaded by a pair of apple trees. A stray green fruit bumped my forehead as I ducked under the branches. A flagstone path stretched out at my feet. I didn't follow it. I was too stunned by what I saw in front of me.

Plenty of old yards have flagstone paths. Very few, however, have a path that spirals gracefully between curving formal beds filled with a summer riot of flowers and herbs.

Now I did move forward, carefully, following that spiral path through the formal plantings. Their rich, green scent hung heavy in the air. I recognized mint, sage, rosemary and thyme as I passed, and suspected there had to be parsley in there someplace. There was definitely lavender and golden echinacea, more roses and marigolds.

It was all beautiful, but there was also an air of quiet mourning here. No one had come around to care for this delightful place in a long time. Grass poked up between the path's stones. Pricker weeds, teasels and volunteer cornflowers were duking it out with the marigolds. The neglected lawn had passed ankle-high and was headed for knee-deep.

The center of this overgrown labyrinth held another surprise. I'd expected a gazing ball, or maybe a goldfish pond. Instead, I found a fire pit with a beaten copper cover. A copper-and-brass chest stood beside it, for wood and kindling, I assumed.

The house in front of me was a snug fieldstone cottage. Pink and yellow rambler roses overflowed their trellises and climbed the walls. The mottled grays of the stone reminded me sharply of Alistair's fur. Its slate roof was a complex landscape of peaks and gables topped by a weather vane in the shape of a crescent moon shot through with an arrow. It looked cozy and picturesque and instantly inviting.

What I did not see was any sign of Alistair.

I turned in place, breathing the green summer scents and drinking in the beauty and the isolation. I liked it here. This house and its garden had mystery and character and contrast. My fingers twitched. I not only wanted my pencils right now; I wanted a trowel, too. I wanted to capture this summer setting, the slow return of the wilderness to the garden, the shadows under the trees and the light on the flower beds. I wanted to trim and tidy and assist, not that I was much of a gardener, but it was never too late to learn, right? When I was done, I could settle back beside the fire pit for the evening with a cool drink in my hand and a cat on my lap, watching the fireflies. A place like this *had* to have fireflies. And chipmunks. And . . .

Wait. I told myself. *Stop.*

This was a Vibe. I hadn't recognized it right off, because it wasn't like any Vibe I'd ever felt. Usually, I knew if a place was full of goodness or badness. If it was a happy house or the reverse. I'd never had any Vibe that felt so much like . . . welcome. That was the only word for it. This place welcomed me.

"Oh, no, you don't." I clenched my fists. "You don't even *start* with me."

The wind gusted, and overhead, the crescent-moon weather vane swung around and pointed west. Even as I thought that, the Vibe shifted. It started in the soles of my feet and traveled up to the pit of my stomach. Something was about to change, and it was about to change forever.

Seriously, universe?

As if in answer, Alistair yowled, sharp, short and impatient. I jerked around to face the cottage again. This time I saw that the back door was open, just a little. Just enough, say, for a cat to slip through.

My sense of standing on the brink doubled, and doubled again. No matter which way I jumped, it was going to be a long climb back. I had to decide.

"Cat," I muttered as I marched toward the house, "this had better be good."

❧ 6 ❧

🐾 SINCE THE COTTAGE shutters were closed, the inside was quite dim. It took a lot of hard blinking before my eyes adjusted. I was standing in a black-and-white kitchen that looked like it had last been updated sometime in the 1930s. It still had the deep enamel farmhouse sink, a wooden floor and tile countertops. Only the stove and refrigerator were from the current decade. The garden window bowed out to make room for a cozy breakfast nook with built-in benches. It was easy to picture the generations of Portsmouth housewives who congregated there for tea and gossip.

And one of them had been Dorothy Hawthorne. She had tended that magnificent garden, picked those apples, and sat here with her cup of tea. Unless she was a coffee person. I wondered what she'd looked like. My brain conjured up a vague Miss Marple sort of image, with white hair, a tweed skirt and big gloves, but somehow that didn't seem to go with the house. Old-fashioned and cozy it might be, but this was not a tweedy sort of place.

I wondered where Dorothy had died, and how. I hadn't

thought to ask Sean, and Valerie had left before I could really get up to speed on my prying. But I did wonder all the same, like I wondered what it was about her death that made "some people" think it was murder.

Curiosity is a terrible thing. You can be having the strangest morning ever and it still whispers tender words to you, like, *You're already inside. A quick look around can't hurt anything.*

"I am not doing this," I muttered as I stepped quickly across the kitchen, almost but not quite tiptoeing. "This is somebody else. This is not me. Annabelle Amelia Blessingsound Britton is way smarter than this."

A swinging door led into the hushed dining room. White sheets covered the chairs and a table and what I took to be a sideboard. The sun shone through a three-paneled stained-glass window set high in the right-hand wall, casting a pattern of red and green tulips onto the carpet. Another door led out to a front parlor. The walls were lined with built-in bookcases, and at the front of the house there was another bay window, this one with a lovely, deep window seat. I passed by the ghostly shapes of more sheet-covered furniture. A pocket door let me into the dark-paneled foyer with its bare floor and simple staircase rising along the opposite wall.

The stairs were at least as steep as the ones at McDermott's. I looked up and saw a railing surrounding the stairwell above that would have been perfect for kids to peek through. Only instead of any giggling kid, it was Alistair who looked down between the spindles.

I meant to tell the cat, and myself, that this was it. No farther. This might not technically be breaking and entering, because the kitchen door really had been open, but it was definitely trespassing. Dorothy Hawthorne might be dead, but the place belonged to *somebody*. They'd left all this furniture. Hadn't Sean the Bartender mentioned a nephew? Whoever he was, he probably wouldn't appreciate my little sightseeing tour.

On the other hand, the state of the garden and the presence of a loose cat said the nephew didn't come around that often.

"Okay, one quick look upstairs and then I'm gone," I told the cat, or maybe myself. "Like into-the-next-county gone."

By the time I got to the top, though, Alistair had vanished again.

I looked around and saw that a total of four doors opened off the short hallway, two in front of me and one at either end. At the same time, all the hairs on the back of my neck stood up. My heart raced too, but not from the climb. That sense of being on the edge was as heavy up here as the smell of warm dust and Murphy Oil Soap. There was something in here. I was getting close. I felt it.

"But close to what?" I murmured.

The minute the words were out of my mouth, a fresh Vibe hit. A sense of expectation surged through my skin and my bones. No, not expectation; something stronger. Eagerness. This house not only welcomed me; it had been waiting for me.

Panic hit hard enough to send the hallway reeling. I pressed my hand hard against the wall. I made myself take a deep breath and hold it. I let it out slowly and paused. And breathed in and held it. And let it out and paused. My heart steadied, and the shock of this new, unexpected and very specific Vibe receded, at least a little.

"Okay, cat," I said. "I get it. Really. You wanted me in here. This . . . this house wanted me here. Here I am. Now, *where are you?*"

Alistair howled, and I about jumped out of my skin. It sounded like he was right over my head.

"Okay, okay," I gasped. "So, there's an attic, right? A house like this is bound to have an attic. Perfect place to hide a cat."

Fighting to regain at least some of my hard-won control, I faced the pair of doors in front of me and picked the one on the right. I put my hand on the knob and rattled it. Locked.

A quick check showed the knob was an elaborate, old-fashioned piece of brass hardware, complete with a keyhole you could have spied through. It was also well past the limits of my skill with a nail file.

"So what now? Do I say 'open sesame'?"

Surely it was a coincidence that right then I felt the knob turn. There was a click. I lifted my hand away. With a long, low creak of antique hinges, the door drifted open.

Alistair sat calmly at the top of a short flight of stairs, entirely unharmed and untraumatized. In fact, his tail swished back and forth as if to say, *What took you so long?*

"You, cat, are a big fat liar, and you have lured me here under false pretenses."

Alistair shrugged, a long ripple of feline shoulders and smoke-colored fur.

I sighed. "Okay. Let's get this over with."

"Mrrp," replied the cat noncommittally. Not that it mattered. I was climbing the stairs anyway.

Dorothy Hawthorne's attic, like her garden, was something out of a fairy tale. Fortunately, it was a cobweb-free fairy tale. There was one big central space, and the slopes of the roof's gables created four low nooks, one in each direction. The pattern of light and shadows looked strange, but that was because while each one of those nooks had a small window, those windows were all at knee height. The central space, where the sloping roof was highest, had been set up as a study, complete with low shelves of leather-bound books and an antique desk topped by a green-shaded lamp. Alistair, perfectly at home, jumped from the desk chair to the desktop and down to the floor again. Then he paced across to what at first glance looked like just a table covered with a green cloth.

But as my gaze followed the cat, I saw it was something else altogether.

That green velvet cloth was decorated with elaborate Celtic knotwork. On it, a white candle in a silver holder stood next to a bundle of dried herbs. I smelled sage and rosemary and lavender and wondered if they had come from the garden. There was a silver cup, too, with some pale cloudy liquid in it, and a little silver dish of something that looked like sugar, or maybe salt.

In the table's exact center lay a length of carved wood and a small square of paper.

"Mar-oow," explained Alistair as he plumped down next to me and began washing his tail.

I picked up the carved stick. I'd never seen anything quite like it. It was maybe a foot long and as thick as my thumb. The pale wood had been carved with a twisting pattern of blossoms, branches and moons—crescent, half and full. Then, as I peered more closely, I realized there were letters carved among the flowering branches as well.

"Quod ad . . . ," I read as I turned it, trying to follow the spiraling words, *"vos mittere in mundum triplici."*

Latin.

There are few advantages to studying classical art. One of them is that you can piece together most stray Latin quotations you come across. "What you send out into the world comes back in triplicate?" I said.

Alistair swatted at me gently with a paw.

"Hey!" I shouted, and then bit down on my next words. I was supposed to be sneaking, right? I moved to put the carved ornament back, but my hand froze. I now saw something else. The velvet cloth that covered the table didn't have just Celtic knotwork for its pattern; there were stars printed on it too. Specifically, five-pointed stars inside golden circles.

Pentacles.

In art school, we'd learned that pentacles were early Christian symbols for the Virgin Mary. These days, though, they were usually symbols of something different—witchcraft.

I backed up an involuntary step. This wasn't a table and it wasn't some random collection of knickknacks put together by an eccentric old cat lady.

This was an altar. A witch's altar.

"Oh, no," I croaked. "No. This is not happening."

Except it was. I was in a witch's attic, and next to me was a vanishing cat. I was holding what could only be a magic wand, and my Vibe and I had been brought to this place by a whole series of very, very strange coincidences.

Alistair meowed and head butted my shins.

"What?" I demanded, because being freaked-out makes me short-tempered. "Has little Timmy fallen down the well? *What?"*

Have you ever heard the noise an indoor cat makes looking out a window at the birds? That set of sharp, creaking, grumpy sounds that must mean something truly insulting in the ancient sparrow dialect? That was the noise Alistair made at me as he jumped onto the altar and off again.

That piece of paper I'd noticed fluttered to the floor. I picked that up, too, and I froze. Again.

The paper was a photograph that had been neatly clipped out of a magazine. I even knew which magazine—*New England Arts Monthly.* They'd published an interview with me about freelance artists and the growing independent publishing industry last summer.

My photo had been on Dorothy Hawthorne's altar.

That was when I heard the footsteps.

🐾 7 🐾

🐾 I WHIPPED AROUND, reflexively stuffing the magazine photo into my purse. Alistair darted between my legs and skidded to a halt at the top of the stairs, his ears pressed flat against his skull.

Down below us, someone was walking. The steps were quick and light, but not light enough to keep the old floors from singing out their warning. Then the tone of the steps changed to hollow thumps. Hollow thumps heading up the stairs.

Alistair hissed, arching his back and puffing up from ears to tail like a Halloween nightmare. Spitting with fury, he dove down the stairs. I shouted, certain he was going to plant his face in the door. But the door opened and the cat streaked through.

In the next heartbeat, somebody hollered in surprise and pain.

I bolted through the open door and into the hall. At the top of the stairs, a man staggered sideways, clutching a screwdriver with one hand and his knee with the other.

"Ow! Damn it! Ahgh!"

Alistair ducked behind me and hugged the carpet, growling low in his throat, his eyes opened so wide I could see the whites. I gaped at the cat and the stranger, not sure which was the bigger threat. This was when I realized I was still clutching the wand.

The man straightened up enough to meet my gaze. He was a white guy. Middle age had hit hard, leaving gray streaks in his sandy hair and lines on his sagging face. The mustache might have made him look younger once but now just looked like it was trying to hide something.

Alistair hissed again. What color there was in the guy's face drained away and he lifted his hand—and that screwdriver. For the life of me, I don't know what made me do it, but I raised the wand and pointed it right at him, like I was channeling Hermione Granger and all the kids from Hogwarts.

"Don't even think it," I said.

The mustached man swallowed. He teetered backward, and then he turned and ran down the stairs.

"Hey!"

I stuffed the wand in my purse and ran after him. Maybe I was worried he'd been hurt by Alistair, who had inexplicably gone into attack mode. Maybe I had some weird feeling of ownership about this house. I mean, I had broken in first. Maybe I was just too startled to think straight. I didn't know then, and I'm still not sure. I did pound down the stairs just in time to see the stranger slam out the front door.

I darted across the threshold and onto the front porch. That was when I heard another set of footsteps and a new shout. Hard hands grabbed me and whirled me around. Now I was staring up at a second stranger.

I think I said something like, "I . . . uh . . . er . . . ack!"

"Who the hell are you?" he—whoever he was—demanded. "What are you doing in my house?"

He was taller than me. His black hair waved back from his broad forehead and his eyes glittered an intense and angry blue. Under better circumstances, I might have realized how much he looked like a cross between Benedict Cumberbatch and Cary Grant. Just then, though, I was completely caught up in realizing that he wasn't letting me go and that he'd said this was his house.

"Frank Hawthorne." I'd blurted the name out. Sean had said that was the name of Dorothy Hawthorne's nephew. Who else would be in this empty house? Aside from me. And Mr. Mustache. And Alistair, of course.

Frank, if that's who he was, let go of one of my arms, but it was just so he could dig his hand into his sports jacket pocket, presumably looking for his phone. "I'm asking you again, who are you and what are you doing here?"

I quickly decided to go with the truth—some of it, anyway. It might buy time before he called the cops. "I, um, I came in after the cat. Alistair? I heard him yowling. I thought he might be hurt or something and the place was all shut up and . . ." I let that sentence trail off. It wasn't going anywhere interesting anyway. "Then I heard somebody else in the house, and . . ."

"What? Crap! Not again!"

The man whipped around and ran into the house, leaving me on the porch with only one question in my head.

What do you mean "not again"?

There were two things I could have done here. One of them was actually smart. I did the other, though, and followed Frank Hawthorne through the door he'd left open.

Don't tell me you're surprised.

Frank was in the dining room. He'd thrown the sheet back from an oak sideboard and pulled open the top drawer.

"All here," he muttered.

"I didn't see the guy carrying anything when he ran out," I said. "Except a screwdriver."

Frank jumped. I braced myself for a fresh, and justified, round of shouting, but all I got was the sound of teeth clicking together as he clamped his jaw shut. Moving very deliberately, he closed the sideboard drawer and then locked it with the old-fashioned key hanging on the ring with his car keys.

"What did you say your name was?" he asked as he pulled the dustcover back into place.

"I didn't. But it's Annabelle Britton."

He nodded. Then he brought a black notebook out of one jacket pocket and a pencil out of another. He flipped the book open and started writing.

There is a special sinking feeling you experience when you realize your bad ideas might be about to come home to roost. "Umm . . . are you a c— Police?"

"Journalist," he answered, which was only marginally better.

"But you are Frank Hawthorne, right?"

His pencil stilled. "And you get to ask that because?"

"Because for all I know, you could be burglar number three. This house is getting a lot of foot traffic today."

The man ducked his head, and although it was tough to tell in the dim light, he might have been trying not to laugh. He also put down the notebook and pencil on the dining table so he could flip open his wallet and hand me his driver's license. Sure enough, the photo that stared out of the plastic rectangle matched the man in front of me, and the name typed alongside was Darius Francis Samuel Hawthorne.

"Old family name?" I asked.

"Old family name," he confirmed. "'Frank' was always the least bad of the possibilities."

"I feel your pain." I also handed him back his license.

"So, you believe I'm me?"

"If you believe I'm me."

"Deal." He held out his hand, and we shook. He had a nicely judged grip, not too firm or too delicate. "So, now that we're all friends, you're going to tell me what you're doing here, right?"

I didn't exactly cross my fingers then, but I thought about

it. "I really did follow Alistair. Valerie McDermott—I'm staying at McDermott's B and B"—I waved in the general direction of the backyard—"asked me to keep an eye out for him. She said he'd been missing, so when I saw him hanging around her back fence, I decided to see if I could find out where he went." *Please don't remember the gate was locked.*

But if Frank remembered, he wasn't letting on. He just kept making his notes. Watching somebody write down what you're saying is surprisingly nerve-racking. I wonder if he knew that. Probably he did.

"Half the town's been trying to get hold of Alistair since the funeral. Why are you the one he comes out for?"

"Half the town has not fed him brisket tacos from the Pale Ale. And even then, he wouldn't exactly let me hold on to him."

The corner of Frank's mouth turned up into a smile that was not entirely voluntary. "Sounds like Alistair. Grab the food and run."

"That's what Valerie said. Anyway, when I got to the house, the back door was open and I heard Alistair inside. I was afraid he might be in some kind of trouble."

"You heard him?" Frank quirked an eyebrow at me.

"He was crying . . ."

Right on cue, an earsplitting, breathtaking, heartrending howl with no visible source split the air.

"Like that," I finished limply, but Frank had already started for the kitchen at top speed. Of course I followed. I am nothing if not predictable. "Where is he?"

"Basement." Frank pulled open the door. "The vents in this place are sound conductors. He used to sit down there and howl just like that if I forgot to clean his litter box." Frank thudded down the dim stairs and there didn't seem to be any reason not to head down behind him.

Until I got to the bottom, and the Vibe hit.

❦ 8 ❧

🐾 SADNESS. SADNESS AND cold and a long, slow falling away, away, away . . . hard hands on my back . . . and the stone walls twisted and the dirt floor tipped and I was sliding away, away into the cold and away from the pain . . .

And hate. Hate and anger that burned. When would this end? Was it over, was it over, hate . . .

"Hey, are you all right?" Frank's voice came from a long ways off, somewhere past the cold and the falling and the twisting, tipping darkness that was trying to swallow the world whole.

"Dead." I'd blurted the word out. "Dead, right here, dead. Oh, my God. Help. Will help. Must help." I was babbling, but I couldn't stop. The rush of feeling was too strong to even try to fight. "Will be right. Must be right. Won't let me down. Won't win. Won't win. Coming for me. Too late, too long. No. Can't believe it. Hate. Hate you. Die this time! No. No! Will help . . ."

"Hey, hey, come on. Sit down . . ."

"No!" I shouted. He was holding me up. Had I fallen? Hands on my back. Hands under my hips. Fallen. Fallen hard, fallen down all those stairs away from hate and into the dark and the cold and new pain. "Out . . . gotta get out . . . please . . . help, help me, will help . . ."

"Okay, okay. But you gotta help me. Ready? One step at a time, okay? Here we go."

He was moving us both forward. My foot found a stair. My hand found the railing. There was an arm under my shoulders supporting and steadying me as we climbed the long, slow way back up.

"Merow?" Alistair. I couldn't see straight, but I knew the cat was there. We'd reached the top of the stairs, and I felt his warm, furry side pressing against my shins.

"Bad timing, cat," muttered Frank.

Except it wasn't, because all at once, my vision cleared and my wobbly legs steadied. I found enough strength to walk the rest of the way out the kitchen's screen door, into the sunshine and onto the flagstone patio, where, thankfully, a white wicker bench waited for me to sit down. Alistair immediately jumped up onto my lap.

"Oof," said one of us. I think it was me.

Frank sat down on the wicker table in front of the bench. Was there some kind of state regulation that said houses with little old ladies and cats must also have a suite of white wicker? I needed Google. What I had was a big gray cat rubbing his head against my chin and purring like an affectionate motorboat.

"I'm okay," I told Frank. And Alistair. It was even true. I was breathing. I could see again and the world had stopped spinning.

"Good," said Frank. "Now, you want to tell me what that was about?"

No. No, I really didn't. I automatically dug into my well-stocked pantry of Lies I Tell About My Vibe.

"Merow!" Alistair gave my hand a firm head butt.

"Not now, cat, okay?" I picked Alistair up and set him on the patio. He jumped back into my lap and hunkered down.

I felt the tiny pinpricks of his claws. If I tried to move him now there would be damage to skin, not to mention my favorite yoga pants.

I sighed in defeat. Frank, on the other hand, frowned in deep and implacable skepticism.

"Those must have been some good tacos."

"Pale Ale's finest."

"You were going to tell me what happened back there?" I wasn't entirely sure if Frank was asking me or Alistair. Alistair, however, looked at me expectantly.

"You aren't going to like it," I told them both.

"I'd say that's a decent bet."

"Mrrp," agreed Alistair.

Me, I did not believe I was having this conversation with either one of them.

I could still lie. I always lied about the Vibe. I was good at it. But as I sat there, both strength and sense drained away, and all I had left was the truth. "Your aunt died at the bottom of those stairs."

"Yes, thank you, I knew that." Frank's words were flat and bitter, and I really couldn't blame him for that.

"I'm sorry."

"You really better not be angling for the job of my psychic friend."

"Believe me—I would give a whole lot not to know this right now."

Alistair swatted at me with one paw. "Hey!"

The cat stared belligerently back at me, blinking his baby blues. Frank, unsurprisingly, did not look at all pleased either.

"So you're not going to tell me my aunt had a last message for me? Like 'Sell the house and give this person all the money'?"

"Um, no. Look. Sometimes when I get to a place, I get a Vibe . . . a feeling. Sometimes it's about something that already happened. Sometimes it's about something that's going to happen." Now that I'd started, words just poured out of me. "I don't need it, I don't want it, but I've never been able to do anything about it and it doesn't matter if you don't believe it or I don't believe it or the cat doesn't believe it—"

"Meow!"

"It happens anyway, and it happened when I got into the garden, and again in the basement. And your reaction is exactly why I hate to talk about it." I struggled under the weight of reluctant cat, but I got to my feet. "And I know you want me gone, so I am out of here. Sorry to have intruded." Very sorry. Completely sorry. So sorry as not to be believed. I started across the lawn, heading for the gate and McDermott's on the other side with no intention whatsoever of pausing or looking back. I clutched my purse strap and tried not to think about the magic wand and the photo inside. I'd figure out what to do about them later.

"Did somebody push her?" called Frank.

So much for good intentions. I not only stopped dead; I turned around.

"What?"

Frank was on his feet and shoving his hair back from his forehead. He stared past me at the garden and the apple trees, like he was hoping they'd have a different answer to his question. Alistair rubbed up against his shins, but Frank ignored him. "This thing—this Vibe or whatever you call it—did it tell you if somebody pushed her down the stairs?"

He was serious. Dead serious. Which was not the expression I wanted in my head right then, but it was the only one that seemed at all appropriate as I met his eyes and saw they'd gone hard and sad.

"The cops say it was an accident," he told me. "They say Aunt Dot must have lost her balance and fell, or maybe tripped over the cat."

"Meow!" Alistair head butted Frank. Frank kept ignoring him.

"What's this Vibe of yours say? Was she pushed?"

"It doesn't work like that," I told him. "It's not like a

vision. It's . . . emotional." I waited for him to make some wisecrack about female intuition, but Frank Hawthorne was, thankfully, way smarter than that.

"So what did you feel?"

I rubbed my hands together. I'd had a few people ask me about what my Vibe meant before, but not like this. Not when it was important, and deeply personal. I swallowed and made up my mind.

I also sat back down on the wicker bench, because I had no idea what was going to happen next. Alistair wound around between my ankles in that snaky way cats do and jumped back into my empty lap. I took a deep breath, and slowly, carefully, I reached for the fading echoes of my Vibe.

It turned out it was a good thing I'd sat down, because I was shaking again. Alistair meowed once and pressed close against my tummy. I put both hands on him, and the trembling eased.

"I got . . . sadness. Worry. She hurt." Frank looked away. "Not for long. I think . . . there was a sense that everything was *going* to be okay." I frowned. There had been thoughts, words, but they were all jangled up with the sadness and the falling. "Help was coming. It . . . something . . . would be made right." *Won't win.* Those were Dorothy Hawthorne's thoughts, Vibed into my mind. *Won't win. Can't win.*

But was that about herself? Was Dorothy thinking, *I can't win*? Or was it about somebody else? As in, *They can't win*? I wrapped my arms around Alistair, and the cat purred, warm and reassuring, anchoring me in place. I didn't want to say what came next. I didn't want Frank to have to hear it, because it would be painful. But he'd asked, and some deep part of me knew it would be wrong to leave this out.

"Hate," I whispered. "There was hate and anger, and . . . and . . . waiting. For things to be over, for this to be done and gone."

A muscle in Frank's cheek twitched. "Who did she hate?"

"She?" I started. "I, no, I'm sorry. I'm not used to this. I don't, I never . . . but it wasn't her . . ." I stopped and played my own words back again, this time really hearing what I'd said and understanding it. "It wasn't her. There were two sets of . . . of feelings. Two people."

Frank was staring at me, anger and tears shining in his eyes. I closed my own eyes. It didn't help, because it was in me now. I didn't want it, but it was not going away. Dorothy Hawthorne hadn't just died in her home.

She'd been murdered there.

🐾 9 🐾

🐾 THE CERTAINTY OF murder leaves a bitter taste in your mouth. It also puts a major damper on the conversation. Fortunately, we were both saved from having to try to come up with any kind of small talk by another voice filtering out from the house.

"Hello? Frank? You in there?"

Frank's face twisted up in disbelief. "Oh, this is perfect," he muttered as he got to his feet. "Just . . . perfect."

Before I could ask any questions, a trim older man in a tan business suit pushed open the kitchen door.

"Hey, Frank, I was heading past and I saw the door open and—" He stopped as if he'd just noticed me. "Oh. I'm sorry. Am I interrupting?"

Alistair hissed, jumped off my lap, and vanished into the bushes. Normal cat style of vanishing this time, not Cheshire cat style. Guess he saved that for special occasions.

"No, you're not interrupting." With a certain amount of effort, Frank relaxed his face into something approaching a neutral expression. "Ellis Maitland, this is Anna Britton.

She's staying over at the McDermotts'. Anna, this is Ellis Maitland."

Son of the very blond, very rich, very regal Elizabeth Maitland. I smiled politely and took the hand Ellis held out.

Banker, I thought. *Or maybe real estate agent.* Every inch of him seemed designed to inspire confidence, from the perfectly calculated handshake to the tailored suit with crisp white shirt to the neatly combed chestnut hair with just the right amount of distinguished gray at the temples. I had the sneaking and rather snarky suspicion the rest of it might be dyed. He was definitely not a young man. Although it was early in the season, he already had a good suntan. He probably got it on the golf course. Ellis Maitland looked like the kind of guy who talked business with a nine iron, or whatever it was golfers used to knock helpless small objects around.

"Pleased to meet you." Mr. Maitland looked from Frank to me and back again, like he'd caught us in the act of something adolescent. "Are you in town on business, Miss Britton?"

"Vacation."

"Something I can do for you, Ellis?" asked Frank.

"I'd heard you finally wrapped up Dorothy's probate," he said to Frank. "That must be a relief."

"Yeah, it is." Frank's answer wasn't exactly hostile, but it sure wasn't welcoming either. I wondered why, but not for long.

"If there's anything . . . ," Ellis began, but Frank held up his hand.

"I'm still not ready to sell."

"That obvious?"

"'Fraid so, yep. 'Specially since you're showing up in the super-agent suit."

I rubbed my face to cover the smile. I'd been right. Ellis Maitland was a real estate agent.

"Okay, I admit it." Ellis chuckled and held up his own hands in surrender. "I want the house. It's a terrific property." He stopped, probably because he saw the genuine distaste that tightened Frank's jaw. "But that's not why I'm doing this, and you know it. Or you should. We've known each other a long time, Frank, and I really do want to help."

Frank's shoulders sagged. "I know, Ellis, I know. It's just . . . it's been a lot . . ." He glanced toward the house, and I knew he was thinking about the basement stairs and what had happened in there. I sure was. "I need more time to think."

"Sure, sure. I just hope that with Dorothy gone you haven't started . . ."

"Do *not* go there, Ellis," Frank snapped.

"Okay, okay. I won't."

Where? Where!

But Ellis Maitland, darn him, had already sighed and moved on. "But it has been six months and—" Ellis paused and glanced at me again. I tried to look harmless, or at least like I wasn't on the edge of my white wicker seat to hear what came next. Frank just shrugged. The combination must have worked, because Ellis kept going. "I know how much you sank into the *Seacoast News* to get it up and running. You're going to need more cash soon, and you know it. Just like you know you risk sinking the whole enterprise if you have to take out another big loan. This house is a real asset. At least it can be if you move on it before the next bubble bursts." He looked at me again. "Unless you've got some other plans . . . ?"

"No. Nothing," answered Frank a little too quickly. His phone buzzed in his pocket and he swore as he pulled it out and checked the screen. "In fact, I'm late to an interview for that newspaper, which, as you so helpfully pointed out, is on shaky ground. So if you both will excuse me. I need to lock up." He fished around in his jacket pocket and came up with his keys. "You'll let me know if you see Alistair again, won't you, Anna? If he's letting you feed him, maybe you can coax him into staying put long enough for me to catch up with him."

"Sure." I got to my thankfully steady feet. Frank and I locked gazes. His said we weren't done here. Mine agreed. It didn't matter that I had no way to contact him. Portsmouth was not a big place. We'd find each other whether we wanted to or not.

Ellis held out his hand to the other man. "We'll talk later, all right, Frank?"

"Yeah, sure." There was no enthusiasm in Frank's answer, or the handshake. Then he walked us back through the shadowy house and out the front door, which he shut on us both. Firmly. That was followed up with the clacking of locks and dead bolts being turned.

"You have to excuse Frank," Ellis said. "Dorothy's death hit him really hard."

"That's not surprising, I guess." I also backed up as much as the small porch allowed. I needed some breathing space. Ellis Maitland was a tall, broad man, and whether he meant to or not, he loomed. "It sounds like they were really close."

"They were, but, you know, there's mourning and there's hanging on to the past for no good reason. It's not like Dorothy was . . ." He stopped and chuckled. "Well, she was a character, right? We all get like that when we pass a certain age, I guess."

He was saying this to the house as much as to me. I wrapped my arms around myself. I really wasn't ready to leave yet. There were too many unanswered questions. They included whether Frank had gone back to looking for stuff that might have gone missing, like the wand from his aunt's altar. Abruptly and ridiculously, I wished Alistair was still here. I wanted something to hold on to.

At the same time, I felt like I owed Frank for what I'd just put him through. The least I could do was get this guy off his porch. There was definitely history there, and not the good kind.

"I heard Dorothy's death was very sudden," I said as I started down the short stone path toward the picket fence and the front gate. "That'd be hard on anybody."

"Sure, sure. Of course." Ellis gestured me through the gate ahead of him. "Dorothy raised Frank, you know, after his mother died. His father did his best, but he was always on the road . . ." There was a sleek black BMW parked at the curb. Ellis paused at the passenger side and drummed his fingers on the roof. "I just wish he could get over feeling guilty about this house."

"Why guilty?"

"He was trying hard to get Dorothy to sell right before she died."

"Oh." I hitched up my purse strap.

"Yeah. Oh." Ellis shook his perfectly groomed head. "I'm sure Frank was really worried about all the stairs in the old place. Dorothy was sharp as a new pin—nobody could say she wasn't—but she was eighty and her balance wasn't what it used to be. A house like this takes a lot of upkeep, too." His fingers stopped their drumming. Instead, he brushed at some speck of dust on the glossy black paint job. "Unfortunately, people knew that they were fighting about the house. So when Dorothy did fall, some of them jumped to a set of really shameful conclusions, which hasn't made things any easier for him."

"It's a reality-show world." I murmured Sean's words. "Nobody wants to believe in normal anymore."

"Exactly. The most dramatic conclusion has to be the right one."

There was one problem. In this case, I happened to know the most dramatic conclusion was right. A murder had been committed. Somebody had stood at the top of those stairs and watched Dorothy die.

"So," I said, with what I hoped was a tone of gossipy curiosity. "You think this house really is a solid investment?"

"Oh, yes. Real estate prices all around Portsmouth have rebounded nicely over the past couple of years." Ellis Maitland was looking at me thoughtfully, but not in a maybe-we-could-be-friends way like Frank had. This was a maybe-she's-useful kind of way. "If you're a friend of Frank's, maybe you can talk some sense into him. Everybody knows how hard it is to make a newspaper pay, even with a good business plan and a strong Web presence. If this house stays empty, it'll turn into a real white elephant. Then he'll either have to sell too fast or he'll lose the paper, and he's worked so damn hard." Ellis shook his head again; then he saw the expression on my face and chuckled. "I know what you're thinking."

I wouldn't bet on it. But I bit my tongue before I said that out loud. Not that Ellis was waiting for me to talk. "You're thinking, 'This guy, he's in real estate. He's only interested in the money.' Am I right?"

"I plead the Fifth."

"Don't bother." He waved his tanned hand again. He had a chunky gold ring on his pinkie, I noticed, but no wedding band. "I know our reputation. But I really do care about Frank, and about Portsmouth. This town is my home. All my roots are here, and I want to see it thrive. A good source of local news is part of that." He fished in his pocket for a set of keys and hit the button on the fob. In answer, the BMW beeped and the driver's side door popped open. "Maybe you could at least find the cat? If Frank knew Alistair was safe in a good home, it might give him what he needs to finally let go."

"I'll do what I can." This statement had the virtue of being both true and completely noncommittal.

Ellis had that thoughtful look on his face again. I had the sense of being sized up, and my shoulders stiffened. "I'm sure I'll be seeing you again, Miss . . . ?"

"Britton," I told him. For a second I debated whether to add the rest of it. Diplomacy and self-preservation said keep quiet. Diplomacy and self-preservation lost. "Annabelle Blessingsound Britton."

Ellis's direct gaze went vague and distant. I could see him scrolling through associations in his mind like he was flicking through his phone's contacts list. Finally, he had it. "Your family's from here, too? A"—he looked at me, and this time I got to watch him estimate my age—"grandmother, maybe?"

"That's right. Annabelle Mercy Blessingsound."

"Well." A half dozen different emotions chased each other across Ellis Maitland's face, momentarily overriding his professional pleasantness. "This is some coincidence. My mother will want to know you're here."

"She does. We met yesterday when she stopped by the Pale Ale." I paused, looking for a properly vague yet leading untruth. "Actually, I was hoping to have a chance to look up some of Grandma B.B.'s old friends while I was in town. Maybe . . ."

"Well, I don't know if she and my mother were *friends* exactly . . . You know how women of that generation can be, especially in a small town. Lots of little rivalries and old grudges."

Nice try. I gave Ellis the calmest smile I could manage. "Maybe we can see about making peace."

"It'd be a worthwhile effort." Ellis tapped the BMW's roof a couple of times, like he was knocking on wood. "I'll send out some feelers. See what comes back. Glad to have met you, Miss Britton." While I was still drawing breath to ask my next question, Ellis ducked into his shiny black car and shut the door on me and the rest of the world.

❧ 10 ❧

❧ I WATCHED ELLIS Maitland's car as it pulled away down Summer Street. Since I didn't have a high-priced automobile, I just drummed my fingers on my purse. "Well, A.B., doesn't look like you're getting out of this mess anytime soon."

Because never mind the wand I'd accidentally taken without permission, or the fact that somewhere on the streets of Portsmouth, there was a startled would-be burglar with a recent cat-inflicted injury. Never mind that Grandma B.B. (who still had not called me back) had once lived in Portsmouth and made an enemy of Elizabeth Maitland and never talked about either event. Even put aside Alistair the Spooky Cat. I still really needed to know just how my picture came to be on that altar in Dorothy Hawthorne's attic.

Dorothy Hawthorne, who I now knew had been murdered.

About then it sank in that I'd been standing there talking to myself for a long time, and Frank—who'd said he had an interview to get to—hadn't come out of the house. I tried to tell myself that it was probably a phone interview. Or he might have gone out the back. My shoulder blades tightened, but I didn't let myself look around. Frank might be watching from the house, and I didn't need to look guilty for him.

It occurred to me right then that there was somebody I could talk to—Valerie McDermott. She and Dorothy Hawthorne had been good friends. At least, she said they had. As soon as I thought that, the events of this long, strange day sort of shifted sideways in my head to make room for a new question. I checked the time on my phone and saw it was nearly five o'clock. I hit Martine's number even though I knew she would be in the middle of getting ready to reopen for dinner. I also walked a discreet distance up the block, just in case Frank Hawthorne really was watching.

"Busy here, Britton," Martine answered briskly after the fourth ring. In the background I could hear a kitchen's worth of shouts and clatter.

"I know, I know. Sorry. I just . . . why'd you pick McDermott's for me?"

"Why? Something wrong with the beds?"

"No. Nothing. It's great. Just . . . why McDermott's?"

Martine's sigh was sharp and short. "I told you. Val's a friend, and she's fighting to keep the place running. You know how it goes. So I was pretty sure there'd be room for you on zero notice."

"Just like that? There wasn't any more to it?"

"What else could there be?"

"Nothing. Nothing. Sorry, and thanks." I tried to sound casual and failed. I also failed to hang up quickly enough.

"What's going on, Anna?"

"I'll tell you when I see you." Because maybe by then I'd know.

Martine paused for a full three seconds. I wondered what she was drumming her fingers on. "Okay. Take care of yourself."

"Working on it."

This time, I not only hung up; I stuffed the phone back in my purse and started walking.

I TOOK THE long way back to McDermott's. The really long way, which went all the way through downtown and paused at the River House for fried clams and a view of the peaceful, beautiful, entirely normal Piscataqua River. I spent the entire meal resolutely checking e-mails and my Hey-Look! page and Twitter and not—I repeat, not—thinking about witches, wands, spooky cats, murder or any old grudges Grandma B.B. might have left behind her.

Right. I wouldn't believe me either. But I did have the fried clams.

By the time I made it back to McDermott's, summer's twilight had settled across Portsmouth. I was no closer to knowing what I could, or should, do about the mess swirling around me. I had, however, managed to gather enough nerve back together that I felt ready to resume my interrupted conversation with Valerie McDermott.

Well, mostly ready.

The great room was empty when I walked in. So much for all that nerve gathering. I puffed out my cheeks. Where should I try next? The kitchen? Valerie and Roger had to have rooms somewhere, unless they didn't live in. I hadn't asked, I realized. There'd been no reason to. But as I turned away, I noticed a glass-paneled door hung with a gold curtain and a brass plaque that read OFFICE.

It also had voices coming from the other side.

"Don't you think I'd know if something was wrong?" Valerie was saying. "Julia hasn't even met her."

Walk away, A.B. Just . . . walk away.

Of course I didn't. I walked forward. Right up to the door, keeping to one side so they wouldn't see my shadow on the curtain. It would be rude to interrupt, right?

"Okay, say she is really answering Dorothy's summons." The second voice belonged to a woman, but she wasn't anybody I knew. "What took her so long?"

She? She's answering Dorothy's summons?

"I love Julia, you know that," answered Val. "But she's listening to her fears. Alistair wouldn't pick the wrong person."

Julia? This put a complete end to any pesky misgivings I might have had about eavesdropping. In fact, I leaned closer.

"We don't know that Alistair's picked anybody," said the other woman. "We just know she saw him."

"He came to her when he hasn't come to anybody else, including Julia," replied Val stubbornly.

"Okay, Val." The other woman sighed heavily. "What if you just give it a couple days? Try to get to know her better before you rush into things?"

"But we don't know for sure how long she's staying. What if she decides to leave before—?"

"If it's real, if it's right, she'll stay. We have to trust that Dorothy knew what she was doing." Other Woman paused. "And we need to trust Julia as well."

"We could call a gathering," Val went on doggedly. "Reinforce the summons. Or initiate a scrying."

"And we will. But . . ."

I didn't hear what came after that. I backed away, one step, two steps. I turned around and walked back to my room. Walked. Did not run. Did lock my door. Did sit down slowly on the edge of the bed like I didn't trust my knees to hold me up anymore.

Summoning. Scrying. A gathering.

Magic.

My friendly, smiling hostess and whoever was with her in there were talking about magic, about witchcraft, like it was a real thing. Not just in stories or on TV. Not just a weird feeling inside my head.

I pulled the wand out of my purse and stared at it. Those

women, those . . . witches were talking about Alistair and
they were talking about me.

I reminded myself that there was absolutely nothing
wrong with an alternative religion or point of view. I
reminded myself that exploration of diverse ideas and life-
styles was healthy.

But once again, myself wasn't listening. I couldn't stop
thinking about the wand and the cat and everything that had
happened to bring me right to this house, right at this time.

Dizziness washed through me. I pressed the heel of my
hand against my forehead. *What's happening?* I stared around
the room. A river of anger and sorrow flowed through my mind
that would not be stopped. How could I have liked Valerie,
even for a minute? She was not normal. Maybe she and her
friends, whoever they were, were harmless crazies, but they
were crazy all the same. Belief in magic was not rational. It
was most definitely not normal. Why was I even still here? I'd
been right before, when I'd thought about leaving. I needed to
be on the road, on my way back to Boston. There was nothing
to keep me here now that I'd seen Martine. Why did I want to
get involved in this place and its problems? I had plenty of my
own problems. I needed to get back to work. My dad was still
recovering from his heart attack. I needed to be there to help.
What would Bob, Ted and Hope think if they found out I'd
gone off the rails and started hanging around with a bunch of
witches in Portsmouth?

"Stop," I whispered, but I couldn't stop. I shouldn't even
be here. I should pack up and go. I didn't belong here.

"Stop it!" I gripped the wand. "Stop it, *now!*"

Outside my window, something screamed. I jumped up
and shoved back the curtains. For a split second, a skinny
goldfinch stared back at me with beady black eyes. I jerked
away, and at that same instant, a silver blur dropped onto the
sill. The bird screamed again, outraged and way too loud for
such a tiny thing. It launched itself into the air, two feathers
falling away behind it like in an old Tweety Bird cartoon.

Alistair, the silver blur, bared his teeth and hissed.

I threw open the window and the cat jumped inside. I scooped him into my arms and buried my face in his fur. Alistair purred and nuzzled me.

"It's okay, Alistair," I said to him, but we both knew I was really saying it to myself. "It's okay. It's okay."

Somebody was pounding at my door.

"Anna? Anna, are you all right?"

It was Valerie.

❧ 11 ❧

❦ ALISTAIR SLID OUT of my arms and did the snaky-curl thing around my ankles, unfazed by the interruption. I didn't feel anywhere near as calm. My nerves were all ringing like Christmas bells. At least all those cold, mocking thoughts had evaporated. I was just me in my own head again.

"What just happened here?" I asked Alistair. He blinked up at me, innocent and trusting.

"Anna?" called Valerie again.

"Just a minute!" I wiped my palms on my pants and stashed the wand under my pillow. I also opened the door.

Valerie stood in the hall, breathing hard like she'd run up the stairs. Considering those stairs and her condition, that was pretty impressive, but not quite as impressive as the African American woman in the blue police uniform right behind her.

"Hey, Valerie," I said, and I nodded at the officer, who nodded back. "Everything okay?"

"Uh, yeah," she panted. "I thought, we thought . . ."

"Are you all right?" The officer had that take-charge kind of voice you hear on the cop shows when there's been an "incident." I recognized hers as the second voice I'd heard coming from the office earlier. "There was some sound of a possible disturbance." She said this smoothly, and she was casually looking over my shoulder, trying to see as much of the room behind me as possible without obviously craning her neck. She was only a little taller than me, with a lean, athletic build and medium brown skin. A spray of dark freckles decorated both cheeks. Her straightened hair was streaked with red and amber and pulled back into a severe bun. She was also in full cop regalia, badge and all.

"This is Kenisha Freeman," said Valerie belatedly.

"Hi," I said.

"Merow," said the cat by my side.

"This is Alistair." I told them. "But, then, you guys know each other, don't you?" Valerie and Officer Freeman both stared. I may have taken a little juvenile satisfaction in having startled them. Alistair, on the other hand, plumped his butt down and started washing a paw. The side effect of this was that the way into my room was now pretty effectively blocked. Smart cat.

"Can we come in?" Valerie spoke the words slowly, and she was still looking at Kenisha when she did. Kenisha nodded.

I glanced down at Alistair. Alistair picked himself up and strolled coolly back into the room.

"Okay," I agreed. I would think about the fact that I had been seeking approval from a cat later. Much later. Preferably with a strong drink in hand.

I stood back to let the women pass. Alistair leapt onto the windowsill and settled down, tucking all four feet under him until he resembled a calm cat loaf.

Valerie took the chair by the fireplace and rested her hand on her round belly. "So."

"So." Officer Freeman went to stand by the window,

which was, coincidently, the best place to keep watch on the whole room. Alistair didn't even flinch. "Who's going first?"

I looked at Valerie and at Alistair. Valerie looked at me. Alistair closed his eyes and yawned.

"Okay," I said. "This morning after breakfast, I saw Alistair hanging around the back fence. Since Valerie said people were looking for him, I went through the gate to see if I could catch up with him—"

"I understood that gate was kept locked," remarked Officer Freeman.

"Really?" I remarked back.

"Really. There was a theft from the house not too long ago. A computer and a few other personal items." If there's one person who can beat a cat at a stare down, it's a trained cop. I was out of my league here and I knew it.

"Then what happened, Anna?" prompted Valerie.

I took a deep breath. This was not something I had planned on saying with a uniformed officer paying close and professionally polite attention to every word. On the other hand, I had every reason to believe that Kenisha Freeman was more than your average officer of the law, and I very much wanted to see how she and Valerie would react to what I did say. "When I got up to the house, the back door was open and I heard Alistair yowling inside. I followed him."

I half expected Officer Freeman to pull out a notebook and start writing, like Frank had. But she just nodded.

Valerie leaned forward, a little, anyway. "Where did he go?"

"Into the attic. Where I found this." I pulled the photo from *New England Arts Monthly* out of my purse and handed it to her. Officer Freeman came around so she could get a good look too.

"You got into Dorothy's attic?" Valerie took my picture. She didn't look surprised or even concerned. If anything, she looked a little misty-eyed. She also said "got into," not "went into."

"Alistair got in first. I heard him crying up there and tried the door. It was stuck, except then it wasn't, and I got in."

I met Officer Freeman's gaze, and we watched each other without blinking for a good long moment.

"Don't worry," she said. "I believe you."

Why? But I didn't ask that, because that is never what you ask when the police accept your crazy story.

"It's starting to look like you were right, Val," said Officer Freeman to Valerie.

Valerie nodded. "She couldn't resist that last, grand gesture."

Which was just about enough. I reached out and plucked my photo from Val's fingers. "Valerie, Officer . . ."

"Kenisha," she said.

"Kenisha. I am having a very weird day here. If you know what's going on, please, tell me. Dorothy Hawthorne, a woman I never even heard of before yesterday, had my picture in her attic, on her altar, under a magic wand." Which was currently under my pillow. That part I was not ready to confess. "Please," I said again. "I really don't understand any of this, and I just want some answers."

"And you'll get them." Valerie heaved herself out of the chair. "We probably should have done this as soon as you told me about Alistair. Just give me a second to tell Roger we're going out. Can you drive, Kenisha?"

Kenisha didn't move. "Don't you think you should maybe call first?"

"No," said Valerie firmly.

"She won't want to talk."

"Then she can tell us that in person."

Kenisha rolled her eyes. "I knew there was no chance of getting to bed early tonight."

"Umm . . . you're going somewhere?" I asked, mostly to remind them I was still in the room.

Valerie faced me. "Anna, I'm taking you to meet a woman who can answer all your questions. She won't want to, and she's not going to like you, but you two need to meet each other face-to-face."

"Oh, no. We're not playing that game. If you know something, you're telling me right here."

"Normally I'd agree with you, Miss Britton—," began Kenisha.

"Anna," I said.

"Anna," she agreed. "But you may have noticed we've got some extenuating circumstances here."

That look of special reluctance must have showed on my face, because Valerie sighed impatiently. "Did something strange happen to you right before we got here, Anna? A sudden flood of foreboding or bad feeling? Maybe even a panic attack? With a really strong urge to get out of the house or out of town?"

My mouth opened but no sound came out.

Valerie nodded. "You were attacked, Anna. Someone tried to cast a spell on you."

"That's not possible," I whispered. "Is it?"

"It is," said Kenisha quietly. "And you need to know what it is and how it's happening. So, please, will you come with us?"

I looked at Alistair.

"Meow," he said firmly.

"Okay," I said slowly. "I'm in." Then, because normal was not even part of the conversation anymore, I looked over at Alistair. "You coming?"

IT WAS NIGHT; it was dark. I was not wearing sunglasses, but I did have the spooky cat curled up on a towel in a lidless Xerox paper box beside me, and I was being driven with professional dexterity toward Market Square by Officer Kenisha, with Val in the passenger seat.

There is a special kind of tension that builds up when you're near people who have answers that they can't, or won't, share. I'd lost my patience with it by the time we reached the second stoplight.

"Merowp," said Alistair, rearranging himself in his box. I took this to mean either *Go for it* or *You're on your own, human.* Maybe both.

So I leaned forward as far as my seat belt allowed. "Okay, I know we haven't actually talked about this yet, but you guys are witches, right?"

"Only witch cop in New England," replied Kenisha without taking her eyes off the road. "In New Hampshire, anyway. Once you get down around Salem, all bets are off."

"And the woman we're going to meet . . ."

"Julia Parris," said Valerie.

"She's a witch too?"

Kenisha nodded. She put on her turn signal, before she reached the intersection even. She also waited for the couple with the stroller to get all the way across before she turned.

"Which means Dorothy Hawthorne . . . ?"

"Was also a witch. In fact, she was the leader of our coven until she was killed," said Val.

"Died," corrected Kenisha.

Valerie's silence was so thick, you'd need a blowtorch to cut through it.

"So what does this make Alistair?" I asked. At the sound of his name, one of Alistair's ears twitched and he rolled over in his box, displaying a broad acre of furry tummy. I did not rub it. We didn't know each other that well.

"He was Dorothy's familiar, her magical assistant," said Val softly. "And now, it seems, he's yours."

As much as I might want to, I couldn't argue with that. I was, after all, the one who insisted the cat come along. I had also stashed a magic wand in my purse, just in case.

Since we were stopped at another light, Kenisha took her eye off the road long enough to give me an appraising glance. "Gotta say, for someone who doesn't know anything about the craft, you're being pretty cool about all this."

"Not really. I just hate having nervous breakdowns in public."

Kenisha chuckled. "Roger that."

"*Do* you know anything about the craft, Anna?" asked Valerie.

I thought about saying I had some friends in art school who got into alternate religions, and the New Age and stuff. That was how I'd recognized the altar for what it was. But that seemed a little like telling Glinda the Good I'd once seen a magician at a kid's party.

"Not a thing. I mean, not about real magic. What do you . . . do?"

Val and Kenisha exchanged a look that could only be described as significant. I tried to do the same with Alistair, but Alistair had fallen asleep.

"You wanna take this one or should I?" Valerie asked Kenisha.

"You do it. I'm driving."

"Right." Val twisted around as far as belt and belly would let her. "There are all kinds of covens and practitioners. Some are congregations that worship nature and the feminine principle; some are societies for friendship and support. Some, for better or worse, try to directly influence events and people." She was thinking of somebody or something in particular as she said that, and it was not a happy thought.

"And your kind of coven is . . . ?"

"We're guardians," said Valerie.

"Of the galaxy?"

"Loved that movie," said Kenisha.

The corner of Val's mouth quirked up. "Just of Portsmouth. We use our magic to divert harmful influences, to help those who need it, and to bring justice if we can."

"Justice?"

Julia nodded.

"Like if there's been a murder?"

"That one's my job," said Kenisha firmly. "We do not go messing around there with the magic."

Something told me that Valerie did not entirely agree with this blanket statement. Maybe it was the set of her jaw. Maybe it was the way she was facing forward again, both arms folded over her belly, and not talking.

"So," I said, only kind of changing the subject. "You guys are the good witches of New Hampshire."

"That's about it, yeah," said Kenisha.

"Is there a bad witch?"

I thought I was joking, but neither one of them answered me. The fresh silence was quickly brushed aside by the business of spotting a parking space, which was followed by the smoothest parallel parking job I've ever witnessed. Then there came the process of helping the pregnant woman out of the bucket seat, gathering up the cat and box, and a quick check to make sure the SUV behind us was in fact the required distance from the hydrant, because, well, cop.

None of this changed the fact that neither Valerie or Kenisha had answered me.

blah blah blah blah blah blah blah blah blah blah
blah blah blah blah blah blah blah blah blah blah
blah blah blah blah blah blah blah blah blah blah
blah blah blah blah blah blah blah blah blah blah
blah blah blah blah blah blah blah blah blah blah
blah blah blah blah blah blah blah blah blah blah
blah blah blah blah blah blah blah blah blah blah
blah blah blah blah blah blah blah blah blah blah
blah blah blah blah blah blah blah blah blah blah
blah blah blah blah blah blah blah blah blah blah
blah blah blah blah blah blah blah blah blah blah
blah blah blah blah blah blah blah blah blah blah
blah blah blah blah blah blah blah blah blah blah
blah blah blah blah blah blah blah blah blah blah
blah blah blah blah blah blah blah blah blah blah

❧ 12 ☙

❧ THE SIGN ON the window of Midnight Reads bookstore did not say CLOSED. It said LOST IN THE STACKS. BACK EVENTUALLY. Despite this, the lights were on, and Kenisha pulled the door open without a problem.

"Julia?" Valerie called over the sound of the jingling bells. "It's us!"

You don't need a Vibe to know you've walked into a good bookstore. It's all in the smell. Midnight Reads smelled like paper, ink, warm dust and lemon polish. Wooden display tables and slanting shelves were piled with the latest bestsellers and beach reads. Hand-lettered signs announced NEW, RE-GIFTED, STAFF PICKS and MUST READ.

Low shelves painted with bright primary colors fenced in a kid's space furnished with beanbag chairs and a Lego table. Farther back, broad bookcases made a series of narrow library-style aisles. Plain plaques on the sides announced the sections: ROMANCE, MYSTERY, BIOGRAPHY, FANTASY/SF, RELIGION AND PHILOSOPHY. I couldn't help thinking the owner might do something more interesting with those

blank spaces that faced the customer. To me, they cried out
for murals. Portsmouth is a city full of murals, and I hated
to see a perfectly good flat surface going to waste. The mystery section, for instance, should have a shadowed drawing
of the corpse, and a butler maybe, and old typewriter font . . .
no, wait, cutout letters like for a ransom note and . . .

No, no, no, *A.B.,* I told myself. *You do not get to make
improvements to this place. You do not want to make
improvements. You are just here to meet this Julia person,
who apparently is not going to like you.*

I set Alistair's box down. The cat shook himself, arched
his back and yawned, unimpressed by his new surroundings.
I braced for any Vibe that might be coming.

What I got was dachshunds.

A pair of miniature, energetic wiener dogs galloped down
the MYSTERY aisle—ears flopping, tails wagging and doggy
toenails clicking madly against the floorboards. They also
barked at the tops of their little lungs. I jumped back, knocking into Kenisha, and frantically wondering what I'd do if
we got into a full-on cat-versus-dog fight.

Alistair sat down on my toes.

The dachshunds scampered straight up to us. One was a
shining coppery brown, the other a sleek black and tan. They
frantically sniffed my ankles and Alistair's tail. Alistair
allowed this, all the while projecting an air of extreme
tolerance.

"Hey, Max. Hey, Leo." Kenisha crouched down, rubbing
ears and patting long backs. "Hiya, boys! Good to see
you too!"

Alistair looked up at me with an expression that clearly
said, *Bored now.* At least, he did until the woman came out
from between the shelves. Then he got to all of his feet and
pressed right up against my shins. Kenisha straightened up
too, and the dachshunds stopped sniffing us and scampered
away to snuffle around her ankles.

The woman, who I had to assume was Julia Parris, ignored

the dogs and concentrated on staring daggers at the three of us. Her appearance was nothing short of striking. Wavy white hair cascaded down her back and shoulders. Laugh lines framed her wide mouth and dark eyes. Her flowing purple blouse and ankle-length black skirt accentuated her strongly curved figure. A pair of reading glasses dangled from the silver chain around her neck and she walked with the help of a black cane that had a blue glass sphere for a handle.

To tell the truth, she looked like a cross between Maggie Smith and Mae West.

"You might have told me." She frowned at Valerie and Kenisha.

"You would have refused to see her," replied Valerie.

"You're correct. I would have."

There didn't seem to be a lot of point in letting this go any further without me, so I stepped forward, over Alistair's back. "Hi. Anna Britton." I held out my hand. "Julia Parris, right?"

It took Julia a heartbeat, but she did hold out her hand, and I shook it. Her hand was light in mine, but I felt the strength there. I also saw the anger and the challenge in her dark eyes.

Valerie broke the stare down. "Julia, somebody tried to breach the wards around my house tonight. It wasn't you, was it?"

Julia Parris snatched her long light hand away. "Why on earth would you even ask such a question?" Funny how she said it directly to me.

Valerie didn't answer. She didn't answer a lot when she was upset, I noticed.

I raised my hand. "Um, breach? Wards? Can I get a translation please?"

"A ward is a spell that protects a specific person or place from harm," said Val. "The wards on the B and B were breached, broken, by whatever, or whoever, was trying to force you to leave." She said all this to Julia. "Since I set up the wards, I felt them break. That's why Kenisha and I knew we needed to make sure you were okay."

Julia said nothing. I said nothing. Alistair washed his whiskers, keeping one eye on those snuffling dachshunds.

Kenisha sighed, irritated. "Julia, I know it's not what we were expecting, okay? But how about instead of standing here making accusations, we sit down and talk? We're going to have to at some point."

Julia looked at each one of us, and she took her time about it. Beside her, the dachshunds did their best to appear staunch and alert. This is difficult when you're only a wiener dog, and a cocktail wiener at that.

"Very well." Julia sighed. "Valerie, will you please lock the door?" She gave me a reassuring smile that I didn't believe for a minute. "We're going to be here awhile, I'm afraid, and I don't want anyone interrupting." Her eyes glittered. I sensed her ticking off a point in the back of a mind that was probably— what was that phrase Ellis Maitland had used?—as sharp as a new pin. "Maximilian. Leopold. Come along."

With that, she turned and walked back into the shadows between the shelves, and her dachshunds trotted dutifully behind.

"Well, that could have gone better," muttered Kenisha.

"Don't worry. We'll bring her around," said Valerie.

Yeah, but to what? I had to suppress a shiver, and I chided myself for it. There was nothing to be nervous about. This was a bookstore, on Market Square, with approximately half the tourists in New England strolling past outside. I was in here with nobody but an old lady and a pregnant woman, for pity's sake. And yeah, okay, an armed cop. And, yeah, okay, they were all witches.

Maybe it was reasonable to be a teeny bit nervous.

I scooped up Alistair and followed Kenisha and Val farther into the store. The cat snuggled down into my arms, and I felt strangely glad to have him there. You know things have gone a long way down the weirdness road when you start thinking the spooky cat is your best ally.

Or your familiar.

The tall shelves took up the central portion of the bookshop. On the other side waited a reading nook complete with cozy furniture, a rag rug and an ancient brick fireplace. A plump brown teapot stood on the coffee table.

I stepped onto the rug, and all at once I got hit with a wave of reassurance. It was one of the strongest Vibes I'd ever felt, and it told me I was perfectly safe. I was among friends—trusted friends, good friends. This was right where I was supposed to be. I could relax and be open and honest. But it was too strong, and too one-sided, and I staggered under the force of it, even as Julia turned a knowing and triumphant smile on me.

Magic. This was magic, and she was responsible.

Without thinking about it, I shoved my hand into my purse and gripped Dorothy's wand. In answer, Alistair meowed sharply. He sprang from the crook of my arm to the nearest chair seat and then to the mantelpiece and the knotwork vase full of cut flowers and greenery. Max yapped and scrambled after him, but too late. The vase toppled to the brick hearth. Vibe and vase shattered at the same time.

"Oh, for the love of mud, Julia!" shouted Kenisha. "What are you doing?"

"That was uncalled-for!" added Valerie.

Julia made no answer. Alistair, shaking each paw in turn, picked his way between shards of vase and the scattered stalks of flowers and fresh herbs. He curled around my ankles, while managing not to take his cat's eyes off the dachshunds, who pressed up against Julia, one on each side.

"What just happened here?" I demanded.

"It was a binding spell," Valerie told me. "It was meant to make you . . . suggestible."

Seriously? We'd just met and this woman was slipping me some kind of psychic roofie? I walked up to Julia Parris, close enough that one of the dogs growled a warning. She'd stopped smiling in triumph, or at all.

"I don't know what you think I've done or what you think I'm going to do," I said. Julia was taller than I was and I had to look up to meet her gaze, but I did it, and I gave my words every ounce of feeling I had in me. I didn't take my hand off the wand. "But the only reason I came here was to get answers about the weird stuff that's been happening to me. You don't want me here? Fine. I'll take my . . . the cat and I'll go and we don't have to see each other ever again."

"But what can I possibly have done?" she replied.

She was going to make me say it. She was going to make me admit it, right out loud. "You're a witch," I said. "And you just tried to work a spell to make me trust you."

"And you not only felt it; you resisted," she said. "Far more strongly than I would expect from someone who *appears* to be completely untrained."

"Come on, Julia," said Kenisha softly. "Give it up. Look at Max and Leo. Would they have let Anna, or Alistair, in here if they had any bad intent?"

Julia did look at her dachshunds, and they looked up at her. It was disconcertingly like the way I'd started looking at Alistair, except Max and Leo wagged their tails anxiously and seemed like they might really care.

Julia sat down slowly. She rested both hands on her walking stick and stared, not at the dogs, but at the shattered remains of the vase. At last, she pressed one long hand against her mouth and then against her eyes and her forehead. Something rippled through the room. I felt it against my skin and up my spine. I tightened my grip on the wand.

It was gone. Julia's shoulders slumped, and she suddenly looked very tired and very old.

"Kenisha, Valerie," she said softly. "I would appreciate

some help cleaning up this mess. Miss Britton . . ." She
turned her face toward me.

"Anna," I said.

"Anna. I'm afraid I owe you an apology. But you see, I've
been afraid for months now that Alistair might have become
corrupted somehow. That he . . ." She swallowed. "He might
even have betrayed Dorothy the night she died."

❧ 13 ❧

♣ "HOW COULD ALISTAIR have betrayed Dorothy Hawthorne?"

The remains of the vase were cleared away and peppermint tea was poured into flowered cups. We all claimed seats around the reading nook, with Julia in the wing-backed chair closest to the fireplace. Maximilian draped across her lap while Leopold sat sentry by her toes. Valerie and Kenisha claimed the flowered sofa, which left me in a green armchair with Alistair curled up so tightly on my lap he could have been mistaken for a gray fur pillow, that is, if gray fur pillows purred like they'd recently swallowed an eighteen-wheeler.

"Alistair is not an ordinary cat," Julia reminded me. "He is, or was, Dorothy's familiar."

"I heard." I scratched the dent behind Alistair's left ear and the purr kicked into another gear. "That's supposed to mean he was her . . . assistant?"

"Assistant and companion. Some familiars act as eyes and ears for their partner, or as messengers."

"Think superhero sidekick," suggested Val.

"If you must," Julia said, sighing. "For a practitioner of the *true* craft, a familiar assists the witch's spell working, each according to his, or her, ability and nature." Julia ruffled Maximilian's floppy ears and he wagged his tail in doggy delight. "Normally, if Dorothy was in trouble, she would have sent Alistair for one of us." She gestured around the room with her free hand.

"But none of us saw him the night she was killed," said Val softly.

"Died," Kenisha reminded her.

Valerie shrugged. "It was like he vanished off the face of the earth."

"Very few things can separate a familiar even briefly from his human partner," Julia said. "Most of them involve powerful magic." Max's tail had stopped wagging and his ears pricked up toward me, or maybe it was toward the cat on my lap. Alistair snuggled closer and I let him. Not that I was starting to feel protective toward the spooky feline or anything. "Alistair vanished when he was most needed by his partner, and when he does reappear, he's bonded to you," Julia went on. "Perhaps you can understand why I might be a little suspicious."

I laid my hand on Alistair's furry side. I thought about how he'd led me to the house and to the basement. He knew what had happened there, and he wanted me to know. If— and it was still a big if—he could do that, why couldn't he go get help when Dorothy needed him?

I also remembered my earlier crack about little Timmy falling down the well. Since Dorothy Hawthorne had fallen down the stairs and Alistair was some kind of witch's assistant who really had been supposed to go for help, that joke suddenly seemed less funny.

And here I was thinking about apologizing to a cat.

Did I say normal had left the building? At this point, I couldn't find normal with a flashlight and a GPS. "The attic wasn't locked," I tried.

"Yes, it was. It opened for you because the house, like Alistair, had instructions to wait for you."

"If you really believe Dorothy wanted me here, why are you so . . ."

"I didn't say Dorothy created the instructions. It could have been someone else." She paused. Max lapped at her hand and his whiplike tail went *thwap-thwap* against her thigh. "Your grandmother, for instance."

Wait. What? I shoved myself up straighter in the chair. Alistair lifted his head and made grumpy noises at me. "You did not just call my grandma B.B. a witch."

"I did," replied Julia. "Because she is one."

I straightened up and got a warning prick from Alistair's claws digging ever so lightly into my pants. Okay, I might be almost ready to believe in magic cats, but . . . Grandma B.B. as a witch? My world-traveling, seashell-collecting grandma? The woman who couldn't bake a cookie to save her life but always knew where to find the best French fries and ice cream in whatever town she was living in, and who sent the best birthday and Christmas presents?

Grandma B.B. was a witch?

"You didn't know?" said Val.

"Come on, Val," said Kenisha. "That is not the look of somebody who knows."

"She didn't tell you." A whole set of different expressions chased each other across Julia's face: surprise, hurt and sadness. "Oh, that is so like her."

Now, I will admit I had my disagreements with Gran, but that did not mean this . . . witch got to go talking down my family. Alistair stood up on my knees and arched his back. Leopold, who was still on guard down by Julia's feet, gave an unhappy growl. The cat twitched his tail, but this time the dog wasn't backing down.

"Julia," said Val. "Please."

This time Julia at least looked abashed. Which represented some kind of progress in our relationship, I supposed.

Alistair finished stretching and climbed up the chair to settle himself on the back behind my head, a portrait of a cat on the watch.

"So, I'm guessing you know why she really left Portsmouth?" I made myself speak calmly. It was not the easiest thing I'd ever done.

"We had . . . call it a falling-out, just before Annabelle married Charles Britton and left us."

Fallings-out with Grandma B.B. were not unusual. She tended to be firm in her opinions, and her drama-queen approach to disagreement took some getting used to. I could easily see her butting heads with this Julia, who was no slouch in the drama department herself.

The black-and-tan dachshund, Leopold, whined up at Julia, thumping his tail on the rug. Alistair glowered down at the dog from his perch, and the dog squirmed uncomfortably. I resolutely refused to smile.

"But if Grandma B.B. left town back in the . . ."

"Nineteen sixty-one," said Julia. "I remember quite clearly."

"Okay, if she left in 'sixty-one but never came back, she can't have anything to do with Dorothy's death."

"Merowp," added Alistair. He also flowed back down into my lap and butted my hand firmly with his furry forehead. I took the hint and started scratching behind his ears again.

"How can I . . . we . . . know that?" asked Julia. "Annabelle didn't stop being a witch just because she left Portsmouth. Perhaps she decided to return to settle the argument in her own favor. Perhaps you are some sort of advance scout, or perhaps you on your own decided to come back and create a place of power for yourself."

I opened my mouth to make some kind of comment, and it probably would have been very snarky, but I felt a warning dig from Alistair's claws and decided against it.

"Besides," Julia continued. "How could you have known Dorothy, if not through your grandmother?"

"I didn't know her. I never heard of her before I got here," I said. "I did find my picture on her altar."

Julia just frowned. "The photo was on the altar?"

"Under the magic wand."

"Dorothy really did summon her, Julia," said Valerie.

"Time out." I crossed my hands in the *T* sign. "What do you mean she summoned me?"

Kenisha answered for the class. "A summons is a spell meant to create the conditions favorable to bringing you to Portsmouth, and to Valerie, and Alistair."

Summoned. I didn't like the word or the idea. Pride rebelled. Common sense would have rebelled, but common sense was whimpering under the bed somewhere and refused to come out.

Alistair yawned and stretched and quickly curled back up. Max yipped, probably scolding him for not paying attention. This had no visible effect on the cat whatsoever.

"If she did . . . summon me, her spell probably busted the boiler in my best friend's building," I pointed out.

"That's why you have to be extremely careful when practicing the true craft," said Julia. "This is not the movies. If I want to bring someone good fortune, I cannot wave a wand and make a pile of money appear. I cannot turn their enemies into toads. What I can do is influence events. I can focus and magnify my wish for their good fortune, and if I've done it right, if my craft is true, events and opportunities will align."

"Or," added Valerie, "maybe I could perform a scrying, to look into the past or the future, and find some helpful information for the person."

"Or," put in Kenisha, "a home or a person can be shielded, warded. It might give them enough safety and breathing space until they can find their own solution."

"Or one could perform a dousing to find something lost or hidden that could help them," said Val.

"Or . . . ," began Kenisha, but I held up my hands.

"Okay, okay, I get it. No toads, but lots of other things."
So much my head was spinning.

"The true craft is subtle," said Julia. "But it's powerful.
Things can be mended or broken. Closed or opened. People
can be kept away or brought closer. Helped or harmed. All
this has very real implications, and one can seldom see all
the consequences."

"But if Dorothy was your friend and she"—*say it*—"worked
some kind of spell to bring me here, why wouldn't she tell you
anything about it, or me?"

"That is the question," muttered Julia. All the anger and
suspicion I'd glimpsed when we first came into the bookstore
was shining in her dark eyes. "Why? She knew something,
or she feared something. Why else would she become so
secretive? She practically barricaded herself into that house.
Why would she waste her last workings on bringing a
stranger to take her place, *without telling me*?" The accusa-
tion in those words was aimed right at me, and it bit deep.
Alistair narrowed his slanting eyes. He shifted on my lap,
getting his paws under him. Max jumped down to the floor
to join his brother. He also drew his lips back until he
showed just a little flash of tooth. Alistair answered with a
low, dangerous rumble deep in his throat.

I took a deep breath and hauled my temper back. I made
myself look at the woman in front of me, really look. Slowly,
I saw past the bitterness that hardened her eyes and her jaw,
down to the anger and the indignation and the deep, sad
confusion.

"I am sorry, Julia. Your best friend was keeping secrets
and then she died. That's terrible and I can't blame you for
being hurt. But that doesn't change the fact that I had *nothing* to do with any of this, until she dragged me in."

Julia scooped Max back onto her lap and rested one hand
against the dachshund's back. By her feet, Leo whimpered
and pawed at her hem. With shaking hands she reached down
and set him next to his brother. Both dogs immediately stood

up with their paws on her shoulders, whining and pushing their noses against her cheeks. She hugged them close, while the rest of us stared at our teacups or the fireplace or the bookshelves, giving Julia a moment to collect herself.

"I owe you an apology as well," Julia murmured as she petted her dogs and pressed them, gently but firmly, back into her lap. "The only excuse I have to offer is it has been an extremely difficult time for us all."

Val nodded in agreement. "You see, Anna, we all *know* Dorothy was murdered—"

"You two *think* Dorothy was murdered," said Kenisha. "Despite all the actual evidence to the contrary."

I bit my lip. Alistair narrowed his eyes at me.

"But Dorothy was murdered," I said to the cat and the witches. "I felt it."

❧ 14 ❧

🐾 ALL THREE WOMEN stared at me with varying degrees of shock and hostility. I guess I kind of deserved it.

"I think," said Julia primly, "that we need a little more information."

"Damn straight," said Kenisha. She didn't sound overly enthusiastic.

I swallowed and rested my hand on Alistair's head. With an apologetic glance at Valerie, I told them the whole long story—from seeing Alistair on the B and B's back fence to finding the wand in the attic, to meeting Mr. Mustache and then Frank Hawthorne, and how we both followed Alistair down into the basement where I almost passed out from the wave of emotion that hit me there.

Julia leaned forward. "This feeling, what was it like? Have you ever experienced something like it before?"

To say that the words came slowly is an understatement. I had to drag them out one at a time. "My whole life. Not all the time, but sometimes. I'll walk into a place and get a Vibe on it. No, that's not right. On something that happened there. It can be a good thing or a bad one. I never know which it's going to be, or if it's going to happen at all."

"But you're sure?" said Val. "This feeling, this Vibe, told you someone did push Dorothy down those stairs?"

"Pretty sure, yeah. I felt . . . hands, and someone hating her hard. And . . . Alistair . . ." *Say this, too. No turning back now, A.B.* "He wanted me down there."

We were all silent for a moment, trying to let this sink in.

"What was Frank's response when you said Dorothy had been pushed?" asked Julia, finally.

"He believed me, I think. He wanted to know if I could tell who'd done it."

"Could you?" Valerie scooted up to the edge of her seat.

"Hold it!" Kenisha put up both hands. "Julia, Val, you swore you'd keep the craft out of any inquiry into Dorothy's death."

"We agreed not to influence events," Val corrected her. "This isn't influencing; this is investigating."

"This is bull . . . ," started Kenisha heatedly, but she caught Julia and the dogs all looking down their long noses at her and swallowed the second half of that. "Nonsense."

Julia pretended not to have heard. "What did Frank say, Anna?"

"He didn't get a chance to say much of anything. Ellis Maitland interrupted us."

"There!" Val stabbed a finger at me. "Ellis Maitland! There's your proof."

"You got a very loose idea about proof, Val. How is a real estate agent showing up at an empty house proof of anything?" snapped Kenisha.

Now it was Valerie's turn to ignore people. She shifted herself to face me. "You were asking about the bad witch of Portsmouth, Anna? If we've got one, it's Elizabeth Maitland."

"Valerie!" cried Julia, genuinely shocked.

"I'm sorry. No, I'm not. It's true and we all know it."

"*I* know no such thing," snapped Julia.

"A little help here?" I pleaded toward Kenisha. "I mean I know Elizabeth is Ellis's mother . . ."

"Elizabeth Maitland hated Dorothy," said Val before Kenisha could answer. "If anybody had a reason to kill her and the power to do it, it was Elizabeth."

"We do not know that," said Julia. "We have seen nothing that leads us to that conclusion."

"And it wouldn't matter if we did," added Kenisha.

"Wouldn't matter!" cried Valerie. "How would it not matter?"

"Because we couldn't prove it. How many times have I got to say that, girl? We got *nothing* I can take to my lieutenant, never mind the district attorney. I tried to keep the investigation open when Dorothy died, but they shut us down," she told me. "Because there was no genuine proof. No physical evidence, no chain of events that would hold up."

"Plus your lieutenant is a blind, stubborn old . . . coot who doesn't care about anything as long as the tourists keep coming and the chamber of commerce stays happy." Valerie's eyes glittered with a dangerously determined mix of tears and anger. "It doesn't matter anyway. We don't need them."

"Oh, no." Kenisha held up one finger. "I did not hear you say that. Because you are not even thinking about taking the law into your own hands."

Valerie threw up those hands. "This is Dorothy we're talking about! Our friend!"

"I don't care if it's Mother Teresa." Kenisha did not shout. Her words were all very soft and very precise. "You do not get to decide who's guilty and who's not. That is the court's job. That is the *law's* job."

"We're supposed to help people."

"Yes, we help people. We do *not* decide somebody needs a little magical visit after dark because the law isn't doing things our way."

"That's not what I'm saying."

Kenisha raised one eyebrow. "Isn't it?"

That made Valerie pull back, at least for a minute. Alistair gave me a sideways look, then jumped lazily off my lap to circle around Kenisha's ankles and then Valerie's.

"Kenisha is right," said Julia before Val could gather any fresh arguments. She spoke gently but with the finality of someone used to getting her own way. "Valerie, we cannot use our power to enforce retribution on someone we only suspect."

"On *anyone*," said Kenisha sharply.

"On anyone," agreed Julia. "If it is not covered by *the* law, it most definitely is covered by our law."

"What's our law?" I asked.

"The threefold law," answered Julia.

"What you send out into the world comes back to you three-fold," Valerie muttered as she slumped back onto the sofa.

"Quod ad vos mittere in mundum triplici," I added, remembering the inscription on the wand.

"Exactly," Julia said, and for the first time I heard a note of approval in her voice. "It applies to the good and the bad, to aid as well as . . ."

"Revenge," I finished, and the word sent a shiver up my spine.

"Yes." Julia set both dachshunds on the floor so she could more easily reach for Val's hand. "I am sorry, Valerie. But at least now we do know it was murder. That's something."

Valerie didn't answer, but I did see how her fingers curled around Julia's, holding on.

All at once, I flashed back on the memory of sitting in a speeding cab on a snowy winter day. Dad had had his heart attack. I'd just flown back to Boston and I was on my way to meet my brother Bob and his wife, Ginger, at the hospital. They hadn't answered my texts in the past twenty minutes. Dad might be dying. He might already be dead. I had no way to know, nothing to hang on to. I was powerless and it was all I could do not to scream at the driver, who was already doing eighty through the Boston traffic, to hurry up!

Dorothy had brought that kind of misery down on her

friends by not telling them what she was doing. What kind of secret could she possibly have been keeping from these women, who clearly cared so much for her?

"I'm sorry," I said to Julia, to all of them really. "Not knowing is what hurts the worst."

Julia bowed her head. "I'm sorry as well, for the way I've acted. Of course you weren't to know, or to blame. Whatever Dorothy thought . . . whatever she was doing, the motivation behind it was hers and hers alone."

Leopold and Maximilian stared at Alistair.

"Yip?" said Leo.

"Mrp," grumbled the cat. They all settled back onto their haunches, and that seemed to be that, for the moment anyway.

"So what happens now?" I asked. "Now that I've been . . . summoned." And handed the spooky cat.

"What do you want to happen?" answered Julia.

"Huh?"

She smiled. "Dorothy's spell did not bring you here to fulfill some kind of mythical, preordained destiny. You are being presented with a choice. You can stay in Portsmouth, take a place in our coven, study magic and maybe learn something about yourself, your family and your life. Or you can walk out the door." Julia gestured grandly toward the front of the store and then frowned. "Once I unlock it, anyway. If you genuinely and freely choose to leave, not even Alistair will follow you."

"I thought I was 'summoned.'" Yes, I made the air quotes. You would have too.

"And you answered the summons. Everything you've done since then has been your choice."

I couldn't deny that, as much as I might want to. I remembered the Vibe I got in Dorothy's garden—that powerful sensation of being poised on the edge and not knowing which way to jump. But I had not only jumped; I'd picked the direction. Was I ready to jump again? This time into a life and a way of looking at the world that I barely understood.

"Mrrp?" Alistair illustrated my dilemma by jumping back onto my lap.

"I don't know." I rested my hand on his warm furry back. "I really don't know. I mean, I've only been here two days and I'm already up to my hips in magic and murder. Why should I let myself in for more?"

The three women looked at one another, and I got the feeling Kenisha at least was trying not to laugh.

"Your 'Vibe,' as you call it," said Julia. "It comes on you suddenly? You can't ever bring it on deliberately?"

"Why would I want to?"

"So you also can't ever shut it out, can you?"

"A little," I answered defensively. Why was I being defensive?

"You learned to hide it," said Val. "That's different."

Julia picked up her cup again and swirled it. "What if you could control your Vibe? Bring it on only when you wanted to? If you ever wanted to."

I was staring, but I couldn't help it. The Vibe was just something I'd always had to live with, work around. Hide. Was she actually telling me I could control it?

Julia saw my shock and nodded. "You are a witch of the bloodline, Anna. That means you have some talents and some limitations that those who come to the craft purely by their own choice—like Valerie and Kenisha—don't have. You will always be sensitive to the vibrations and influences around you, but it doesn't mean you have to live at the mercy of those feelings."

"You're serious?" My jaw was hanging open again. Julia nodded, and I saw she was perfectly serious. "I could learn to control my Vibe?"

"Control it, and call on it to help you," said Julia.

I wanted it to be true. I'd always wanted to be a person who didn't have to brace herself whenever she walked into somewhere new. Now Julia was telling me I could be.

All I had to do was become a witch.

❧ 15 ☙

🐾 "I'M SORRY ABOUT what I said about Elizabeth," said Valerie to Kenisha as we stepped onto the sidewalk. Behind us, Julia was turning off the bookstore's lights and pulling down shades, closing up for real this time. I'd said I needed more time to think. She said it was just as well, because she had a business to run and needed a good night's sleep to do it. Kenisha reminded us she wanted to change out of her uniform, and Valerie mentioned she had guests who would be wanting breakfast and clean rooms tomorrow.

I hugged the empty box to my chest. Somewhere between the reading nook and the front door, Alistair simply ceased to be following me. As much as it would have killed me to admit it, I already missed him.

Kenisha shrugged. "We can't do anything on suspicion, Val, even our kind of suspicion. We need proof."

"I know. I do." Val hung her head. "I've just felt so helpless."

"Roger that." Kenisha touched her friend's shoulder

briefly. "How about we get you home? Do you want a lift back, Anna?"

I stared across Market Square. The evening was warm enough that the cool breeze off the river felt welcome. A lively combination of tourists and locals headed in and out of the bars and shops that filled the center of Portsmouth, even though the church clock had just chimed ten. Somebody zipped by on a turquoise Vespa scooter and I suddenly missed my motorcycle. Mom had taught me how to ride on her Harley. I'd ridden mine all the way through college before I decided I needed more carrying capacity and switched to the Jeep. I still missed it.

Sometimes when you've got a monumental decision, a whole set of little things comes crowding around. It's like once you've opened your mental closet, the old questions and wishes spill out in a heap, and the possibility of a motorcycle mixes up with wondering what would happen to the cat who used to be in the empty box you're carrying if you decided to leave, and that mixes up with wondering if you're really about to become a witch.

"What I want," I said slowly, "is a drink. How about you guys?"

Kenisha stared at me, startled; then she shrugged. "Why not? I've only been in this uniform fourteen hours. Another couple won't make a difference. How about you, Val?"

"Very pregnant here, in case you forgot."

I smiled. "It just so happens, I know a place where you can get a really amazing mocktail."

LIKE THE SQUARE, the bar at the Pale Ale was full of cheerful people and cheerful voices. As soon as we got through the door, the three of us automatically started craning our necks to see if the shifting crowd had left anyplace to sit. I spotted Sean on duty behind the bar. He raised his hand to wave hello and pointed toward a free stretch of banquette in the corner. I waved back and led the other women over.

"You know, we could be the opening line of a joke," I said as we shifted and slid to make room for one another around the little round table. "Three witches walk into a bar . . ."

"You're not a witch yet, remember." Valerie picked up the wine list, gazed at it like an old friend, and put it back down. "Being a witch involves commitment and study. I'm glad you're thinking about it, though."

"I reserve the right to backtrack at any moment."

"Fine," said Kenisha. "But what's got you thinking?"

"The idea I might be able to learn how to control my Vibe. That and . . ." Val nodded in encouragement. It was going to take a while to get used to talking about my Vibe in public. As it was, I felt strangely exposed, like I'd taken off my shoes in public. "If somebody is trying to use . . ." Nope. No good. This was a conversational bridge too far.

"Magic," Valerie said it for me.

"You'll get used to it," added Kenisha. "Admitting you have a problem is the first step."

I shrugged. "Okay. Hi. My name's Anna and somebody's trying to use magic to get me to leave town."

"Hi, Anna," chorused Val and Kenisha, and I couldn't hold it in anymore. I threw back my head and I laughed.

"Good evening, ladies." Sean stepped up to our table, wiping his hands on a clean white towel that he tossed across his shoulder.

"Young Sean!" Kenisha slapped palms sideways with him. "Aren't you supposed to stay back there?" She nodded toward the antique oak bar.

"Like I'm going to let somebody else take care of New Hampshire's finest? Not to mention my boss's best friend. What can I get you, Miss Britton? Ginger Lady? Maybe with prosecco instead of the seltzer this time?"

"Perfect."

Kenisha raised that eloquent eyebrow of hers. "Ginger Lady? This is new. Can anyone play?"

Sean laid one hand over his heart and bowed. The guy was clearly something of a showman. "I'd be delighted to make you a Ginger Lady, Officer Freeman. Anything for you, Val?"

"Cranberry spritzer."

"My pleasure." Sean gave another little bow, with added sparkle, and headed back to the bar. When I turned back to Kenisha and Val, they were both looking at me.

"What?" I asked testily.

"Nothing," they said, again in perfect unison.

I might have been tempted to start an argument, but the sight of a red coat moving through the crowd distracted me. "Martine!" I called, raising my hand.

"Hey, Anna. Sean said you were out here." Martine gave me a peck on the cheek and extended her hand to Officer Freeman. "Kenisha, good to see you. Hi, Val. You guys don't know what a miracle you're seeing. Normally, Anna here turns into a pumpkin around ten."

"I do not," I said indignantly. "I am the total party girl."

"Uh-huh. The kind who parties with the cop and the pregnant lady." Martine turned to a passing server. "We need the French fry tasting for the table, Beth," she said.

"Yes, Chef!" Beth said immediately, and changed direction, heading for the kitchen.

"Martine . . . ," I began, but she turned her chef's eye on me.

"You have something to say, Miss Britton?"

"No, Chef. Sorry, Chef."

Martine laughed. "We're still doing Monday, right? If this is the company you're keeping, I'm guessing we've got things to talk about. Good to see you all." She nodded to the other women and left us, cutting a professionally straight line through the crowd.

"How long have you known Martine?" asked Val.

"Since we were kids. We roomed together in college for a while too, before she switched over to culinary school."

We talked a little about where we'd grown up and how each of us came to be here. It turned out Kenisha's family had roots in Portsmouth, but Val was a relatively recent arrival from Chicago. From the way she danced around it, I guessed the situation she left there had not been good.

I was maybe halfway through the list of places I'd lived since college when Sean edged his way back to the table carrying a heavily laden tray.

"Right on time, Young Sean!" said Kenisha as Sean set the glasses in front of us.

"Why Young Sean?" I asked.

"Because my dad's Old Sean, and it keeps me from being called Sean-Boy." In addition to the drinks, he set down three wire holders containing paper cones of French fries, and a trio of sauce-filled ramekins. Kenisha and Val were watching me again. I really wished they'd cut that out.

"And here I've just been calling you Sean the bartender." I sipped my Ginger Lady. It was spicy and sparkling, and just what I wanted.

"Ah, well, see, there's a problem with that, because my dad tends bar too. It's a family thing. Now, then." Sean gestured toward the array of dishes. "We have here the sweet potato fries, the zucchini fries, and the double-dipped potato fries, my personal favorite. The sauces here are a spicy aioli, a lavender mustard, also my personal favorite, and a soy ginger." Something back at the bar must have set his bartender sense tingling, because he glanced over his shoulder. "I have to get back to manning the barricades. You have a great evening." I did not particularly notice that he was looking at me when he said this. There was no reason for Val to give that low whistle or for Kenisha to become deeply fascinated by the sweet potato fries.

I opened my mouth to point this out, but Kenisha leveled a French fry at me. "Trust me, Anna—now would be a good time to remain silent."

"So, what are your plans?" said Val, very intelligently changing the subject. "You said you were only going to be in town a couple of weeks."

"That's a really good question." I swirled a zucchini fry in the soy ginger sauce and popped it in my mouth. They were fabulous, but then, they came out of Martine's kitchen and she did not accept anything less. "I guess it's going to be for longer than that now." All things considered. "But I'll need someplace to else to stay." I couldn't afford the B and B for more than a couple of days, even with the discount, and Martine and I had tried the long-term roommate thing once. It did not go well. I am, as I've mentioned, a morning person. Martine, on the other hand, had never voluntarily gotten out of bed before ten in the morning when the house wasn't actually on fire.

"That shouldn't be a problem," said Kenisha. "There are plenty of apartments in town."

At Portsmouth rents. I tried not to wince. Those rents would get jacked up to new heights for a short-term lease. Plus, it'd have to be a place that would take spooky cats. I wondered if the local landlords would charge extra for the spooky part.

Before I could say anything about this, though, Valerie started waving to somebody over my shoulder. "Laurie! Over here! Laurie!" she called, half standing to be seen better.

I twisted around to see a woman in a pale blue sundress making her way toward our table. She had a brown leather purse slung over her shoulder and under her arm she clutched a black portfolio, the kind used to hold prints and sketches. I had been through about a thousand of them since school.

"Hello, Val. Hello, Kenisha." The woman, Laurie, smiled. She looked a little older than me, and recently sunburned. She'd French braided her straight brown hair, but the wind off the river had had its way and wisps of hair straggled across her forehead and down the back of her neck.

"Laurie Thompson, this is Anna Britton," Val introduced us, and we shook hands. "She's thinking about moving to town. Here, have a seat."

"Thank you." We all shuffled around to make room for Laurie and her portfolio. "I'm meeting Brad and Colin here. My husband and my oldest," she added for my benefit. "But I haven't seen them yet."

"You're an artist?" I gestured toward her portfolio.

She blushed. "Oh, well, no, not really. I do some watercolors. Martine was nice enough to say she'd hang one here."

"Anna's an artist," said Kenisha.

"Are you? You look familiar . . ." She snapped her fingers. "I know. I saw that article in *New England Arts Monthly* about art and the Internet. You sounded very upbeat. Half the time people talk like the Web is going to bring about the end of the world."

I smiled and thanked her and we chatted a little about change and art. Both Val and Kenisha looked at me expectantly, and I knew what it was they expected. Because I wanted to be friends with them, I took another swallow of the Ginger Lady and nodded at Laurie's portfolio. "Can I see what you've got?"

"Oh, well. It's not really that good. Not professional or anything." As Laurie fumbled with the portfolio tie, I started lining up polite, noncommittal compliments.

As it turned out, I didn't need them.

The painting inside the portfolio showed an extreme close-up of a stone tide pool, with a cluster of shells and pebbles nestled in the hollow. The tiny, complex scene was richly rendered in sepia ink and bold watercolor on cream paper.

"This is terrific." It wasn't framed, so I took it carefully by the edges and held it toward the light.

"Do you really think so?" I could tell by Laurie's voice the blush was back.

"Yes, I really do. You've done a great job with the details and the light." In fact, the light seemed to glow from the depths of the paper. It's a beautiful effect that's tough to achieve, and even tougher when you're representing water. "Martine's getting herself a find."

"Thank you. That means a lot." I laid the painting back

down into the portfolio and Laurie flipped the cover closed, like she was trying to trap the praise. "I'd been hoping to maybe get something into one of the galleries in town, but so far I've had no luck."

If this was a sample of what she could do, the gallery owners of Portsmouth must be blind. Not only was her painting good; it was perfect for tourists looking for something to take home with them. I opened my mouth to say all this but did not get the chance.

"Hi, Mom. Sorry. Didn't see you there at first."

Two men came to stand beside our table, both carrying overloaded paper grocery bags. The one who called Laurie "Mom" was a boy who looked like he was in high school. Tall and thin, he was still at that all-knees-elbows-and-ears stage, like he hadn't caught up with his final growth spurt. His white coat and checked trousers announced he had a summer job at one of Portsmouth's many restaurants.

"Hi, Colin," said Laurie. "How was work? Hi, Brad."

The second man, Brad, came out of his son's shadow and stooped to give Laurie a quick kiss. All the sound in the bar faded away into the background as I took in Brad Thompson's sagging cheeks and his mustache, and the way his pale skin turned dead white as he straightened up and saw me.

"Hi," I said. Which was not original, but it was better than *So, Mr. Mustache, we meet again.*

Because Brad Thompson was the other burglar.

❧ 16 ❧

♣ "SO, LIKE, YOU guys know each other?" Colin Thompson's narrowed eyes shifted from his dad to me. A minute ago, I'd been glad the bar's lighting was good enough that you didn't have to strain to read the menu or see a painting. Now I wished for a total blackout, because this kid most definitely did not like what he saw.

"Oh, do you?" Laurie also looked from me to Brad, but thankfully without the sting of cutting-edge adolescent suspicion.

Brad, on the other hand, looked about ready to pass out. "Miss, um, she was considering some properties and wanted some advice."

"Just thinking about possibilities," I mumbled and took a quick swallow of my Ginger Lady.

You know that awkward moment where what you really want to do is flee the scene, but you can't, because that would make people ask the wrong questions, so all you can do is stay put and pray nobody asks the wrong questions anyway? That was this moment, and the questions I did not want included either Kenisha or Val wondering why I was "thinking about possibilities" with Brad Thompson when it had been pretty clear to all concerned that I hadn't been planning to stay long-term in Portsmouth until an hour ago.

After a brief but serious struggle, Brad pasted a smile on his face. "In fact, I'm glad I ran into you." He shifted his grocery bag to the crook of his elbow and started fumbling in all his jacket pockets in rapid succession. "We didn't get to talk as much as I would have liked the other day. Maybe we could meet up tomorrow, or Monday? Monday would be better, I'm sure. No need to do business on a Sunday if we don't absolutely have to, right?" He finally produced a slightly battered business card and held it out.

"Sure." I tucked the card into my purse. "Sounds like a good idea."

Colin watched the whole show. I'm not even sure he blinked. Laurie's polite smile started showing distinct signs of strain.

"Well." Brad tried to sound brisk. That didn't work any better than trying to sound nonchalant had. "I'd better get my family home. Nice to see you all again."

"Yes, it's getting late." Laurie got to her feet, holding her portfolio against her chest. "Just let me drop this off with the manager." There were whole volumes of things not being said among the three Thompsons, but Laurie didn't look angry, just tired. "See you soon, Val, Kenisha. Nice to meet you, Anna."

I nodded. Brad shot me a last pleading glance and hurried after her. Their son, though, stayed just long enough to make sure I couldn't miss the way he was glowering at me.

Once Colin had finally strolled out of earshot, Val slapped both hands down on the table. "Well! That was interesting."

"Sure was," agreed Kenisha.

I looked at the bottom of my empty glass and wished Sean would pick now to make another appearance.

Val levered herself to her feet. "Unfortunately, the pregnant woman needs the restroom. Don't start without me."

But as soon as she was gone, it became clear that Kenisha had no interest in obeying her instructions.

"So." Kenisha folded her arms and leaned them on the table. "That thing there, with Brad and family. Anything you want to tell me about that?"

If we'd just run into Brad on his own, I would have told her straight-out, I think. As it was, though, I couldn't stop remembering Laurie's exhaustion and Colin's suspicions. Something bad was going on there, and as much as I already liked Kenisha, she was the police. I saw her sharp eyes, and her uniform with the patch on the shoulder of her dark blue shirt, reminding everyone she was here to "Protect and Serve." Telling her that Brad had broken into Dorothy's house would open a whole new can of worms for the Thompsons, and it was pretty clear they'd already been through a lot.

"No," I said.

Kenisha sighed and tipped her glass toward her, measuring the amount of cocktail still in the bottom. "Didn't think so."

"Sorry."

"Let's just hope it doesn't lead to more sorry. We've had too much of that." She plucked another fry from its paper cone, dipped it in lavender mustard sauce and chewed. "Listen, Anna. You need to think long and hard about what you're actually doing here, because you're jumping in the deep end."

"I did notice," I said, to my drink and the last zucchini fry. "Is . . . Is Laurie another . . . you know . . ."

Kenisha rolled her eyes. "Will you please get over this stutter of yours? Is Laurie a witch? A member of the guardians' coven? No. She's just somebody who's had a hard time and could use a break. Now, here comes Val. Since you've got nothing to say, we should probably get you guys home. If I don't get a shower soon, we are all going to regret the heck out of it."

* * *

BY THE TIME we got back to McDermott's, I owed Kenisha a whole boatload of favors. She hadn't let Val sit back down at the table, but stuck to her story about needing a shower, even adding that Sunday was her one day to sleep late, and she wanted to enjoy every second of it. She also mentioned that Roger was going to kill her if she let Val stay out too late, because he was deep into the whole nervous-father routine. In short, she didn't give Val any time to ask the kinds of questions she was clearly dying to.

I may have owed Roger a few favors too, because he had waited up for us. While Val was kissing him and telling him at least something about where she'd been for so long, I was able to sneak upstairs.

I set the box down and unlocked the door. My plan was to shut myself into the room, quickly. But when I put my hand on the knob, I remembered how the last time I'd been alone in this room, I'd gotten a vibe that was not just bad, but actively hostile in a new and personal way. Almost before I realized what I was doing, I reached into my purse and curled my fingers around the wand.

"Okay," I breathed. "Okay. Getting over the stutter thing. If I'm doing this, I'm doing this all the way." I gripped the wand firmly and shouldered the door open.

The room was dark, but moonlight streamed through the white curtains, illuminating the furnishings and the gray cat sitting in the middle of the bed.

"Merow?" Alistair inquired, in a tone that could only mean *What took you so long?*

"You know, I really shouldn't be surprised." I kicked the box in and shut the door behind us. "I take it this means the coast is clear?"

"Meow." The cat stretched out his front legs, toes spread and claws extended.

I dropped into the cozy armchair by the fireplace. I barely had time to put my purse down before Alistair was in my lap, butting his head against my hand.

"Okay, okay." I dutifully rubbed him behind the ears. "So, Alistair, since you're so eager to talk, where *were* you the night of Dorothy Hawthorne's murder?"

Alistair had been purring. Now he stopped and mewed, pitifully, painfully, like a lost kitten. He rolled over in my lap and started trying to burrow down behind me.

"Hey, hey, it's okay." I pulled him out gently and gathered him into my arms. "I'm sorry. It's okay. Really."

As I've said, I'm not a cat person, but even I know sad and scared is not a normal feline state of being. Except that's what Alistair was. He was actually trembling in my arms.

"We'll figure it out," I whispered, scratching behind his ears and under his chin. "I promise." I had just made a serious promise to a cat. We were definitely not in Kansas anymore. "But you are going to have to give me some help. I mean, I can't just wave that wand and say 'abracadabra,' right?" I paused and lifted Alistair up so we were brown eye to blue eye. "Right? I need some answers."

And, like it or not, I knew where I had to start. I settled Alistair on my lap, pulled out my phone and hit Grandma B.B.'s number.

❧ 17 ❧

♣ "ANNABELLE AMELIA! I'M so sorry I didn't call back." It was three hours earlier in Arizona, so either Grandma B.B. was on her second cup of herbal tea for the evening or she'd been out gallivanting with some of her gal pals. My bet was gallivanting. "But I was out with Margie and Patty, and I'd forgotten to plug my phone in last night and, well, that's that. Where are you this time, dear?"

This last was Grandma B.B.'s usual opener when I called. Out of all my family, Gran was the only one who never got impatient with the extended road trip that was my life. When Grandpa C. was in the navy, he and Gran moved all around the country. Once he retired, they traveled for fun—from Belize to the Himalayas and back again.

I could picture my grandmother sitting in the sunny little house in Sedona, Arizona, with the souvenirs of her busy life spread out across shelves, coffee tables and mantelpieces. There'd be framed photos of her children and grandkids, with the budding crop of great-grandkids in between. The last photo she'd tweeted (yes, Gran tweeted, and Pointred and said HeyLook!—she loved new tech) showed that she'd started wearing her hair in a Roaring Twenties–style bob with a sparkly orange lily barrette. That was how I imagined her now, as she leaned back on her sofa, anticipating a cozy chat.

Sorry to disappoint, Gran.

"I'm in Portsmouth," I said. "New Hampshire," I added.

I know I did not imagine the pause, or the hollow ring underneath her cheerful answer. "*Portsmouth?* Really? What on *earth* for?"

Grandma B.B. lived in italics. She was not a hinty, sit-in-the-dark-and-don't-mind-me kind of grandmother. She made sure everybody knew exactly what she meant when she meant it.

"I am—at least I was—visiting a friend," I told her. "You've met Martine Devereux, right? She's got a job as executive chef at the Pale Ale."

"Oh, yes, Martine, of course." Gran's relief was just as real, and just as marked, as the pause had been. Alistair looked up at me, blinking both eyes. Yeah, he heard it too. Never mind how. "I would have thought *Portsmouth* would be a bit out of the way for her, but I suppose everybody's got to take *whatever* they can find these days. She should come down *here* to Sedona. The town is *absolutely* booming. Margie and I had dinner at this *wonderful* little . . ."

"Gran," I cut her off before she could really get going. "I met an old friend of yours here. Julia Parris."

Silence. Long and completely uncharacteristic. Silence with italics and underlinings.

"I don't remember you ever mentioning her," I went on. "Or any of your other old friends from Portsmouth."

She took a deep breath. "I never thought you'd be interested in the little details of my past. Children usually aren't."

Oh, no, Gran. You aren't getting out of this that easy. "I'm not a child anymore, Gran. Julia told me you and she and some other women had a huge falling-out before you married Gramps and moved. What was that about?"

"I'm not even sure I *could* tell you, Annabelle. After all, it's *ancient* history, even to me. It can't possibly matter to you, dear."

"Mer-oww," remarked Alistair.

"Do you mind?" I said to him. "This is a private conversation."

"Mer-oww," he said again.

"Is someone *there* with you?" demanded Gran. "*Really*, Annabelle Amelia. I *know* young people have *no* concept of privacy anymore, but your *mother* taught you . . ."

"It's just the cat, Gran," I told her. Then I added, "His name is Alistair."

There was that silence again. I was starting to feel bad. You shouldn't deliberately make your grandmother uncomfortable. It wasn't nice. I knew that. But then again, I was pretty sure the usual etiquette rules didn't apply here.

"He's kind of adopted me," I went on. "Julia Parris says he belonged to a woman named Dorothy Hawthorne. She died recently."

"*Dorothy's* gone?" Unlike the cheerfulness and the outrage, the shock was real and it hit me like a splash of cold water.

"About six months ago."

"*Oh*. My. Oh. Annabelle, I'm having one of my dizzy spells. I need to hang up *now* and lie down."

"I'll call back," I said. "I'll call back a whole lot."

"I can't believe *you'd* be so inconsiderate, Annabelle Amelia, my *favorite* grandchild."

"I'm only your favorite because I'm the one on the phone with you right now. I'm also in the middle of something very strange, and I need your help. Please." I paused and let her spin out another silence, but not for too long. "It does matter, and it matters a lot. Grandma, are you a witch?"

I waited for her to explode, to demand to know how I could talk to my *poor, aging grandmother* like that. There'd be italics on her italics and extra exclamation points, and bold type.

Except I was wrong. There was only a soft murmur of regret. "I used to be, Annabelle. I used to be."

"And you didn't think maybe you should tell me about this?"

"Well, how was I to know you'd go back to Portsmouth? You were always so happy in the city."

Which city? I pinched the bridge of my nose and did my best to rein that burst of temper in. To be fair, I'd thought I was happy too. A little too restless maybe, but happy.

"So. Okay. You did know Julia Parris and Dorothy Hawthorne. What happened, Grandma?"

"Oh, *dear.* Really, Annabelle, this is all too *much.* I *can't* possibly." I heard her drawing in another huge breath and pictured her pulling her round shoulders back and shaking her bobbed white hair. "*No.* No. I *will.* You're right. You *should* know the *truth.*" She stopped again, and I could practically hear her deciding what that truth should be. I steeled myself to be firm. I was *not* letting her pull a conversational fast shuffle on me. Not this time.

"You asked about witches," Gran said. "Yes. *It's* true. There are, or were, a *few* families in Portsmouth that practiced the *true* craft and followed the *old* traditions. It was always kept very quiet. You knew each other, of course, but you never, *ever* discussed craft or family matters with *outsiders.*" I heard the soft shudder underneath that word. "Dorothy wanted to change all that."

"Change it? How? Why?"

"Oh. Well. You have to understand, dear, it was a *very* different time back then. The war was over, everything was *supposed* to be back to *normal*—men at the office, women in the home, children all clean and happy and in bed by eight o'clock. My mother *tried* to be that way, even after she'd worked three years at the shipyard. But somehow, the world kept going from strange to stranger. There was rock and *roll,* and all these new *books,* and the *bomb* and *Iron Curtain* and the *Red* Scare and . . ." *And the kids with the hair and the clothes* . . . I covered my mouth. Alistair gave me a knowing look, and I stuck my tongue out at him. He very pointedly curled himself up so his face was tucked into his belly.

". . . and we were all so young and excited about everything," Gran went on. "But Dorothy, she was, well, *radical*. I mean, we all smoked and went *completely* gaga when we discovered the *Beatles*, but Dorothy had *ideas*. You see, back then, if you had the old ways, *the ways to get and guard*— that's what we called them; sounds *unbearably* quaint now, doesn't it?—you used them *strictly* to look after your family. Perhaps a few *close* friends, but we were all taught that magical abilities were a *consequence* of heritage, bloodline, breeding, all *those* things that were *supposed* to make our family, well, better. *Special*."

Alistair peeled open one eye. "Merow?"

"Don't rush me," I muttered.

"What was that, dear?"

"Nothing. So, what was it Dorothy Hawthorne did back then that got everybody so upset?"

"Dorothy decided to break tradition. No, that's not strong enough. Dorothy decided to *shatter* tradition. She started saying *anyone* could learn witchcraft—the real craft, the true magic—not just the songs and meditations like some of these airy-fairy New-Agey selfie-help sorts go on and on and *on* about.

"Now, it would have been one thing if she'd limited herself to talking, but one day she announced she was going to actually start teaching people, *regular* people. It sent a shock wave through all the old families, I can tell you."

"What happened?"

"The families lined up against her, of course. First they tried to shame her into silence. Some tried to threaten her, but most just shunned her."

She was trying to change tradition in hardheaded, granite-souled New England. Of course they shunned her. "Most, but not all?"

"Well, she *had* her friends and supporters. And some of us were sure it would all blow over. We didn't believe there'd be that many . . . seekers. True craft is internal, and nondramatic, and takes a long time to learn. It can be difficult to hold on to a belief in its possibilities, even when you do see the results. But when Julia Parris joined Dorothy's coven . . . well, I at least knew the argument had shifted. The Parrises were the oldest of the families, and Julia was their sole heir. If she changed her mind, everyone else would too, eventually. I thought."

I found myself wondering how this fit in with how prickly Julia had been toward me when we met. "What happened?"

"The worst thing possible," said Gran. "It turned out Dorothy was right. She took in a gaggle of girls and even a few boys without even half a bloodline between them, and they successfully learned the true craft.

"Well, there was explosion and splits right down the middle of the old families. People who had been best friends stopped talking to each other overnight. Most of the town thought it must be over men or money or something of the kind. Only those of us on the inside knew the truth."

"Which side were you on?" I asked.

"Oh, dear. I'm not proud of this, Annabelle." Which was as shocking as any confession she'd made yet. "It was very confusing. Dorothy was so confident. She was trying new things, looking at the world in a new way. She thought everyone should have a chance to excel, each according to their lights and their passion. I mean, it seems obvious now, doesn't it? But it was so different back then. Everyone was so angry, and called her such *ugly* names. What they called her students was even worse. And there I was, the last of the Blessingsounds. I wanted to support my friend. I thought she was right, but *my* mother and my aunts wouldn't see it; they *couldn't* see it . . ."

"Julia said you guys had a falling out before you married Grandpa C. and left. Was it because of Dorothy and Elizabeth's feud?"

"What? Oh, no, no. It was my *mother*. Mother badgered

me and badgered me to swear that I would only follow tradition. That if I taught the craft, I wouldn't ever teach outside the family, that I would only teach a daughter . . . It got to be too much. I gave up the practice and I just left. Your grandfather . . . he proposed rather than lose me."

She stopped. This wasn't the drama-queen grandmother I knew and most of the time loved. This was an old woman reliving an old hurt.

"Merow." Alistair rubbed his head against my hand. "Merow."

"But you never told anyone that was why you were leaving."

"It seems a little foolish now, doesn't it? But I didn't want to air our dirty laundry in public, not even about this. I thought I might make things worse."

"Did you . . . ever offer to teach Dad magic? Or were you sticking with the tradition?"

"I did offer. Mother would turn over in her grave, but I did. Once. But he . . . he didn't believe me, at least not at first. Then, when he did start to believe, he got scared, or at least he got angry, and he asked me to never bring it up again. So I didn't."

"And that's why you never told the rest of us? You didn't want to get Dad angry?"

"I didn't want you to have to choose sides, Anna, not like I had to. It was rather ironic actually. The whole battle had started over a desire to be open about the craft, and here I was unable to even tell my own family. I kept thinking I'd go back to Portsmouth one day and straighten things out for good and all between me and Dorothy, Elizabeth and Julia. But there was your grandfather and his postings, and I was always busy with my own family. I told myself I'd go back once your father, Robert, was settled, or when Charlie retired. But by then there just didn't seem to be much *point*. You and your brothers and sister were all growing up, and none of you had inherited the family talents."

"Uhhh . . . Gran?"

"Yes, dear?"

"That's not quite true."

"Annabelle Amelia . . . do you mean . . . ?"

"I've got some kind of magic talent, Gran. Turns out I've had it for my whole life."

"Oh, *no*! Oh, *dear*! Why didn't you tell me?"

Anger bubbled up in me, left over from all those years I'd spent being afraid of walking through doorways because of my Vibe.

"Well, it's not like it was something I could bring up at Christmas dinner!" I snapped.

"No, of course not," murmured Grandma. "I'm sorry, Annabelle. I should have . . . checked."

"Merow." Alistair batted my elbow with his paw. I pushed it away. I did also sit on my temper. Hard.

"It's okay, Gran," I said, and mostly I meant it. "But, listen . . . do you think there was anybody who might, you know, still hold a grudge about what Dorothy did?"

"Good *heavens*, Annabelle! This is small-town New England. This is *families*. Of *course* somebody still holds a grudge."

I gripped the chair arm. "Gran . . . Dorothy Hawthorne was murdered."

❧ 18 ❧

❀ THERE WAS ANOTHER of those pauses. For a minute, I thought the connection had dropped out. Then I heard
a soft, hiccoughy sound. "Oh. Oh. Oh."

I swallowed. Grandma B.B. was crying. I had no idea
what to do. If I'd been there, I would have hugged her and
handed her a handkerchief. Gran hated Kleenex. But all I
could do now was wait for her to find her voice again.

I didn't have to wait that long. "Do they know *who*?"

"No. So far, the police think it was an accident, that she
just fell down her stairs."

"Oh, poor Dorothy. She was always so passionate, so
interested in justice and making things right." Justice. It was
the word Julia Parris had used. "Sometimes she just refused
to see how angry people could get."

"Grandma, Julia and some others think Dorothy used
her magic to bring me back to Portsmouth just before she
died. Was it possible somebody was using magic to keep
you, and the rest of us, from coming back before that?" It
was an idea that had formed on the ride back from the Pale

Ale. I mean, if somebody could use a spell to try to make me leave, couldn't they have used a spell to keep Gran from being able to come back once she did leave?

More silence. Alistair jumped off my lap and paced restlessly from the door to the window and back again.

"It could be," Gran said at last. "Yes. It might very well be. I never thought about it. No. I never *wanted* to think about it."

"But why, Gran? Why would someone want to keep you away?"

"Because of the seeing, I suppose."

"Seeing?"

"Yes." I pictured her nodding vigorously. "Different practitioners have different strengths and talents. As you practice your craft, these talents are uncovered. Some do run in families, like an eye for color or an ear for music. We Blessingsounds, we're seers. We can tell what has happened to a place or person, or what will happen sometimes, or . . ."

"Wait. Wait. You're telling me *you've got a Vibe?*"

"Annabelle, will you please speak standard English?"

"When you walk into a place, you get an impression, a feeling about it."

"Oh, no. I can only read palms, not places. But if you can read places . . . Oh, I'm sorry, Anna. I never knew."

"But you are saying somebody might not want me here, because I . . . my magic might be able to see what they were really up to?"

"That's exactly what I'm saying," Gran told me. "If murder's been done . . . Annabelle, you have to leave. You could be in danger."

Alistair jumped back into my lap, and I wrapped my free arm around him.

"No, Gran," I said firmly. "I'm not running away. I'm going to stay and figure this thing out."

"I love you, Annabelle Amelia. Whatever you do, it has to be because *you* want it. But you have to be careful, dear.

The craft is a force for great good, but only when the intention of the practitioner is good."

"What you send out into the world comes back threefold."

I couldn't see it, but I knew she was nodding again. "Promise me you will be careful."

"I promise, and I'll call you back really soon." I paused. "Uh, Gran, when Ginger was tracing the family history, she said she found an Innocence Blessingsound in, um . . ."

"Oh. Yes. She would. Well, no point in not saying it, I suppose. The family did originally settle in Salem, and yes, we left during the trials before anyone in the family could be called out."

"That's what I thought."

"Anna . . ."

She was going to apologize again, and I found myself smiling. "It's okay, Grandma. Really."

"Do you mean that?"

"If I don't, I will soon. I love you. I'll call tomorrow, okay?"

We said our good-byes and I hung up and hugged Alistair. Alistair put up with this for a while and then slithered down to curl up in my lap and resume his important napping. I scratched his ears, because that's what you do with a cat in your lap and I'm only human, even if he wasn't only a cat.

Which got me thinking about the other strange animal I'd been seeing recently.

"So, Alistair . . . That yellow bird, the one on the sill? It really was a familiar, like you, and Julia's dogs?"

"Meow," said Alistair, which I took to be an affirmative.

"Swell." I sighed. "Well, what do we do now, big guy? Get a spiral notebook and a number two pencil and an apple for the teacher at witch school?"

Alistair jumped back down to the floor and padded over toward the window. I blinked, and he wasn't there.

I probably swore. I know I jumped to my feet and pushed the curtains back and stared out at the moonlit lawn. I watched a plump shadow slide across the grass and jump up onto the fence that separated McDermott's garden from the Hawthorne house. Alistair paused on the fence and I know he looked up at me. I could feel it in the pricking of my thumbs. Then he jumped down onto the far side and disappeared. Possibly literally.

I knew what he was telling me. If I really wanted to figure this out, I needed to get myself back into Dorothy's old house.

❧ 19 ❧

❧ DESPITE THE (BY my standards) late night, I woke up bright and early. The sun flooded in through the windows. Alistair was nowhere in evidence, but there was a warm cat-shaped dent on the spare pillow next to me, which said he'd come back sometime during the night.

I got up, showered, dried my hair and pulled it back into a ponytail. This was definitely a comfort-clothes day. It called for soft old jeans, a loose red V-neck T-shirt and the scuffed flats. I even unearthed my Red Sox cap from Thing One. Then I stuffed my laptop, sketchbook and purse into my backpack. I also made sure I had the wand. What a difference a day makes.

I'd fully intended to slip out the front door without being noticed, but luck was not with me. When I got down to the entrance hall, Valerie was already there, setting a fresh vase of cut flowers onto a table covered with colorful brochures for local attractions.

"Good morning, Anna," she said as she wiped her hands on her apron. This one was bright pink and read QUEEN OF ABSOLUTELY EVERYTHING. "Did you sleep okay?"

"Yeah, I did. Thanks."

We stood there, and all kinds of awkwardness stretched out tight between us.

"So," I began. "Which of us is going to say, 'Uh, about last night . . .'?"

Valerie laughed, and at least some of that tension dissolved. "I think that's my line." She adjusted the angle of the vase on the table. The bouquet wasn't simply cut flowers, I saw. Rosebuds and leafy apple branches and some spiky things I didn't recognize were mixed in with delphinium, foxglove and rosemary. The vase was covered in pale green and gold Celtic knotwork. In fact, it reminded me a lot of the one Alistair had broken back in Midnight Reads.

"Redecorating for the season?" I asked, casually, of course.

Val glanced past me, making sure no one was coming down the stairs, before she said softly, "I'm resetting the broken wards. The vase and the herbs serve as a point of focus for the protective spells that keep the house safe from harmful influences or magic." Footsteps sounded overhead. The other guests, who presumably were not all into the witch thing, were stirring. Val glanced at the ceiling. "Let's take this into the kitchen, okay?"

McDermott's kitchen was huge, and where it wasn't black and white it was stainless steel. It also smelled wonderfully of bacon and cinnamon. We caught Roger in the act of pulling a tray of muffins out of the top oven.

"Morning, Anna. Early riser? Great. Sit. Food." He hoisted the tray in our direction. This morning, his apron read COFFEE: IF YOU'RE NOT SHAKING YOU NEED ANOTHER CUP. Clearly these two were collectors. "Coffee?" he asked as he flipped the tray over so the muffins tumbled into a towel-lined basket. "Bacon?"

"I can see why you fell in love," I said to Val as I climbed up on one of the kitchen stools.

"Can't believe I got to him first." Val did not try for a

stool but lowered herself into an armchair that had probably been brought in from the great room.

Roger immediately brought over a muffin on a napkin and set it next to her. "How are you doing?" Val smiled and nodded. He laid a gentle hand on the curve of her belly. I realized that the terrace was really lovely. So were the checkered curtains and the sunbeams on the spotless white floor.

"Okay, Anna." Val laughed. "The public display of affection is over. You can look."

"Just giving you guys the moment," I said, magnanimously, I thought.

Apparently Roger did too, because he set a plate of muffins and bacon down on the counter in front of me. "First course," he said. "Eggs up in a sec."

I bit into the crispy bacon, noting idly that the perfectly golden brown muffin top was thick with streusel. Which was all wonderful, and just what I needed, but how were we supposed to talk magic and spooky cats and murder with Val's doting husband in the room? I poured myself coffee from the big silver carafe on the counter and tried to think of excuses to get Val someplace more private. Maybe something about my bill . . . ?

Before I could come up with anything, though, Roger waved the spatula in our direction. "Go ahead. Talk witch stuff. Not going to bother me."

"You *know*?" I admit there may have been a dropped jaw here, and perhaps a tiny bit of eyeball bulging, but that was no excuse for Val to start laughing again.

Roger confined himself to a smile. "Of course I know. Val told me about her practice before we got engaged."

"I couldn't have married him otherwise," said Val. "I didn't want to have to hide who I am."

"I admit, it was a lot to take in, and it took a while to accept the real magic."

"True craft," said Val and I together. We stared at each other.

"Jinx!" she said.

"Seriously?" I felt my smile slowly fade.

Val snickered. "No, but you do owe me a soda."

"What I was trying to say," interrupted Roger firmly, "is that I know what you're going through." I have no idea what kind of look came over my face at that moment, but Roger grimaced. "Okay, maybe not all of it, but I do know some part of what you're going through."

"It's just all so different. I've spent my whole life trying to hide what happens to me."

"Yeah." Val sighed. "We both know about that too." She smoothed her hand across her belly. "Which is why I was thinking . . ." She looked from Roger to me as she did, gauging our reactions before she'd even given us anything to react to.

I gripped my cup. I could already tell I was not going to like this. So could Roger.

"What is it you were thinking, Val?" he asked carefully.

"Don't look like that. I was just thinking that since we now know for certain that Dorothy was murdered, we should go back into her house and find some kind of definite proof Kenisha can use to get her lieutenant to open the case up. That's all." She added this calmly, like she'd never heard the words "breaking and entering" in her whole strawberry blond life.

It seemed that Roger had heard them, though, and he'd heard them enough to be more than a little freaked. "Valerie, you can't be serious. You . . ." He bit down on whatever it was he was going to say and turned back to his pan, turning off the burner and carefully scooping scrambled eggs onto the waiting plates.

"I know, I know," Val said in answer to whatever it was Roger hadn't said. "But what else are we going to do? It's only a matter of time before Frank sells the house or something, and then any chance we have of proving the murder even happened is gone. Besides, Alistair has already let Anna in. He wouldn't do that unless there was something important in the house, right?"

"Maybe she's already found it," said Roger. "You told me she got Dorothy's wand."

"But there still might be something else," said Val stubbornly. "We won't know until we look. Really look."

I was all set to agree with her until I saw the look in Roger's eyes. He'd raced straight past simple worry and was headed toward heartbreak. A black hole waited underneath this conversation. It was old and deep and I had absolutely no idea where it came from.

"I know you're open about your practice, Val." Roger was straining to keep his words even. "But you know and I know very few people believe in the reality of your magic. Somehow I don't think any local judge is going to be all that sympathetic if either of you try to say, 'It's all right—the cat let us in.'"

Val probably answered him, but I wasn't paying attention to her. I was paying attention to the prickling sensation in the back of my neck.

"Uh, 'scuse me," I said. "Roger, could you check the back door?"

Roger frowned, but he did open the door to the terrace. There sat Alistair, bolt upright on the welcome mat with his tail wrapped neatly around his paws. As Roger looked down, the cat sauntered inside and jumped up onto the stool next to mine, and then onto the counter.

"Hey!" shouted Roger, outraged.

I picked Alistair up and put him on my lap. "Are those eggs ready yet? I think somebody wants breakfast."

Roger gave me a plate, and I put it on the floor. Alistair meowed, leapt heavily down and started eating.

"That can't be good for him," grumbled Roger, although I wasn't sure if it was because he was really worried about Alistair's health, or annoyed because I'd given his perfectly cooked eggs to the cat. "He should be eating cat food."

"Tell him that."

"You should be eating cat food."

Alistair didn't even look up.

"That's what you think, puny human," I translated.

"Yeah." Roger sighed. "Got that. Thanks."

"You two do realize it's not a coincidence he showed up just when we were talking about searching Dorothy's house?" mumbled Val around her mouthful.

"You mean breaking into Dorothy's house." Roger slid the rest of the eggs onto two fresh plates. "I'm sorry, hon, but I can't go along with this one."

They exchanged a long look, the kind that's filled with layered, telepathic communication. I sat there wondering what I wasn't hearing and, unlike Alistair, letting my eggs get cold.

"What should we do, then?" asked Valerie at last. "Sit around and wait for . . . whoever it was who breached the wards to make another magical attack on Anna?"

"It's okay," I said to them both. "I have an alternate plan."

"You do?" The relief in Roger's face was as real as the heartbreak had been a moment before. I could have said my plan involved motorcycles and light sabers, and he would have thought it was swell.

"I'm going to talk to Frank Hawthorne today," I said. "Hopefully, he'll let me back into the house."

Val frowned. "Any reason why he should?"

"Because I've got his aunt's magic wand and her missing cat," I said. "And because when I told him Dorothy had been murdered, he believed me."

❧ 20 ❧

🐾 FRANK HAWTHORNE TURNED out to be an easy man to find, even on a Sunday. Since I knew he was the publisher for the *Seacoast News*, all I had to do was look up the paper's address. My only experience with newspapers was as an occasional reader, but I was fairly sure any small paper would have a small staff. So it made sense that the guy in charge would put in a lot of overtime.

I decided to leave the Jeep at McDermott's and walk downtown. First, because it was a gorgeous day, and second because I'd been sitting enough lately that I was starting to feel distinctly blobby. Plus, I wanted time to plan what I would say when I actually faced Frank Hawthorne. *Can you let me back into your house so I can see if I pick up any more Vibes or clues about your aunt's murder?* lacked a certain something.

The *Seacoast News* occupied the second floor of a converted brick warehouse overlooking the river. As a workspace it was fairly bare-bones. The desks were all cheap, industrial and probably secondhand. Whatever start-up money there was had clearly been lavished on the laptops, outsized monitors and, at my count, four different printers. Men and women—or maybe I should say boys and girls because some of them looked like they were still in high school—worked the keyboards, flicking through windows and sites with dizzying speed. A kitchen space took up one corner and the aroma of fresh coffee mixed with Portsmouth's morning breeze where it drifted through the open windows. The only decorations on the bare brick walls were framed enlargements of *Seacoast News* front pages hung between movie posters for classics like *All the President's Men* and *Sweet Smell of Success*.

The photo over Frank's desk was a big black-and-white portrait of a solemn-looking man in a suit who I suspected was the legendary journalist Edward R. Murrow.

Frank was not wearing a suit, dark or otherwise. He had on a blue BOSTON STRONG T-shirt and khaki pants. A brown sports jacket with, I promise you, real corduroy patches on the elbows hung on the wooden stand behind him. He was frowning hard at a yellow legal pad and he held the receiver of an ancient, industrial beige telephone between his ear and his shoulder, until he saw me.

"Annabelle Britton," he said as he set the receiver back on the cradle. "Speak of the devil."

It was not the greeting I'd been hoping for, but it was understandable. "Frank Hawthorne," I answered. "Good morning."

"Casing the joint?" His tone was so bland and his face so serious, it actually took me a minute to be sure he was joking. I decided then and there I should never play poker with this guy.

"Nah. Robbing a newspaper is like robbing a church. Not a lot of return for the trouble."

The corner of his mouth quirked up, reluctantly. "I see you have grasped the essentials of modern journalism. Can I help you with something?" He gestured toward the folding chair in front of his desk. "I suppose it's too much to hope you want to take out an ad."

"Sorry." I hitched up my backpack strap and glanced around at his staff, who were all busy trying to look like they were not sneaking glances. "Um, it's personal business. Maybe we should go somewhere . . . else?"

Frank gazed across his exposed-brick domain, and apparently he saw the same thing I did—an open room full of potential busybodies, aka journalists. He glanced at the little space behind him that had been partitioned off for a conference room but discarded that possibility out of hand.

"Do you drink coffee?" he asked. "There's a terrific place right around the corner. Northeast Java."

"Sounds perfect."

Frank got to his feet and grabbed his jacket from the stand. "Magda, hold the fort, would you? And text me if anything comes up."

"You got it, Chief." A young Latina woman with sandy brown skin and waving black hair who I assumed was Magda snapped a quick salute.

"Chief?" I quirked an eyebrow as we headed down the stairs.

Frank shrugged. "People who want to be journalists love drama."

"Never would have guessed."

NORTHEAST JAVA TURNED out to be a little coffee shop on a riverbank lane that could only loosely be called a street. What it actually was, was an honest-to-God cobblestone walkway that stretched down a flight of steps from the main square. Nothing but a handrail and a three-foot drop separated the street from the river. A shadowy and entirely too intriguing vintage shop waited on one side of the coffee shop, and Annabelle's (no relation) Ice Cream on the other. If you didn't know the café was there, you would easily miss it. It was cramped and had a low ceiling and a chipped door with the hours painted on it, but no sign. The abandoned appearance was not helped by the stack of wooden crates piled by the door. But the warm and wonderful odor of fresh roasted coffee swirled out from the open door and let you know you'd stumbled across something special.

"What can I get you?" Frank pulled out a wrought-iron chair from one of the tiny round tables that perched on the uneven paving stones and gestured for me to sit. A flock of sparrows quickly assembled on the river's guardrail, in case we might be about to drop any interesting crumbs.

I started to protest that I could pay for my own coffee, but Frank held up his hand. "This is a business meeting. What can I get you?"

I ordered a cappuccino. Frank ducked into the low doorway and returned a few minutes later with a mug of what looked like solid black coffee, and my cappuccino in a widemouth cup. The barista had drawn a fern leaf with the milk foam. I have never figured out how they do that. Foam is not exactly a stable medium.

"So, would you be surprised if I said I'd been checking up on you?" Frank asked as he gulped down a good quarter of a mugful of solid black coffee. I watched, fascinated and appalled.

"I'd be surprised if you hadn't," I said when I could speak again. "What did you find out?"

"Let's see . . . Annabelle Amelia Blessingsound Britton?" He pulled out his notebook and laid it on our marble-topped table so he could flip one-handed through the pages. "Graduated State University of New York at Buffalo with a BA in fine arts and a minor in business. Not your usual combination . . ."

"I figured it'd take a while to make it as an artist, so I needed a backup plan."

"It seems to have worked. You freelance, specializing in book covers and illustrations for independent authors, and commercial art like posters and murals, but you also have some gallery shows to your credit"—Frank turned a page—"and some good reviews from critics and a few specialty publications. Probably not married . . ."

"Definitely not married."

"No arrests, no outstanding warrants, no mortgages or bad car loans, no debts in collection . . ."

"You can find that out?"

"I am a trained professional. Want to know your age and weight?"

"No, but I'm thinking of canceling my HeyLook! account."

"Too late." He tucked the book away and took another long swallow of black coffee. I winced. The man must have a cast-iron stomach. "But the long and the short of it is, you probably are who you say you are."

"Just like you."

"Just like me, and more importantly, you do not seem to be making your money or reputation off bogus psychic predictions or ghost hunting." Frank leaned back and crossed his ankles. A few sparrows switched positions on the guardrail, and several others fluttered away, maybe heading out to get reinforcements. Frank just kept looking at me. His pose was relaxed, but that relaxation wasn't genuine. His whole attitude remained as closed and as neutral as his expression. Two plump women in purple T-shirts and bright red hats trotted down the stairs from Bow Street and ducked into the vintage store. Frank waited until the door shut behind them.

"Are you sure about what you said?" he asked quietly. "You're certain Aunt Dot wasn't alone when she died?"

"Positive." I paused. "You do believe me, right?"

"Yeah." Frank stared out across the river. "I wish I didn't, but I do."

It was a long moment, and several more sips of coffee (well, sips for me, gulps for Frank), before either one of us spoke again.

"Did you know your aunt was a witch?" I asked softly.

To my surprise, Frank laughed loud enough to scatter the sparrows.

"Are you kidding? Everybody knew. She was proud of it. She had a Web site and a HeyLook! page, for Pete's sake, Northeastwitch.com. Dressed up in the pointy hat and green makeup every Halloween. You should have heard her doing her Wicked Witch of the West imitation: 'I'll get you, my pretty.'" He hooked his fingers into claws.

"And your little dog too?"

He chuckled. "Especially the little dog."

"But did you know she actually . . . worked magic?"

Frank considered his mug for a moment. "I knew she thought she did. I saw one or two things that made me wonder. And then there's Alistair, who is definitely not a normal cat and never has been." He took another swallow of coffee. "So, let's say I've got an open mind on the whole magic question." He paused. "How about you?"

"Me?"

"Are you a witch? Is that why you were able to . . . do that thing you did down in the basement?"

It was a serious question and it deserved a serious answer, especially after that "thing I did" down in the basement. "I'm not really a witch, yet. But I'm exploring the possibilities."

He nodded. He also took a deep breath and let it out again. There was something opening up inside him. I couldn't tell if he liked it, and I was pretty sure he couldn't either. "But you still don't have any idea who it was with Aunt Dot when she died?"

I shook my head. "Sorry."

He nudged the handle of his empty mug back and forth a couple of times. "Could you find out?"

"Maybe. I don't know, and if I did find something . . ." I met his gaze. It was surprisingly easy this time. "I don't know if it would be anything that would stand up in court."

He nodded and nudged the coffee mug handle again. I resisted the urge to tell him to stop that.

"Are you asking me to take a look?"

He nudged the mug handle back. "Yeah, I guess I am."

"Why? You don't know me from Adam's off ox. I could be anybody."

"Ah, but you're not." He patted the pocket with his notebook in it. "You're Annabelle Amelia Blessingsound Britton, and your grandmother was friends with Aunt Dot, and Alistair likes you." He paused. "And you're not me."

"Sorry, but why is that important?"

"Because Aunt Dot's friends don't like me very much. At least, some of them don't."

"By some of them, you mean Julia Parris?" I guessed.

Frank nodded. "Julia, among others. They won't talk to me about what Aunt Dot was doing those last weeks, or much of anything else. It's made it hard for me to find what I need on my own."

"Okay. I'm going to ask the obvious question. Why don't they like you?"

"I'm going to give you the obvious answer. They think I'm the one who killed Aunt Dot."

❧ 21 ❧

🐾 HERE'RE A FEW things I've learned when it comes to talking about murder:

1) As a topic, it generates more than its fair share of long pauses.

2) Long pauses, in turn, generate copious amounts of staring into the bottoms of cups.

3) When you're tired of staring into the bottom of your cup, across the river is a decent substitute.

4) There are a lot of really fat sparrows in Portsmouth.

I was working through option number three on this new list, and realizing the full truth of number four, when I heard myself ask Frank, "Is there a reason somebody might think you murdered your aunt?"

"Probably because I inherited the house, and everything

else. Probably because . . ." He sank into another of those long pauses. "Because they know Aunt Dot and I were fighting over it right before she died."

"Which it? The house?"

"The house. The money." He swirled the last of his coffee before he gulped it down. "Aunt Dot was . . . on edge a lot during those last weeks. I thought she might be having health issues."

"Like with her balance?" I said. There is such a thing as a look of pure poison, and Frank was leveling it at me now. "Sorry," I mumbled. "That was inconsiderate of me."

His expression said he agreed, but he shrugged again. "For the record, what I was worried about was dementia. She'd stopped going out. She wasn't keeping her usual appointments with her book group and her garden club. Those can be signs."

"So, you wanted her to move?"

"Move, or at least get an aide. We would have found the money. But she insisted everything was fine, and we argued."

"Did you tell Julia about this?"

"I tried to." He frowned at the bottom of his mug, as if disappointed that it was not spontaneously generating more coffee for him. I understood the feeling. "Julia doesn't believe me."

"Why?"

"I don't know. She won't talk to me, remember? But a couple of her good friends were talking to you last night at the Pale Ale."

"You know where I was last night?" That snapped my head back around. Several consternated sparrows took off for less disturbing begging grounds. "Gosh. That's in no way creepy. Or stalkerish."

"I was in the bar having a beer with some of my staffers," answered Frank calmly. "We were celebrating getting the latest issue to bed, and I saw you there. Right out in public and everything."

I folded my arms and went back to looking out over the river. I also wondered how I'd missed seeing him. It seemed a big thing to miss. I tried telling myself, *Well, the bar was awfully crowded last night, and I was a little distracted.* I have no idea whether myself planned on buying that or not, because movement caught my eye. A teenager careened down the cobbled river walk on his battered bicycle, causing the sparrows to launch themselves off the guardrail. When the birds reassembled, they had a new friend: a surprisingly skinny goldfinch.

My heart thumped, and I groped for my backpack. "Sorry," I muttered.

"Phone call?" asked Frank.

"Something." But the flurry of wings sounded behind me, and I glanced back. The sparrows, and the skinny finch, had all taken to the sky again. But this time it wasn't any kid on a bike scaring them off. Alistair galloped out from under the wooden crates like a furry gray avenger. Sparrows chirped and birdy-cursed and Alistair meowed. He also retreated under our table and wrapped himself around my ankles.

"*Again?* You're kidding me," breathed Frank. "You are really, absolutely effin' kidding me."

There was no answering this, largely because it wasn't very coherent.

"Hello, Alistair." I lifted the cat onto my lap. He meowed complacently and rubbed his face against the table edge.

Frank opened and closed his mouth several times, before he apparently decided to give in and accept the situation. "Hey, Alistair." He scratched Alistair behind the ears. "Where've you been, huh? I've been worried about you."

The cat proceeded to demonstrate his repentance by sticking his face into my empty cappuccino cup and licking up the remains of the milk foam.

"Your human concern is touching," I translated as I petted Alistair's back, "and has affected him deeply."

"Don't worry. I'm used to it. We pretty much grew up together."

Alistair meowed again, possibly in confirmation. Then he leapt off my lap and darted back under the stack of crates.

"What the . . . ," began Frank. Then his face twisted up. "Oh, for Pete's sake."

I twisted around in my chair in time to see Ellis Maitland trotting down the stairs from the square.

"Hello, Frank," Ellis called. "Magda said I'd find you here."

"Magda should remember who's signing off on her summer internship," Frank muttered, but when Ellis held out his hand, Frank shook it, mostly as a polite reflex, I thought. "What can I do for you?"

"Mind if I sit?" Frank clearly did mind, but he nodded anyway. Ellis pulled up a chair from the other table and sat. Today's suit was crisp, creamy linen, which is really tough for a guy to wear without looking like an escapee from a Southern Gothic.

"Good to see you again, Anna." Ellis offered me one of his professional smiles. I smiled back, but it was like Frank's handshake, a polite reflex. I also snuck a glance toward the crates. If Alistair was still lurking, I couldn't see him.

"I just wanted to apologize," Ellis was saying to me. "Brad shouldn't have come at you sideways like that."

"What are you talking about?" asked Frank before I could even get my mouth open.

Now Ellis frowned and turned to me. "You didn't tell him Brad caught up with you last night at the Pale Ale?"

"No, she didn't tell me," said Frank. He was going to have to stop stepping on my lines, not to mention frowning at me like this was all my fault.

"We hardly spoke," I told him. "Mostly I was looking at a watercolor painting his wife, Laurie, did. He gave me a card, in case I wanted to see some properties later. But that was it."

"Really?" Ellis settled back, crossing his legs at the knee. "Oh, well, I must have misunderstood."

"And just what was it you misunderstood?" asked Frank. He'd tucked his hand into the pocket where he put his notebook but seemed to think better of it and brought it out empty.

"Oh." Ellis waved his hand vaguely. "I thought Brad said he'd been talking with Miss Britton here about Dorothy's house."

The silence couldn't have lasted more than a couple of seconds, but it felt much longer.

"Why would Brad Thompson tell you he'd been talking about Dorothy's house?" I asked.

"Brad works for me." Ellis tilted his head toward me. "You didn't know that?"

"No. I'm new around here."

Ellis chuckled. "You're not new. You're back. Whole different kettle of fish."

"Not that I ever actually lived here," I reminded him.

He shrugged. "But your family did once. With the old families, you can never really get away, can you?" The way he said "old families" made my neck prickle. It reminded me too much of the conversations with Julia and Val. Was he trying to tell me he knew Grandma B.B. was a witch, like Julia? Not to mention his mother, Elizabeth?

"Brad's not in any trouble, is he?" asked Frank abruptly. "I'd hate it if he was on the outs again over Aunt Dot's house."

I gripped my cup and ordered myself not to make a sound, no matter how startled I was. Why would Frank care about Brad Thompson? Were they friends? If they were, what was Brad doing breaking into his friend's house?

That was when I remembered I had so far neglected to tell Frank I knew who the second burglar was.

Ellis's eyebrows shot up in an attitude of surprise that was at least as genuine as his smile. "Huh? Brad in trouble?

No, no, of course not. Brad's a good man. Focused. Works hard. No. It's all good there. I'm just a little confused; that's all." He leaned his elbows on the table, which brought him in close enough for me to smell his aftershave. "Why would Brad think you, Anna, would have anything to do with decisions about Dorothy's house?"

A fresh silence settled over us, with both men waiting for me to fill it. My options for that, though, were really limited. I was not going to tell Brad Thompson's boss he'd been doing a little casual B and E on the weekend. Not even to see his reaction, although I had a feeling that reaction would be truly interesting and informative.

"What confuses me, Mr. Maitland, is why this is your business," I said. "It's not your house."

"No, but Brad is my employee, and what he does affects my business." Ellis spread his hands. "You may be just passing through, but I have to live here. If I get a reputation for sneaking around, nobody's going to want to deal with me. So, maybe Brad thought there was some connection between you and Frank that he could work on to get hold of the house, you know, maybe score some points with the boss." He gestured toward himself. "But if that's the case, he's stepped over the line, and I want to know about it."

He was fishing for something. I knew it, and from the look on Frank's face, he knew it too. I knew something else too.

Somebody around here was lying.

Either Brad had lied to Ellis, or Ellis was lying to the both of us right now. But was this really about the house, or could the cause be something to do with Dorothy herself? Both Julia and Frank said Dorothy had grown secretive before her death and practically barricaded herself in her home.

The home Ellis Maitland was so very interested in.

"I've known Brad a long time, Ellis." Frank's eyes narrowed slowly. I would have given anything to know what he was thinking right then. "If he's stepped over a line, I've got to ask myself, when did he decide to take that risk? It didn't come out of nowhere."

"That's something I've been asking myself." Ellis's answer was smooth, and was not, I noticed, a real answer. "Anyway, it won't happen again." Ellis climbed to his feet and slapped Frank's shoulder on the way up. "I'll have a word with Brad, and we're all good, right?"

"But you still want the house."

Ellis threw up his hands. "All right, *yes*! I still want the house. Because I want to *help*, Frank. What's it going to take to get you to believe that? Are you going to live in that house? No, or you would have already moved in. Can you afford the mortgage? Oh, excuse me, mortgages, because Dorothy took out a second there, didn't she? No, you can't afford it, because you're pouring every penny into that paper of yours." He stabbed a finger behind him. "Dorothy's house has been empty for six months and counting. No matter how often you're over there, it's going to start falling apart. Now, if you hurry, and if you get yourself a decent agent, you might still catch some of the summer buying season. If you don't, it's going to be standing empty over the winter. After that, no matter how good the location is, you're going to be taking a hit on the sale price. Look, cards on the table, okay?" He glanced at me. "You don't mind, do you?" He pulled out a notebook, wrote something down, tore out the sheet and handed it to Frank. Frank unfolded the paper.

First, his eyes popped. Then he frowned, hard.

"Final offer," said Ellis. "After this, you never hear from me again."

Was it just me, or did that sound as much like a threat as a promise?

Frank folded the paper up and slid it into his pocket. Then he pulled out his cell phone and hit a number. All the time, he kept his eyes on Ellis Maitland.

Somebody must have answered, because Frank started

talking. "Hello, Enoch? Hi. Listen, I think I've found a solution about what to do with Aunt Dot's house. Yeah, I know, about time. No, not selling after all." He kept his gaze fixed on Ellis. "I want to do a summer rental. Yes, I've got somebody in mind."

Now Frank was looking at me.

I opened my mouth, and I closed it again. Ellis Maitland let his head fall back, so he was staring up toward the sky in a wordless plea, or maybe curse; it was hard to tell from this angle.

"Yes, I need a lease," Frank was saying to whoever was on the other end of the line. "That's why I'm calling. Yes, I know it's still Sunday. Can you draw something up for me? No. She's . . . a friend of the family. We can be a little loose, can't we? No, I didn't say she was family, just a friend." He paused again. "Thanks, Enoch. I owe you. Ha-ha, yes, I'll see it on the bill. Bye."

He hung up and put his phone in his pocket.

"Well," Ellis snapped. "That's that. You sure showed me, didn't you, Frank?" The edge on his words could have cut glass. "Hope it works out for you. Good luck with him, Anna." I shook his dry hand. "I did talk to my mother about you and maybe mending fences. I'm sure you'll be hearing from her."

He gave us both a final nod before he turned away and strode up the stairs, back stiff, fists curled, like he was heading into a fight. Or heading away from one.

I thought about how he said, "Good luck with him." Not "with it" or with "the house," but with "him."

"You know Elizabeth Maitland?" Frank asked me.

I ignored the question. There were far more important things for us to talk about. "When did we decide I was renting your house?"

Frank had the grace to at least look abashed. "Yeah, sorry about that. But it just hit me we could kill two birds with one stone. If you're living in Aunt Dot's house, you have unlimited access, and you can invite anybody in you want, right? Like all Dorothy's old friends, for—I don't know, tea and a cozy chat? Does anybody do that anymore?"

"I'll check my *Miss Manners*. But there is no way I can afford to rent a whole house in Portsmouth for a week, let alone the summer."

He shrugged. "It'll only be a nominal rent, if any. After all, you're doing me a couple of major favors. You'll be taking care of the house, and you'll be finding out what really happened to Aunt Dot."

"So . . . you're really *hiring* me?"

"I guess. Kind of. Not that I'd be able to really pay you or anything . . ."

I was back to looking in the bottom of my coffee mug. I had no idea what to think or to feel just then. I already didn't like this mess. There were too many lies being told. There were also way too many people circling around those lies, looking for openings and answers.

And all this activity centered around that house, and the murder of an old woman.

What if you don't like what I find? What if I don't like what I find?

"Anyway," Frank said, "if nothing else, I'll finally be able to get Ellis to stop badgering me."

I thought about those mortgages on the house. I thought about how if I said yes to this, this guy became my boss. And my landlord. "You *still* haven't actually asked me if I want to go along with any part of this."

"I said I was sorry."

I looked at him. I reminded myself that at bottom he was a guy and probably couldn't help himself. It was at that moment that Alistair strolled back out from the crates he seemed to have adopted as his personal fortress. He stopped next to my chair, sat down with his tail curled around his paws and also looked up at Frank.

"I see I am outnumbered." He sighed. "Okay. You're right.

I'm sorry. I should have asked you first. Both of you," he added to Alistair. "Anna, would you please consider staying in Aunt Dot's house for the summer? It'd really help me out."

It was a good idea, darn him anyway. It would be a perfect cover for me and for anybody else I wanted to be in Dorothy's house looking for whatever clues there might be. It would also be an excuse for me to keep in touch with the man sitting across from me, in case some of those clues led back to him. There were only a couple of problems:

1) I would be sleeping in a house with the deepest, coldest Vibe I'd ever experienced.

2) At least one person I'd met recently had reason to believe that my new landlord (and kind of employer) was a murderer.

Alistair, as if sensing my discomfort (which, let's face it, he probably was), got up and rubbed himself against Frank's ankles and then gave me a look full of feline meaning and import.

"Okay," I said slowly. "But, I warn you, I can't be sure what I'm going to find out. You really might not like it." And I really might not, either.

"But at least I'll know," he said softly. "I owe Aunt Dot that much." Frank pulled his phone out to check the time. He also swore. "Look, I've got to get back to work. Who knows what else Magda's been doing while I'm gone." He wrote an address down on a page of his notebook, tore off the sheet and handed it to me. "Meet me here at nine tomorrow?"

I took the paper and looked at the address. I also made up my mind.

"Okay," I said as I stashed the sheet in my purse. "See you then."

Frank said good-bye and started up the stairs toward the square. I sat and watched him go, but I didn't really see him.

In my mind's eye, it was Ellis Maitland walking away again. I heard his protest that he wanted to help and his revelation about the second mortgage on the house.

"So," I breathed to myself, and to Alistair, if he was there to hear. "What have we got? One. Brad Thompson, who works for Ellis Maitland, broke in to that heavily mortgaged house with a screwdriver." And, incidentally, A.B. Britton had failed to mention this fact to her new . . . what? Landlord? Employer? Client? Why had she done that? But I knew the answer. It hadn't changed. Something was wrong with Brad, and it was wearing down his family. I wanted an answer for them before I opened my mouth and maybe made things worse.

"Two. Ellis Maitland wants to find out if there's something going on between me and Frank, possibly involving Brad and the house. Why?"

No answer came to this question, not from inside or outside.

"Three. Dorothy Hawthorne stopped talking to her best friends before she died. She was showing signs of something that might have been dementia. Or . . ." I swallowed as several of the things I'd just heard all dropped into place. "Or it might have been fear."

❧ 22 ❧

🐾 I GRABBED UP my backpack and trusted Alistair to follow if he felt like it. I needed to get to Midnight Reads and find Julia. There were questions she could answer for me, including, but not limited to, just why she thought Frank Hawthorne might have murdered his aunt.

Then there was that skinny goldfinch. I was really starting not to like that bird.

It was a short walk from the coffee shop to the bookstore. Downtown Portsmouth is convenient and dangerous that way. But the minute I put my hand on the doorknob and looked through the window, I saw I had picked a very bad time to arrive.

Julia stood by the BEACH READS table, leaning heavily on her cane and saying something to the woman in front of her. It took a second, but I recognized that other person.

Julia Parris was arguing with a perfectly turned-out and perfectly furious Elizabeth Maitland. I could hear the rhythms of their raised voices through the door glass but couldn't make out any of the words. Mrs. Maitland gestured harshly, and Julia stabbed one long finger right back. Max and Leo flanked Julia's ankles, their necks and noses thrust forward. Neither one of them had his tail wagging, and somehow they looked a lot less adorable and goofy than they had the other day.

Mrs. Maitland turned on her heel. I ducked back from the door, suddenly not wanting to be seen, but not at all sure why. She stormed out past me, setting the bells jangling and clanking in her wake, and strode down the street, her back perfectly straight. Julia came and stood by the window, her face twisted up in a hard, angry knot.

Max put his paws up on the door and barked. Julia jerked her head around and saw me. She closed her eyes briefly, maybe asking for strength, before she beckoned me inside.

I went in and closed the door behind me. Softly.

"Dissatisfied customer?" I asked.

"No. No. That was . . . personal. It's all right, boys," she murmured to the dachshunds, who had started snuffling around her shoes, whining and wagging. "Really. It's over."

"That was Elizabeth Maitland, right?" I asked. "I met her briefly at the Pale Ale. Mm . . . somebody said you two didn't get along."

"Who told you that?" she snapped. I stood there and didn't answer. Julia rubbed her eyes. "We have certain disagreements, but Elizabeth remains a sister witch, and that's a special relationship, as you will find out." She paused, clearly shaking off the last of her bad temper. "So, Anna." She folded her hands on her cane. "What can I do for you?"

Where to begin? I hitched up the strap of my backpack. "I wanted to let you know I'm staying in town, at least for the summer, and . . . I talked with Grandma B.B. last night."

Julia said nothing. Her face went very still. Even the dachshunds stopped snuffling.

"She told me about you and Dorothy. And Elizabeth. And the . . . feud."

Julia's face remained unreadable. She also glanced toward the door, but at the moment, everyone on the sidewalk was strolling right past. "It's good that you know."

"I've also just talked to Frank Hawthorne. He asked if I'd be interested in renting Dorothy's house for the rest of the summer." Which was mostly true. It would take too long to go into the details of how he'd asked right now.

I don't know quite what I was expecting when I dropped this little bit of news, but it wasn't to see Julia flush bright red.

"Did he say why?" she croaked.

"He said he wants me to help him find out who killed Dorothy."

The black-and-tan wiener—Leo, I remembered—yipped sharply. Julia scooped him up in the crook of one arm and turned away. Leaning on her cane, she limped over to the counter. I followed slowly. A battered blue calico dog bed waited beside the counter, and she deposited Leo in it. "Stay," she murmured. Leo ignored her and scrambled out to join his brother on sentry duty by her ankles.

Maybe these two had more in common with Alistair than I thought.

"Did . . . Did Frank tell you I think he killed Dorothy?" asked Julia.

"Yeah, he did. Is it true?"

"Is it true that I think it, or is it true that he did it?" She crossed to the shelf labeled NEW ARRIVALS and began minutely straightening the bright hardcovers.

"Both, I guess." It was strange to see her being so hesitant. After our first meeting, I'd come away with the idea that this was a woman who could look anything in the eye.

That anything, however, did not include me, at least at the moment. Instead she moved to the children's nook, picking up drawings left behind on the table. I set my backpack down by the register and started gathering the scattered crayons and loading them back into their boxes. The scent instantly reminded me of rainy afternoons. Hope and my brothers might be glued to their game systems, but if I had my crayons, I had the whole world.

"I need you to understand something, Anna," Julia said at last. "When you told us Dorothy had definitely been murdered, the bottom fell out of my world. This is my home. I live here; my family has lived here for generations. If Dorothy was murdered, then someone in this town who I know—perhaps a friend or a colleague, or a child I have watched grow into an adult—deliberately took her life." She pulled a fresh pack of construction paper out from under the counter. "This is not easy."

It also didn't answer my question, but I kept my mouth shut. Julia had something she needed to say, and I needed to give her the time to say it.

"Frank shares a lot of Dorothy's energy and passion. He has never shown any interest in magic, but he is another crusader. Like her, he never lost the notion that he could make this corner of the world better. The paper became his way to help and protect. He's poured everything into it. Maybe too much. I talked to Dorothy about it." Leo yapped and nudged her shin. Julia sighed. "Oh, all right. I argued with Dorothy about it. I thought she should try to moderate Frank's crusading ideals, temper his dreams with reality. But Dorothy thought he should be encouraged."

"Ellis Maitland said Dorothy took out a second mortgage on the house."

Julia nodded. She pulled the big box of Legos out from under the play table and started tossing stray pieces back into it, making the plastic bricks rattle. "To help Frank finance the paper. This was after she took out the first one to help him through school."

I crouched down and picked up some red bricks off the carpet. Max waddled over and started nosing around under the shelves for runaways. "Where's his father?"

"Goodness knows," Julia answered bitterly. "On the road somewhere. Darius is the eternal salesman, always chasing some new deal and leaving Dorothy to take care of things at home. Half the time I'm not even sure what he's selling."

"So Frank always depended on Dorothy."

"Sometimes without considering what his dependence cost her. She never had any children, just Frank, and . . ." Julia shook her head as she pushed the Lego box back into its place. "When it became clear that Dorothy was not going to listen to me, I confronted Frank directly. I told him he was asking too much of Dorothy. That he should consider what she needed for a change. We argued. More than once, I'm afraid."

"Do you think that was maybe what she'd been so secretive about? Maybe she was over her head financially with the loan payments, and she didn't want to tell you because you'd blame Frank."

Julia hung her head. Max and Leo crowded close. Leo got up on his hind legs and rested his paws on her shins. She made no move to push him down. "It's possible. In fact, I've been afraid of something like that." She touched the corner of her eye.

There was a Kleenex box beside the register. I handed one to Julia, and she accepted it with a tiny nod of thanks.

"Julia . . . you said you didn't know for sure Dorothy had been murdered. Why didn't you . . ."

"Work a spell?" Julia finished for me. "Use my magic?"

"Well . . . yeah."

"I tried. I spent months trying to find a scrying . . . that's a way to conjure a vision of a place or event. But I can't clear my mind enough. It's all . . . jumbled. Even Maximilian and Leopold couldn't help." She lifted her head. "I've been very much hoping you can."

"I don't seem to be making a very good start."

"On the contrary, you're making an excellent start. Just your presence here is forcing things into motion."

"What if that motion turns out to be a train wreck?"

Julia smiled, and that strength and confidence I'd seen

during our first meeting all came rushing back. "It will be better than being permanently stalled on the tracks."

I was going to have to think about that, because I wasn't sure I agreed. But there was something else I needed to say first. "Julia, Frank was the one who came up with the idea of me living in the house. That's got to be an argument for his innocence. It'd be too risky to get somebody looking into a murder you committed."

"Or a perfect way to control the inquiries, not to mention to feed the investigators misinformation."

"I hadn't thought of that." And I did not like thinking of it now. I shivered, and I wasn't the only one. Leo and Max both shook themselves and suddenly had their noses to the floor, snuffling around for something unseen.

"What is it?" Julia asked me quickly. "Do you feel something?"

"No, not really. I . . ." I swallowed. "Is there anybody in your coven who has a yellow bird as a familiar?"

Yes, that was me, asking that question with a straight face. Day. Difference. Dealing with it.

"No," said Julia. "No, there is not."

Max was growling at the darkness under a bookcase and scrabbling at the boards. I shivered again.

"Are you sure? Because I've been seeing that bird a lot, and Alistair doesn't seem to like it much."

"Alistair, for all his other fine qualities, is still a cat. He doesn't like any bird much." Julia smiled. Leo barked sharply. "You're right," she said to the dog, and then to me: "Have you ever heard of medical students' disease?"

"It's something that happens to young doctors, right? When you start reading about all kinds of diseases, you start thinking you've got all kinds of symptoms."

"Something like it can happen when you start practicing the craft, too. You start attributing everything you see to magic. In your case, you've got more reason to do so than the average new witch. Wait one moment." She, and the dogs, went back into the religion and philosophy section and pulled a couple of books off the shelf. "Why don't you take these to read? They'll help ground you in some basic principles about the craft, at least the way we practice it in our coven."

"Thank you." The first book was *The Spiral Dance* by Starhawk. I'd heard of that one. The second was *Ways of Magic: History and Practice*. I slid them both into my backpack.

"Of course, these are both just overviews. To really understand you should read . . ." She hesitated.

"What?"

"I'm sorry. I'm still getting used to this. When you take possession of Dorothy's house, you should find a set of books in her attic. Her Books of Shadow."

"Books of Shadow?" I repeated.

"Yes. They're sort of . . . magical journals. Most serious students of the craft keep them. They're notes of ceremonies and workings, as well as thoughts and experiences about the craft in general."

"Sort of spell sketchbooks," I said.

"If you like." Her eyes found mine and I saw a softening that hadn't been there before. "I'm sorry you've been thrown into this so suddenly, Anna. It is not the return I would have wished for anyone in Annabelle's family. Do you . . . do you have the wand with you?"

"Yes. I packed it this morning. I thought . . . I don't know, that I might need it."

"You have good instincts. The wand is not magical as the term is usually understood. But such tools, the words and the symbols all serve to sharpen the witch's focus and bridge the gap between the internal wish and the external world. The wand will help you focus and increase your natural attunement to the world around you."

"And summon my familiar?"

"Certainly it will make it easier." She smiled.

"Julia," I said suddenly. "Do you have a picture of Dorothy around here?" Maybe it was all the talk about focus that

reminded me. I was in the middle of this very strange journey full of very strange discoveries, and I still didn't know
what the woman who started it all actually looked like.

She looked startled, but only for a moment. "I do." She
and the dachshunds all went into the back of the shop. When
they came out, she had a silver-framed picture in her hand.

The photo had been taken on a beautiful fall day. A solid
fireplug of a woman stood under a brilliant scarlet maple.
She had the classic black witch's hat on her head and looked
at the world through a pair of huge rhinestone-decorated
glasses that should have been consigned to the seventies.
Alistair, looking smug and tolerant, curled up in the crook
of one arm. She raised a wineglass high with the other,
toasting the camera and the photographer. She wore jeans
and a purple T-shirt with a yin-yang symbol on it, only the
yin and the yang were a pair of curled-up cats.

But it was her face that really touched me. Dorothy had
been caught in the act of laughing, wide mouth open. This
woman who made no apologies for her full years. Her face
was tanned and spotted and an absolute road map of wrin-
kles, and her dark eyes were all but lost in a lifetime's worth
of laugh lines. She was someone who spent her days in the
sun and her nights sitting up late with friends. She didn't
care what people thought of her looks, or her attitude. She
was going to live and laugh and love and the rest of the world
could like it or lump it.

I liked it. I liked her.

"Thank you," I said and started to hand it back.

"You can keep this," Julia told me. "I've got others." Then
she took a deep breath and laid a hand on my arm. "I'm glad
you're taking Dorothy's house," she said. "If for no other
reason than it should be lived in and loved. Will you let me
know when you've signed the lease? With your permission,
I'd like to bring over some of the coven members. We could
help you move in."

"Thanks. I think I'd like that."

All at once, a herd of children exploded into the store, followed closely by a group of women in shorts and sun hats. Julia smiled wanly at me and turned away, shifting from worried witch to happy bookstore owner without batting an eye. The dogs scampered up to the squealing kids to be hugged and petted.

I nodded to them all, understanding. We would finish this later. It was probably just as well. I already had more than enough to think about.

Like what those "certain disagreements" between Julia and Mrs. Maitland were, and if they had anything to do with Dorothy's murder.

Julia had accused Frank of trying to control what kind of information I got about Dorothy and her death. But as little as I liked the idea, I could say the same thing about her.

❧ 23 ❧

🐾 THE CHURCH TOWER was chiming noon. I thought about going somewhere for lunch. I thought about going back to McDermott's and curling up with the books Julia had given me. I dismissed this. I wasn't ready to start in on my homework yet.

I stopped at Popovers on the Square for coffee and a sandwich (and a popover, of course). Then I traced the winding way down to the riverbank until I came to a lovely little park. I made way for joggers and dog walkers as I strolled under the trees, past green lawns and flower beds and onto a wooden pier.

The wind off the river was pleasantly cool. I sat on the sun-warmed bench, ate my lunch and sipped my coffee while a red tugboat full of tourists chugged past, trailing a flock of hopeful (and loud) seagulls. I watched the traffic on the Memorial Bridge and the slow-moving cranes over in the shipyard.

I pulled out my notebook and started on what I meant to be a sketch of the river in front of me. But the river wouldn't

come. Instead, I found myself incessantly doodling faces—
Julia, Kenisha and Valerie. Frank Hawthorne was there too,
and Brad Thompson. And down around the edges, one fat
cat with slanting eyes.

I wasn't really surprised. It was tough to concentrate on
anything except what I'd been through since I got here. In
the clear light of a summer day, so much still felt impossible.
But I had to accept it. All of it.

I pulled out the silver-framed photo again and looked at
the woman in the pointy hat.

"Okay, Dorothy, where do I start?" I asked. Dorothy just
laughed and saluted me with that glass of red wine. I put
the photo away and stared at my sketch pad.

Did I search the house? I slashed my pencil across the
paper, making an outline of the cozy cottage exterior with
its roses and its crescent-moon weathervane. I definitely had
my way in now, but what would I even be looking for? Did
I talk to the people around Dorothy? Gather all the suspects
in the dining room à la Hercule Poirot and interrogate them?
No, probably I was supposed to question them one by one
before then.

But whom did I actually suspect? And why?

I sighed and doodled a question mark. I definitely needed
to find out what Dorothy was up to before she died. Frank
said he didn't know. Julia said she didn't know. They were
the two people who were supposed to be closest to her.

The truth was, despite having the photo from Julia, I
really didn't know much of anything about Dorothy Hawthorne. I knew she was a witch, and proud of it. I knew she'd
withdrawn from her friends and family before she died. I
knew someone had been angry enough with her to let her
die, if not actually kill her. I gave my question mark a
frowny face, eyelashes, horn-rimmed glasses and Cheshire
cat stripes. When it came to all the details that make up a
person's life, that wasn't actually a whole lot.

Maybe that was why I couldn't understand what was

going on. I'd been seeing myself as being in the middle of this mystery, but I wasn't. The person who was really at the center of this puzzle was Dorothy Hawthorne herself. If I wanted to untangle the riddle, I didn't just need to search the house; I needed to untangle Dorothy.

Frank had mentioned a HeyLook! page and a Web site. I dug my laptop out of my bag and flipped up the lid. I opened the search window and typed: *northeastwitch.com*.

"Okay, Miss Hawthorne," I murmured as I hit Enter. "What have you got to say for yourself?"

THE NORTH CHURCH clock had chimed noon when I left Midnight Reads. It was chiming six when I crossed Market Square for what I really hoped would be the last time today. I'd spent the entire afternoon crisscrossing downtown Portsmouth, looking for people who had known Dorothy Hawthorne. This turned out to be half the town.

Modern technology is a wonderful thing. I might not be a highly trained professional, like Frank, but I could run a decent online search. It did feel kind of strange accessing the Web and HeyLook! pages for someone who was dead. Recently dead, I mean. I looked up dead artists all the time.

Not only were Dorothy's pages still up and running; they had collected long strings of comments from people who mourned her passing and wished one another hope and comfort. Some of those comments came from Portsmouth residents who used their real names and left a lot of personal profile information open to public view. Those names, in turn, led to Web and HeyLook! pages for the businesses, restaurants or cafés they kept, and listed the addresses in the brick-and-mortar world.

Which was how I ended up hiking along the steep, curving streets between places like Gabrielle's Nail & Beauty Salon, the Left Bank Gallery and Annabelle's Ice Cream. At this last, there may have been some slight indulgence in salted caramel ice cream with chocolate sprinkles, but hey, I needed to keep my strength up. Discovering my inner Nancy Drew was giving me a new and immediate appreciation of the term "legwork."

It turned out just about everybody I met had their own Dorothy story. They told me how she'd helped them, or annoyed them, or prodded or pushed them in some direction that was exactly the way they were supposed to go, although they might not have realized it until much later. Most of them could also point me toward somebody else who also had a Dorothy story.

I had decided I should take a hint from Frank Hawthorne and keep notes about what I'd heard. I ended up scribbling across so many pages in my sketchbook, I had to make an extra stop at Mrs. Morgan's Fine Papers & Stationery and buy another. There, I not only got a fresh sketchbook; I got a story about the time Dorothy turned up to order fifty engraved announcement cards for an engagement that everybody else was sure would never happen. "My present to the happy couple," she'd said. "You wait and see."

"So did it happen?" I asked Mrs. Morgan, a plump, energetic woman who looked at the world from over the rims of old-fashioned half-moon glasses. "The wedding?"

"Sure did," Mrs. Morgan answered as she rang up my receipt. "Happy couple picked up their announcements less than a week later. I think Dorothy knew it was all a go before the pair themselves did. But that's how she was—one step ahead, and one over the line."

That had been several hours ago, when I'd felt much more chipper and social. Now my throat and my feet were informing me they'd had more than enough healthy outdoor activity for one day, thank you very much. Plus, never mind the recent salted caramel ice cream with sprinkles in a waffle cone, I was starving. I needed to hole up in my room for a while and go over my notes. My plan was to organize my thoughts and lay the whole thing out in front of Martine. It would be good to have an impartial observer at this point. Assuming, of course, that impartial observer didn't decide to read me the riot act for getting involved in something that was none of my business.

Then it occurred to me that there was one important person I hadn't talked to yet. One person, aside from Julia Parris, who had known Dorothy, not to mention Grandma B.B., back when their split happened, and who might have some idea what was driving Dorothy those last few weeks of her life.

I stepped into the shade of the nearest storefront, pulled out my smartphone and brought up the search engine. After a few minutes, I had the number I needed. I dialed and waited while it rang.

"Maitland residence," said a woman's lightly accented voice.

"May I speak with Elizabeth Maitland, please?"

"Who shall I say is calling?"

"Annabelle Blessingsound Britton."

"One moment please." I waited. "I'm sorry, but Ms. Maitland is not available. Would you care to leave a message?"

"Could you ask her to call me?" I gave my number and listened while the woman read it back. I thanked her and hung up.

Would she call? I wondered. If she did, what would I say? *What were you and Julia Parris arguing about? How come nobody around here likes you? What do you know about your son's business, oh, and Brad Thompson?*

I shook my head. When Mrs. Maitland called, if she called, I'd just have to play it by ear. Right now I had other things to worry about. Like dinner. I'd spotted a little Indian place about a block back. Some tikka masala and naan bread sounded like just the comfort-food ticket.

Raja Rani proved to be small and kind of bare-bones, but it was filled with a warm, spicy aroma that made me certain this was a good decision. The hostess led me to a table by the window and handed me a menu. I ordered my masala medium hot because I am not a daredevil, and my naan without garlic because I had to live with myself. I got a cup of chai, too, which was strong and full of spice. I hate it when chai tastes like milky sugar water.

I stared out at the street, sipping my lovely chai, losing my worries in quiet contemplation of the passing pedestrians and important questions of the day like whether I wanted to hop the bus back to McDermott's. Then one of those pedestrians stopped dead in front of the window and stared right at me.

It was Brad Thompson.

I SET MY cup down carefully. I also pressed my hand against my backpack, right where I could feel the shape of the wand in the outer pocket. I immediately felt silly. I knew I shouldn't judge by appearances, but it was tough to imagine somebody who looked less dangerous than Brad Thompson. If I drew his portrait, I'd use charcoal, all soft and gray and fading at the edges. Plus, he was wearing a pale blue button-down shirt and khaki pants, which is not the fashion choice of somebody who wants to give off that danger-man vibe.

Outside, Brad glanced over his shoulder, then back at me, then over his shoulder again. I didn't know what he wanted to do. Come forward? Run away? I'm not sure he knew either, at least at first. At last, he steeled himself and started toward the restaurant's door.

I unzipped my backpack pocket, yanked the wand out and slid it under the napkin I had spread on my lap. I wasn't sure what I planned to do with it, but Julia said it could help me focus. Right now, focus sounded very useful.

Brad waved away the hostess when she bustled up to him. He walked over to my table carefully, like he expected the floor to give way underneath him.

"Is this where I get to say we have to stop meeting like this?" I asked.

I'm pretty sure Brad meant to chuckle, but the sound came out more like a titter. "Or ask if I'm, uh, stalking you or something. Which I'm not," he added quickly. "Please believe me—I'm really not. But . . . I . . . uh . . . yeah. I, um, might be able to help you. I think."

"Oh?" I frowned at him. He shrank back and I honestly didn't know what to do. Part of me was impatient. Part of me was confused. Things must have gotten pretty bad in this man's life if a five-foot-something artist with a cup of spiced tea looked scary.

"I, um, yeah, do you mind? Could I sit down?" Brad gestured toward the empty chair.

"Go ahead," I told him, and Brad sat, or rather, he perched on the edge of the chair. The waitress brought a glass of water and a menu. He ignored both.

"So." I rested my hands on my lap and, incidentally, my magic wand. "You're not stalking me, Mr. Thompson . . . ?"

"Brad, please. I, uh, think we can be casual, right?" He laughed, that same nervous titter, and looked down at his fingertips. His wedding ring was a simple gold band, and now that we were face-to-face, I could see his left shirt cuff had frayed and his buttons didn't quite match. That told me they'd popped off and had been sewn back on at least once. I was struck again by how tired Brad looked and remembered that same exhaustion in Laurie's eyes.

"I'm sorry about everything when we met at the house. I was just startled." Brad spoke quickly, like he was afraid he'd lose his nerve in the middle of a sentence. He also glanced out the window, yet again. I had the sudden feeling he would have been more comfortable in a dark alley than sitting here where all of Portsmouth could get a very good look at the company he was keeping. "I should have known you were one of Dorothy's friends, but I couldn't be sure until I saw you with Val and Kenisha." He glanced back again, and then leaned toward me. "So," he whispered, "did you get the copies?"

❧ 24 ❧

🐾 A WHOLE SERIES of potential responses to Brad's question flashed through my mind. Most contained the words "What copies?" They also might have involved grabbing him by the shoulders and shaking.

But before my hands could move, a voice inside me whispered, *Let him talk. Find out what's going on.*

Seems my inner Nancy Drew was a calculating little thing, or maybe it was the magic wand under my palm. Whichever it was, I listened.

"No, I didn't find the copies." Which was the truth, as far as I knew, anyhow.

Brad's mustache twitched and he twisted his wedding ring. "But she told you where they are, right?"

"Uh, no. She never got the chance." Which was also, you'll notice, the truth.

The waiter brought my tikka masala and naan along with a dish of jasmine rice and set them all down. He looked expectantly at Brad, who entirely failed to notice him. He was too busy twisting his wedding ring. I waved the waiter away.

"But at least Frank hasn't found them, right?" The note of hope in Brad's question was painfully sharp.

"I don't think so," I answered slowly. "He didn't say anything about them."

"Okay, well, that's something, I guess."

"I thought you and Frank Hawthorne were friends." I curled my fingers loosely around the hidden wand. I expected to feel that low prickling under my skin that I was beginning to associate with magic. But there was nothing. The man sitting opposite me just looked sadder. Deflated. Defeated.

"Things change."

"Is that why you need those copies now? Because things changed?" I asked gently.

He also didn't answer me, not directly, anyway. "I really hoped you'd found something in the attic. I tried to get in before, but that is one tough lock." He twisted his wedding ring back and forth some more. "I was coming back to try to get the hinges off the door when we . . . met. I guess Dorothy sent you the key or something?"

"Yeah, well . . . are you sure the . . . copies . . . are in the house?" I helped myself to rice and chicken tikka so I had an excuse not to be looking at him right then.

"Where else would they be? Unless she had a safe-deposit box or something?"

"Not that I know about." I pushed the basket of naan toward him. Brad shook his head.

Then I remembered something Frank had told me. "I do know Dorothy's computer got stolen. Was that you?"

"No. I was too slow. I've been trying for months to find out who took it. It's been making me crazy. I'd hoped for a while it was one of her . . . in-town people."

"By hers, you mean Dorothy's?"

"Of course Dorothy's." He frowned hard at me, and I forked some food into my mouth to keep myself quiet. "But when nobody lowered the boom, I figured it was pretty obvious who actually got hold of it."

No! No, it really isn't! I screamed in my mind.

"Well, there are two of us now." This time, Brad did help himself to a wedge of the buttery flatbread and nibbled the corner. "We should be able to pick up the pieces pretty easily. What took you so long to get here?"

I shrugged. "I had stuff to tie up, and I thought . . . things here might take a while."

"You got that right." Brad tore his piece of naan in half, popped one piece into his mouth and chewed, for a long time. "So, okay, if you got the keys from Dorothy, we should be able to get back into the house while—"

"Actually, I've got some good news." If I was playing the coconspirator, I might as well go all the way. "Frank Hawthorne is going to rent me the house."

"What? You're kidding." All the blood drained from Brad's face, and I got the slow, creeping feeling that I'd just made a terrible mistake.

"We're drawing up the lease tomorrow."

Brad swore. He stared and he swore again. "That means they're gone!" he croaked. "He got them, or he knows where they are!" He shoved his chair back and climbed heavily to his feet, getting ready to leave in some kind of panic before I'd even kind of found out what he was talking about.

"Brad, please, calm down. You . . . we can't be sure he found anything."

"I can't be sure? He hasn't let anybody near that house for six months and then you show up . . ." He stared at his hand, which still clutched that piece of naan. "You show up and he's renting it out and oh, my God, I'm such an idiot!" He swore again and hurled the bread down onto the table. The hostess and the waiter were staring at us from the podium by the door. "Dorothy would have told you about me! I should have known something was wrong when you didn't come straight out and say it!"

"Look, Brad . . ."

"Is there a problem, sir?" the waiter asked smoothly as

he hurried over to us. He was only about as tall as Brad, but he was in much better shape, and right then, much calmer.

"No," I said quickly. "Sorry. Thank you."

The waiter looked at me, and he looked at Brad. Brad sat back down, slowly. Over his shoulder I could see the hostess pull a cell phone out of the podium drawer and flip it open.

"You've got to calm down, Brad," I said evenly. "Otherwise they're going to throw us both out."

Brad clenched his fists and made an effort to control himself. He actually shuddered doing it. Then he leaned across the table until we were almost nose to nose. "You lied," he whispered furiously. "You're not working with Dorothy! You're working with Frank!"

"I'm not working with anybody." Except, of course, I was.

"Then who the hell are you?" He grabbed my wrist and squeezed hard. "What are you doing here?"

"I'm just trying to help, and you *really* want to let me go right now."

I tensed myself, getting ready to put that self-defense class I took at the YMCA into action. I also clutched the wand under my napkin. The hostess had turned away from us and was talking into her phone.

This time, I felt it, that warm, prickling current. Something in the air around me shifted and Brad's panicked grip loosened.

I pulled my hand away, gently. "Look, Brad. I can tell you want to talk to somebody about . . . all this. That's why you're here. Whatever you tell me, I promise, it won't go any further without your say-so." *For your family's sake, if nothing else.*

There it was, the pricking under my skin, the shifting in the air. I felt it stretch out, and I willed Brad to trust me. I wanted him to trust me. I needed him to. It was important.

Tears glittered in his eyes. Then the air shivered and the connection broke.

"I know I'm a freakin' coward and I look like some kind of idiot," he whispered. "But you better keep your mouth shut. I swear that if you bring my name into whatever game you're playing, I can still break you, and Frank. You tell your new landlord that."

He stomped out, shoving his way hard through the door. I fell back in my chair, crumpling my napkin in my hands.

The hostess closed her cell phone and turned to greet the new family who'd come through the door. The waiter brought me my check and offered to wrap up the rest of my dinner to go. I couldn't blame him. I didn't want me in here anymore either.

IT WASN'T UNTIL walking—okay, tiptoeing—through the door at McDermott's that I realized I'd left my carryout bag on the bus.

I tried to shrug it off, but somehow it really bothered me. You know how it is, when you've got so many big things going wrong that somehow it's the last little thing that seems to bring the world crashing down.

"Anna?"

I jerked around, wobbling dangerously on the stair. Roger came into the foyer from the threshold of the great room, drying his hands on a striped dishcloth. He wore a green polo shirt and jeans and his dark hair was tousled. He looked so intensely nice-guy normal, it was almost embarrassing. Here I was worrying about witches, theft and murder. He was probably worrying about whether his quiche was going to gel, or whatever it was those sneaky quiches did when you weren't looking.

"Good day?" asked Roger, like his quiche hadn't a care in the world.

"Oh, yeah. It was just . . . long." I started up the stairs. I needed to be away from this guy and all his normalcy. I was tired, I was confused and I was entirely without the tikka masala that had been supposed to make things better.

"You do remember I know what's going on, don't you?" said Roger to my back. "We're here if you need to talk."

He was trying to be nice. Considerate. I made myself smile. "Thanks. Really. But what I need right now is some space."

"I understand. Call down if you need anything else, okay?"

Up in my room, I closed the door and locked it. I pushed back the curtains on the window and checked the sill. There was no evidence of Alistair. At that moment I didn't know whether to be relieved or worried. I dropped my stuff and myself down on the bed.

I had wanted Brad Thompson to tell me what he was doing in Dorothy's house, and he had, except now I was more confused than ever. So confused, I'd tried to use magic to get Brad to tell me more, and it had kind of spectacularly failed to work.

"So what *was* that?" I asked the world in general as I ran both hands through my hair. "A lesson in being careful what you wish for?"

"Merowp."

I jumped and tumbled over on the bed. Alistair was sitting on the windowsill, tail twitching back and forth and big blue eyes blinking calmly.

"Jeez, cat!" I pressed my hand against my chest. "You can't do that!"

He blinked again. *Do what?* Then he jumped down and stuffed his face into my purse.

"There's no food in there," I told him. "I left it on the bus." I might have been a little grumpy when I said it, but I was tired. Tired of turning all this mess over in my mind. Tired of talking to nobody but the cat.

"Mmmrp." Alistair gave my purse a shove, knocking it off the bed and, incidentally, spilling the entire contents onto the floor.

"Oh, for Pete's sake!" I bent down to start scooping things back in, but Alistair was already in the middle of the mess. He was batting at a scrap of paper with his paws, and of course it was getting away from him. Therefore, it must be chased after, and pounced on, and swatted for good measure, because clearly it was a most dangerous scrap of paper.

I shook my head. Julia was right. Whatever else he was, Alistair was still a cat.

I was about to drop my cell phone back into my purse, but I hesitated. What I really needed right now was to get out of my own head, which was too full of mystery, magic and murder.

"Merow," said Alistair with an air of strained patience. The paper was holding still, but he didn't trust it, and crouched down, ready in case it tried to make a break for it.

"That's it, big guy; you show it who's boss." I hit my brother Bob's number.

"Hey, Annie!" shouted Bob when he picked up. Members of my immediate family are the only living beings allowed to call me Annie. "How's it going? How's Portsmouth?"

"Hey, Bobby," I answered him. "Portsmouth is great . . . In fact, I'm thinking I might stay for a while. If everything is good there. How's Dad?"

"Dad's great. Watching the Red Sox." I heard a shout behind me, but I couldn't tell if it was good or bad.

"Hello, Annie!" shouted Dad. "Whaddaya mean he was out! The ump's blind!"

"Instant replay doesn't lie, Dad," I heard my sister-in-law, Ginger, reply. "Hi, Annie!"

"Hi, Ginger!" I shouted back, picturing my brother's grimace as he yanked the phone away from his ear.

"Instant replay my . . . ahhh, hooey . . . ," grumbled Dad.

"Hooey!" The shout came from my small, enthusiastic, and consistently oversugared nephew, Bobby Britton III. "Hooo-EEEE!"

"Tsk, tsk, Robert Sr.!" cried Ginger. "Look what you're teaching your grandchild!"

I was smiling. I couldn't help it. "You guys clearly got it under control," I said to Bob.

He laughed. "For certain values of control. You sure everything's all right? You sound kinda down."

"No, no, I'm fine. I just . . . I wanted to check in."

He was willing to let it go, and, as it turned out, so was I. We would work our way around to touchy subjects later. Right now, we could chat about the usual small family matters; who'd heard from whom most recently, how things were going in preschool and whether Ted was finally going to propose to his girlfriend.

Eventually we ran out of gossip, or Bobby wanted to get back to watching the Red Sox trounce Satan's baseball team (otherwise known as the Yankees), or both. "Good to talk to you, sis," he told me. "Let us know what your plans are. And hey, you know if there really is anything wrong, me and Ted will be up there in a hot minute, right? Nobody messes with our sister."

"I know." *Darn it, big brother, I do not need your protection,* I thought. Except if that was how I really felt, why was I smiling and feeling that odd prickling behind my eyes, not to mention an easing of the tension in my shoulders? "I'll call back soon."

We said good-bye and I hung up. I was still smiling. Whatever happened before, whatever happened next, I was still Annabelle Amelia Blessingsound Britton. I had my Yankee pride and my New England stubbornness, and I was a long, long way from being alone. For starters, there was Martine, who would have skewered me for ever doubting she had my back. Behind her, and me, stood the whole Blessingsound Britton clan. No matter what I faced, my family was with me. All of them.

"I needed that," I told Alistair.

Alistair wasn't paying any attention to me. He was still glowering at the Very Dangerous Scrap. "Merow!" he snapped.

I laughed and rubbed his ears to apologize for not taking his paper-chasing prowess seriously enough. Then I heard footsteps outside and a soft knock on the door. I shot a look of inquiry at the cat, who responded by vigorously cleaning his tail. I went and unlocked the door, but there was no one outside. Somebody had been there, though, and they'd left a small folding table, a tray with a covered dish and a note:

YOU LOOKED HUNGRY.

I bowed my head and started laughing. I couldn't help it. Julia said I had no mystical destiny. She was wrong. I was clearly destined to be fed by compulsive cooks.

I did pick the tray up and carry it inside.

"If it's quiche I really am leaving," I told the cat as I lifted the cloche. It wasn't quiche, but it was some lovely roast chicken and green salad and new potatoes. And a cup of that amazing blackberry grunt.

"Hungry, Alistair?"

His nose shot up in the air. "Merp!"

I carefully shredded some of the chicken to make sure I didn't get any accidental bones, forked the results onto my napkin, and set it on the sill. The presence of chicken apparently changed Alistair's mind about just how dangerous that paper was, and he leapt up onto the sill. The cat ate. I ate. It was simple and delicious, and I felt better. I was also able to start thinking again. If talking to a cat can be considered a sign of thinking.

"So, did I really screw up today, or what?"

Alistair, however, was too busy nosing the napkin to see if he'd left any shred of chicken to venture an opinion.

I pulled the wand out of my purse and turned it over in my fingers. It was a beautiful thing, and it felt warm and comfortable in my hand. I traced the delicately carved pattern with my fingers, following the branches as they turned from bare to blossoming to full leaf. I circled the tip of my finger around a crescent moon, a half-moon and a full. I peered at the Latin inscription of what Julia had called the threefold law.

*Quod ad vos mittere in mundum triplici. What you send
into the world comes back threefold.*

I closed my fingers around it. What had I sent out into
the world when I had tried to use the wand, and the magic,
on Brad? I wanted him to calm down. I wanted him to trust
me. Talk to me. I wanted him to open up, whether he wanted
to or not.

My thoughts skidded to a halt. Wasn't that exactly what
Julia had tried to do to me when I first walked into Midnight
Reads? And how had I reacted? Angry, hurt, betrayed,
because this woman I didn't even know had tried to trick
me. And I'd just tried pretty much the same trick on Brad,
and it hadn't worked any better.

I swore and laid the wand down on the nightstand. In its
place, I dug my new sketch pad out of my backpack. I started
scribbling down everything I could remember about what Brad
had actually said to me. It was me, of course, so there were
also plenty of doodles, a caricature of Brad sweating bullets
and tearing a piece of bread in two, and stacks of documents
with question marks floating in the air around them.

Brad was looking for copies. That implied there were
documents of some kind out there. Dorothy had copies of
important documents, and Brad knew about them, but he
didn't know where she had hidden them. He wanted to find
them so badly he broke in to her house, more than once.
He'd planned on taking her computer but somebody beat
him to it. Which implied that there was at least one other
person who found these documents—whatever they were—
of vital interest.

"Merow!" Alistair jumped onto the bed and ducked his
head under the paper, pushing it up. "Merow!"

"Oh, for Pete's sake." I picked the scrap up. I intended to
roll it into a ball and toss it for him to chase, but I stopped.
This was the photo of me I'd found on Dorothy's altar.

My fingers tingled.

"Mrrp," said Alistair, curling his tail around his feet, like he was satisfied.

I stared at my photo, and my photo stared back. I turned the paper over. On the other side, I saw what had once been part of a car ad. But along one edge there was some very small handwriting that I hadn't noticed before. It was so small, in fact, I had to bring it almost to my nose and squint before I could read it.

"Aka Dorothy Gale."

"Merow!" announced Alistair proudly.

I stared at the cat. I stared at the piece of paper in my hands. This was a clue. This was absolutely and without a shadow of a doubt a clue, deliberately left for me by a woman who knew she was in danger.

The problem was, I had no idea what it could possibly mean.

❧ 25 ❧

♣ THE BUSINESS ADDRESS of Enoch Gravesend, Esq.,
LLC, PLLC, and M-O-U-S-E, for all I knew, turned out to
be a Federal-style house in Portsmouth's historic district. This
basically meant it was a pale yellow box of a building with a
peaked roof and shuttered windows. The office was on the
left-hand side of a flagstone foyer, and it contained everything
you could possibly want from a lawyer's office: wood paneling, overflowing bookcases, solid, comfortable chairs and a
broad desk with a green blotter and a green-shaded lamp.

"Ah! Miss Britton! Come in, come in!" The lawyer himself came out from behind that expanse of antique oak to
shake my hand and pull back the chair Frank hadn't claimed.
"Please, do sit down."

Like me and Frank, the gray-haired and portly Enoch
Gravesend was a card-carrying member of Ye Olde Family
Name Society (New England branch). He also had more
than enough personality to handle it. Enoch wore a linen
suit and bright blue vest with gold buttons. His face was
ruddy and his handshake delicate without being limp. I'm

not a fan of the theatrical, especially in a lawyer, but Enoch's smile was instantly charming.

"Now." Enoch settled himself back in his padded leather chair. "Let's see where we are. Miss Britton, how long were you thinking of staying with us?"

"Errrm . . ." I let my glance slide sideways toward Frank. It felt strange to be sitting in a lawyer's office with someone I'd only just met. Personal somehow.

"I see," said Enoch gravely. "Perhaps three months, then?"

Frank nodded first, and I nodded back.

Enoch laughed loudly and tossed his pen onto his desk. "Come off it, you two. You are not getting married. At least, if you are, there's nothing about it in the lease. Frank, are you sure you're ready for this?"

Frank took a deep breath. "Yes," he said. "Yes, I am."

"Fine. Miss Britton, shall we say three months?" I nodded and Frank nodded, and the lawyer nodded. "Now, the rent is, as I understand it, being waived in return for you, Miss Britton, living in the house and keeping the property clean and up to a saleable standard."

He glanced at Frank, and I wondered what the lawyer was thinking about him, and about me.

"That's right," said Frank calmly.

"All right. Given the nature of the agreement, and the property, and since Frank does not rent out any other buildings, the law gives us some flexibility here, so we can take advantage of that and keep the process at least somewhat informal." He said this in a way that indicated informality was not his first choice. "You will, however, need to put down a security deposit." He wrote down a figure on a piece of paper and pushed it toward me. I read it and I winced.

"That's his idea," said Frank.

"And it will of course be returned at the end of the lease." Enoch folded his hands on his desk and gave me a look of unruffled calm that rivaled one of Alistair's.

"No, that's okay. I mean, I could be anybody, right?"

"Just so," said the lawyer.

I reminded myself that I had a plan. I'd come up with it last night before I'd fallen asleep over Julia's books, my head full of the cycle of nature, the feminine principle in the divine, the sacredness of the earth and all creation. I'd read about meditations and ceremonies for cleansing the mind and spirit; the symbolic importance of circles, spirals and directions; the four elements of earth, air, fire and water; not to mention several chapters on the threefold law.

Including the fact that I might not want to believe it, but I could be sitting next to the murderer right now.

"There is one more thing," I said slowly.

"Yes, Miss Britton?"

"I'd like to know if the house is . . . encumbered at all."

"Encumbered?"

"Are there any outstanding liens or delinquent payments on a second or third mortgage, or anything else that might cause it to be sold or foreclosed, or repossessed, before the lease is up."

Both men were staring at me. I stared right back. Books about witchcraft, ancient and modern, weren't the only things I'd been reading last night. I'd also spent a large chunk of the evening poring over my notes and surfing the Internet trying to work out what kind of "copies" Brad could have been talking about.

My best guesses included:

1) Something to do with that second mortgage that
   people kept bringing up, or

2) The house being used as collateral for some kind of
   deeply subprime loan on the equipment needed to
   open a newspaper.

Frank was frowning, but Enoch remained cool.

"There's nothing that I know of, and I was Dorothy's

lawyer for the last twenty years. Frank?" Enoch swiveled his chair and steepled his fingers. "Has anything changed?"

"Since probate wrapped up? No."

"Just checking," I told them.

"It's good to be thorough." Enoch made another note. "Is there anything else?"

"Not as long as the house is in good repair." I paused. "And I'm assuming it's okay if I keep a cat?"

Frank chuckled. "If Alistair wants to stay with you, he's more than welcome."

"We are in agreement, then." Enoch made a few more notes. "Good for you both, less good for my billing sheet, but we can't have everything. Now . . ." He rifled a stack of papers and extracted one page to hand to me. "This is the results of the inventory and the walk-through that Frank did up for me. It has the details on the condition of the house and so on. You can either do your own walk-through before you rent, Miss Britton, or accept the list and submit any corrections afterward."

"I'm sure it's all fine." I skimmed the list. On the inventory, there was a lot of furniture and dishes in the kitchen. As for the condition of the house, there was a loose shutter and some dampness in the basement. Frankly, I would have been shocked if there wasn't some dampness in the basement.

Enoch favored us both with another appraising look. Then he sighed and shook his head. "I am going to have to assume you two know what you're doing here. But, Frank . . ."

Frank held up his hand. "I know, Enoch. You don't approve, but I'm doing it anyway."

"Which is your prerogative." Enoch ran one thick finger down his legal pad. "Miss Britton, you'll want to be sure to note or photograph anything that needs repair so that you are not charged with the damage. That is everything I have here. Is there anything more for either of you? No? Good, better, best. If you two will excuse me, I will type up the remainder of this and we will be finished shortly."

Enoch rose. He also—I swear I am not making this up—gave me a small bow and disappeared through a side door. A moment later the heavy metallic clatter of actual typewriter keys sounded from the next room.

"Wow," I said.

Frank chuckled. "I know. But don't let the theatrics fool you. Enoch's the best lawyer in town, especially when it comes to contracts."

"Sounds like I should read this lease pretty carefully."

"Do you want to back out?"

"No. But . . . you haven't told him anything about why you're doing this, have you?"

"No more than necessary. Enoch pretty much thinks I'm just trying to get Ellis Maitland off my back." Frank paused and looked down at his hands. "I was thinking, maybe, would you like to get some lunch?" He glanced toward the side door. The rattle and clatter of typing had stopped. "To talk about . . . things."

It was a good idea. We did need to talk, and it was probably not smart to be bringing up any amateur investigator stuff in a lawyer's office, even if he was Frank's lawyer.

"Thanks," I said, and I did mean it. "But I think I need to spend today getting settled, and you never know—I might find . . . something else we need to talk about."

Our gazes met and locked, and Frank nodded. "Well, how about dinner tomorrow? Assuming everything goes okay?"

"Sounds great," I said, just as the door opened.

"And here we are." Enoch reappeared holding a sheaf of legal-sized pages. "Now, if you will write the check, Miss Britton, and you two will sign here." He passed the lease across that acre of desk.

I admit, I hesitated. If I signed this, I was finally, truly, legally committed, and not just to the house, but to Portsmouth and all that implied.

It implied a whole heck of a lot right now.

I took a deep breath. I read, and I signed. Frank read and

Frank signed. I wrote the check for the deposit with a minimum amount of wincing and handed it to Frank. Frank squinted at the name of the bank. Then he pulled a ring out with three keys on it and handed them over to me.

"Congratulations, Frank." Enoch held out his hand. "You're a landlord."

"Ugh. Not sure I like the sound of it."

Enoch gave him a smile of fatherly tolerance. "You'd like handing over those keys to Ellis Maitland and his mother a lot less, and you can trust me because I'm saying this as your lawyer." My ears pricked up at the mention of the Maitlands, but Enoch had already moved on. "Now, I must ask you both to excuse me . . ." He pulled out a pocket watch. He actually pulled out a pocket watch. It was big and silver with a complicated pattern etched on the back. I felt the urge to check the calendar to make sure I hadn't accidentally slipped into the wrong century. "I have another client. I wish you both good morning."

Enoch stood and gave another of those little bows, and we stood, and everybody shook hands, and the lawyer ushered me and Frank out his door.

"So, we're good, then?" said Frank as we walked down the path to the sidewalk.

"I guess so, yeah." *Except for this whole situation being more than a little strange, and awkward.* "Do you want to come with me and . . . walk through the house or anything?"

I could tell he wanted to say yes, but his phone beeped in his pocket. He pulled it out and hit the mute button. "Duty calls," he said. "But I'll see you tomorrow?"

I agreed that he would, and Frank headed up the street toward the square. He did glance back a couple of times. I thought I read a little regret on his face. Was that because he still didn't want to give up his aunt's house, or because he was he afraid of what I'd find in there?

I found myself thinking about the missing computer again. Frank could have taken it, easily.

"But that doesn't make sense," I said out loud. "Frank was Dorothy's heir. He wouldn't have to steal anything. That computer belonged to him." After she died, anyway. Now, there was a pleasant thought. I thought about the photo and the clue she'd left me, hidden in the room she'd locked with her magic. That was an awful lot of trouble to take. In fact, it might look like she was hiding it from someone who could easily search the house.

This entirely cheerful thought was followed fast by another. There was somebody else who knew Dorothy was keeping secrets and was interested in them. Angry about them, in fact. Someone who could also have easily searched the house.

Julia Parris.

❧ 26 ❧

❖ WHEN I PULLED into the driveway of Dorothy's house, Alistair was waiting on the porch. I kicked the Jeep's door shut while I dug one hand in my purse to find the keys Frank had given me. In the other, I carried a couple of straining grocery bags. I'd stopped at the Market Basket for a few necessities—cheese, crackers, peanut butter, toilet paper and, of course, coffee.

"So, you're okay with this?" I said to the cat, or maybe the house; it was tough to tell which. I admit to being a little nervous. Memories of the Vibe in the cellar, and the one on the second floor, and the one in the garden, had me rethinking my entire plan.

I told myself I had a lease. I'd put down a deposit, which left me with barely enough in my account for gas money out of town, never mind a hotel room. I was looking into mysteries and I'd made promises that I was not ready, or willing, to break.

And I still wasn't going in. I stood on the porch, inhaling the rich scent of rambler roses, with the keys in one hand

and the eco-friendly recycled paper bags in the other. Alistair meowed and rolled over on his back, waving his paws in the air, as cute as any Internet cat video.

"Okay, I get it. Nothing here's going to hurt me. It's just . . ."

I was interrupted by the sound of an engine and turned to see not one, but three cars pull up to the curb and park in a ragged row. Their doors all opened and out climbed a small crowd of women, led by Julia and Val.

"Good morning, Anna!" Val waved while balancing a large Tupperware tub on her hip. "I told Julia you were moving in today! We thought you could use some help getting the place clean."

Kenisha was there too. She opened the trunk on a silver Toyota to pull out paper grocery bags, which she handed to a suntanned woman with auburn hair and heavy nerd-girl glasses. Julia carried a mismatched pair of handled tote bags with publisher logos on them. Max and Leo scampered ahead of her as she made her careful way up the path toward the porch. The dogs sniffed the fence, the tiny front lawn and the roses, all the while yipping urgently to each other about whatever it was their busy doggy noses found. Behind them a sturdy, dark-haired Caucasian woman who wore a plain apron over her loose green T-shirt and black jeans was pulling a truly impressive number of buckets and mops out of her car. She passed these to a Chinese woman with bobbed black hair who wore a pair of faded jeans and a Red Sox T-shirt.

I looked down at Alistair. He shrugged and yawned and washed a paw, clearly unconcerned about these new arrivals.

"Now, you haven't had a chance to meet everyone," said Val. "That's Didi Paulson there." She gestured toward the woman with the apron, who raised a bucket in salute.

"And Shannon Yu." Julia pointed her cane at the Red Sox fan, who waved back. "And here's Trisha Robinson," she added as the auburn-haired woman arrived at the porch alongside Kenisha. Trisha wore jeans and a sweatshirt with the sleeves cut off to show a truly impressive pair of arms. Somebody in this group worked out *way* more than I did.

"The good witches of Portsmouth?" I guessed.

Val smiled and shifted the tub she had balanced against her hip. "And Pregnant Woman declares this stuff is getting heavy."

What could I say to that? "Well, I guess you better come in." I found the key labeled FRONT DOOR. It turned smoothly in the lock and the door opened easily. Alistair, tail in the air, sauntered across the threshold.

VALERIE, OF COURSE, had brought food to this work party, and she wasn't the only one. The women piled the kitchen table with plastic tubs of cookies, deviled eggs, empanadas, and fresh fruit, not to mention two loaves of fresh bread and the butter to go with them. Julia brought bagels, cream cheese and orange juice. I plugged in the coffeemaker and measured out the fresh-ground beans I'd bought, before I joined the cleaning crew.

What followed was what is traditionally known as a flurry of activity. Didi Paulson's mops, buckets and brushes were deployed with brisk efficiency. We threw open the windows and shutters to let the sunshine flood the dim rooms. We pulled dustcovers off the furniture, turning the spaces once populated by ghosts into comfortable areas for living. We plumped and turned the velvet cushions in the window seat and dusted the shelves on the built-in bookcases.

Dorothy, it turned out, had great taste. Most of the furniture was Shaker-style, all clean lines and polished wood. There were a few pieces of an older vintage, like the armchair in the front parlor and the mahogany dining table and chairs. If I had to guess, I'd've said they were Victorian. With their carved curlicues and deep red velvet, they were certainly a lot showier than the Shaker pieces, but not so much that the place felt uncomfortable. This was a house for living in, not for showing off.

The women were all old friends, and they talked and laughed and teased one another as they worked. Valerie got out her smartphone and started up a classic rock playlist. Julia's dachshunds were inside and outside, barking at everything with great authority and satisfaction. At least, they were until Alistair decided he'd had enough and cuffed them upside the head with an even more authoritative paw.

I was so busy working and discovering and laughing, it took me a while to realize there was more going on than just cleaning. Shannon was hanging bundles of herbs in the windows: rosemary and lavender and a few things I couldn't identify. Didi pulled a big bag of kosher salt out of her purse and dissolved a huge handful in one of the buckets before she used a fresh sponge to wipe down the thresholds, front door, back door and all the windowsills.

"What's happening?" I asked Val.

"Cleaning," she answered simply. "And warding, and protection and blessing. Making the house a safe place again."

Magic. This was magic going on around me. I turned in place, watching. There was something else too.

"I don't feel it," I murmured.

"Don't feel what?" asked Julia as she came up beside Valerie.

"The Vibes." I turned again, as if I'd see them in one of the kitchen cabinets that Didi was wiping down. "When I first got here there were a bunch of Vibes. They were mostly good ones, but they were scary strong. I haven't felt them at all since I walked in." In fact, I wasn't even feeling weird about being in Dorothy's house. Somewhere, somehow, it had become just a place. Well, not just a place; a beautiful, comfortable place, with my name on it.

"That's good." Julia nodded. "This"—she swept her hand out—"is supposed to renew and refresh the house's spirit. If you're not feeling your Vibes, that means it's working. Did you read those books I gave you?"

"I started them."

Julia laughed. "It's a lot, isn't it?"

"It's going to be a lot for a long time."

"I feel your pain," said Val. "And that's okay. You're not alone."

"No." I listened to the sounds of music and clatter and cheerful voices. When was the last time I had a house full, or even an apartment full, of friends? I couldn't remember, but that was okay too, because I had it now.

I reminded myself this was strictly temporary. I had this place for only three months. I could not get too attached.

Myself was, once again, not listening. Myself needed a little reminder.

"What about . . ." I gestured toward the basement door.

Julia followed my gesture, her eyes both steely and sad. "We'll get to that," she said quietly. "Very soon." She shook herself and turned her back on the door. "But first things first. I wanted to ask if it would be all right for us to hold a ceremony in the garden tonight."

"What kind of ceremony?"

"One to ask blessing and good fortune for the house and its occupants. Expressing gratitude for the blessings we already have. Maybe a little request for prosperity and protection thrown in."

"Sounds great." Considering what I'd been through since I got to town, a little extra protection wouldn't be a bad idea, but I decided I didn't need to bring that up right now. We still had work to do.

Despite Julia's reassurances, I was still a little nervous when I climbed up to the second floor. But the atmosphere had changed as much up here as it had downstairs. Shannon moved from room to room, throwing open the casement windows and letting in the summer air. The cheerful sound of Joni Mitchell singing "Chelsea Morning" echoed out of the black-and-white-tile bathroom where Didi was scrubbing a claw-foot tub big enough to do laps in. I could say the last of my doubts about taking the house vanished right there, but it wouldn't be true. They did, however, close their suitcases and check the bus schedule.

There were two bedrooms. Trisha told me the one at the front of the house was Dorothy's. It let her feel like she was in the middle of what was going on, even when she was asleep. I laughed at this, because it fit so well with everything I'd heard about the woman.

But my heart was lost the minute I saw the back bedroom, the one Dorothy had kept for guests. The front room would make a terrific studio. It had built-in bookcases and a bay window with diamond panes, just like downstairs. The room I wanted for my private sanctuary, though, looked out over that magnificent garden. I could see the spiral path curling between the flower beds. In fall, the apples would shine red on the trees. I could just about see McDermott's as well, a reminder that some of my new friends were also my new neighbors.

The back bedroom was sparsely furnished, just a double bed with a Shaker-style headboard and a matching dresser. The walls were bare except for the black-and-white picture hanging over the dresser. I lifted it carefully off its nail to get a better look. It was a still from the movie *The Wizard of Oz* and showed the Wicked Witch of the West writing SURRENDER DOROTHY! across the sky. Somebody had written *Margaret Hamilton, 1939* in black marker at the very the bottom.

More evidence that Dorothy Hawthorne had a boundless sense of humor. Less comfortably, it reminded me of the magazine photo I now had tucked in my wallet and its tiny *aka Dorothy Gale*.

"What do you think, Alistair?" I asked as the cat jumped up on the bed. I held the picture out toward him. "Should we keep it?"

Alistair meeped very softly, like a lost kitten, and rubbed his face against the corner of the frame. "Meow."

"Oh, hey, I'm sorry." I set the photo down and gathered him into my arms. "It's okay, big guy. I know you miss her."

I didn't feel the least bit strange saying it, either. There was a whole lot of change going on today. Alistair shivered and buried his face against my shoulder. I rocked him like I would a baby and petted his back. I also remembered what Julia had said, how the night Dorothy died no one had seen Alistair. I wondered what had happened to him.

I wondered if it had been something bad enough that he was still scared.

❧ 27 ❧

🐾 I DIDN'T GET to sit and wonder for long. Alistair licked my chin and jumped from my arms to the middle of the bed and began washing himself frantically.

Nothing to see here, human. Move along.

"Cats!" I laughed.

I walked out into the hallway, fully intending to leave him to his grooming. But as I reached the attic door, I found Alistair was already there. He wasn't doing anything, exactly, except providing a very effective block to my pulling it open.

Joni Mitchell wasn't singing about Chelsea mornings anymore. It was James Taylor and he had Carolina on his mind.

"Everything okay, Anna?" Didi poked her head out of the bathroom and pushed her glasses up on her nose.

"Ask him." I put my hands on my hips and glowered at Alistair.

"Sorry. *No hablo el gato.*" She ducked back into the bathroom. There was the sound of running water, and James Taylor gave way to Paul McCartney, who wanted someone unspecified to let 'im in.

"That's a song cue, Alistair," I said. "Are you going to let me in?"

Alistair blinked up at me but didn't move.

"Pretty please?"

Alistair gave one of his big unconcerned yawns.

"There's some tuna in it for you."

He got up and stretched his front paws out and stalked away.

"Now I know how you got that belly," I muttered as I pulled on the doorknob. It came open as easily as the front door had. There was no resistance and, just as important from my point of view, no Vibe. Just a door that opened onto a staircase, and a fat gray cat bounding up ahead of me.

"Anna?" called Julia from down below.

"Up here," I answered. I turned quickly to see if Julia needed help. That flight of stairs was short but really steep. Julia, however, waved me back and, with the help of her cane and the railing, finished the climb on her own.

Maybe I didn't catch a Vibe up here anymore, but Julia clearly did. She swayed at the top of the stairs for a moment and then drifted over to the altar. The faraway look in her eyes told me she was deep in her own memories, so I kept myself quiet. Alistair curled around her ankles, the first gesture of affection I'd seen him make toward her. He merowed once. Just then, Max and Leo came scampering up the stairs. They wagged and whined and snuffled, checking out everything. Alistair jumped up onto the desk out of dachshund range and tucked his paws under himself.

I thought about asking Julia if she wanted a private moment, but I made myself keep quiet. I desperately wanted to like and trust Julia, but I couldn't ignore my suspicions. She was another person who could have quickly and easily searched the house, in person or by magic. If Dorothy had needed to keep secrets from Julia, she would have taken extra precautions. Like sealing the attic door.

Julia looked at the altar for a long moment; then she went

over to the desk and opened the central drawer. Alistair narrowed his eyes but didn't interfere.

"I was hoping Dorothy might have left something here," she said, and my heart skipped an uneasy beat. "To let us know what she'd been up to before she died."

She did. She left a great big honkin' clue. Max was snuffling around my shoes now, and I felt the prickle of perspiration beginning on the back of my neck.

"Merow!" Alistair bounded across the attic to the garden window. Both dachshunds raced after him, wagging and nosing the glass.

My hero. I let out the breath I'd been holding.

Julia closed the central desk drawer and opened the one on the top right-hand side. "If she'd sealed the room, the thieves who took her computer wouldn't have been able to get inside." She pulled out another drawer. "So she may have left something important behind."

"Are these the Books of Shadow?" I crossed to the set of low shelves I'd noticed when I was up here the first time. It was filled with old leather-bound journals slotted in between three-ring binders in a rainbow of colors. They must have smelled very interesting, because Max and Leo were sniffing them up, down and sideways.

"Yes," murmured Julia.

Now that I looked closely, I could see each volume had a date written on the spine; 1958, 1959 . . . 1965 had two binders, and 1977 had three.

"Busy year."

"It was." Julia's smile was faint and distant. "Floods, and then one of the worst nor'easters ever that winter. We were very busy." She touched the book briefly.

"Would Dorothy have written something in here?" I suggested. "About, you know, what she was doing toward the end?"

But Julia shook her head. "These are her personal writing about magic, her craft and practice. Even Dorothy wouldn't use them for . . . worldly matters."

There were three for 2001, I noticed, and another three for 2012, the year of Hurricane Sandy. But only one for 2013. On impulse, I pulled out a random volume. The label said 1979. I leafed through the heavy, wrinkled pages. I was expecting instructions for standing out under the full moon with a bubbling cauldron, or something. What I found was carefully written quotes, philosophy, theology, observations and anecdotes. There were newspaper clippings and invitation cards taped to brown paper pages, along with fading Polaroid photos. Truth be told, it reminded me of my mother's old collection of recipes she'd snipped from magazines, newspapers and those pamphlets that Jell-O and Campbell's Soup used to publish.

"What should I do with them?" I asked. "Do you want them?"

Julia looked around her, clearly weighing a whole set of decisions. "Let's leave things as they are for now. If you decide you're not staying permanently, the coven will take charge of the books and tools. There are rituals for passing on such items. You still have the wand, I take it?"

"Yeah. I've kind of been carrying it around. I hope that's not, I don't know, disrespectful or anything."

"Not in the least. It means you feel an affinity to it. But I would like to use it in the blessing ceremony tonight. We can pass it on to you formally then."

"Okay. I guess."

My hesitation made Julia smile. "You'll get used to it. Just give yourself time."

"If you say so."

She laid her hand on my shoulder. "I do, Anna."

"Meow!" announced Alistair from his spot by the window.

I jumped and nearly dropped the binder. "What!"

"Merow!" he tried again. He also whisked past Julia's dachshunds and jumped onto the desk.

"Oh, no. We're not playing Timmy down the well today, cat. What is it?"

Alistair grumbled and jumped up on the bookcase. He also pawed at the open binder in my hand.

It hit me then that I hadn't told Julia about my meeting with Brad and how he was looking for copies of . . . something he believed Dorothy kept. I looked at the binders with their pages full of clippings and photos and bit my lip. Tears prickled the back of my eyes. I did not want to believe this woman had been working against Dorothy. I liked her and her friends. I wanted to learn what she had to teach me. But until I knew more, I had no choice. I had to hold back.

But what if I told her just a little, just to see how she reacted?

"Julia." I hesitated. "You know when I first got into the house, there was somebody else already here?"

She nodded.

"It was Brad Thompson."

"Brad? Laurie's husband? What on earth was he doing?"

"Trying to get in here."

Julia staggered. I caught her arm, but she jerked away. I opened my mouth to ask if she was okay, but right then Leo yipped and Max's ears perked up and they both scampered toward the stairs.

"What is it?" asked Julia then.

I looked at Alistair. Alistair was staring daggers, and right at Julia.

"Anna!" Val's shout sounded from the hall below. "Martine's here!"

Martine! I had called her after I had finished at the lawyer's and left a message to let her know where I was and what I was doing. I'd also apologized for messing up our planned girls' day out. But there was so much else happening, I'd clean forgotten she'd never called back.

I looked at Julia. I didn't want to break off this conversation, but she was waving me on. I bit my lip and hurried downstairs, trusting her to follow when she was ready.

Martine stood in the cottage doorway. I was in no way surprised to see she'd brought her own Tupperware.

"Hey, Martine!"

"Hey yourself." We hugged, and she handed me the Tupperware so she could put her hands on her hips and look around her. "So, this is the house."

"This is it." I wrapped my arms around the industrial-sized tub she'd given me. "Come on in." I led her toward the kitchen. "Everybody! This is Martine. Martine, this is . . . everybody."

Everybody called hello back. Including Didi and Julia, who both came down from upstairs. Whatever it was that had upset Julia about finding out that Brad Thompson had been in the house, she'd set it aside and was all smiles now.

Martine said her hellos and shook hands as we all congregated in the kitchen. Her arrival seemed to signal the need for rest and food, and everybody started getting out the plates and silverware. I made more coffee.

It turned out Martine knew not only Kenisha and Val; she was friends with Shannon and Didi. It also turned out she'd brought a huge salad of tomatoes and mozzarella dressed with balsamic dressing, cracked pepper and fresh basil. We heaped it onto plates for lunch along with thick slices of Roger's homemade bread.

"And here I thought you didn't know anybody in town." Martine gestured to the busy, gossiping gathering with a slice of bread.

"Except for you. I didn't. These are . . ." What was I going to tell her? As it turned out, I didn't have to tell her anything.

Martine rolled her eyes. "Dorothy's coven."

"Um, yes."

"Thought so," she said. I stared at my plate and tried not to squirm. "What?"

"Am I the only person in the world who thought this stuff had to be kept secret?"

"Now, how would I know that?"

"Good point."

"Dorothy didn't know what secret was," said Shannon, from where she leaned her butt against the counter and sipped her coffee. "Have you seen her HeyLook! page?"

"Not to mention the Web site," added Didi, who came in from the garden terrace to help herself to another cookie. "And you really should have seen this place at Halloween. She always spent a solid month on the decorations."

"Yeah, and didn't the witch on the hill just love that," added Trisha.

"Trisha!" Julia thumped her cane once, and Trisha, who ran a gym and had been shoving the heaviest furniture around without breaking a sweat, looked instantly like a guilty schoolgirl.

"Anna!" called Val from the foyer. "We got another visitor!"

Martine laughed. I shrugged and went out to see who it was this time.

To my surprise, this time it was Sean the bartender. He wore a tweed flatcap that matched his tweed vest.

"I heard the news," he said as he handed me a bottle of red wine. "Welcome to Portsmouth, Anna Britton."

"Thank you. Won't you come in?" Sean stepped inside just as a plump gray shadow slid casually into the foyer. "Meow."

"Well, look at that!" said Sean. "I guess he was just waiting to come home."

"Yeah, I've been adopted." I smiled as Sean reached down to skritch Alistair behind his ears. The cat submitted to this and even consented to purr just a little. "I never had a chance to thank you for your help with him the other day."

"All part of my dastardly plan to make a positive first impression," said Sean as he straightened up. Only guys who wear hats can use words like "dastardly."

"Well, I should warn you, if you keep trying to ply me with alcohol, I'm going to start getting suspicious."

"I'd try food, but with the chef and company here, I figured you'd have more than enough." He smiled and I felt myself starting to blush. I turned around quickly, planning on inviting him in. The words were cut off by the sight of Martine standing in the parlor doorway.

Martine was not smiling. "Young Sean," she said. "What brings you here?" Her words might have been addressed to him. Her look, however, was most definitely aimed at me.

"Actually, I got a message for you, Chef," Sean told her. "Ken says there's been a snafu with the beef deliveries for tomorrow, and he texted you but . . ."

Martine had her phone out before he could finish. Whatever she saw there made her swear and sigh. "It would be today. All right." She stuffed her phone back in her jeans. "Tell him I'm on my way."

Sean hesitated, but Martine raised an authoritative eyebrow. "Yes, Chef." He nodded, put his cap back on and retreated out the door.

Martine stepped up from behind and took the bottle out of my hands.

"He's been asking about you, you know," she said as she examined the label. "Nothing direct, but you've definitely come up in conversation. And here he shows up with a bottle." This she held up as Exhibit A. She also eyed the label. "And pretty good wine, too. It's kind of cute."

I had absolutely no answer for that, which apparently was answer enough for Martine. She sighed and handed the bottle back. "Okay, I get it. Nothing to see here. And unfortunately, no rest for the chef. I gotta get back." She put a hand on my shoulder. "It's great to see you settling in, Anna. This bunch, they're good people."

"Yeah, they are. So are you." We hugged. "Will you call when you're free? There's been some stuff happening, about Dorothy Hawthorne and how she died . . ."

"Anna." Martine backed up until she held me at arm's length. "You're not getting involved in that whole business, are you?"

"No, no," I said, resisting the urge to cross my fingers behind my back.

"Too bad. That Vibe of yours might come in handy." Martine grinned at me, waved and headed out the door before I picked my jaw up off the floor.

Alistair looked up at me. If he were a human, he would have been shaking his head.

"Yeah, okay, you're right. I should have known," I told him.

I walked back into the kitchen with the bottle. All the women were watching me.

"What?" I asked them all.

"Nothing," said Val.

"Nice bottle," remarked Kenisha. "Newer vintage, though, isn't it?"

"Bet it's got good legs," murmured Trisha.

"And a really smooth finish," added Didi. "Audacious, with hints of oak and tweed . . . I mean tannin."

"All right, all right." Julia climbed to her feet before my blush could really get started. "You will all remember we're here to help, and there's one place we haven't cleansed yet."

Very deliberately, she walked over to the basement door and pulled it open.

❧ 28 ❧

🐾 "NO. I CAN'T." I stared down into the dark basement stairwell like I thought it was going to swallow me whole. "It's too soon."

"You cannot live here if you're afraid," Julia answered firmly. "You need to know you can control what you feel, from the start."

"You pull the Band-Aid off all at once, don't you?"

"Every time," she answered.

I glanced around at the women who filled the kitchen, all my new friends. I saw sympathy and support. What I did not see was one person who was going to make a case for me backing out of this.

Alistair slid up beside me. "Merow," he told me as he rubbed his head against my shins.

"And that makes it unanimous." I took a deep breath and tried not to let my voice wobble. "All right. Let's do it."

Kenisha got to her feet. "I'll go first."

If that was meant to be reassuring, it didn't work. "You don't really think there's bad guys or something down there, do you?"

"I don't know," she replied coolly. "I do know a whole lot of horror movies would be about five minutes long if somebody just let the cop check the spooky basement first."

Kenisha flipped on the light, walked down the stairs and ducked around the corner. At the same time, Leo and Max came trotting in from the terrace. Julia didn't so much as whistle, but both dogs scrabbled and plopped down the stairs right behind Kenisha. I rubbed my face to keep from smiling, but something inside me eased. Dachshunds have that effect.

"Merowp," grumbled Alistair.

"Don't worry. My heart belongs to you, big guy," I said.

Somebody laughed and I smiled.

A few seconds later, Kenisha and the dogs reappeared at the bottom of the stairs. "Clear!" she called.

Julia laid a hand on my arm. "Are you ready, Anna?" I nodded, and so did she. "I'll go first." She started down the stairs.

"And I'm right behind you," said Val.

"We all are," added Shannon.

I swallowed and stepped up to the threshold. I told myself this was a perfectly ordinary set of basement stairs. The only thing remotely strange here was that they were cleaner than average. But it was cold, and it was dark, and the air smelled of dirt and damp. Like a grave.

Julia paused on the third stair and looked up at me. "It's just the memory that's bothering you," she said. "You remember being afraid."

"Right." I agreed. But I still didn't move.

"Merow," said Alistair, right beside me. I bent down and scooped him up. He didn't object. In fact, he purred.

I gritted my teeth and walked down two steps. It was cold. So cold and lonely.

"You're not alone," said Val from behind me. "We're right here."

"Right," I said again. Two more steps. I was shaking. What was I doing here? How had it come to this?

"Breathe," said Julia, walking down two steps in front

of me. "Breathe and focus on the present. The past is over. It's done. What's here is only an echo, and an echo cannot hurt you."

Says you, lady. But I did breathe. Deep breath in. Hold. Deep breath out. Hold. Two more steps. Six more to go. Kenisha and the wiener dogs were already down there, waiting patiently.

Alistair pressed his warm head under my chin and purred like a motorboat.

"Echoes only." Julia walked down the last three steps to stand beside Kenisha. "Fading, as we speak. Focus on the present. This moment."

"Shouldn't there be, you know, magic?" I tried to laugh, but I couldn't.

"What makes you think this isn't magic, Anna? Here we are. We are maiden, mother and crone. We are breath and head and heart. You are safe with us. You are safe with Alistair and this house. Just three more steps."

Three more steps. Three left. *Finish it, A.B.,* I told myself. *Pull off the darned Band-Aid.*

Holding the cat between me and the nightmare, I clomped down the last steps and straight into a tidal wave of cold and dark. I was filled with gentle, fading sorrow, burning anger, terrible yearning hope and bitter impatience. It was all at war inside me. I couldn't breathe. I couldn't see. I was falling away down into the dark.

A sudden sound cut through the black chaos. I felt the vibration through my chest and down to my toes.

Purring. There was a cat purring. I felt the warm rasp of his tongue on my cheek. An impatient meow sounded somewhere beyond the anger and the fear.

"Come back, Annabelle. Focus." Julia gripped my hand. "Listen to me. Listen to Alistair. Breathe. Feel the stone under your shoes. Come back to us, Annabelle Britton."

Slowly, reluctantly, the dark receded. As my vision cleared, so did my head, or maybe it was my heart.

Alistair squirmed and slid out of my arms. I barely noticed. I turned around in a tight circle. I saw the walls and the flagstone floor. I saw Val and Julia and Kenisha, my new friends. I could see. I could breathe. I was all right. Oh, I could still feel the uneasy knot of emotions all around me, but it was no longer overwhelming. It was a troubling background sound, like being stopped next to a car where the bass is turned up too far. I didn't like it, but I could tolerate it. I could even set it aside.

For the first time in my life, I could set it aside.

I punched a fist into the air. "Yes!"

"Meow!" shouted Alistair.

We all laughed, and the Vibe faded even further.

"Was that it?" I said to my friends. "All I had to do was walk down here and take calming breaths?"

Julia's smile was a little tight. "Not really. You did have help."

Val held up her hand with two fingers pinched together and mouthed, "Just a little."

"But this is a good beginning," Julia went on. "As your practice progresses, you will be better able to tap into your gift—your Vibe—and more accurately interpret what it tells you. In the meantime, I believe we have more work to do upstairs."

"Um, shouldn't we look around a bit while we're down here? In case there's something . . . ?"

Kenisha looked toward heaven for patience. "All right. I'll look, but only if you promise me you'll believe me when I say there's nothing to find."

"Promise. Really and truly," said Val. "Thank you, Kenisha."

Kenisha shrugged like she already regretted it and headed into what even I could see was a largely empty basement. The rest of us went back upstairs to join the others helping clean and organize what I had started to think of as my house.

Eventually, Kenisha came up out of the basement, as serious as a migraine, but she just shook her head at Val's

hopeful look. Whatever there was to find in this house, it
wasn't down there. Then she rolled up her sleeves and helped
Trisha and Didi break down the bed so we could move it
from the front room to the back, and then bring the desk
down from the attic into my new studio.

By dinnertime, we were all starving again. So when Roger
arrived through the back garden with a massive pot of white
bean chili and a basket of cheddar cheese biscuits, we hailed
him as a true hero. We uncorked the wine Sean had brought
and toasted him and one another. Alistair contented himself
with tuna. I might accept that he was no ordinary cat, but I
was not going to deal with the consequences of feeding him
anything containing beans and serrano chiles.

Which reminded me, I was going to need a litter box and
the name of a local vet. I was pretty sure even spooky magic
cats needed their shots.

How old was Alistair anyway? Frank said they'd grown
up together, which meant he had to be far older than any
normal cat. I needed to talk with Julia about the care and
feeding of familiars. As I looked across the kitchen to where
Julia sat laughing with Didi and Shannon, I remembered
how she'd gotten so upset when I'd told her about Brad.
Clearly, taking care of my familiar was not the only thing
I needed to talk with Julia about.

As the gold-and-magenta sunset spread over the garden,
the atmosphere around the little house changed. Everybody
started packing cleaning supplies away into car trunks, and
instead brought out lovely wooden boxes and embroidered
bags. From these they pulled colorful scarves and flowing
caftans. There was a line outside the two bathrooms so
everyone could wash up from a day's hard work and change.

"Anna," said Julia, who had draped a bright blue robe
decorated with white stars around herself. "Would you go
out into the garden and light the fire?"

The request felt solemn and I agreed right away, even
though I hadn't lit a campfire in years. I went out into the

garden and walked the spiral path to its center. Alistair followed me, cool and collected. I opened the copper chest and found kindling, twists of paper and some fluffy stuff that looked like dryer lint. It was a mess in here. Clearly the local squirrels had been busy. I had to do some rummaging to find what I needed, but at last I came up with a box of matches in a zip-topped bag.

The night was warm and still around us. A flash caught my eye and I grinned.

"I was right," I said to Alistair. "Fireflies."

"Merow," he answered. *Of course.*

Girl Scouts was a long time ago, but I still remembered the basics. The kindling and sticks were dry and there was plenty of paper, and that lint was a great idea as a fire starter. It took only three matches before the clear yellow flame caught and spread.

In answer, the lights in the house winked out. The back door opened and the women—the coven—in their bright robes walked slowly across the terrace and onto the path.

Julia led the way with a basket slung over her arm. Max and Leo trotted beside her, two small sentries. Val wore red and looked absolutely vibrant. She carried an unlit candle in both hands. Didi followed, in bright blue like Julia. She carried a cup and Sean's bottle of wine. Next came Kenisha, wearing a shimmering emerald robe embroidered with black and gold. A matching band held her hair back from her forehead. She carried an iron kettle. *Cauldron,* I reminded myself, recalling my research reading. Last came Shannon dressed entirely in shimmering black and holding a lighted lantern.

I knew them all, but I didn't know them. The atmosphere they carried with them as they followed the curves of the path was charged with electricity. Julia came to a halt in front of me and set her basket down on the chest. Slowly she turned. She looked like a queen standing there in her bright robes, holding her cane like a scepter.

"Blessed be," she said.

"Blessed be," answered the women.

"Mrp," muttered Alistair.

"We are gathered to cast the blessed circle. We welcome the sacred powers of the world to witness our gathering and ask the favor of their blessing."

"Blessed be," said the others, and this time, I said it too.

Alistair butted my shin, shoving me forward with surprising strength. I swallowed and took the hint. I also walked up to Julia. Julia pulled the wand out of her basket and held it up to the sky.

"We invite the spirit of the East, the spirit of air and inspiration, to our circle." She handed me the wand and nodded. I went to stand beside Alistair, who sat bolt upright with his tail curled neatly around his paws.

Val stepped up next and gave Julia her candle. Julia lit it from the fire and held it up. "We invite the spirit of the South, the spirit of fire and creation, to our circle."

Once Val had returned to her place, Didi came forward with the cup and the wine.

"We invite the spirit of the West," said Julia, "the spirit of water, healing and cleansing, to our circle."

Next came Kenisha carrying the cauldron. Julia poured something white into it, probably salt. "We invite the spirit of the North, the spirit of Earth, the source from which all life comes and to which all life returns."

Once Kenisha had returned to her place, Julia raised her arms. In response we all lifted our hands, whether we held tools or lights, to the black sky and the rising moon. It felt awkward for a minute, but only for a minute. I don't know if it was the atmosphere around me that changed, or the attitude inside me. But gradually I began to feel a current of warmth, of connection, winding around us all. I saw it in the swirling sparks that rose from the fire to the stars. I sensed it in the breeze against my skin, the rustle of the tree branches, the heavy green scent of the garden, and even the press of the earth against my shoes. I felt it in my breath and heartbeat and fingertips.

"Blessings upon this house and those here gathered," said Julia. "Blessings upon our sister Annabelle Amelia Blessingsound Britton, whom we welcome to our circle. Blessings upon our sister Dorothy, who has begun her journey on the night side. May we all walk in the light, in truth and justice, kindness and mercy."

"An' it harm none, so mote it be," answered the women. Their voices formed a chorus, rising along with the sparks and the firelight. I lifted my eyes and saw the moon looking back down on us all.

I didn't feel awkward anymore. I felt whole. More. I felt like I had finally, truly come home.

✥ 29 ✥

♣ I SLEPT SOUNDLY. The Shaker-style bed was incredibly comfortable and the pillows smelled like warm lavender. I didn't dream. I didn't agonize. I didn't worry.

That is, until I felt the large warm weight on my chest and a cold nose against mine. Even then I didn't worry. I did shout, though.

"Gah!"

"Meow!" Alistair jumped sideways as I scrambled backward.

I shoved my hair out of my face and blinked. My room was dim, but the beams of morning sunshine that streamed through the closed curtains told me it was a lovely day outside. Despite this, Alistair paced restlessly across the foot of the bed.

"What is it? Is it an emergency?"

"Meow!" Alistair leapt down and ran out the door.

"Shoot!" I grabbed my old pink robe out of the suitcase. With all the cleaning and everything yesterday, I hadn't found time to unpack. I wrapped the soft flannel around myself and hurried downstairs, my heart in my mouth. What was it this time? Should I have stopped for the wand, or the cell phone? Did I need to check the house Vibe? Maybe I should get Julia, or better yet, Kenisha, on speed dial or . . .

Alistair trotted into the kitchen and circled around a cracked china bowl somebody had put next to the stove.

"Meow!" he announced.

I stared at the empty bowl. I stared at the cat.

"OMG, Alistair. All that because you're *hungry*?"

"Meow!" Alistair pawed the bowl.

"Of course, of course. The cat's hungry. Clearly, this is a national emergency." I stumped over to the refrigerator. I was grumpy from being woken up so suddenly, but also because I realized that with all the bustling around yesterday, I hadn't thought to buy cat food.

"Maybe there's some leftovers or something." I yanked open the fridge.

There were leftovers, and they crowded the peanut butter and cheese I'd bought to one side. There were eggs and milk too, which I was pretty sure I hadn't bought, and lettuce and tomatoes in the crisper, another loaf of bread and some neatly wrapped packages of what might have been cold cuts.

I was going to be writing a lot of thank-you notes.

"Scrambled eggs okay again?"

"Mer-ow," answered Alistair, his tone indicating some reservations about my culinary skill. Clearly, he'd been talking to Martine.

"Tough," I told him.

I'll be the first to admit my cooking's nothing to alert the media about, but I can manage a decent scrambled egg. I whisked in the milk, added some salt, and dropped a pat of butter in the pan to melt. Alistair leapt up on the counter to watch the proceedings.

"Down, cat."

He looked at me like I was nuts. I had a feeling I was going to have to get used to that. I'd add it to the list.

It was going to be a long list. The house—my house—was

comfortable, but a little stark. The bedroom would benefit from a throw rug or three, and I'd need more towels for the bathroom. Some people are clotheshorses, but any of my old roommates will tell you I am a towel horse. And then . . .

"Whoa, girl, settle down," I muttered to myself as I stirred the eggs in the pan. "You can't go loading up on stuff. You're only here for three months at most."

I told myself this firmly, but I couldn't quite believe it. I portioned the eggs out onto Corelle plates (the kind with the green flowers) and set one down on the table for Alistair. I buttered some toast for me and brought it to the table along with my mug of coffee. I watched Alistair nibbling for a minute, and I realized that if I left town, I'd probably have to leave him too.

My throat tightened up for no readily apparent reason. I decided to change the mental subject.

"The question is," I said as I dug into my own eggs, "if we're not redecorating, what are we doing today?"

Alistair didn't so much as look up from the eggs. Evidently, he'd decided my cooking was minimally acceptable.

"I really have to get some work done," I went on. "If I don't bring in some fresh cash, we're both going to be in a really deep hole really soon. But, you know, I'm worried about what happened . . ."

"Knock, knock!" called a familiar voice.

I twisted around in time to see Val lean in through the kitchen door, which I'd evidently forgotten to lock last night. I waved her inside. I also straightened my robe over my sleep shirt and ran a hand over my hair. Val laughed at me.

"Good morning! Good morning, Alistair!" She scratched his ears. He cleaned a whisker at her and returned to what was left of his eggs.

"Good morning." I pulled out a chair. "How're you doing? I'd offer you some coffee, but . . ."

"I know." She patted her belly. "And I really can't stay anyhow." Despite this, she did sit down. "I just wanted to stop by and see how you're doing, after last night and everything."

"I'm good, really," I told her, and I meant it. "It all feels . . . right. Weird, but right."

"I'm so glad." Val smiled, and she hesitated. "I don't want to bring up anything contentious, but, did you feel . . . anything last night? Maybe after we left?"

I eyed her over the rim of my coffee cup. "You mean did I get any new Vibes about Dorothy's death? No. Sorry."

"Oh, well. We probably just have to give it time."

I swirled my coffee, and Alistair butted my elbow, making things slosh. "Okay, okay." I scratched his ears. "Um, Val, I can't believe I'm about to ask this, but what was Dorothy's relationship with Brad Thompson?" I'd work my way around to my interrupted conversation with Julia later. After that, I'd tell her about *aka Dorothy Gale*. Maybe.

I expected a frown, but Val leaned forward eagerly. "You did pick up something! What was it? Does it have something to do with that argument you and Brad had in Raja Rani the other day?"

"You saw that? How did you see that?"

"Portsmouth is not a big town. I didn't have to see it. I heard about it."

I considered my coffee and my new neighbor. Was I ready to tell Val about Brad's mysterious copies? She might decide to start tearing into the house to look for them, even though we'd been over the place from top to bottom yesterday. But that wasn't the real problem. The real problem was if I told Val, I'd have to explain to her why I hadn't told Julia, and that wasn't going to lead anywhere good.

I took a deep breath and punted. "Were Brad and Dorothy friends? Or business partners?"

"Not as far as I know, but you could ask Laurie Thompson."

"Riiighht," I drawled. "I could go to her house and say, 'Hey, Laurie, I want to talk about your husband and the dead witch.'"

Val demonstrated her essential maturity and stuck her

tongue out at me. "You could go over and talk about art. I mean, you said that painting of hers was really good, didn't you?"

I did, and it was. I drummed my fingers against the table. "They're in trouble, aren't they? The Thompsons? Is it money?"

Val nodded. "Brad was out of work for a long time before he got his job with Maitland and Associates. The debts piled up. You know how it goes."

"Yeah, yeah, I do." I drummed my fingers some more and glanced at Alistair. He licked his whiskers and strolled over to bump his head against my purse where it was hanging on the back of the chair. "Hang on," I said to Val. I unearthed my phone and hit a number. It was too early for anybody to be in the office, but I got voice mail.

"Hey, Nadia, it's Anna Britton. Call me back when you get a chance. I've been looking at some work by a new artist out here, and I think they're somebody you're going to want to see. Bye." I hung up. Val was staring. "A friend of mine runs a gallery down in the Hamptons. It's not huge, but if I can talk her into hanging one or two of Laurie's pieces, it could lead to something."

"Seriously? That's wonderful!"

I shrugged. "I can't promise anything, and I'll need to find out if Laurie's even interested." I smiled. "So, I guess I'm going to have to talk with her after all."

"That's fantastic! I knew you could do this! I'm just sorry I can't come with you."

"You've got a business to run. I swear, I'll report back as soon as I'm home."

Val gave me her number to add to my phone list and we said good-bye. I closed the door behind her but watched as she crossed the garden and let herself out through the gate. I realized I was smiling.

"I think I'm going to like this friends-and-neighbors thing," I said to Alistair.

He responded with a grumpy rumble and nosed at his

now-empty plate. "No more for you," I informed him as I cleared the table and carried the dishes to the sink. "I've got places to go and people to meet. I can't spend all day feeding the cat."

When I looked down to see Alistair's response, he wasn't there.

I SHOWERED AND dried my hair. That is, I dried my hair after I unearthed my blow dryer from the depths of Thing Two. In honor of the fact that I intended to go visiting, I put on my batik-print skirt and a mostly unwrinkled sleeveless blue blouse. I was going to need an iron, or at least time to hang stuff up. There was a washing machine in the basement. It would mean going down into the cellar again, but I could handle it now. Probably.

As I headed to the foyer to grab my purse and keys, which I'd left on the table, I was startled by a low rumble from the doormat. Alistair was back. He was also flattened out in front of the door, growling.

"That's not about your dish being empty, is it?"

He grumbled a response. I walked gingerly up to the door, undid the dead bolt and peered out. The little porch was empty; so were the yard and the street. The morning was already warm, and the air was full of the smell of roses.

But Alistair wasn't taking all this emptiness calmly. He stalked past me and started prowling the narrow front yard. I found myself automatically looking for that skinny yellow bird neither of us liked. What I found instead was a white envelope sticking out of the mailbox.

"What's this?" I asked as I pulled it out. Alistair showed no interest. He was busy patrolling the picket fence, shoving his face into the weeds and lashing his tail.

At first glance, the envelope looked normal enough, although it was a little thicker and heavier than the usual office supply store paper. Then I saw it had been addressed by hand, in the precise, slanted cursive you hardly ever saw anymore. There was even a seal on it, but no stamp. Somebody had put this into the box him- or herself.

"What the hey?" I broke the seal and pulled out a sheet of notepaper, which was a match for the envelope. The handwriting looked the same as for the address.

I read:

To Miss Annabelle Blessingsound Britton:

I am writing to invite you to have coffee with me Tuesday morning at eleven o'clock. I recognize you do not know me and have no objective reason to agree. However, if you will come, I promise I will be able to shed some light on certain events that have occurred in your proximity since you arrived in Portsmouth.

> *Sincerely,*
> *Elizabeth Maitland*

The address was over on Newcastle Island.

Alistair climbed back onto the porch, tail still lashing.

"Hey, Alistair." I crouched down and held out the letter. "What do you think of this?"

Alistair sniffed the paper and shrank back with a growl.

"Yeah, me too. Should I go?"

Alistair growled again.

"Okay." I tucked the note in my purse. "Change of plans. I can talk to Laurie Thompson later. Right now, I'm going to meet the bad witch."

❧ 30 ❧

❧ I KNEW THAT the mouth of the Piscataqua is a maze of islands. I hadn't realized several were large enough to hold their own communities. Newcastle felt like a country town, all winding roads, big trees and clusters of old houses interspersed among the new gated "communities" (read, groupings of big houses planted behind massive garages and wide lawns with no sidewalks, all built to order from preset patterns, carefully spaced so you didn't have to actually get too close to your neighbors).

Yeah, yeah, I'm an old-town snob, and that's not changing anytime soon.

The GPS led me past three "communities" and around a bend to a sloping road where the oaks were so huge and so close together, I was plunged into twilight.

"Destination is on your left," the voice informed me.

Except when I looked to the left, all I saw was more trees. I had to squint and slow down before I could tell that the winding path between them actually was wide enough for a car. I downshifted and turned the Jeep onto the shadowed path.

Past the first screen of trees, I came to an old stone wall, complete with a pair of wrought-iron gates. They were, at least, standing open. I was expected.

"Criminy," I muttered as I eased the Jeep through. "She really is old money."

It took another couple of minutes of carefully negotiating the drive's multiple curves before I reached the edge of the grove and came out onto a sun-drenched lawn. Now I could see the Maitland house, and it was, quite literally, the big house on the hill. A redbrick house, specifically. It was built in the high, square, Georgian style with a curved brick porch and a slate roof. The drive might have been left in wilderness, but the lawn and the bushes that surrounded the house were trimmed within an inch of their lives. I half expected to find a gardener in a smock and floppy hat to be stooped somewhere among those perfect plants.

I thought about flexing my new magical muscles and trying to find a Vibe but decided not to push my luck. I was already on edge just walking up the flagstone path to the semicircle of a brick porch. I felt a long way from home here, like, a hundred miles and a hundred years away.

Instead of a pushbutton, the doorbell was the antique kind that turns. A Hispanic woman with gray streaks in her black hair and wearing a black dress and white apron opened the door.

"Miss Britton?" she asked, and I nodded. "Good morning. You are expected. This way, please."

"This way" took us through a formal front room and a formal middle room and what had to have been a breakfast parlor of some kind. I felt the twenty-first century slipping further away with each step.

The back parlor was as grand as the front room. Plaster rosettes and garlands decorated the ceiling. French doors framed in stained glass looked out over the terrace. No white wicker furniture graced Mrs. Maitland's terrace, I noticed, just wrought iron, like the gates. Her immaculate back lawn sloped down toward more trees and a green-and-brown pond.

"Miss Britton is here, Mrs. Maitland," announced the maid.

"Thank you, Marisol." Mrs. Maitland rose from her seat on a graceful Victorian sofa upholstered in a deep moss green and came forward to shake hands. "I'm so glad you decided to come, Miss Britton."

"Thank you for inviting me, Mrs. Maitland. What a lovely home you have." This was me being polite as well as truthful. The place was gorgeous. It also had all the warmth and life of a museum display. I kept expecting to see velvet ropes set up to keep me away from the glass-topped tables and delicate Louis XIV display cases.

"Thank you." Mrs. Maitland gazed about that cool room with satisfaction. "My . . . let me see, five times great-grandfather Diligence Maitland built the house shortly after the family arrived here. Won't you sit down?" She gestured toward a velvet and mahogany chair of the same vintage as the sofa. "Marisol will be back shortly with . . . Ah, thank you, Marisol."

The woman who had answered the door walked in with a tea tray (silver), loaded with china cups and a pot and plates of little ham sandwiches and mini tarts.

"Lemon or milk?" Mrs. Maitland inquired. "This is a lovely first-flush Darjeeling I'm sure you'll enjoy. And please, help yourself." She handed me a cup and saucer, waved at the food, but didn't take any herself, I noticed. That trim figure came at a cost.

I put a sandwich on my saucer and sipped the tea. It was very good, but, then, I didn't expect it would dare to be anything else.

Mrs. Maitland sipped her own tea. She also contemplated me over the cup's rim. I had to resist an urge to smooth my blouse down. This flawless room was working its effect on me, and all at once I felt too awkward and too rumpled.

"I cannot get over how much you look like your grandmother," she told me. "How is Annabelle Mercy? I entirely lost track of her after she left us."

"She's doing well, thanks for asking."

"She and Charles both?"

"My grandfather passed four years ago."

"Oh. I am sorry." But Mrs. Maitland didn't sound sorry. She sounded more than a little satisfied, like she'd just had her suspicions confirmed. Something inside me curdled. I took another sip of tea to try to settle it.

"Were you two close when she lived here?"

"I thought so," murmured Mrs. Maitland toward her tea. "But that all changed when she met Charles."

"Really? I was under the impression you had an argument before then—you and Grandma B.B. and Dorothy Hawthorne."

Not one perfect hair turned; not one immaculately mascaraed lash blinked. "I see you've got at least some family history in your pocket. Or maybe I should say ancient history." Mrs. Maitland shook her head. "One hopes that private quarrels will stay private. However, that's not really possible for people like us."

"Like us?"

"People from the old families." That euphemism had been polished perfectly smooth. "What the rest of the world chooses to forget or ignore, we do not, or cannot."

It wasn't just a faint ring of pride I heard in her words; there was a whole ancestral chorus. I set my teacup down. Carefully.

"I appreciate your inviting me, Mrs. Maitland . . ." I waited for her to say, *Call me Elizabeth*, but she didn't. "But your note said there were things you wanted to talk about?"

"It's straight to business, then. Very well." Mrs. Maitland took a final sip of tea before she set her cup and saucer down with a definitive click. "I understand you've rented Dorothy Hawthorne's house for the summer."

"That's right."

"Darius has been extremely reluctant to let it go. You must have been very persuasive."

I opened my mouth to ask who the heck Darius was; then I remembered. "Are you talking about Frank Hawthorne? Or his father?"

"Frank, of course. I forget sometimes he changed his name."

"Oh. Well. I wasn't that persuasive. It's only a short-term lease." I smiled. "I haven't made up my mind about staying in town yet."

"Why that house?" she asked.

"I'm sorry?"

"Why that house in particular? There are many summer rentals available." Mrs. Maitland waved her perfectly kept hand, indicating the river, and Portsmouth. "You must see things from my perspective. Annabelle Mercy's granddaughter returns after many years' absence. She's a dynamic young woman who, I gather, has traveled the country, has a glamorous career in the arts . . ." Hardly. She was trying some left-handed flattery on me and wasn't making a very good job of it. "But what does she do now? She takes up with Annabelle's old friends, rents another old friend's house. I have to wonder, what has made her so suddenly and so very determined to stay in a place like Portsmouth and spend her time with old women and their old ways?"

She was watching me closely, looking for cracks. I summoned all the cool I'd learned from dealing with difficult clients and fussy gallery owners. It wasn't easy.

"I don't know that I am determined to stay," I said. "I just needed a change of scene for the summer. As for old ways . . . well those ways are part of my family history and I'm interested. That's all."

"You'll forgive me if I don't believe you."

"You'll forgive me if I wonder why it's any of your business."

"Because I don't want to see you taken advantage of."

That stopped me. "I beg your pardon?"

Mrs. Maitland clasped her hands on her knees. For the first time since I came in, she seemed uncomfortable. "Julia Parris is a bitter, tired woman," she said softly. "Just like Dorothy Hawthorne was. But they both also come from old families like mine, and yours."

My patience with her indirect language snapped. Like the house around us, it felt designed to intimidate and exclude. Blessingsounds, you may have figured out by now, do not take to being intimidated real well. Neither do Brittons.

"Mrs. Maitland, it's just us here," I reminded her. "We don't have to be coy. Dorothy and Julia and my grandmother"—*and me*—"are all witches. So are you. You practice magic—excuse me, the 'true craft'—and you use it to . . . arrange things."

It seems I'd finally gotten over the stuttering thing. Kenisha would be so proud.

Mrs. Maitland did not answer immediately. It seemed to me like she was considering how far she really wanted this little conversation to go. "I ask you to understand, Anna," she said at last. "I was raised to keep the craft a strict secret, as was my mother and her mother before her. Not only was this the way our family avoided the persecutions that rather famously overtook others, but it is how we keep the power out of the hands of those who might use it unwisely." She paused. "Did Julia tell you that she and Dorothy disregarded all precautions to go public with their practice?"

That choice of words was no accident, and I needed to be careful how I answered it. "Julia told me Dorothy wanted to teach anyone who wanted to learn. It went against tradition, and there was a fight. Julia took Dorothy's side, eventually."

Mrs. Maitland's mouth tightened into a little moue. "I'm sure that's how she remembers it. And perhaps that is how it happened. I was not . . . admitted to all their discussions." She tried to say this with indifference, but it didn't work. She might accuse Julia of being bitter, but Mrs. Maitland was angry. No. She was furious. "Of course they said that they were working in the interests of freedom. Equality. That it wasn't fair for any power or knowledge to be restricted according to family and heritage. They said . . ." She shook her head hard. "It was a time of change, radical change. Old ideas were being thrown out left and right, without any consideration as to the purpose that such traditions serve. Dorothy and Julia thought they would bring a revolution to our little corner of the world, and perhaps they did. But they went too far, and they never recovered." She lifted her gaze, and it was as hard and cold as the room around us. "In sharing the power of the true craft, they diluted it. They let it bleed into the river of nonsense that gets called 'New Age.' Their students came and they went, while the two of them stayed and withered." She shook her head. "Instead of powerful teachers and leaders, they became sniping spinster women, reduced to petty attempts to destroy those around them."

"Destroy? Destroy how?"

Mrs. Maitland picked up her teacup like she meant to read the leaves, which she did, for all I knew. A long silence stretched out between us. I could hear the ticking of the massive grandfather clock and the wind rushing through the tree branches. What I couldn't hear was the sound of any other person in the house. I thought about how we hadn't seen anybody since Marisol left. Mrs. Maitland was entirely alone here in this perfect big house. I wondered where Mr. Maitland was. I wondered if Ellis ever came by.

"Dorothy was a blackmailer," said Mrs. Maitland.

"What?"

Mrs. Maitland set down her cup. Her expression had gone sad and serious. "She had run out of money. Bad investments, like so many of us." She shrugged. "And, of course, all those loans to her nephew. When the recession came, she was ruined." She looked down at her fingertips. "She turned to blackmail to try to make ends meet."

I didn't believe it. I couldn't. Not Dorothy Hawthorne, with her beautiful house and beautiful garden, her cat and all her friends. I saw the woman in the photograph, laughing and wearing her witch's hat. The same woman who kept a picture from *The Wizard of Oz* around the house because it tickled her funny bone. I would not believe that this woman could be so . . . wicked.

"Have you got proof?" I heard myself ask. Why was I even asking? It didn't happen. It was impossible.

Oh, yeah? murmured a treacherous voice in the back of my head. *And just how many impossible things have turned out to be true since you got here, A.B.?*

"I thought you'd want to see evidence." Mrs. Maitland got to her feet. She walked over to an inlaid cabinet table and pulled a ring of keys out of her pocket. She unlocked the center drawer and brought out a piece of paper. Her hand shook as she handed it to me. "I never wanted to show this to anyone, but . . ."

I took the letter. I recognized the small slanted handwriting. I'd seen it in the journal in Dorothy's attic. In fact, it looked a lot like Elizabeth Maitland's handwriting, which made sense, I supposed. They'd have learned at the same time, and probably from the same teachers.

I read:

> *We're not finished yet. I will not let you go halfway on this. It will ruin you. Bring the rest with you on Saturday, then we will both be free.*
>
> *D.H.*

That was smart, I thought. *Using an actual paper letter. Easy to create, easy to destroy, and no unauthorized copies floating around the Internet to come back and bite you.*

That was stupid, I thought. *Using an actual paper letter. Handwriting can be recognized, and then you go and put your real initials on it?*

Instead of, say, D.G., for Dorothy Gale.

That last hit me so hard, my hand shook briefly.

"So." I drew the word out. I needed time to wrap my head around what I was seeing, and what Mrs. Maitland was saying, even if I really didn't want to. "You're telling me Dorothy Hawthorne tried to blackmail you?"

"Oh, no, not me. Bradley Thompson."

❧ 31 ❧

❧ *THIS MAKES NO sense.*

I forced my hands to relax before I crumpled the letter. In my mind's eye, I saw Brad Thompson, sitting across from me at Raja Rani. He was worried. No, he was frightened. He was looking for copies of documents, or something, he thought Dorothy had left in her house.

That much certainly fit with the idea of blackmail. It was the rest that was all wrong.

Brad Thompson had wanted to talk to me, but only as long as he thought I was working for Dorothy. When he decided I was working for Frank, he lost it.

If Dorothy was blackmailing him, that all should have been the other way around.

Unless . . .

Unless Dorothy wasn't the blackmailer. What if it was Frank himself? That D. in the D.H. could stand for Dorothy, or it could stand for Darius.

I looked at Mrs. Maitland. Did she believe what she was telling me? I couldn't tell. She was too practiced at holding her emotions in for me to read anything on her smooth, perfectly made-up face.

Something else didn't make sense.

"If Dorothy was blackmailing Brad, how did you get this?" I held up the letter. "Don't tell me Brad gave it to you."

"I got it from Ellis." Elizabeth took the paper from my hand and locked it back in the drawer. "My son cares a great deal about our town and its people. He listened to Dorothy when she told him Brad deserved a fresh start. She reminded Ellis that Brad was a family man who had fallen on hard times, and said he deserved a new beginning."

"Dorothy got Brad the job with Maitland and Associates?"

Elizabeth nodded. "My son has been trying to bridge the rift between me, Dorothy and Julia for years. As I said, he cares about this town and about the old families. He doesn't know everything, of course. The craft is passed from mother to daughter, not mother to son. I cannot go against that, no matter how much I might want to. I'm not like Dorothy. I cannot simply disregard the rules because they do not suit me personally." She took a deep breath and dragged her thoughts back onto the paths she wanted to follow. "Dorothy wanted Brad to work for Ellis, but not because Brad needed the job. She wanted Brad to have access to certain sensitive documents about various loans and real estate transactions. Dorothy could then bully him into finding out what she wanted to know." Mrs. Maitland's hands curled into bony fists. "Laurie Thompson found that letter. She showed it to Ellis, and Ellis brought it to me."

Which certainly would explain the exhaustion in Laurie Thompson's eyes. "But none of you thought about going to, say, the police?"

Mrs. Maitland laughed, and it was a brittle, mirthless sound. "Oh, yes, the lady from the manor descends and uses her influence with the police. That would work so very well." Her voice lowered. "You may have noticed, Anna, I do not have the gift of making myself liked. My mother used to tell me that's the one unforgivable sin in a woman. I do try, but I simply do not make friends easily." Her words grew softer, like she was at the end of her strength. "But I believe in loyalty, and I believe that we must help our own. I offered to help Dorothy when her money started to run out, but she turned me down flat. She'd never forgiven me for not taking her side all those years ago. Oh, she could hold a grudge with the best of them." Mrs. Maitland bit her lip. With an effort, she lifted her head and her voice returned to a normal conversational tone. "You were asking why I did not go to the police. I didn't go because I do not have evidence of actual wrongdoing. I have a single unsigned letter that has passed through any number of hands. If I went to them with my story, I would be patted on the head and sent home. I would also, of course, instantly alert Dorothy that I knew what she was up to."

"Because Dorothy had a . . . friend on the force?"

"A friend. Yes. Exactly. Dorothy, you see, had the gift I do not. Everyone loved her. Me, they simply tolerate for my name and my money."

Jealousy filled her voice as she said this, but so did pain. If she had been anyone else, I might have reached out to touch her.

"Why are you telling me this?" I asked.

"I'm worried about Bradley. It is my hope that whatever Dorothy dragged him into can be cleaned up, quietly, so that his family doesn't have to suffer anymore. With Dorothy dead, that should be possible, especially if it's just a matter of papers that were, shall we say, misdirected?"

And here we were, back to finding Brad's copies.

"And if it's not just papers?" I asked. Mrs. Maitland must have heard the rumors about Dorothy having been murdered.

"Then the police must be called," she said firmly. "It would be painful, of course, but if poor Bradley was driven that far . . ." She was talking to the French doors and the empty yard and the still, brown pond. "But perhaps it will serve to expose Dorothy and the chain she was part of."

"What you send out in the world comes back threefold," I murmured.

Elizabeth's head jerked around. "Yes. Exactly. You do know something of the craft, then."

"A little," I admitted. "I'm learning more all the time."

"I could help with that. If you wanted." A trace of wistfulness drifted through those words. I felt all the silence pressing heavily against us.

"I'll think about it, thank you." There was something else. "Why did you wait so long to start looking into this?"

She smiled. "Because in the end it seems I am a naive old woman. I wanted the whole matter to simply go away. I thought with Dorothy's death, it might. But, clearly, that was a foolish and, indeed, an irresponsible hope." Her jaw tightened. "With your arrival, and the rumors all starting up again, it became quite clear I must act." Mrs. Maitland stretched out one hand hesitantly. "Annabelle . . ."

"Anna."

"Anna. Your grandmother and I were friends once. When you're an old woman who does not have many friends left, you think a great deal on the ones you used to have. I would wish . . ."

There was a soft knock at the door. Elizabeth jerked backward like she'd been burned. "Come in."

The door opened and Marisol stepped through. "Excuse me, Mrs. Maitland, but there's a phone call from Mr. Ellis."

"Please take a message, Marisol. I will call him back as soon as I am finished here."

"He won't leave a message, ma'am. He says it's urgent."

A spasm of annoyance flickered across Mrs. Maitland's face. "I'm sorry," she told me. "I should only be a moment."

Once she left, the polite thing to do would have been to stay sitting here in my assigned chair. Maybe eat a few of the finger sandwiches that Marisol had probably worked hard to make.

Of course that's not what I did.

First I wandered over to the door that led to the hall. I eased it open, and I listened. I've got no excuses. This was straight-up, blatant eavesdropping. Unfortunately, it was also useless. Wherever Mrs. Maitland had gone to take that call, it was too far away for me to hear anything.

I wandered over to the French doors and looked out at the sunshine and the tangle of the wilderness beyond the little pond with its cattails and water lilies. Then I examined the landscapes on the wall. They weren't by anybody I recognized, but they were not only original; they were extremely well done.

I tried the drawer on the cabinet table, but Dorothy had locked it again. I thought about my trusty nail file.

"Annabelle Britton, what are you doing?" I muttered, turning my back on the table. I ran both hands through my hair. I was trying not to think; that's what. Because I was confused all over again. Dorothy Hawthorne couldn't be a blackmailer. It was the mirror image of everything I'd heard so far. Everyone I'd talked to had loved Dorothy.

Except the Thompsons. Who might have been bullied or blackmailed or bribed.

And Dorothy really was a witch. She knew about secret influences. She knew how to pressure people in ways that couldn't be tracked because the rest of the world thought they were impossible.

Could Julia and the others be trying to cover up Dorothy's blackmail? No. They couldn't possibly know. Not even Julia. If Dorothy was a blackmailer, she'd be a complete idiot to tell anybody at all. Another unwanted memory pricked my mind.

She'd become so secretive lately, Julia said. *She used to be so outgoing, and all that stopped.*

No. I shook my head. It didn't add up. Not when you looked at it all together. Brad's reaction to me didn't fit with any of the rest of what Elizabeth said. Unless . . .

I froze.

Unless Brad Thompson wasn't Dorothy's victim. Unless he was her partner in the crime of blackmail. That would explain everything. If Brad and Dorothy had been working together, he would naturally want all the copies of whatever incriminating documents she had kept. Because:

1) "Incrimination" is also an ugly word.

2) He could continue their blackmail business on his own.

3) If Frank found the copies and uncovered the scheme, it wouldn't matter if the police believed it. Frank could just publish the whole story in the *Seacoast News*, naming all the names when he did.

I was cold, so cold I was shaking. What if . . . what if . . . Frank *had* discovered Dorothy was a blackmailer? How angry he must have been, how hurt and betrayed. Angry enough to shout, maybe angry enough to push her.

Maybe angry enough to give her a shove when she was standing at the top of the basement stairs.

Stop it, A.B., I told myself. *You don't know. You don't know anything.*

I turned away again, searching the room for something, anything, to take my mind off this. There was a door in the right-hand wall I hadn't tried yet. I put my hand on the brass push plate and listened for a moment. When I didn't hear any sound of returning footsteps, I pushed it open.

On the other side of the door was a small library. The built-in shelves were filled with old leather-bound books, just like you see in all the movies. Actually, they reminded me a lot of the ones in Dorothy's attic. There were no landscapes on the walls in here, but there was a pair of portraits, done in that early American style where everybody looks a little flat and heavy. The first was a man dressed in Puritan black and white. He was bareheaded, and his flowing locks were streaked with gray. The shining hat with its gleaming gold buckle that he held in both well-gloved hands spoke of respectable prosperity.

Five-Times-Great-Grandfather Diligence, I presume.

To the grandfather's right hung a portrait of a woman. She wore a lace cap with dangling strings, but the rest of her clothing was as plain and severe as her husband's. They made the perfect Puritan couple. Except for one thing. Grandmother Diligence didn't hold any hat in her hands. Instead, she held a tiny golden cage, and inside there was a tiny yellow bird.

I sucked in a breath and I stared. The artist had lavished as much care and detail on that bird as he had on the woman. It was thin and it had an intelligent light in its beady black eye.

Nothing ends up in a picture by accident or coincidence. If it was in there, it was because it was important enough for the artist to take time over, or for the client to request. One way or another, that particular bird was very important to Five-Times-Great-Grandmother Maitland.

That bird belonged to the Maitland family the way Alistair belonged to the Hawthornes and to me. It was their familiar.

Which meant Julia must know about it.

Which meant Julia Parris had lied.

❧ 32 ❧

🐾 I PROBABLY SHOULD have waited for Mrs. Maitland to come back. I'm sure Nancy Drew would have waited. But I couldn't remember Nancy ever suddenly finding out she'd been lied to by her new friend, who incidentally was trying to talk her into becoming a witch.

Unfortunately, given the nature of our recent conversation, I couldn't exactly trust Elizabeth Maitland as a source of information either. Especially since it turned out she was spying on me in a particularly spooky way.

So, instead, I found Marisol and asked her to give Mrs. Maitland my apologies, but I was called away to deal with an urgent matter for an important client, and I got the heck out of the house. I did glance back as I was unlocking the Jeep, and saw Mrs. Maitland's shadow in one of the upstairs windows. She was gesturing to thin air and talking into the phone. I wondered if it was her son she was arguing with on the other end of the line, or somebody else.

I'd worry about that later. In fact, I probably wouldn't be able to avoid it.

Back in Portsmouth, I found a parking spot right across from Midnight Reads, which was stronger proof than anything I'd seen yet that magic does happen. Unfortunately, the bookstore was doing a brisk business today. Even from where I sat I could see it was full of happy, browsing customers. I fished out my phone and considered calling. No. I put it back. This was not a conversation anybody wanted to have where customers might overhear.

So, if I wasn't going to talk to Julia yet, what should I do? I drummed my palms against the steering wheel. No matter which way I looked, all the roads to actual answers led back to Dorothy, the house and the missing documents. Which meant they also led to Brad Thompson.

"Back to Plan A, I guess," I said to myself as I threw the Jeep into gear. "Laurie Thompson. Then Julia. After that . . ."

Well, after that, there was nothing on the schedule except dinner with Frank Hawthorne.

This was turning out to be one heck of a day.

THE THOMPSON HOUSE was the kind of place that gets described as "modest." In this case that meant it was small with a plain peaked roof and white aluminum siding that was starting to peel in a couple of places. The lawn was mowed but weedy. Everything had the air of not quite enough time and not quite enough money.

I parked my Jeep and walked up to the door, wondering if I should have called first. Well, I was here now. I stepped up onto the plain concrete porch, pushed the bell and waited.

The door flew open, and there stood Laurie Thompson, pale and out of breath. When she saw me, her whole body sagged.

"I . . . I'm sorry . . . ," I said.

"No, no," she answered, rallying quickly. "Hi, Anna. Sorry. I was . . . expecting someone else. I . . ." She glanced behind her. "Would you like to come in?"

I would, but I hesitated. Laurie was a stranger. I had no business intruding, but at the same time, I didn't like to leave her alone when something was so clearly going wrong. "If you're sure? I mean, this doesn't look like it's actually a good time for you. I . . ."

"No, no." Laurie looked behind her again. "Sorry. I need to get that."

She hurried into the house. I pushed back my rising doubt and stepped over the threshold.

The inside of the Thompson house was a match for the outside—small, plain and straining at the edges of its resources. I walked past the small but tidy living room and through the kitchen, which opened into the family room that was clearly the center of the Thompson life.

As I came in, Laurie was flipping her cell phone closed.

"Please, have a seat." She gestured toward the worn leather sofa. She also cleared a slanting stack of mail off the coffee table, in that self-conscious way you do when unexpected visitors show up. "Would you like something to drink?"

"No, I'm good. Thanks." I sat and pulled my purse onto my knees. "Are you sure this is an okay time?"

"Oh, yes. It's all fine," she answered as she tucked a stray lock of hair behind her ears.

"I actually was hoping I might get a look at some more of your paintings," I said. "The one you showed me the other day was really lovely."

"Oh. Oh. Well. That's very nice of you. I . . . just a moment . . ." She got up and went into a side room that I suspected served as her studio space. I waited, looking around, not sure what I was looking for exactly. Books, papers, toys and game systems were scattered across the various surfaces. The walls were decorated with family photographs down several generations: weddings; graduations; smiling young men in the uniforms of at least three different branches and eras of service; boys and girls grinning and hoisting sports trophies into the air. It all looked breathtakingly normal, and it should have been happy, except it wasn't.

Footsteps thumped down the stairs. A girl, maybe ten years old, darted around the corner into the kitchen, a book clutched in one hand. She stopped dead when she saw me.

"Hi," I said, demonstrating the full extent of my way with children.

"Hi," she said back. "Mom?" she called.

"Yes, honey?" Laurie answered from her studio.

"Can I go over to Margot's?"

"Oh, yes. Go ahead, but nowhere else, okay? I . . . just, you stay with Margot."

"Okay." The girl gave me another point-blank stare and then slammed out the door.

Kids these days. They hadn't changed much.

Laurie came back out; she was carrying a portfolio. "This is really nice of you," she said, laying it on the coffee table. "I mean, I'm mostly self-taught, and, well . . ."

She undid the tie and opened the portfolio.

I looked through the pages. Laurie's work was heavy on the local landscapes, but not panoramas. She did mostly small studies: a single stone on the riverbank, one gull on a broken piling, a man in his overalls and waders sitting and staring out across the waters, his tired face rendered simply but with individuality. I would recognize this person if I met him on the street.

"These are really good," I said. "I mean that."

"Thank you." She rubbed her hands together as if she was cold, even though it was warm in the room. I sympathized. It's always nerve-racking to watch someone looking over your work. "I've tried to sell some," she said. "But, honestly, it's so hard to know how to start. I mean, my daughter Jeannie wants me to set up an online store, and there are art fairs and everything, but . . ."

"Actually, that's what I wanted to talk to you about," I said.

"I might be able to help." I told her about Nadia and her gallery. "Would you mind if I took some snaps of these to send her?"

"I . . . that would be wonderful! Thank you!"

"I can't promise anything, but . . . well, there's a possibility." I pulled my phone out. The snaps wouldn't be great, but they'd be enough to give Nadia an idea of Laurie's range.

"I really can't thank you enough for this, Anna," said Laurie when I tucked my phone away. "Are you sure I can't get you something? Some coffee?"

"No, no, really. I just stopped by for a minute." I hesitated again. There really was no good way to work around to this. "Listen, Laurie, you're sure everything's okay?"

"Yes. Fine. Especially now." She wasn't looking at me as she said it, though. She was picking up her paintings and sliding them carefully into her portfolio.

"I'm really glad. Because I was up talking to Elizabeth Maitland and . . ."

"Mrs. Maitland!" A sketch of the pier slid out of her fingers and fluttered to the floor. We both bent down to grab it, but Laurie got to it first. "I didn't realize you two knew each other."

"She was a friend of my grandmother Blessingsound, back when Gran still lived in Portsmouth."

Laurie closed the portfolio. When she looked up again, her expression, which had been so welcoming and hopeful a minute before, was closed off and cool. "You're a Blessingsound? I didn't realize."

"My father's mother is Annabelle Mercy Blessingsound," I told her. "She and Mrs. Maitland grew up together. And Mrs. Maitland seemed to think there might be a problem, between Brad and Frank."

Laurie picked up the portfolio and turned away. The speed of her movement sent another stray lock of hair drifting down from her braid. "Is this what Brad wanted to talk with you about at the restaurant the other day?"

Now it was my turn to be distinctly uncomfortable. "Oh. You heard about that?"

"I heard Brad ran into you. I didn't hear what you talked about."

I hesitated. I really hadn't planned this far ahead. "We talked about the house, and how I liked it."

Laurie wasn't buying it. "And Dorothy?" she prompted.

"A little. I didn't know her, of course."

"Of course," she answered. "She really was a wonderful person. She recommended Brad for his job with Maitland and Associates."

"Yeah, Mrs. Maitland mentioned that." I paused again. Maybe there was a community college course I could take in asking leading questions. Until then, I was just going to have to shove my way through this. "Laurie, I need to ask you something, and it's not a good question. It's also probably not my business."

"Okay." She attempted a smile. "Now I'm concerned."

"Is it possible Dorothy was blackmailing Brad?"

My brief acquaintance with Laurie Thompson had gotten me thinking of her as an essentially nervous person. Now her head snapped up and her spine stiffened. "Who told you that?"

"Somebody showed me a letter. They said it had come from you and that it was a blackmail note."

Laurie was silent for a long moment. I watched her expression shift as she tried to get hold of her anger and failed. "Was it Frank Hawthorne?" she asked at last.

"Laurie, I can't . . ."

"But it was, wasn't it? I swear, he's never going to let go!"

Well, she was talking. She wasn't happy about it, but you can't have everything. "What happened between them? I thought they were friends."

"The newspaper, that's what happened. Frank lost his mind over it. Completely obsessed with the idea. Who opens a paper nowadays?" Laurie threw out her hands, looking around the family room and the world at large for an answer. "At least, not without really deep pockets."

I nodded in agreement. There's an old joke I'd heard from a friend of mine who illustrates kids' books: How do you make a small fortune in publishing? Answer: Start with a large fortune.

"Brad tried to get Frank to see some sense," Laurie went on. "He thought maybe Frank should start small and work his way up. When he heard about how short the money really was, he got worried enough that he tried to talk to Dorothy about it."

"And that didn't go well?"

"Frank accused Brad of trying to take advantage of Dorothy."

"What? How?"

She shook her head. "At the time, Brad was coming home late some nights. He was very tired. He didn't want to tell me what was wrong, but eventually he did. He told me Dorothy was looking to sell the house, to raise money for Frank and his business. He tried to talk her out of it, but she wouldn't budge. Oh, she was a good woman, but she could be absolutely blind where her nephew was concerned. If anyone was taking advantage . . ." Laurie's clamped her mouth shut, but I didn't need to hear her say it. In her considered opinion, if anyone was taking advantage of Dorothy, it was Frank.

"Anyway. Dorothy didn't want Frank to find out she was thinking of selling. They'd already starting arguing about her finances, so whatever she did had to be done very, very quietly, or Frank would never accept the money. Brad told me he'd agreed to help, although it was difficult. They couldn't put anything online, because Frank publishes the real estate deals in the paper, so he watches the sites for interesting bids and buyers."

"So, I guess Brad and Dorothy were spending a lot of time together."

"And even though they were being careful, Frank found out, and he jumped to the conclusion that Brad was badgering Dorothy about the house. They argued. In fact, they argued the night Dorothy died."

I bit my lip and ran my hand over my purse. I felt the wand underneath. A low prickling ran up my palm. I didn't know what to do with it. I didn't know what to do with any of it. Because this story Laurie was telling me was so very different from what I'd been hearing from other people.

"This must all be really hard for you," I said.

"Well, it hasn't been easy. Still." She shrugged and brushed her straggling hair back. "Maybe now . . ."

She was cut off by the sound of the front door slamming open. "Hey, Mom!" shouted Colin. "You here?"

Laurie shot to her feet. "Colin!" she called back. "Did you . . ."

Colin loped into the kitchen. He saw me and he stopped dead. I seemed to have that affect on the Thompsons.

"What's she doing here?" he demanded.

If ever there was a cue to exit stage left, that was it. "Thank you for your time, Laurie." I shook her hand. It really was cold. "I'll let you know as soon as I hear anything."

"Thank you, Anna," she murmured.

"Well. Gosh. Since you're going, I'll walk you out." Colin stepped aside to make it easy for me to head for the front door, all the while making it very clear that this was exactly what I should be doing right now.

Of course his mom noticed this.

"Colin," said Laurie sternly. "This is not a problem."

"Course not," he answered. "Didn't say it was."

I didn't say anything at all. I just smiled politely and headed out the Thompson's front door, very aware of the young man who followed me down the driveway to make extra sure I didn't turn around and bother his mother anymore.

I didn't. But when I reached my Jeep, I did turn around and bother Colin. "I'm not here to make trouble," I said. No points for originality there, but at least I meant it.

"Suuurrre," Colin drawled. "Why would I think that? Especially since you're going away now, and you're not coming back."

"I was here to help. I might have a gig for your mom, for her art."

That startled him, but he was not at all ready to back down. "We've had enough help."

"What do you mean, Colin?" I laid my hand over my wand. My palm prickled. Julia said magic was about focus and concentration. I tried to concentrate on what *I* meant. I meant to help. I meant to be a friend. I meant to get to the bottom of what had gone wrong.

Colin shifted his weight and looked away. "I mean since Dorothy Hawthorne 'helped' Dad, he's been acting all crazy. It was bad enough when he was out of work, but this . . ." He folded his arms and stared out across the street.

"What's 'this'?" I took a step closer and did my best to focus. *Tell me. I can help. Please, tell me.*

"He's supposed to be at work today, but he's not," whispered Colin. "Nobody knows where he is." He slapped his palm over his mouth and for a second he looked panicked. "Don't tell Mom, okay? Please?" The hostility was gone. This was just a worried kid who was having to grow up a lot faster than he should.

Personally, given how she was acting when I showed up, I figured Laurie already knew. But I nodded anyway. "I won't say anything to her, I promise."

"Thanks. Look, I'm supposed to be going to work now. Just . . . leave Mom alone, okay? She's got enough problems."

"I'm going, I'm going," I told him. "But if there's anything I can do . . ."

But Colin had already turned away and headed back toward the house.

I climbed into the Jeep, started the engine and drove. When I was two blocks away and around the corner, I pulled over and hit Kenisha's number.

"Freeman," she answered. "What's going on, Anna?"

"I've just been over at the Thompsons'. Brad Thompson's missing."

"Missing?" she repeated in her calm, controlled, cop voice. "How long?"

"Just since this morning, but he's not at work, and Colin is really worried. I think Laurie is too. It's got to be twenty-four hours before they can make out a report, right?" Kenisha made an affirmative noise. "I know you don't like to do anything without proof, Kenisha, but I'm sure something's going on here."

"You've been talking to Val too much."

"No, that's not it. I swear."

Kenisha sighed. "All right, all right." All at once, her voice dropped. "I can't talk now." I pictured her glancing over her shoulder and wondered if that lieutenant everybody kept muttering about had come within earshot. "But I can keep an eye out for Brad. Is Colin home with Laurie?"

"For now. He says he's got to go to work soon."

"Okay. Maybe I can phone later . . . thanks for the heads-up."

We said good-bye again and hung up, and I sat there for a while, both hands on the wheel, not going anywhere. I'd done what I could, for the moment. I had just a few problems:

1) Brad Thompson was probably lying to his wife about why he'd been spending so much time with Dorothy Hawthorne.

2) Elizabeth Maitland was probably lying to me about how she got her hands on that blackmail letter.

3) Julia Parris was definitely lying to me about the little yellow spy bird.

4) How in the heck was I supposed to make small talk with Frank Thompson with items one, two and three hanging over my head?

❧ 33 ❧

🐾 DESPITE THE LIST of lies and worries that I seemed to be accumulating, the day brought some good news too. Nadia *loved* Laurie's work. Capital *L*, italics, exclamation points and blinky smiley faces loved.

"Do you have her e-mail?" Nadia demanded. "I showed her stuff to a couple of my clients who do high-end office decor, and they want to see her originals, like, yesterday!"

At this time, I was curled up on the living room window seat with Alistair purring in my lap, and looking proud enough that you'd think the whole thing had been his idea.

After I hung up with Nadia, it felt a whole lot easier to believe that everything could be cleared up with a few phone calls and a few pointed questions. I was singing old Beatles tunes as I showered and changed to go meet Frank.

Alistair did not stick around for the second chorus of "A Hard Day's Night." Smart cat.

Frank and I had agreed to meet in front of the North

Church, and he was already sitting on one of the tourist benches when I arrived.

"You look like you want to change your mind," he said as he got to his feet. Apparently, I hadn't been able to keep all my worries and doubts out of my expression.

"No, no. I'm sorry. I just . . ." I glanced around, searching for an excuse. I couldn't tell Frank straight-out about all the things I'd heard today, not if I wanted him to keep talking to me. Which I did. Kind of a lot, all things considered. "I was just wondering where we should go." From where I stood, I could count at least five busy restaurants between the clothing and souvenir shops.

"How about the Pale Ale?" he said. "I know you like the place, and the new chef is really terrific . . . And you've got that look on your face again."

I laughed. "Sorry. It's just that the new chef is my best friend, Martine Devereux, and if we go to dinner there, she might see . . . us."

Frank raised both eyebrows. "And Best Friend Martine would care because . . . ?"

"Because she'd think we're . . . that this is a . . . you know . . ."

"Oh." Frank nodded sagely. "Is she pro or anti you know . . . ?"

"Oh, pro, but I'm taking a break from . . . you know."

"And she doesn't get it, and she's going to give you all kinds of best-girlfriend grief if you walk in with some random guy, especially if he just happens to be your new landlord."

"Hey, you're good at this."

Frank grinned. "It's those killer journalistic instincts. Okay, Pale Ale probably not the best idea. How do you feel about chowder?"

"I feel that chowder is nature's perfect food."

"I was hoping you'd say that. Come on, Anna Blessingsound Britton. It's time you were introduced to Joe King's Chowder Shack."

JOE KING'S CHOWDER Shack proved to be just that—a shack. It was a little white clapboard building by the river sandwiched between a Circle K quickie mart and a gas station. Across the street, a fake tiki bar blasted techno dance music from the roof patio. It was early yet, but the bar's parking lot was packed and clearly the party was in full swing.

Inside the shack, there was barely room for me and Frank, the battered counter, and the smiling man who tended the pair of steaming kettles.

"Hey, Manny!" called Frank as he held the screen door open for me. "How's it going?"

"Hey-yah, Frank. Cahn't complain. Cahn't complain."

Manny was a little round man with leather brown skin and black hair slicked back under a black flatcap. He also had big hands, a genial smile and the thickest old-school New Hampshire accent I'd ever heard.

"What's on the fire today?" Frank leaned both elbows on the counter and inhaled the fragrant steam.

"Oh, let's see heyah. We got the clam chowdah, as always, and we got a lobstah bisque, mighty good. Get'cha a taste?" he asked me.

"That'd be great," I answered.

Manny produced a couple of small white cups filled with delicate pink broth and a chunk of sweet lobster floating in each. I sipped. The bisque was light and savory and sweet. In short, perfect.

Frank was watching me and grinning. "I think that'll be two, Manny. And some of Marisol's bread, okay?"

"Comin' right up." Manny started carefully ladling soup into disposable bowls and wrapping bread in brown paper.

"Marisol?" I said to Frank. "The housekeeper at the Maitlands'?"

"You've met Marisol?" Frank asked.

"Elizabeth Maitland invited me over for tea yesterday."

"Did she?" Frank did not sound very happy about this coincidence. Considering his opinion of Ellis Maitland, I guess I should not have been surprised. "What for?"

Before I could answer, Manny put two white paper sacks down in front of us. I reached for my purse, but Frank waved me back.

"Let me."

"Oh, no. You got the coffee last time. This is mine."

Frank made a face. "You're working for me, remember? Boss buys bisque."

I made a face of my own but relented. Frank paid, and we headed out, each carrying a paper bag. Frank winced at the noise from the tiki bar. "Maybe we should walk a ways?" He gestured up the river. "There's a park by the North Mill Pond, just across the bridge there."

"Sounds good."

The park turned out to be a lovely green space around a big irregular sidewater of the Piscataqua. Dragonflies chased midges across the water's dark surface. We found a lopsided picnic table to sit at and flattened the bags to use as place mats for the chunks of crusty bread. Unlike some people (Martine), Frank Hawthorne did not get all judgey when I dumped an entire packet of oyster crackers into the satin-smooth bisque. Seagulls clustered on the rocks, a feathered mafia waiting for their chance to make a move on our turf, and our dinner.

"So." Frank dunked bread into bisque. "Have you had a chance to look around the house yet?"

It was not exactly a subtle lead-in, but I'd been ready for something like it. "A little," I told him. "In fact, I noticed the furniture's there, but Dorothy's personal papers aren't. The old bills and checks and stuff like that. Have you got them?"

"Yeah, I do."

"Have you been through them?"

He cocked his head toward me. "Not thoroughly."

I stirred soup and oyster crackers and said nothing. Frank made a sour face. "And you are wondering why I haven't gotten off my duff and really dug into them?"

"I have never said the word 'duff' in my life."

"It was one of Aunt Dot's favorites." He sighed. "I did look. I had to get the records together for probate and everything, but it all seemed . . . normal. I mean, I already knew that Dorothy was up-to-date on all her payments, and the mortgages were both fixed rate, really conservative and straightforward."

A strange feeling of disappointment surged through me. If there wasn't any money trouble, that shot down several of my best theories about Dorothy's murder.

Unless, of course, the reason she didn't have money trouble was that she'd been bringing in some extra money on the side. I bit my lip.

Frank, of course, saw this, and he pounced. "You have found something. What is it?"

I found out your aunt is a blackmailer. Unless it's Brad Thompson. Unless it's you.

I did not say this. Frank, it turned out, was not in a mood to let a good silence stretch out.

"Is it something to do with what you and Brad Thompson were arguing about at the restaurant the other day?"

"I should have known you'd find out about that."

Frank smiled, but it was not a happy expression. "Yeah, you really should have."

I dipped my spoon into the bisque and turned it over. "Seems like Brad was fighting with a lot of people," I said. "Including you."

Frank winced. "You've been talking to Laurie, haven't you?"

"I'm supposed to be figuring things out, remember?" I sipped a spoonful of bisque. "And as it happens, I'm putting her in touch with a friend of mine who might be able to sell some of her watercolors."

Frank wasn't looking at me. He was spooning up soup and struggling with something hard inside. "That was nice of you," he said, and he meant it. I remembered how he'd tried to protect Brad when he thought Brad was about to get into trouble with his boss.

"Were you and Brad good friends?" I asked.

Frank nodded. "He was older than me, so we didn't exactly grow up together, but you know how it is in a small town; there are just some people who are always . . . around. Our families knew each other, and I didn't have siblings, and Brad, he kind of took over the part of my big brother. He looked out for me when I got into high school. Made sure I made it home okay when I'd gone to a party or two I maybe shouldn't have." He turned over his bread a couple of times like he was looking for something in the crumbs. "I accused him a couple times of ratting me out to Aunt Dot when he probably didn't." Frank yanked off a chunk of bread and pitched it at the gulls, who set up a massive ruckus as they all dove after it. "Brad was one of those straight-arrow guys we were all supposed to imitate. Studied hard, ran track and field, got into a good college, got out with a good business degree. Came home, married Laurie, bought a nice house, had nice kids. Everything by the book, everything smooth. Until all of a sudden it wasn't."

"What happened?"

Frank shrugged. "Life. He got downsized at work, and then his dad got sick and the insurance wasn't covering half of what they needed, and . . . it all just melted away: savings, house, everything. We were all hoping things would get better for them when he got the job with Ellis Maitland, and for a while they did. But now . . ." Frank tore off another hunk of bread to pitch toward the gulls. "Something's gone wrong again. It's probably nothing, really. He's probably just scared it'll all fall apart again."

Except that wasn't all there was to it. But how much could I, or should I, tell Frank about what I knew? I thought about

Brad's search for the "copies." I thought about how Frank had just told me he had all Dorothy's personal papers. I thought about how frightened Brad had been when he realized I might be working with Frank.

I thought about how Dorothy had left her clue in a room she'd made darn sure her nephew would have trouble getting into.

Her nephew, or anybody else.

"I should have told you before," I said slowly. "When I . . . was in Dorothy's house the first time, the person Alistair and I chased out was Brad Thompson."

Frank made no answer, at least not right away, but his whole body tensed. A whole lot of something was going on inside his head, and none of it was taking him to his happy place.

"You're sure?"

"We got a very good look at each other."

He sighed and tossed the spoon into the empty bowl. "You know, when you described the guy, I thought, jeez that sounds like Brad, but I told myself it couldn't be."

"Why not?" I asked, and when I saw the glare he turned on me, I almost wished I hadn't. Almost.

"Because it's not the kind of thing he'd do! Brad's a good guy, a good, regular guy. Maybe we're on the outs, but that's only because he cared about Dorothy almost as much as I did!"

"Then, they were close? Laurie told me Dorothy and Brad had been spending a lot of time together."

Frank didn't answer. He got up and paced over to the pond and stared at the busy dragonflies.

"You asked me to help find out how your aunt died," I reminded him. "You said you wanted to know, no matter what turned up. Well, this is what's turning up."

"You've got to understand; Aunt Dot . . . she was all I had," Frank said softly. "My mother died when I was a kid. My dad . . . he was, is, always off somewhere chasing the next big thing. Aunt Dot raised me, and Brad looked out for me. And this is what I'm supposed to go tearing apart?" He stopped. "I know. I'm a journalist. I'm supposed to go after the truth, whatever it is. But how can I do that when it might hurt the people I care about? Or ruin my memory of them?"

Which is why you asked someone else to look for you. I swallowed and nodded. *You had to know, but you weren't sure you could follow through on your own.* Julia had said something like this too, about the pain of finding out people you'd known your whole life might not be what you thought.

My purse, with the wand inside, was beside me on the picnic bench. I laid my hand on it, and I watched Frank as he stared across the pond. I tried to study him like I was going to paint his portrait—breaking his face down into its component shapes and shadows, seeing through skin to the lines of the bones and the shape of the person.

I felt my palm prickle, and this time I understood at once. I was looking at someone who was lonely. Really, truly lonely, and he had no idea what to do about it.

"Brad's missing," I said.

"What?" Frank whirled around.

"Colin said he didn't turn up at work today, and Laurie's worried."

Now Frank did swear. Journalists have a large vocabulary, and he used it all. "Why didn't you tell me? I have to . . ." He yanked his phone out of his pocket, hit a number and waited while it rang. "Hi, Laurie, it's . . ." I heard the sound of shouting from the other end. "Yeah, yeah, okay, I know, but is Brad . . ." More shouting. "Okay, I'm sorry." He hung up.

Worry dug into me. "He's not home yet, is he?"

Frank shook his head, and he shoved his phone into his pocket. "And she's still mad at me. Doesn't matter." He took a deep breath. "I'm going to go check a couple of spots. Last time . . . well, Brad can drink too much when he gets depressed, and . . ." He stopped. "Somebody needs to find him."

I nodded. "Go on. I'll clean up here."

"Thanks." Frank squeezed my hand briefly, turned on his heel and took off back toward downtown at a good fast clip.

I gathered up bowls and bags and spoons and stuffed them into the trash can. My head was spinning. I didn't know what to think or whom to believe. Every time I thought I had the people around me figured out, they showed me an entirely new side and sent all my theories into a tailspin.

"Merowp?"

"Speaking of tailspins." I turned my head, completely unsurprised to see Alistair sitting on the picnic table with his tail curled around his toes.

"I know what you're here to tell me," I said. "If we're going to send Frank looking through the old financial documents, it's about time I got off my duff and really went through Dorothy's attic, isn't it?"

"Merow," answered Alistair.

Well, who was I to argue with that kind of logic?

❧ 34 ❧

🐾 THE ATTIC WAS warm and stuffy. The windows were sticky from disuse, but I eventually got a couple of them open to let in the breeze. It was still hot, but at least it wasn't so close. I needed to get a fan up here. Another thing for the shopping list.

I faced the bookshelf. The books faced me. Alistair, in true cat fashion, came over to rub his face on the corner of the case.

I thought about Frank Hawthorne and how he'd been unable to answer all his own questions about Dorothy and Brad because he was afraid of what those answers might be. Standing in front of the journals, I could really sympathize. Whom would I find in here? The kind, laughing woman in the picture Julia had given me? Or the bitter, heartless woman reduced to blackmail and revenge who Elizabeth Maitland said was all that remained of her friend?

"So, where do we start?" I whispered to Alistair.

"Merowp." Alistair rubbed his face against the corner of a battered black journal that stuck out of the end of the shelf. It was labeled 1954.

"Begin at the beginning." I pulled the book out and carried it over to the chair. Alistair was in my lap as soon as I
sat down, so I balanced the book on the chair arm and
started to read.

TWO HOURS LATER, I had a crick in my neck, itchy
eyes and dry fingers. Stacks of journals and binders teetered
on the floor and the footstool. The sun had set, so I'd turned
on all the lamps.

I also had a picture of a life that had nothing to do with
blackmail.

I'd skimmed years of clipped articles detailing all the
small-town triumphs. There were pieces about school plays,
bake-offs, scholarships, high school graduations, town hall
meetings, candidate lunches, successful fund-raisers for local
causes. The library opened; it expanded; it struggled for fund-
ing; it had a successful casino night and raffle. The high school
teams went to the National Spelling Bee and to the state cham-
pionships for ice skating and hockey. People met and married
and raised families. There were articles about the opening of
Midnight Reads, and the ad for Didi's business, the Cleaning
Fairy Housekeeping Services (It's magical!).

If an article showed that some hoped-for event had come
to pass, Dorothy decorated it with underlinings and exclamations, and lists of related magical ceremonies were jotted
down in the margins. Smiley faces too. Dorothy Hawthorne
was a deep believer in the smiley face, not to mention the
heart and exclamation point. No wonder she and Grandma
B.B. had been friends.

Between the articles were pages of handwritten notes.
These were the details of Dorothy's magical life. The phases
of the moon were faithfully recorded. There were descrip-
tions of the coven ceremonies Dorothy attended or created,
along with their blessings and wishings and workings.

I read about blessings and incantations for clarity of mind

before acting and for attracting luck, prosperity and, yes, love. Dorothy was all about bringing people together, or bringing in the good and banishing the negative.

"That was her specialty, wasn't it?" I said to Alistair as I scratched his ears. "Attraction, connection." I paused. "Summoning."

"Merow," Alistair agreed.

I read about meditations for calm, for acceptance and for forgiveness. I read about cleansing before rituals and closing the circle afterward, and how some spells had to be tended for days if not weeks before they could come to full strength.

There was a lot about the garden as well. Dorothy listed her various cuttings and plantings. She made notes about the weather and clipped yet more articles about natural methods to fight pests, from aphids to green flies. She listed which herbs were good for cleansing and healing and which were best for mundane uses, like marinara sauce or soothing teas.

There were pages about her students, too. Names and photographs were pasted on pages like a handmade year-book. There were years' worth of letters, going from hand-written to typed, and finally printed e-mails. They discussed the philosophy of magic, sometimes curious, sometimes angry or confused, but always trying to move closer to an understanding of the world and themselves. There were letters of thanks sent as students moved away, looking for their own paths.

I found a picture of Val, looking sullen and unfamiliar as she stared out from under a set of long, slanting punk-rock bangs. I found another of Kenisha, who looked at the camera like it was pronouncing a life sentence.

I found Frank. Not that it was difficult. Dorothy had detailed his life with maternal pride. There were photos of birthday parties, of Frank in his peewee hockey gear, and of him hugging a very patient Alistair around the neck. Teenage Frank held up the keys to an epically battered Ford Mustang. He wore a fast-food uniform and waved a paycheck over his head. He stood in his graduation cap and gown beside a gray-haired man who must have been his father. Neither one of them had an arm around the other. In the last journal, Frank stood in the doorway of the *Seacoast News*. He held up the keys to the office with the same triumphant pride with which the boy had held up the first paycheck or the keys to the first car.

But where was the hard, petty woman Elizabeth Maitland had described to me? I closed the journal and laid my hands over it. She wasn't in here. Everything in here was cheerful, loving. Oh, there were obituaries, but nothing cantankerous, let alone bitter.

"It makes no sense," I said to Alistair. He was lying on the rug beside the bookshelf, playing with a loose thread. "Why would Mrs. Maitland tell a lie that I could disprove so easily?"

Alistair rolled over on his back and looked at me upside down.

"Unless I'm missing something." I frowned at the shelf. "What's not here?"

Alistair vanished.

I jumped. I may have also made a slightly undignified sound that could have been mistaken for a scream by the uninitiated.

"Meow?"

Alistair reappeared on top of the bookcase, blinking at me. *What's your problem, human?*

"Don't do that!" I pressed my hand over my heart, which was now going a mile a minute. "When I said what's missing, I didn't mean you!"

Alistair leapt from the bookcase to the floor, slid between two crooked stacks of journals and vanished again.

"Fine, stay gone. Be missing . . ." I stopped. "Missing," I said again.

I scrabbled through the piles, yanked out some older journals from the sixties, and started flipping through pages.

This time I saw it.

A number of the pages had blank spaces. Scraps of yellowing Scotch tape were still stuck on the corners, showing where photos or articles had been attached but then removed.

What I didn't find was any mention of Grandma B.B., who was supposed to be one of Dorothy's girlhood friends. I didn't even see her name in the yellowing newspaper announcement of the graduating class from Portsmouth High School. I found the picture of a young Dorothy in a white cap and gown, clutching her diploma. But it wasn't a complete photo. I ran my finger down the right side. The rest had been cut away. I turned more pages, scanning the faces, scanning the names in the articles. Some names, I saw, had been carefully and solidly blotted out with black marker.

Dorothy had edited Grandma B.B. out of her life as thoroughly as Grandma B.B. had edited out Dorothy, and Portsmouth itself. I grabbed up the more recent books and flipped through them too. Not only had the Blessingsounds been blotted out; so had the Maitlands. Mostly. There was one long, gossipy article about Elizabeth Maitland's divorce from Albert Maitland, her husband of thirty-two years. But when I leafed back through, I found no mention of the marriage. I found articles following the New Hampshire district attorney's probe into Maitland and Associates' finances, but nothing about when the office opened, or how it had grown.

"Oh, Dorothy," I breathed. "You really did carry your grudges, a long way." Elizabeth had been telling the truth about that at least. I looked around at the heaps of books and binders. "But nothing about Brad," I said to Alistair. "And no copies." I tapped the cover of the binder in my lap. "Not of anything obvious, anyway." I stopped. My hands stilled. "No copies and sure as heck no originals." I stopped again. There was something there. Something I'd missed before. Alistair climbed up onto my lap and onto the binder and sat staring at me.

I scratched his ears. "How come Brad was worried about

finding copies?" I asked him. "Whatever these documents are, why wasn't he worried about finding the originals?"

"Merow." Alistair jumped onto the footstool, sending a whole stack of binders and journals crashing to the floor.

"Hey!" I shouted, and went down on my knees to pick the scattered books up. Alistair, of course, jumped in the middle and scrabbled in the pages.

"Cut. It. Out." I picked him up and, I admit it, dropped him to one side. But he just came right back, unfazed, and head butted the book I was holding so hard it slipped out of my hands.

"Hey!"

"Merow!" he repeated as he leapt across the book, the motion rifling the yellowing pages.

I yanked the book off the floor, intending to put it safely back on the shelf away from further cat interference. But then the page headline caught my eye.

AUTOMATIC WRITING

I looked at Alistair. Alistair looked at me. I looked at the book. This time I read:

> *Automatic writing or psychography is an alleged psychic ability allowing a person to produce written words without consciously writing. The words are claimed to arise from a subconscious, spiritual or supernatural source.*

"What? I'm supposed to try this?"

Alistair sat bolt upright and looked at me, steadily and expectantly.

I sat back on my heels. Was I really thinking about this? Well, why not? Grandma B.B. said that clairvoyance was the family talent. She also said somebody might have been trying to get me to leave town because they were afraid of what I might be able to see.

"Meow." Alistair rubbed his head against my elbow. I scratched his ears briefly as I read the page again. This might not produce any evidence Kenisha could use with her stubborn lieutenant. In fact, it might not produce anything at all. But maybe, just maybe, it would give us an idea where we should be looking.

"Okay," I told Alistair. "But we need to do this the right way, don't we? Like it says in the books and Dorothy's notes. We need—I need—to set up a circle, right? Like for the blessing ceremony? So I can . . ." I dug down to remember all the reading I'd been doing and the lectures I'd been getting. "Focus my intention."

Creating a space for focus was something I could just about wrap my head around. The times when I had my own dedicated studio, I always decked the space out with pictures, colors, motivational sayings, anything I found beautiful or interesting, really, to draw down the inspiration for my work.

Now I looked at the altar that stood in the center of the attic, and at the cat.

"I'm sure you'll let me know when I get it wrong."

"Merow," promised Alistair.

We'd finished the bottle of red wine Sean had brought, but I still had the bottle of white that had been Shannon's contribution. I brought it up and poured some into the silver cup. I didn't have any kosher salt, but I had plenty of the ordinary kind, and I refilled the silver dish. There were white candles in a box in the kitchen. I grabbed one for the candlestick and stuck a pack of matches in my pocket. I also grabbed the kitchen shears and went out into the garden. Alistair accompanied me.

I looked up at the moon. It was half-full, and waxing, I thought, which was supposed to be propitious.

"Lavender's green, dilly, dilly," I muttered as I snipped some branches. "Lavender's blue, dilly, dilly . . ." I snipped a branch from the apple tree, with a small green apple on the end. "What else? Rosemary? For remembrance, right?" I found the big bush and added some of that to the bundle. "Is that enough?"

Alistair was already headed for the house, so I assumed the answer was yes.

Back in the attic, I set the herbs on the altar and lit the candles. Then I laid down the wand, right where I'd first found it. I opened the book on the history and practice of magic to a page on invocations. Alistair claimed the armchair while I sat on the floor cross-legged, with my sketch pad balanced on my knees. It reminded me of when I was a kid and I'd sit alone in my bedroom, drawing unicorns and rock stars and whatever I saw out the window.

I cleared my throat and tried not to feel awkward.

"In . . . in reverence I call," I read from the book. "In hope I ask. Let that which is hidden be made clear. An' it harm none. So mote it be."

I held my pencil poised, and waited. I took deep, meditative breaths. I tried to keep my mind open to possibilities and to focus on attracting good and useful thoughts.

Nothing happened, except my back started to get tired.

Alistair made an exasperated huffing sound. He jumped off the chair, flopped down next to me and started purring, a long, slow wave of sound. I took another deep breath and stared at the candle flame. I smelled smoke and rosemary and lavender. My pencil rested against the paper. The wind rushed through the branches outside and a breeze curled through the attic, setting the candle flames flickering.

How did I even get here? What made me think any of this was my business, let alone my responsibility? I kept asking myself those same questions, and I kept not getting any answers. But it didn't seem to matter. Every step took me deeper into the mysteries and deeper into my involvement with the people of this town—Julia, Val, Kenisha, Frank, Sean, Laurie and Brad.

Especially Brad. I wondered if Frank had found him yet. I wondered if he was home with Laurie and Colin, where he belonged. I hoped he was. I saw him again in my mind's eye, angry, confused, hurting so deeply. My hand was moving, sketching, outlining eyes and the shape of a face. I distantly realized I was drawing Brad Thompson, whose exhaustion masked his anger. Who was he angry at? At Dorothy? Probably. At himself, certainly. He'd run into a brick wall. Bottomed out.

What am I doing here? he'd asked himself. *This isn't me. I have to find a way out. I know what I have to do.*

The feelings shifted, like the rustling of pages. All Brad's certainty was bleeding into fear. Random snippets of thought and feeling drifted through me.

No. No. I don't want this.

Well, one more, maybe. Just to take the edge off.

Acceptance rose. *Maybe this doesn't mean the end of everything.*

Can still do what's right and not hurt anybody anymore.

Feelings shifted, softened and blurred. Soppy, sentimental, relieved. There was help now. A friend to drive. A way to get home. Wife. Son. Not hurt them anymore. Even laughter. The world spinning.

Shift again. A fresh page. Awareness fading in and out as the world became a blur of cold and rushing sound and the wind around an aching head. Something's wrong. Stone hit hard and balance was gone and there was nothing but cold all around. Fear rose with the darkness.

Where am I? What am I doing? Where is . . . where is . . . gotta get out of here. Cold. Cold. This is wrong. Wrong.

Falling.

Gotta get up. Gotta get out. Cold, heavy and cold and . . . and . . . and . . .

"Gotta . . . gotta . . . get help."

The pencil slid from my fingers and I was falling too.

ॐ 35 ৬

✿ THE WORLD CAME back as a pinhole of light that slowly opened outward, like in an old black-and-white movie.

I blinked up at the ceiling.

There was a weight on my chest, and it purred.

Thoughts and sensations steadied, and I realized I was lying on my back on the four-poster in my new bedroom. Morning sunlight filled the room.

Morning? It had been nighttime a minute ago. I shoved myself upright. At least, I tried to. First I had to get Alistair to move his furry butt.

"Carefully, young woman!" said Julia. "You've been unconscious since last night."

"Last night!" I pushed myself back on the pillows. Details flooded back, of being in the attic and the candle flames and the smell of herbs. The pencil in my hand.

Brad. Memories and visions, not about Dorothy and her murder, but about Brad Thompson.

"My sketch pad," I gasped. "Did you find it . . ." I tried

to shove the blankets back, but a wave of dizziness sent the room spinning.

"Oh, no, you don't." Julia pushed me back onto the pillows. "What on earth possessed you to try such a powerful working on your own? You could have done serious damage to yourself."

"No!" I struggled to sit back up. Somebody was really going to have to get this room off spin cycle. This time I managed to get my feet on the floor. "Where's my phone? We've got to call Kenisha. Now!"

"All right, all right. Calm down." Julia put her hand under my chin like Mom had when I was a little girl and made me look up at her. "Talk to me, Anna. What's happened?"

"Brad Thompson's in trouble! I saw it! I drew it!"

"What!" cried a new voice. Valerie walked through the door carrying a tray with bowls and cups on it. I smelled hot cereal and toast.

"Begin at the beginning, Anna," ordered Julia.

"I was in the attic, looking through Dorothy's journals. Alistair found an article about automatic writing . . ."

"Alistair did?" Julia frowned.

I nodded. "I thought I'd try it, to harness my Vibe, like you said, and maybe find out something more about how Dorothy died. But I didn't get anything about Dorothy. It was all about Brad Thompson."

Val deposited the tray on my lap. "I saw your sketch pad in the attic. I'll go get it."

"My phone . . ." I started to get up again, but Julia pushed me back down.

"Stay," she said, like she might have been talking to Max and Leo. "Shannon!" she called over her shoulder. "Bring my purse up here!" She faced me again. "You have to eat and drink. You've drained your energies and if you don't replenish them, you're just going to faint again."

I wasn't hungry. At least, I didn't think I inhaled the fragrant steam from the bowl of steel-cut oatmeal, with lots of brown sugar and cinnamon. But I picked up the spoon and started wolfing it down like I hadn't eaten in a year.

Then I thought of something else. "How did you get in here? I locked the door."

"Alistair let us in," Julia said. "He came to get me; I suppose it was after you passed out. He told me you were in trouble."

"He *talked to* you?"

"Of course not." She sniffed at the very notion. "He told Maximilian and Leopold there was trouble, and they told me."

"Oh. Of course." I petted the cat slowly. Alistair suddenly got very busy washing his tail.

"But you did find out something?" Valerie edged past Julia and handed me my sketch pad.

"Sort of. I think. I was . . . I don't know . . . it was like I was remembering things. Bits and pieces, scraps, but all from Brad Thompson's point of view. It felt so real." Real enough that I was still kind of surprised I didn't have a hangover. Real enough that my hands and feet carried the memory of cold water. "Except I don't think I actually wrote anything." I flipped the pad open and all three women crowded around the bed. "I more sort of drew."

"You certainly did," murmured Julia.

They were not finished sketches. They were more doodles than anything, but they were pretty clear. There was a caricature of Brad Thompson with his head bowed into his hands. Then Brad on a stool clutching a highball glass. There was a hand on his shoulder. In the next scene, Brad was looking up and reaching out. Hands clasped his and helped pull him to his feet. Then, it was Brad in the car with a shadow in the passenger seat beside him.

Then it was the car, with water up to the window.

Then it was a man lying in the water, facedown.

My throat closed up again, sad and sick with what I remembered.

"Who was it?" Julia touched the passenger shadow.

I shook my head. "I don't know. A friend, I think. Somebody he knew, somebody he thought would help. He . . . he'd done something wrong. He was regretting it. He'd made up his mind to put things right. He was thinking, 'This isn't me.'" I stopped and swallowed. I tasted salt and iron. I tried to tell myself it was just the oatmeal, but I knew it wasn't. It was river water. "He wanted to go home to Laurie and his kids. He wanted to get back to being himself." I ran my fingers across the shadow in the passenger seat. "But somebody doesn't want him to." A fresh surge of panic hit. "We've got to find him! It might . . ." I couldn't make myself say the words.

"Already be too late," whispered Val.

Shannon pressed her hand against her mouth.

"We don't know that," said Julia firmly. "Anna, your Vibe has given you premonitions before, is that right?" I nodded. "Very well. It is possible this hasn't happened yet. We may still have time."

Julia grabbed her black purse from Shannon's hands and pulled out her phone. She hit a number and held it to her ear.

"Hello? Mr. Thompson, please . . . No, no message. Thank you." She hung up. "He's not at the office."

"I'm telling you!" I stabbed my spoon toward the sketch pad.

Julia had already called another number. She held up one finger, signaling me to wait while it rang. "Hello? Colin? Yes, it is. No, wait . . . I need to talk with your father . . ." I heard the young man on the other end yelling, and I heard the click.

Julia closed her eyes for a moment. "He says his father's fine and we need to get off his back." I suspected there were a few unprintable adjectives in there.

"Not believing that somehow," breathed Shannon.

"Me neither." Val sank onto the edge of the bed and gripped my hand.

Julia just dialed again. "Kenisha? Yes, it's Julia. We need

your help. We think something may have happened to Brad
Thompson. No, no evidence, but Anna's had a vision about
him . . . a car accident, perhaps by the river. I know . . . I
know. Do what you can. Thank you." Slowly, thoughtfully,
Julia tucked the phone back into her purse.

"Tell me we are not just going to sit here," I snapped.

"We're not. Valerie, Shannon, can you drive down to the
river? Check the beaches?" She flipped through the sketches.
"There's not much background, but maybe go out on the
islands? And there's that little stretch of sand by the coast
guard station. I'll need to get back to the bookstore. I can
set up a scrying there and see if I can find any additional
clues." She picked up her cane where she'd leaned it against
the nightstand. "Max. Leo." Slowly, she bent down to riffle
her dachshunds' ears. "I need you on the scent."

The dogs went absolutely still, ears and tails alert and
quivering. Max barked once and the pair of them whisked
away, noses down to the floorboards.

Julia straightened up and turned to me, absolutely serious.
"You stay here and gather your strength, Anna," she said.
"We will call the rest of the coven, and between us, we will
find him."

She meant it, and it was all for my own good. I sank back
onto the pillows.

"Okay," I said. "I don't think I could get up anyway."

"We need to check on where Elizabeth Maitland was last
night too," murmured Valerie. "And what she was doing."

"We have no reason to believe Elizabeth had anything
to do with this."

I hadn't told them about my teatime visit yet, I remembered. Or that I knew about Elizabeth's familiar.

"We have every reason," Val was saying to Julia. "Considering the amount of trouble she's made for Dorothy and
you. Why can't you even consider that she might be up to
her perfectly plucked eyebrows in this?"

"Now is not the time," I snapped. "We've got to find Brad!"

"We will, Anna. I promise," said Valerie, but she didn't stop glowering at Julia.

The three of them gathered their things. Julia extracted fresh promises from me to stay put. Alistair stayed sitting upright on the pillow beside me. Shannon brought my purse up from downstairs so I could have my phone. She also brought the wand down from upstairs. I tucked it under Alistair's pillow.

Then I lay there staring at the *Surrender Dorothy* photo on the dresser and thinking about that photo, that movie, and how Dorothy Hawthorne and Brad Thompson had been spending time together. All that time, I listened to the women's footsteps and voices as they moved down the hall and down the stairs. I thought about copies and originals and questions nobody had remembered to ask yet.

I thought about how Frank had said Brad would drink when he had trouble. I thought about how I'd started Frank looking for Brad. And how in my vision, Vibe, whatever it was, Brad had been so very drunkenly glad to see a good friend.

Downstairs, the front door creaked as it opened and thumped softly as it closed.

Alistair meowed and sprang to the windowsill. "Merow," he said again, and I understood him perfectly. He meant, *All clear.*

I kicked back the covers and scrambled to my feet. "Come on, big guy. We're getting out of here."

Don't tell me you're surprised.

❧ 36 ❦

🐾 ACCORDING TO THE GPS, I had to drive to the offices of Maitland and Associates, LLC.

I unearthed my straight black skirt, pink blouse and conservative pumps. I dressed and brushed my hair in between gulps of oatmeal and bites of toast. Maybe I wasn't ready to stay in bed, but I didn't want to pass out again either.

I had no idea whether I'd find Brad at work. And if he was there, I had no idea whether he'd talk to me. I didn't really care. I just wanted to know he was safe. Okay, that wasn't the only thing, but it was the most important thing. Julia, Val and the rest of the coven were out combing the river and beaches. This was the base left for me to cover. Yes, Julia had called, and yes, she'd been told he wasn't in. But that was before. He might be there now. There were lots of reasons he might be running late. Construction season was under way, and the traffic was heavy on the highways. Also, he had been out drinking. Maybe the reason Colin was so upset when Julia called was that his dad was still in bed with a hangover and Colin was trying to protect him but was angry about needing to.

What I saw, what I drew; it didn't have to be about last night. It didn't have to have happened yet. Maybe, maybe we could prevent it. And if we couldn't, it didn't mean that the friend, the silhouette I'd drawn, was Frank. It could have been anyone. Right?

The offices for Maitland and Associates turned out to be in a brand-new office building, one that was as much glass as it was brick. Solar panels glinted on the slanting roof. The atrium was all big windows and terra-cotta tile with metallic abstract art pieces hanging on the walls and planters filled with ficus and hosta and peace lilies arranged in the corners. I found Maitland and Associates on the building directory and rode the escalator up to the second floor. My palms were sweating, despite the air-conditioning. Part of this was because I was still feeling the aftereffects of the visions I'd called down. Part of it was because I was absolutely sure I was getting close to the heart of the mystery.

Last night, I'd asked myself why Brad was interested in copies and not the originals. As I lay there in bed, looking at that movie photo, I'd come up with two answers to that question:

1) The originals had been destroyed.

2) Brad already knew where they were.

If the real answer was choice two, I was hoping I'd be able to find out at this office, whether Brad was there to tell me about it or not.

I walked into the bland gold-and-brown reception area. Its furniture was modern and generic. The atrium's abstract art had been replaced by landscape photographs—all fields and wooded hills, presumably waiting for houses and shopping malls.

"Can I help you?" asked the perky brunette receptionist.

"I'm here to see Brad Thompson," I said in my best professional tones.

Her perfectly made-up face fell. "I'm sorry, but Mr. Thompson isn't in yet this morning. Did you have an appointment?"

Time for Plan B. And yes, I had one. It started with a smile.

"No, no appointment," I told her, and hoped I sounded casual. "I was just coming in to pick up some papers. He hasn't left anything?"

The receptionist pulled some manila folders from her in-basket and checked the labels. "What name did you say?"

"Gale," I answered. "Dorothy Gale."

Because "aka" stands for "also known as." I checked. And while I was at it, I ran a search on Dorothy Gale and found out that "Gale" was the last name of the very famous Dorothy in *The Wizard of Oz*.

The receptionist set the folders down. I tensed and waited to find out if I'd jumped to the absolutely wrong conclusion.

"I haven't got anything here," she said. "Maybe he left it in his office. If you wait here a moment, I'll go see."

"Thank you."

The receptionist disappeared into the side office, and I gripped my purse strap, struggling to stay calm. This was ridiculous. There was no way Brad had left important documents here. I'd told myself that the best place to hide important papers would be with a whole bunch of other papers, but nobody would really do that, would they? I was wasting time. I should be out helping to find Brad. Or at least Frank. I didn't know where he was either, and that might also be extremely important for all kinds of reasons.

That was when a door did open and Ellis Maitland walked out. He was in the act of straightening his blue silk tie.

"Miss Britton." He smiled, but his eyes slid across me, looking over my shoulder toward the door, like he thought there might be somebody else behind me. "Good morning! To what do we owe the pleasure?"

I was ready for this. I hadn't expected to walk into Ellis Maitland's office during business hours and not see the man himself.

"Good morning, Mr. Maitland."

"Ellis," he corrected me.

"Ellis. I was just stopping by to talk with Brad, but I understand he's not in yet."

Ellis hesitated, just a little. His professional smile flickered. "No, I'm afraid he's not. Is there something I can help you with?"

"Maybe. I was hoping to talk about some commercial space."

I had thought his eyes would light up, but it was exactly the opposite. What I got from Ellis Maitland was a very suspicious frown. "Really? I was under the impression you didn't plan on staying in Portsmouth that long."

"Well, I've been thinking it over and I've decided it's time for me to move past freelance work. A woman's got to think about her future."

This was when the receptionist walked back out of Brad's office with a thick manila folder in her hands. "Here you are, Miss Gale . . ." She saw the boss and stopped.

Ellis Maitland had inherited a whole lot of his mother's self-control, because he barely blinked. "What have you got there for . . . Miss Gale?" he asked.

"Some papers Brad left for her," answered the receptionist, her eyes darting from Ellis to me and back again. "Since he wasn't in yet . . ."

"Of course. Why don't you give me those, and Miss *Gale* and I can go over them together?"

She handed him the file and smiled. And Ellis smiled and gestured toward his office. I smiled and walked through the door. What else was I going to do?

Ellis closed his office door behind me, and I heard the

snickt as the lock turned. He circled me to stand behind his desk. I felt his gaze like a cold weight the entire way. I pressed my hand against my purse, trying to feel the wand I'd tucked inside, but my hands had gone cold and I couldn't feel anything at all.

Ellis rolled his eyes. "Oh, come on, Miss Britton. I'm not going to bite. Just . . . sit down. Please." He gestured to the squared-off chairs as he took his own seat in the padded leather chair behind the desk. He laid the file on the desk in front of him. "Now, what's this visit really about?"

Well? I asked my inner Nancy Drew desperately. She, of course, chose this moment to clam up. *Think,* I ordered myself. *Think about this man in front of you, about what you know about him and . . .*

I had it.

"It really is about finding commercial space." I folded my hands over my purse. "It's also about Frank Hawthorne."

"Frank? What about Frank? I thought from the way you were talking the other day, you two were . . . close."

"No. Nothing like that. I think he really just rented me the house to make you angry, and because he was out of options."

Ellis nodded. "That could be, but it doesn't explain why you're here now."

Now was the time for a small, but sharp, burst of honesty.

"You know some people think Dorothy Hawthorne was murdered?"

Ellis didn't even flinch. "Some people have too much free time."

"My grandmother is one of them." This was true. Now, Grandma B.B. only thought this because I'd told her, but we didn't need to go into that.

"I thought your grandmother hadn't been in town for years."

"It turns out she and Dorothy were still in touch. Grandma B.B. was worried about her."

Ellis narrowed his sharp eyes at me. He tapped his fingers against the folder, considering. Considering what? What did he see? I pressed my hand against the purse, but there was no sensation of magic. Somebody didn't believe hard enough, and it was probably me.

"I don't want to get Brad in trouble," I said. "But he knows something about Dorothy and Frank. He tried to tell me about it the other day. I thought maybe it involved the house, and he might have something here at the office . . ." I gestured toward the folder.

Ellis didn't like this either, but he did believe it; at least, he seemed to. "And you didn't consider coming to me directly?"

"I probably should have, but there's the possibility that, well, murder has happened."

"Suddenly everybody has to start acting like we're in an episode of *Columbo*. I understand." He sighed. "All right. Let's see what we've got here."

The Dorothy Gale file was a thick one, full of documents of various colors and sizes. I watched him flipping through pages of what I assumed were contracts of some sort. There was a lease, and a mortgage, and a purchase agreement, but that was all I could see. I'm pretty good at reading upside down, but not fine print legalese.

As he leafed through the contents of that folder, Ellis Maitland's frown deepened. The office was absolutely silent except for the rustling of the pages and a sense of concentration so thick I thought one of us might suffocate. I knew I was having a tough time breathing. I glanced toward the door. I glanced at the clock. When was the phone going to ring? When was somebody going to call and say they'd found Brad and he was okay? Heck, at this point, I'd even be glad to see Alistair appear, although he'd be awfully tough to explain. I didn't care. I just wanted to know.

At last, Ellis closed the folder and slid it into the center drawer of his desk. Then he got up and walked over to the window. He stared out across the parking lot for a very long time.

"These . . . people who think Dorothy was murdered," he whispered. "Is one of them Kenisha Freeman?"

"I can't say for sure," I said. Noncommittal was rapidly becoming my middle name. "Is . . . What have you found?"

He turned around, and one look at his face told me he'd made a decision. "Can I trust you, Miss Britton?"

There aren't a lot of ways to reply to that question when you're being asked it by a virtual stranger. But there was only one answer that would get me the answers I needed. "Yes."

"The papers in here, they're—well, I'll spare you the technical details—but they're all real estate documents. I expect you noticed that." He gave me a brief, and not very warm, smile. "They are also all signed by my mother."

My thoughts, which had been racing through a thousand different possibilities, skidded to a dead halt. And those possibilities? They evaporated into a big cloud of smoke. Poof.

"I don't understand," I told him. "Your mother's a wealthy woman. Your family is supposed to have some serious real estate investments of its own. What's wrong with that?"

"I handle the family investments, Miss Britton," Ellis snapped. "These"—he gestured toward the desk—"these purchases, and . . . other things . . . they haven't gone through this office, or any office I know about. So, I have to ask, What's my mother been doing? And why does Brad Thompson have the documents?"

"Brad was asking me if I'd found some copies at Dorothy's house . . ."

"What's in that folder are originals. Brad thought Dorothy had copies of something? Copies of what?"

"That he didn't say."

"And you haven't found anything?"

"Not yet."

"And you haven't heard anything about this from Frank?"

My skin started to prickle, and it wasn't just from the

air-conditioning. Something was wrong. I felt it in my hands and the back of my neck.

"Those documents," I said slowly. "Could Brad have gotten them, I don't know, under the table somehow?"

Ellis stared hard at me. The bluff and hearty real estate agent was entirely gone. This was an executive manager in front of me now, and he looked like he wanted more than anything to fire me out of his particular shark tank.

"What are you talking about?"

"I mean, if these documents came to light, could they be . . . damaging?"

"You want to know if they're fraudulent somehow," said Ellis slowly. Since that was in fact one of the things I wanted to know, I nodded. "You're suggesting my mother may have been committing fraud and that Brad was going to . . . what? Blackmail her?"

"It might be blackmail," I said. "Or maybe he was just going to give the papers to Frank so he could publish the story."

I'm sorry, Brad. I'm sorry, Dorothy. I didn't want to believe it. But after seeing the way Dorothy had so carefully written the people who disagreed with her out of her life, I had to consider the possibility.

No, I didn't forget that Elizabeth Maitland had lied about how she got that letter she showed me. There was another possible explanation for that.

Ellis looked at his desk again, like he was seeing the folder through the dark wood. Slowly, a grim, cold smile spread across his handsome, trustworthy face. I shivered.

"It is possible," he whispered. "Very, very possible." He lifted his eyes to mine. "I need to call my mother," he said. "Find out what she'll tell me about . . . this." He gestured to the drawer and the folder. "I don't expect it'll be much."

"Brad . . ."

He shook his head. "If he tried to tangle with my mother, then I'm very sorry for him. She doesn't like to be crossed, as I expect you noticed. It may be . . ." He paused and then shook his head. "Anyway. I need to call her. You'll excuse me."

"Of course," I said, because I couldn't think of anything else to say, and I got to my feet and turned toward the door.

"Miss Britton?" said Ellis to my back. "I'd appreciate it if you kept quiet about this. At least until we've talked with Brad. I want to give him a chance to explain."

I nodded and I smiled and I got out of there as fast as my little black pumps and pencil skirt would allow.

Back in the Jeep, I sat for a long moment, just trying to fit all the pieces together.

Elizabeth knew Dorothy was capable of carrying a grudge. She showed me a letter that suggested blackmail. She said she'd gotten it from Ellis. Ellis did not seem to know anything about it. There was another place Elizabeth could have gotten a letter like that from.

Julia Parris. Julia was ready to defend Elizabeth to the other members of the coven. She had not wanted to take sides in the old feud. What if she had found out Dorothy had finally carried her old grudges too far? She might have gotten hold of the letter, by fair means or foul.

Or magic. After all, Grandma had called magic "the ways to get and guard."

I could see Julia taking that letter up to Elizabeth in her lovely sitting room. I could understand neither one of them wanting to tell me the truth about it, because I had been brought here by Dorothy, and Julia was torn in her loyalties, and Elizabeth was wounded by years of distrust.

It all fit, except for one thing. I could not envision any circumstances under which Julia Parris would help cover up a fraud. Especially when that fraud was tied so tightly to murder.

Something here was still seriously out of whack.

I dug my phone out of my purse and hit Valerie's number. I figured Val would spend less time chewing me out for leaving the house than Julia.

"Hello?" Val answered her phone. "Anna, is that you?"

"I know what Dorothy was doing," I said, to forestall that chewing out I mentioned. "Well, I don't *know* know, but I kind of know."

"And you've kind of stopped speaking English," said Val.

"Dorothy was working with Brad Thompson to get hold of a bunch of suspicious real estate documents. Those were the copies he was looking for. Now . . ."

"Anna," Val cut me off, but softly. "Brad Thompson's dead."

❧ 37 ❧

♣ "HE WAS FOUND in the river. Beside his car."

Kenisha was reading from her notebook. The coveners and I all huddled together in the front parlor. We'd pulled in every chair from the dining room so there'd be enough seats. Martine was there too. I'd called to tell her about Brad because when you've just found out about a death like this, you kind of desperately need to talk with your best friend. She'd insisted on coming over, especially when she heard the coven would be here too. I mentioned her usually needing to supervise lunch service right about now. Her answer was unprintable.

The coffeepot was out and everyone had a cup, but no one was drinking. Thanks to Roger and Martine, we had plates of sandwiches and pastries, but no one was eating, either. We all just sat and listened to Kenisha read her notes.

"According to the medical examiner, the probable cause of death was suffocation resulting from aspiration of water or other fluid." Kenisha carefully turned over the page. "Brad was probably incapacitated, maybe even passed out, when the car went into the river. From the looks of things, he tried to climb out, slipped on the rocks and drowned."

Didi murmured something and Shannon closed her eyes as if in prayer. I sat on the window seat with Martine beside me. Alistair curled up on my lap, and I could tell he listened to every word as attentively as the rest of us.

"You said he was incapacitated?" asked Val. She was on the window seat too, running her hand across her belly, but I couldn't tell if she was trying to soothe the baby inside or herself. Probably both.

Kenisha closed her book and tucked it away. "Alcohol was definitely a contributing factor." I noticed how fully she'd retreated into formal police language. "We found the bottles in the backseat. We think he'd been sitting on the beach, drinking."

Just one more. Just to take the edge off. Memories shifted and sloshed through my thoughts and I shuddered. Martine saw and laid her hand on mine.

"Has anyone been to see Laurie?" I asked. "She must be devastated."

"I have," said Julia. Julia sat in the armchair by the fireplace. Max snuggled up beside her and Leo was sitting on the hearth. "Or at least, I tried to. Colin didn't want to let me in." Max growled and she patted his head.

"No surprise," I murmured. Given the way he felt about Dorothy, Colin wouldn't deal well with her old coven showing up after his father's death.

"No, I suppose not." Julia sighed. "I decided not to press the issue. I can say Laurie is in a very bad way. Her sister's arriving from Philadelphia tomorrow, though, and I think there's other family coming as well."

"Roger's taking over some food this afternoon," said Val. "Maybe he can talk to her."

"Why's Colin so angry?" I asked. In the back of my head, I was hearing Elizabeth's story about blackmail and Brad

Thompson and Dorothy Hawthorne. "What happened between the Thompsons and Dorothy and . . . you?"

"You mean why didn't we help them?" snapped Julia.
"Why have the women who declare themselves to be the
guardians of Portsmouth failed this particular family?"

"That's not what she meant, Julia, and you know it," said
Kenisha.

Julia rubbed her eyes. Leo whined and wagged and
pawed at her skirt. "Yes, I do know. I'm sorry, Anna. I
thought we had been able to help. We did try."

"We cast several protections and blessings for the family," murmured Val to her teacup. "Wishes for prosperity."

"And there were a couple times when maybe I should
have written up that kid, or Brad, and kind of didn't," Kenisha added grimly. "Maybe I should have. Maybe if he'd felt
the consequences sooner . . ."

"It's not your fault," said Didi. "Everybody did what they
could. I had Colin helping me with some of the houses on
weekends. We were all keeping an eye out for ways to get
Laurie some kind of part-time income, but it was difficult,
with the kids and Brad . . ." She smiled at me. "I heard about
the possibility of her selling some of her art."

I'd almost forgotten about that. I'd tried to help too, and
in the end, it hadn't been enough.

At least when Mom died, we had some time. It was hard,
it was terrible, but we were more or less ready for it. We'd been
able to say good-bye, and when she was gone, we had one
another and we were all adults. But Colin wasn't much more
than a kid, with a younger sister and a devastated mother.

"I can go over there today," said Martine. "Maybe get an
idea what Laurie needs. Colin might have a serious mad on
at Dorothy's . . . friends, but I don't think he's going to turn
away his boss."

"Boss?" I turned to her. "Colin works for you?"

"Just started in May. You didn't know?"

I shook my head. I'd seen him in the signature white

cook's jacket, but it hadn't occurred to me that he might be working at the Pale Ale. Maybe I should give up this Nancy Drew life. I clearly was not up to seeing the big picture.

"Thank you, Martine," Julia was saying. "I think that would be very helpful."

Martine nodded.

"But *why* is Colin so angry at you?" I asked again. "And Dorothy?"

The women glanced back and forth at one another. I shifted my weight. I didn't want to ask this question, but I couldn't just let it go.

It was no surprise that they all let Julia answer. "We've never been able to find out. I asked Dorothy, but she wouldn't say. We argued over it, but she just kept saying it was better if the coven stayed out of this for the moment."

There it was again, Dorothy keeping her secrets from her friends. Like she had something serious to hide. Or like she'd found out she couldn't trust them.

Which is it? I demanded angrily, silently. *Which is it?*

All at once, a whole series of thoughts tumbled together into my brain, and the pattern they made was not pretty.

I found myself on my feet without realizing I'd moved. "I'm sorry. I need . . . I need you to go." I hurried into the foyer and grabbed my purse off the table there. I also didn't look anybody in the eye. "I've got some calls coming in. I'm sorry," I said again.

The women all glanced uneasily at one another. One of the dachshunds yipped at Alistair, and Alistair meowed back noncommittally. Seems that not even the dogs believed me, but everybody got up from their chairs anyway, and they all filed out the door.

All except Martine. She closed the door firmly behind Julia's back and turned to face me.

"Okay, Britton," she said as she folded her arms. "What's going on?"

I thought about telling her that I couldn't say, or I didn't know. But the set of her jaw told me that wasn't going to work.

I sighed and retreated as far as I could, which was back to the parlor and the window seat.

"You were saying?" Martine prompted from the threshold.

Alistair jumped into my lap, purring and pressing close. I petted his back, grateful for the warmth. He blinked up at me, and I knew what he was saying. I still had doubts about Julia's motivations, and Frank's. Heck, I even had them about Val. But Martine? Not a one. Ever.

"I saw Elizabeth Maitland the other day."

"You got in to see the queen bee?" Martine sounded impressed. "Well. *Somebody's* the special girl."

One corner of my mouth twitched, trying to smile. "She sent a written invitation and everything. She told me . . . well, she told me a whole bunch of things. One was that Dorothy Hawthorne was a blackmailer, and that one of her victims was Brad Thompson."

Martine drew her chin back. I saw her want to ask if I was sure, but she didn't. She just let out a long, slow breath.

"It's not the sort of thing I could bring up with all of . . . them." I waved my hand over my shoulder.

"The coven," said Martine. "Go ahead and say it, Anna. It's okay."

"You know, I've got to get over being surprised that nobody's surprised," I muttered. "Did you know the stuff they do actually . . . works?"

"I didn't, but I believe it." I'm not sure how much surprise showed on my face just then, but it was enough to make Martine roll her eyes. "Now, why wouldn't I believe in magic, Anna? I've known about you and your Vibe for years. Not to mention the fact that my mother's parents are from Haiti. I grew up with magic in the air." She dropped onto the other end of the window seat. "Have you gotten any kind of bead on what these ladies really think about Dorothy?"

"You mean has anybody admitted their collective BFF was a blackmailer?"

Now I was the one getting angry. Even if Dorothy didn't entirely live up to the good-witch image, it didn't follow that her friends knew about it. I so very much wanted to like these women, even Julia. Maybe especially Julia. She might be stiff and imperious, but she was a good person. But Julia might be lying about more than Elizabeth's familiar.

On the other hand, Elizabeth might be lying about much more than where that blackmail letter came from.

"Talk to me, Anna," said Martine. "You know you can tell me anything."

I did know that. I had always known that. I might be making a whole set of new friends, but Martine had known me since we were both in grade school. She was the one who'd been there for every little triumph and every lousy breakup. If there was one person in my life outside my family I trusted, it was Martine.

So, I took a deep breath, and I started talking. I told her everything, from confronting Brad when we both broke in to the house, to how I found out Dorothy really was murdered. I told her about the magazine photo and the clue on the back. I told her about visiting Elizabeth and visiting Laurie, and my scene with Brad in Raja Rani.

I told her about how Frank had gone looking for Brad and how I'd tried my little trick with the automatic writing to do the same, and I saw what happened to Brad. Some of it, anyway.

Martine put her hand on my shoulder but said nothing.

"So, while everybody else was looking for Brad this morning, I went to see Ellis Maitland," I said. "I was hoping Brad would be there, but he wasn't. I did find a file under the name Dorothy Gale, but Ellis caught me before I could read it."

"How'd he take it?"

"Surprisingly well." I frowned. "He's been saying all

along that he wants to help Frank. Maybe he means it. Anyway, Ellis said the file was full of real estate documents, and that they were all signed by Elizabeth."

"I don't get it," said Martine.

Alistair shifted in my lap. I rubbed him behind the ears, but he wasn't purring anymore. "I don't either, at least not entirely. But maybe Dorothy found out Elizabeth was involved in some shady real estate deals and went to Brad to get confirmation. Either that, or Brad found out and went to Dorothy for advice on what to do."

"Then Dorothy confronts Elizabeth and Elizabeth kills her?"

I nodded. "Val thought it was Elizabeth from the get-go. You see, nobody could find Alistair the night Dorothy died. They think . . . there might have been a spell cast to keep him away from her, so he couldn't go for help."

Alistair hid his face under his tail. Martine was silent, but only for a moment.

"What do you think?"

"I think I don't know," I answered. "Martine, tell me not to do this. Tell me to quit trying to play Nancy Drew and go back to Boston and move back in with Bob and Ginger."

She snorted. "I am not your pastor, and your brother's already looking after your dad." She paused. "Maybe I can help."

"You sure you want to? I mean, this road had been pretty crazy so far."

"I liked Dorothy, and I like the Thompsons. Besides, Kenisha Freeman's been pretty sure something was wrong for a long time now, and Brad's death doesn't make it better."

"She has? How do you know?"

She looked down her nose at me. "It's a small town, Anna. Smaller for some of us. Anyhow, she has, but she hasn't got anything to take to the higher-ups. And then there's this lieutenant who's a real hard . . ."

"Yeah, I've heard." I rubbed Alistair's ears. My head was

spinning, and for once, the coffee and the cat weren't helping clear anything up.

"This whole mess revolves around five people," I said slowly. "Dorothy, Frank, and Brad. Ellis and Elizabeth."

"And now two of them are dead."

"Yeah." I shivered. "But that's not the question. The question is, Which of them were working together? Was Dorothy working with Brad? Or was Brad working with Elizabeth, and Dorothy found out about it?"

"Or was Brad working with Ellis, and Dorothy found out and ratted them out to Elizabeth?"

"Yeah, there's that possibility too."

"Or Ellis found out Dorothy and Brad were involved in Elizabeth's fraud, and killed them to keep them quiet."

"I don't like that idea," I whispered.

"Yeah, I can see that," answered Martine with a lot more calm than most people would. "Because that would make you a target now too."

"Yeah." I gathered Alistair even closer. He made no protest. "Me and . . . oh, crud."

"What?"

I jumped to my feet, and Alistair jumped to the floor with an annoyed rumble. "The coven's been so focused on Brad and his family, I bet nobody's checked in on Frank Hawthorne."

❧ 38 ❧

🐾 I SENT MARTINE back to the Pale Ale, reminding her she had actual work to do. She didn't want to go, but I held firm. The truth was, I didn't want her to see what I really planned to do next.

Frank, it turned out, lived in an apartment in a large Italianate mansion that had been subdivided sometime during the Great Depression. It was one of those places that's so old the stairs have been creaking and grumbling to one another for longer than anyone in town's been alive.

I carried an aluminum pan covered with plastic wrap and foil up three flights. I didn't pick up any Vibes, thankfully. Unfortunately, the building completely lacked air-conditioning, and I was perspiring by the time I made it to the top landing. I didn't want to imagine what it must be like up here in August.

I balanced the baking pan against my hip and knocked on Frank's door. There were thumping footsteps and creaking floorboards and the door opened a few seconds later.

"Oh. Hi." Frank looked like he hadn't slept in a week.

His hair was tousled and his face was drawn tight across the bones.

"Hi," I said. "Can I come in?"

"Yeah, sure."

It was cooler in here, because the kitchen windows were all opened wide. A gigantic chestnut spread its branches right outside, making the whole place feel like a tree house. A black cat with bright gold eyes sat on the windowsill and watched as I followed Frank into the living room.

"So, this is it." He spread his hands. "The inner sanctum."

Frank might have been a longtime bachelor, but his place was in no way the stereotypical man cave built around a massive flat-screen TV. In fact, it took me a while to see the TV stuffed back in its corner. The most prominent feature of Frank Hawthorne's apartment was books. There were books on shelves and books on top of shelves and books on tables. Books waited in stacks on the desk and on the floor. Paperbacks, hardbacks, new, used, all mixed in with piles of newspapers and magazines. The wall behind the desk was a mosaic of corkboards with papers, maps and photos pinned to every inch.

"It's nice," I told him. "It looks like you." Which it did. It was the home of someone who preferred comfort over appearance, who was insatiably curious and a little offbeat.

The cat jumped off the sill and came to curl around Frank's ankles. The animal moved so easily, it took me a minute to realize it was missing a back leg.

"And this"—Frank stooped down and picked the cat up—"is Colonel Nick Kitty."

"Great name." I held my hand out. Kitty sniffed and licked my fingers enthusiastically.

"It's after Colonel Nick Fury. You know, from the Avengers?"

I nodded. I had a friend who worked on the comic books for Marvel. Plus, the guy who played Thor in the movies? Totally swoon-worthy. "Is he a rescue?"

"Kind of. The day after I moved in here, I opened the window to get some air, and he jumped in and didn't leave."

Colonel Kitty finished licking my fingers and moved to my thumb. Frank raised his eyebrows.

"Tuna," I told him and held out the aluminum foil pan. "I made you a casserole." Tuna noodle casserole, specifically, made with cream of mushroom soup and Velveeta. I'd just have to hope Martine never found out. I'd never hear the end of it.

"Thank you." Frank put down the cat and took the pan. "I guess you heard about Brad?"

"Yeah," I said. "I wanted to see how you were doing. I stopped by the paper, but they said you went home early."

"Not setting the best example there." Frank stashed the pan in the battered Frigidaire. Colonel Kitty watched wistfully.

"Do you want to sit down?" Frank started clearing books off a worn leather armchair. "Can I get you anything?"

"I'm good, thanks." I sat and put my purse on the nearest pile of books. "I'm really sorry about Brad."

Frank dropped onto a sofa about the same vintage as my chair. His hands dangled between his knees. "I looked for him everywhere I could think of. I even tried that stupid tiki bar. I asked Sean and his dad, but they hadn't seen him. I thought . . . I thought maybe he'd just gone on a long drive someplace. And I went home." He ran both hands through his hair. "I should have kept looking. I should have . . . done *something*."

"Like what?"

"I don't know." Colonel Kitty loped over to his side and, with only a little bit more strain than for the average cat, jumped up onto the sofa's seat and then onto the back. The cat hunkered down and started nuzzling Frank's neck. This was clearly something they were both used to, because Frank just smiled a little and rubbed Kitty's ears. "I mean, I *knew* things were bad. If I'd started looking earlier, if I hadn't been so afraid of what I'd find . . ."

"You were trying to protect your aunt and her memory."

"And myself," he said. "Don't forget myself." He folded his arms, which meant he wasn't scratching the cat's ears anymore. Colonel Kitty mewed in protest. "Some crusading journalist I make. What if . . ."

"What if what?"

"What if the reason I haven't tried hard enough to find out what was really happening to Aunt Dot is because I don't want to find out I was the one responsible for her death."

His words jolted me hard. "What do you mean?"

"I'd been so focused on getting the newspaper up and running, I didn't pay attention to what was going on with Aunt Dot."

He was obsessed, Laurie Thompson had said. *He didn't care.* But Laurie was angry, and from the outside, it could be tough to tell the difference between passion and obsession.

"I was so used to her being able to take care of . . . well, of anything. If I look into this stuff, into the house and Brad and the Maitlands . . . what if I find out there was something I could have done, or should have done, to save her life, and Brad's?"

"Then you need to know that."

"Why?" he asked me, and Colonel Kitty, and the world in general.

"Because no matter what you find out, not knowing is worse. You'll never be able to stop imagining the possibilities, and it'll eat you alive."

His jaw tightened, and for a minute I thought he was going to argue. Colonel Kitty licked his cheek. Then, in a display of that special feline indifference, he turned around and started vigorously cleaning his hindquarters.

I watched for a minute. "Frank?" I said.

"Yeah?" He blinked heavily.

"Um, I've got some news for you."

"What?"

"Colonel Nick Kitty is a girl."

Frank stared at me. Then he stared at the cat. Colonel Kitty lowered her one back leg and turned, and Frank stared again.

"Awww, Nick," he groaned. "You been holdin' out on me!"

"Maybe she was afraid you wouldn't respect her lifestyle choice."

"I'm a bleeding-heart journalist. I am all about diversity!"

I laughed and he laughed and Colonel Kitty got to her feet and stalked away to the windowsill with great dignity, which just got us laughing again.

"Thanks," said Frank when we finally quieted down. "I needed that."

"Thank the cats," I said. "Alistair's been a real help since this whole thing got started."

I expected him to make some snarky comment, but he didn't. "Well, maybe I can start living up to the family standard. I started looking into a few things since we talked." He waved one hand toward the map of Portsmouth taped to the wall. I went over to get a closer look. "Maitland and Associates has been on a buying spree."

"Maitland and Associates has?" The map was decorated with red and blue pushpins as well as lines of yellow highlighter. "The company itself? Are you sure? Have you got copies of the documents?"

"Yes, I'm sure, and of course I do," Frank said as he came to stand beside me. "I was trying to find some kind of pattern in the purchases, or any significant difference between the properties Brad handled and the ones Ellis handled himself, and . . ."

"Can I see them?"

Frank frowned, but he shrugged and rifled through one of the stacks of folders on the coffee table. Colonel Kitty strolled over to sniff my Keds in case I'd accidentally dropped any bits of tuna. I perched on the sofa arm and picked her up. Alistair was having a bad effect on me. I was finding it hard to think straight without a cat to hold on to.

Eventually, Frank came up with a thick sheaf of legal-sized paper. I had to set the cat down so I could flip through it. I also may have uttered a few of my brothers' more colorful exclamations.

"Something wrong?" inquired Frank.

"I can't tell if they're the same ones!"

"Same ones as what?"

"I went to Brad's office before . . . before I'd found out he was dead. I thought with all his talk about Dorothy having copies of something important, there might be some clue there, or maybe even the originals of whatever the heck had gone missing."

"And?"

"I was right. There was a whole file there, with Dorothy's name on it, or at least her alias."

"Aunt Dot had an alias?"

"Or maybe Brad assigned it to her. I don't know. It was Dorothy Gale."

"Why am I not surprised? What happened then?"

"I didn't get out fast enough," I admitted. "I ran into Ellis Maitland instead. Anyway, he looked over the documents and said they were for a whole set of properties he knew nothing about. He also said the papers had all been signed by his mother."

Frank stared at the map and ran his hand through his hair. "Did you actually see the signatures? Can you remember any addresses?"

I shook my head. "He put the file away before I could see anything at all."

"Okay. Okay. We need to be logical about this. We cannot be talking about the same set of properties. Ellis isn't stupid. If he was committing fraud, he wouldn't be altering documents that had already been filed. It'd be too easy to check."

"Darn. I was hoping it would be something obvious."

"Maybe it is. Maybe Brad was working with Elizabeth Maitland to commit real estate fraud."

Brad and Elizabeth in this business together? That wasn't a combination I'd considered. I'd been too fixed on Brad and Dorothy.

"They could be buying properties up cheap and then flipping them, or something like that. Or using shell companies or straw-man buyers to hide the profits from the IRS."

"I thought the Maitlands were rich. Why would they need to do something like this?"

Frank made a face. "I've never met a rich person who didn't want to be richer. It also means Elizabeth could afford to bribe Brad to help her."

Brad, who had been out of work for so long, and who had a house and a car and two kids who would eventually need college tuition. He must have been going out of his mind trying to figure out how he was going afford it all. I could tell Frank was thinking something similar.

There was another possibility. I bit my lip. If Brad was taking bribes from Elizabeth to help commit fraud, he could also have been taking them from Dorothy, who might have wanted to expose Elizabeth.

I was still figuring out how to say this to Frank when a hard knocking sounded through the door. We both jumped. Colonel Kitty meowed loudly and disappeared behind the couch.

"'Scuse me a sec," said Frank as he went to open the door.

I saw Kenisha first. She was in uniform, radio clipped to her shoulder and sidearm clipped to her belt and everything. I swallowed. This was an official visit and she wasn't alone. A short, white, beefy man in a pale blue sports coat stepped into the apartment and held out his hand.

"Hello, Frank."

"Hi, Pete." Frank shook the man's hand. He looked disappointed, but in no way surprised. "Hello, Officer Freeman. I thought you guys might be coming around."

Pete shrugged. "It's the job."

"Hi, Kenisha," I said.

"Hi, Anna." She nodded to me, but her expression remained closed. This was going to be strictly business.

"I guess you must be Anna Britton." Pete shook my hand too. "Detective Pete Simmons."

So, not the famous lieutenant, then, which was something. I couldn't tell, though, if Detective Simmons was any improvement. Kenisha's face was as set and still as stone.

"Nice to meet you."

Pete Simmons was a rumpled fireplug of a man with broad hands and a round, red face. His sandy hair had started to thin. His blue sports jacket strained around the shoulders and his checked shirt had seen better days.

"Well, I guess it's like I told you on the phone, Frank." Detective Simmons stuck his hands in his pockets and jingled his keys. "We're asking some questions about Brad. Just making sure about things. If you want to do this later . . ."

"No. It's not going to be any better later." He glanced at me. "Should Anna go?"

The sharp glance the detective gave me was at odds with his awkward act from a moment before. "Actually, we've got a few questions for Miss Britton as well. So, if you wouldn't mind staying . . . ? This shouldn't take long." He pulled out a notebook and flipped through it.

While Frank cleared a stack of books and papers off the other leather armchair for Detective Simmons, I pulled a chair out from under the dining nook table and sat. Colonel Kitty immediately jumped up on my lap and rubbed against my shoulder.

"Okay, okay," I muttered, and scratched the cat's ears.

"You and cats," Kenisha came over and rubbed Kitty's back. But then her whole tone changed. "What have you been *doing*?" she breathed.

I swallowed and stared at her. Kenisha frowned back at me, scared and angry. This could not be about the tuna

casserole. She must have found out about my visit to Maitland and Associates, which meant the rest of the coven knew
about that too.

Before I could muster a reply, Kenisha took up a post at
Detective Simmons's shoulder. A shiver ran up my spine
and I hugged Colonel Kitty closer.

"So, Frank, I understand you and Brad had been arguing
lately?" Simmons was saying.

"That's right," said Frank.

"What about?"

"I rented Aunt Dot's house to Anna." He nodded toward
me. "Brad had been angling to get hold of the property, and
he was pretty upset about it."

Detective Simmons made a note. I watched Kenisha,
hoping for some kind of sign, but she was busy looking
around the apartment, at the books, at the map, at Frank, at
anything and everything except me.

That shiver was back, and it was spreading.

"From what I hear, the real estate market's been pretty
brisk lately," said Simmons. "You wouldn't think one house
would mean that much."

Frank shook his head. "Brad and Ellis have both been
after the house since Aunt Dot died. I've never been able to
figure out why."

"Huh." Pete flipped a few pages. "Now, Miss Britton,
according to Officer Freeman, you and Brad were seen arguing in Raja Rani recently. You want to tell me what that was
about?"

Of course the police would be interested in Brad's move-
ments over the past few days. How was I going to steer them
toward looking for the other person—the one who maybe
helped Brad and his car into the river—without implicating
Frank? I couldn't exactly tell Simmons about my Vibes and
visions.

I opened my mouth to answer, but Kenisha cut me off.

"Better tell him about the break-in, Anna."

"Break-in?" said Simmons.

I might not be picking up any Vibes, but I suddenly had a very bad feeling about this conversation.

It turned out Pete Simmons was an extremely patient man. He listened while I told the whole story about following Alistair into Dorothy's house, about looking around for the cat and finding both the cat and Brad Thompson. Simmons didn't interrupt, not once. He didn't even ask any questions until I'd finished.

"But Brad was gone before Frank got there?"

"Yes."

"What made you stop by that day in particular, Frank?"

Frank shrugged. "Nothing, really. It had been a while and I wanted to check on the place. There'd been a break-in before."

"Sure, sure, sure. I remember that." Pete made another note. "And Brad said he was looking for something?"

"It wasn't the first time he'd been in there, either." I told Simmons about our conversation/argument in Raja Rani. "He seemed to think the computer had been stolen because somebody else had been looking for these 'copies.'" I paused and looked at Kenisha again. She wasn't looking at me. She was staring out the window. "I think I know what the copies were of," I said slowly.

Pete arched his eyebrows. "Oh?"

I told them about how I'd gone down to Brad's office the morning he died and about what happened afterward. If, as I suspected, they already knew, it would be better for everybody if I just came clean, myself included. I also I told them about my little talk with Ellis Maitland. Detective Simmons remained entirely calm, taking notes with professional speed. Kenisha kept her gaze on the window and the chestnut tree outside.

"And this was all before you knew Brad was dead?" Pete asked. "You're sure?"

"Yes. I'm sure."

"What was it took you down there in the first place?"

Warning bells sounded in the back of my mind. This was going no place good. Especially since I could not tell Detective Simmons the truth; at least, not the whole truth.

"I was trying to figure out why Brad was so interested in the house that he tried to break in," I said. "Since he was only worried about copies, I thought he must know where the originals were. I thought if he had them, he might have decided to hide them in plain sight somewhere."

"In plain sight?" Detective Simmons flipped a page. "Under the name Dorothy Gale?"

Everybody was looking at me, Kenisha and Colonel Kitty included. "Yes."

"Where'd you get that name?"

"I guessed it," I said, but that sounded hollow even to me. "Dorothy Hawthorne was a fan of *The Wizard of Oz*."

"That's some guess." Simmons tapped his pencil against his page. "So, Miss Britton, after having a public argument with Brad Thompson, you go his office. You don't know him well, you don't know he's dead, but you're interested enough that you give a false name to get a hold of some documents that don't belong to you, and that you had not at that point told the police about. Then what?"

There are moments when you feel the world crack apart and reassemble around you. This was one of them. My vision spun and whatever I'd meant to say dried up in my throat.

"I was just looking for some kind of connection between Brad and Dorothy," I croaked finally. "That's all."

"What kind of connection?"

"I . . . I don't know. But I figured there must be something. Brad was so interested in the house."

"Sure, sure, sure," said Pete again. He was looking at Frank, at the map, at me. "The thing is, it's pretty common knowledge that Dorothy and the Maitlands did not get along.

I'd really hate to find out that feud was getting ugly." He got to his feet.

"What you mean, Pete," said Frank, "is you'd hate to find out I'd put Anna up to something."

He shrugged. "I think Miss Britton here is capable of getting up to all kinds of things on her own. Ellis also told us that her grandmother and Dorothy were still in touch, isn't that right, Miss Britton?"

Oh. No.

Oh, no, no, no.

"Well . . . I . . . yes, I did tell him that, I think."

Pete's smile was patient. "So it sure looks like this whole thing is moving along family lines, doesn't it?" Detective Simmons read over his last page one more time before putting the notebook into one pocket and the pencil into the other. He got up and strolled across to the map with its pushpins. "Working up an article about the real estate market, Frank?"

"Maybe," answered Frank carefully. "It's big news these days. Recovering local economy and so on."

"Well, good luck with that." He was looking around again. "I think I got everything I need. Miss Britton, I might want to talk to you about one or two more things. You'll be in town?"

"Um, yes." I had the sudden feeling I'd better be.

Detective Simmons fished out a card and handed it to me. "If you've got anything else you want to say, you can call me at this number. You too, Frank."

"So, you're treating Brad's death as suspicious?"

Detective Simmons smiled. It was a very engaging smile. Probably it put a lot of people at ease. "Now, you know the lieutenant would have my head if I said anything to a reporter."

"Off the record, Pete. Brad was a friend. I was out looking for him half the night."

"Yeah, Sean and Sean McNally said you looked pretty

upset too." I felt a lump form somewhere in the pit of my stomach. I should have been relieved. Because if Sean and his dad were speaking up for Frank, it meant he had an alibi, right? Right?

The detective was jingling his keys again. "Off the record, Frank, I think Brad knew something he couldn't live with anymore." He turned, but he turned the long way around, so his gaze swept across the entire apartment, me included.

Kenisha didn't look back as she followed him out the door. I could feel her worry and anger beating against my skin as Frank closed the door.

"I thought you said your grandmother hadn't talked to anybody in town for years," he said.

"She hasn't." I'd thought I was being so smart. How had I failed to see how this would look to the police? Because I hadn't thought about it. I'd never thought Ellis would actually tell the police about what had happened. But then, I hadn't known Brad was dead either. "I lied to Ellis when I was in his office to try to get him to talk. I didn't think he'd tell anybody about it."

"Uh-oh," said Frank.

"Yeah," I agreed. "Uh-oh."

❧ 39 ❧

❧ I DIDN'T DO much over the next few days. Nobody did. It was like Brad's death had drained all the initiative out of us. I rattled around Dorothy's house. I read her journals. I tried to work. I tried to pick out some furniture and rugs for the house, but I couldn't even focus on shopping on the Internet. I pulled what I recognized as weeds from the garden and dug grass up from between the flagstones. Alistair prowled the house with me and slept curled up on my pillow. Martine came over every day. So did Val. None of us saw Kenisha. Julia said she was focused on the case.

I wished I could focus on anything else.

I didn't go to the funeral. Maybe that was cowardly. What I told myself was that I was staying out of the way. Considering Colin's attitude about anybody associated with Dorothy, I didn't want to risk setting off a public argument. At least that was what I told myself. The truth is, I didn't want to risk running into Pete Simmons at the funeral and having to answer any more of his questions.

Yes, okay, I was hiding. I admit it. But hearing the official police version of my little attempt at amateur investigation had seriously shaken my confidence.

I did write Laurie a letter, and send flowers. I called Nadia to let her know what had happened. She was sympathetic. She said Laurie should call her when she was ready.

I also spent a lot of time at Frank's apartment going through Dorothy's personal records. Like he'd said, Frank had kept them, and after our disturbing interview with Pete Simmons, he was more than willing to bring the boxes out of storage and pile them in his already crowded living room.

"What is it you're really hoping for?" Frank asked as we cut through the packing tape on yet another cardboard box.

I still hadn't figured out how to tell Frank about Elizabeth's blackmail accusations, so I went with Plan B. "Online accounts."

"Sorry?"

I pulled out a stack of manila folders. I was truly beginning to hate that shade of beige. "I've been thinking about documents and copies." Thinking about them, talking about them, making myself a little crazy about them while wondering what Ellis Maitland was telling the police about them. Kenisha had pretty much stopped talking to me. "I thought, Who keeps paper around anymore?" Frank held up his handful of papers and eyed me. "I mean paper that isn't absolutely necessary," I said. "Maybe Dorothy made computer copies of whatever it was she got hold of with Brad and put them up in an online storage space. That way, it wouldn't matter who got hold of her computer or got into her house."

Frank nodded. "Not a bad idea. I mean, she did have a UrSpace account, but I've been in it, and there was nothing . . . serious. Photos, some music and videos, that kind of thing. Nothing worth . . ."

Killing over. Neither one of us said it, but I'm sure he thought it as quickly as I did.

* * *

DOROTHY, AS IT turned out, believed in keeping the regulation seven years' worth of receipts, bills and checks, which made an astounding amount of paper. Frank and I sorted and stacked and read, and reread and shuffled, working side by side, mostly in silence. Colonel Kitty helped by jumping in and out of the boxes and chasing papers across the floor. We all ate tuna noodle casserole until it was gone, and then we sent out for Chinese. I couldn't face an order of Indian food.

There were no signs of any sudden infusions of income, and no bank accounts or bills that Frank didn't recognize. Not even anything convenient like a receipt for a safe-deposit box or a wall safe. Julia came over once and helped us sort checks, scanning them for the name Dorothy Gale or any other alias. Val came over with sandwiches and helped sort phone bills, looking for calls to the Maitlands or the Thompsons.

At long last, we got to the bottom of the last box. Colonel Kitty jumped into it to make sure all was clear.

I sat back on my heels and looked up at Frank.

"Nothing here," he said bitterly.

"Nothing," I agreed. "What do we do now? We know there is still something that could incriminate the murderer out there."

"Unless that something was Brad," said Frank quietly. "In which case . . ."

"No," I snapped. "I don't accept that. There is something and we will find it."

Frank folded his arms and stared out at the chestnut tree. The leaves rustled in the summer breeze, filling the apartment with a sound like the ocean. "*If* there's something, it must be back at the house," he said. "It's been about that house from beginning to end."

I stared at the boxes, deep frustration burning in my

brain. In the time since Brad had died, I'd been over the house with a fine-toothed comb, and so had the rest of Dorothy's coven. Julia had turned the dachshunds loose in it, much to Alistair's annoyance, but they'd come up empty. Val and Didi had helped me go through the Books of Shadow yet again, and still nothing.

I was about to tell Frank all this, but in the depths of my purse, my phone rang. I pulled it out and checked the number. It was Martine.

"Martine!" I said as I walked over by the open window. Kitty followed and jumped up on the sill. "What's up?"

"Colin Thompson's come in to work."

"You're kidding."

"I know you're still trying to find out about Brad and Dorothy. So, if you come on over, I can maybe help you . . ."

"I'll be right there." I hung up and turned to Frank. "I've got to go."

"Anything I can help with?"

"Not yet. I'll call you later, okay?"

He did not like this, but he just sighed. "Okay. And thanks again."

I left him there, but it wasn't easy.

THE PALE ALE'S kitchen was in full swing when Martine walked me in. The restaurant shut down between three p.m. and five-thirty so they could switch over from lunch to dinner. Chefs hollered and chopped, line cooks hollered and sautéed, waitstaff came and went and hollered. The only people who weren't hollering were the dishwashers, and I wasn't sure about them, because I couldn't really hear them over the sounds of the spray and the clattering pans.

"Chef on deck!" hollered somebody.

"Thompson!" bellowed Martine.

"Yes, Chef!" Colin turned away from the soup pot he'd been stirring. I hadn't been able to tell him apart from the

other white-coated young men, despite the fact that he was
wearing a blue bandanna over his hair instead of the omni-
present baseball caps.

He saw me standing next to his boss, and he went white.
Then he went red. For a minute I thought he was going
to run.

"Alvarez, take over. Thompson, with me."

"Yes, Chef!" they both said. Colin fell into step behind
us. I could feel the resentment rising off him in waves as he
followed us into Martine's cramped office. She closed the
door and motioned us to chairs. I sat. Colin didn't. He just
folded his arms.

"Am I in trouble, Chef?"

"Not that I know of." Martine sat down behind a desk
piled high with folders, papers and multicolored invoices.
Here was the glamorous life of the executive chef in a nut-
shell. "However, it would be a favor to me if you would
answer some questions for Miss Britton."

No one can sneer like a teenage boy, and Colin turned
his up to eleven. "Oh, yes, Chef. I'd be delighted to help out
Miss Britton. Yahsureyoubetcha. It's not like I've spent the
past week talking nonstop to the police or anything." Now
he did drop into the chair, kicking out his ankles as far as
he could. Not that there was a lot of room. "Maybe she wants
to hear about the TV crews camped out on my mother's
lawn, or how we've had to unplug the phone because it won't
stop ringing because the media ghouls want to know what
drove my father . . ." His voice broke and he didn't finish
the sentence. "Maybe she wants to hear how I had to take
away my little sister's laptop so she wouldn't see all the crud
on HeyLook and Pointr, or how my mother hasn't stopped
crying for three days and how the insurance a . . . jerks are
saying they're not going to pay out on Dad's policy because
it might have been suicide and we're still inside some kind
of time window on the stupid crap policy and . . . !"

"I know it's a nightmare, Colin . . . ," I began.

"You don't know jack!" he shouted. Martine leaned forward.

"Tone it down, Thompson."

"Oh, yes, Chef. That I will, Chef."

I swallowed and tried again. "You said the other day, you thought Dorothy was responsible for your dad's problems."

"Oh, look!" drawled Colin. "Somebody else here to defend the sacred memory of Dorothy Hawthorne. What a surprise!"

"No. If she was . . . if there was something wrong, you might be the only person who knows, and I want to hear about it."

"Why? It's all too effing late. What could you do?"

"I don't know," I admitted. "And I won't know until I hear what you've got to say."

Colin's narrowed eyes shifted from me to Martine. He yanked off his bandanna and ran his hand through his long hair. He looked like what he was, a high school kid who already knew too much about adult life, but hadn't known until now how much worse it could get.

Then he lifted his head and the anger slid right back into place.

"You want to know what Dorothy was doing? She was effing hounding my dad. She was always calling him, at home, at work, everywhere. He kept going over to her house and sitting with her for hours."

"How do you know?"

"I saw them," he said. "Mom had found out Dad wasn't in the office a couple of nights when he said he was. I was worried. I thought maybe . . ." He shook his head. "Doesn't matter. I was worried and I followed him and I saw him go into her house. They were locked in there a couple hours before he finally came out and went home."

"Did you tell the police this?"

"Did you think about minding your own business?" he shot back.

"I wish I could," I said. "But your dad was involved in some kind of real estate fraud," I told him, and I hated myself for doing it. "So was Dorothy Hawthorne. And you knew it."

Colin climbed to his feet, both hands clenched in white-knuckled fists at his sides. "You watch your mouth, lady."

"Thompson," said Martine quietly. "Back it down. Your mom doesn't need any more trouble right now."

Colin dropped back into the chair and slumped backward. It was an attitude of total defeat.

"We don't know he was committing the fraud, Colin," said Martine. "He might have been trying to expose it."

Colin's head snapped around. *"What?"*

"It's possible," I agreed. "But if we're going to prove it, I need you to tell me about these meetings with Dorothy."

"I . . . I . . ." He was shaking; his face had gone dead white. "I don't know anything," he whispered.

"Colin . . . ," I began.

"I don't know anything!" he shouted, and dug both hands into his hair, like he was trying to literally hold himself together. "I only thought . . . I . . ." A tear ran down his cheek, ignored, and dripped off his jawline. "I'm outta here," he muttered and got to his feet.

"Colin . . . ," began Martine, but Colin had already slammed out the door and bellowed something into the chaos of the kitchen. I sat back in my chair. I watched my friend circle her desk and consider calling him back, but she stopped. Grim and silent, she returned to her crowded desk. There hadn't been a lot of times I'd seen Martine look diminished, but this was one of them.

"That could have gone better," she said.

"Do you think he was telling the truth?" I asked her. "He didn't know anything?"

"I think he's a smart kid who has been helping take care of his family for a long time now. He probably picked up on way more than anybody wanted him to, but not quite enough to figure out the truth."

"Laurie should talk to a lawyer about the insurance money," I said. "There must be something that can be done."

"Maybe." Martine tapped her pen on the edge of her desk and stared at her piles of papers and folders. I watched the calculations running back and forth behind her eyes. "I'll talk to Gravesend, see if we can work something out." I must have been looking at her funny. "What? Colin's one of mine. I do not leave my people out in the cold." I wasn't surprised. Martine might not have had kids of her own, but that didn't stop her from being one of the biggest mother hens out there. But there was something I had to say. Not that I wanted to.

"Martine, what if it turns out Brad Thompson's death really was a suicide? Or even just an accident while he was drunk? What if . . ." I stopped and started again. "Pete Simmons said he thought maybe Brad had found out something he couldn't live with anymore."

Martine picked up her phone. "Then, the family's really gonna need that lawyer." Her hand hovered over the buttons. "If there is anything, and I mean *anything*, you can do about this, Anna Britton, you do it fast."

I nodded and I got out of there, making a beeline through the kitchen. All I could think about was getting to my Jeep and getting home. Martine was right. I had to figure this out and figure it out fast.

Because what this little interview had done was raised another real, terrible, possibility. There was somebody, besides Frank, besides the Maitlands, who was visibly upset with both Dorothy and Brad; upset enough and protective enough to act in anger.

And who had all but told us he might have been in the vicinity the night Dorothy died.

Colin Thompson.

❧ 40 ❧

❧ EXACTLY HOW I would figure out the truth surrounding Dorothy's and Brad's deaths when all my sleuthing and magicking had failed so far was a mystery. It remained a mystery all the way out the door and across the parking lot, and during all the swearing and muttering while I dug down into the very bottom of my purse trying to find my keys.

When I finally looked up, it was to see a man's hand pressed against the Wrangler's door. Young Sean McNally had walked right up next to me and I hadn't even noticed.

"You," he said. "Are in no shape to be driving."

"Your bartender sense tingling?" I muttered.

He folded his arms and leaned one hip against the car door, all casual-like. "That, and I saw you walking across the dining room, but I don't think you saw me. Or the dining room."

"I wasn't drinking." He wasn't moving, I noticed.

"I didn't say you were, but you're scared and you're angry about whatever the heck it was you and Chef heard from Colin." He held out his hand. "And that's no way to be behind the wheel. So, I'm driving you home."

"No. Thanks. I'm fine. Really."

Somehow, this cogent argument entirely failed to convince him to step away from my car.

"You're not fine," he said. "There's been a death and it's close enough to you that you were interrogating the dead man's really unhappy kid with his boss. If you don't want me driving you, fine. Take a cab. Come back for the car tomorrow when you've had a chance to cool down."

I fixed my best glare on him. I'm not in Martine's league, but I do okay. "You better not be accusing me of being hysterical."

"I'm accusing you of being a feeling human being. Which is it going to be? Me or the taxi?"

"You won't make it back before you open for dinner and you'll get in trouble with Martine."

"For getting one of her best friends home okay? I don't think so."

He wasn't moving, and apparently neither was I until I gave in. "All right, all right," I muttered. "Can you drive a stick?"

Sean grinned. "Watch me."

I climbed into the passenger seat, folded my arms and in general attempted to silently signal my disagreement with his utterly unreasonable assessment of my mental state and driving capacity. Unfortunately, Sean turned out to be not only a first-rate bartender, but very good at ignoring grumpy people. He adjusted the seat, turned the key, smoothly shifted into reverse and eased the car onto Bow Street.

It was not a long drive. I spent most of it staring stubbornly out the window. Sean didn't seem to mind. I might not feel like admitting it, but he was a comfortable person to be around. He didn't push to know what Martine and I had been talking about, or how I liked Portsmouth or what I thought about Brad's death. After all those days of doing nothing but wonder and worry, it felt terrific to be with someone and just relax, even if it was only for about fifteen minutes.

Sean pulled into the driveway and shut the engine off.

"Thanks," I said as he handed me back the key. "For everything."

"Anytime," he answered. He also peered through the window at the cottage. "I'm glad somebody's living here," he said. "A house like this should be lived in."

"Did you know her?" I asked.

He laughed. "Everybody knew Dorothy. She was more Dad's friend than mine, but we both did some odd jobs for her sometimes, when Frank was busy or out of town. Or she knew Dad needed some extra. Bartending's not the steadiest job in the world." I smiled. That sounded like her. "So, he'd do roof repairs, tree trimming, things like that. I helped her set up her Wi-Fi and UrCloud accounts."

"Really?" I laid my hand on my purse, right over the wand. *Tell me more, Sean. Please. If you want to,* I added silently.

My fingers tingled. Sean wasn't looking at me. He was still looking up at the house.

"It was kind of weird, you know? Setting up high tech in the witch's cottage. Man, she loved to play the part." He chuckled. "You should have seen her at Halloween. She'd be out in the yard with a cauldron, broom, pointy hat, the whole thing. And man, that laugh and the whole 'I'll get you, my pretty, and your little dog too!'" He hooked his fingers and clawed the air. "It was great."

"Yeah, I'd heard about that, and . . ."

And I stopped. And I backtracked. "Accounts?" I said. "Sorry?"

I stared at Sean. "You said you helped Dorothy set up online accounts. Plural. Did she have more than one?"

"Yeah, she had a couple. She said she wanted an extra for privacy and emergencies." He frowned. "Made some joke about Frank's naked baby pictures . . ."

My heart was pounding. My thumbs were pricking. "What was the name? On the other account?"

Sean was frowning. "I'm not sure . . ."

But I was. "It was Dorothy Gale, wasn't it?"

"Yeah," he admitted slowly. "But don't ask me the password, because I don't . . ."

"I gotta go." I scrambled out of the Jeep while trying to dig in my purse for my keys. It was not graceful. "I . . . erm . . . you okay to get back?"

"No problem," he said easily. "Are you okay to stay here?"

"I'll let you know." Before he could ask any more questions, I sprinted into the house.

Alistair was already there, sitting on the desk next to my laptop. "Meow!" he announced, like he was saying *Finally!*

"Yeah, yeah, I know," I muttered as I flipped the lid open and opened up a new search. "I'm slow. But I'm here now." I paused for a second. "Should I get the others over here?" I asked the cat. He turned around three times and sat down with his tail around his paws. "Right," I said. "Time for that after we know if we've found anything."

I clicked keys and called up the UrCloud homepage. "Question," I said to Alistair. "How could Dorothy keep a secret online account off her credit card bills? Answer: She used a free service and a fake name." Alistair blinked and rubbed his face against the corner of the laptop. "It's easy to set up a secondary e-mail address," I told him. "You don't need ID. You just need a friendly tech-savvy bartender who'll play along and show you the basics."

I clicked on the user ID box and typed: *dorothygale*.

"Now. There's a password box." I pointed for Alistair's benefit. "You do not tell anyone your password, because you are security conscious. But you also know somebody might need to find it one day. So you hide it in your house, but you hide it in plain sight on your favorite piece of memorabilia from your favorite movie."

And I typed: *margarethamilton*.

And I hit Enter. Seconds ticked past. Then the screen flashed INVALID PASSWORD.

Alistair growled impatiently. I tried to keep breathing.

"Right, right. Because for a secure password, you need numbers or symbols."

I typed: *margarethamilton1939.*

Seconds crawled by. I gripped the edge of the desk until my fingers hurt. Alistair came over and head butted my shoulder. I ignored him.

"Come on," I said to the computer, and then in case it didn't get the hint, I added, "Come on, come *on*."

The computer beeped. The screen flickered. I felt my nails bend as I clutched the edge of the desk and leaned forward.

A list of file names scrolled up the screen, including one that read MA PROPERTY.

I clicked on that one.

Dorothy had been busy. Page after page of documents flickered past on the screen: mortgages, leases, purchase agreements.

The copies. We'd all been so sure they must be on paper, tucked away in the house somewhere. Why? Because Dorothy was an old woman. Because she still kept a checkbook and paper bills and wrote everything down in notebooks. So everybody, me included, had just assumed that these records would still be hard copies too. So we'd all focused on searching the house and ignored cyberspace.

She'd outfoxed us all. Again.

I clicked through the documents, scanning them as quickly as I could, until I found a page with a signature on it. There it was, cramped and pointy, and it read: *Elizabeth Maitland.*

"Ellis was telling the truth." I slumped backward. Elizabeth Maitland had been into some kind of shady real estate dealings.

"It doesn't make sense," I said out loud. "It's . . . it's undignified. It'd disgrace the family. It . . ." I stopped. "The family," I repeated.

Alistair jumped off the desk and shoved his face in my purse, nosing around. "What? Did I leave a sandwich in there?"

Alistair's meow was muffled. I thought about pulling him away. On second thought, I pulled my purse away instead and upended it on the desk. Alistair jumped up and, in the way of all cats, immediately sat on the one piece of paper.

Realization crept into my mind, slowly. I moved the cat onto my lap and picked up the paper. It was that letter inviting me to tea I'd received from Elizabeth Maitland. I hadn't even realized it was still in my purse.

"You're not serious," I said to Alistair.

"Meow," he answered me, and I knew what he was thinking, because I was thinking it too.

I held the paper up next to the screen and stared. I looked at the elaborate *E* on the invitation, and the much simpler one on the document on the screen.

"It's not the same," I told the cat. "Somebody's forged her signature." I stopped. "Ellis forged her signature."

Alistair jumped into my lap and rubbed his head against my shoulder.

"I should call Kenisha," I said as I automatically petted his back. "Right now. That's what I should do first."

But I couldn't help thinking about Elizabeth Maitland in her lovely, empty house on the hill. I thought about family ties and traditions that could tie a person up like iron chains. I thought about kindness, and I thought about what you send out into the world coming back in so many different ways. I thought about how despite everything, Julia, whom I liked and trusted, defended this woman from the accusations that came at her from all kinds of directions.

I dialed the phone and waited while it rang.

"Maitland residence," answered Marisol.

"Marisol, I need to speak with Mrs. Maitland. It's urgent."

"One moment, please."

I heard Marisol put the phone down. Alistair curled around

my ankles, trying to reassure me while I waited, yet again. It was a good try, but I was past being reassured. I stared out the window at the summer twilight. I didn't want to be right. I really didn't. I understood now why Frank and Julia had been so reluctant to go digging into this mystery. It was nothing at all like you saw on TV. It was just sad and a little scary.

"Hello?"

I swallowed my doubts. I had come too far. Like it or not, I had to finish this. "Mrs. Maitland? This is Annabelle Britton."

"Is there something I can do for you, Miss Britton?"

"Mrs. Maitland, I have some . . . difficult news."

"Which is?"

"Somebody's been trying to frame you, Mrs. Maitland."

She paused. I pressed my palm against the desk and forced myself to wait. "Frame me?" she repeated finally.

I nodded, even though I knew she couldn't see me. "For real estate fraud."

There was no answer except the sound of harsh breathing. When she spoke again, her voice was tight. "Are you certain?"

"Fairly certain."

"Was it Dorothy?"

I swallowed. Of course. She still had that letter, the one Ellis said he'd gotten from Laurie and that was supposed to have been written by Dorothy.

"I don't know. It . . ." How did I say this? I closed my eyes. There was no good way. "It might be Ellis."

"I see." The two words were stone-cold.

"I wanted you to know before . . . before I went to the police."

"To cushion the blow?" she said icily. "Well. Thank you for that, I suppose. I am assuming—and it may be a rather large assumption—that you have some proof of what you're saying. I'd like to see it."

"Sure. Can you meet me at the police station?"

"I cannot," she snapped. "You will come here."

"It really would be better . . ."

"Miss Britton, you clearly need my assistance with something. You would not be calling if you did not. You would already be talking to the police. I assure you, I will say nothing and do nothing until I have seen evidence of wrongdoing. So, unless you intend to accuse me of a crime you know I did not commit, you will come here, and you will present your evidence."

"And then what?"

"If someone is trying to tarnish my family name, you may be certain, Miss Britton, I will do everything in my power to make it stop. No matter who is responsible."

This I believed. "I can be there in twenty minutes."

"We will be expecting you." She paused again. "Anna? I . . . Please don't tell the others about this. You know who I mean. I . . . If it is as you say, it will all come out soon enough and I would like to preserve some measure of my pride until then."

"Okay, Mrs. Maitland," I said. "I won't say anything."

"Thank you. I'll make sure the gates are open."

I hung up and looked at Alistair. His right ear twitched.

"Darn right, I lied," I told him, and hit Kenisha's number.

❧ 41 ❧

🐾 THE GATES TO the Maitlands' house were standing wide-open when I got there. The summer shadows stretched across the lawn as I climbed out of the Jeep and trotted up to the front door and rang the bell.

I hitched up the strap on my purse while I waited. I had my backpack slung over my other shoulder. I considered backing away. But I was too late. The door opened.

It was Elizabeth Maitland.

"I sent Marisol home," she told me. "I didn't want her overhearing our next conversation."

That made sense, but it didn't make me feel any better as I followed her into the sitting room. The house's silence was so thick, I felt like I was wading through it.

"Mrs. Maitland," I said. "I'm very sorry about this. I know it must be . . ."

"Yes," she said. "Yes, thank you. Please, will you show me what you've found?"

I pulled my laptop out of my backpack and opened the file with the papers in it. "Dorothy had these in an online account," I said. "I compared the signature on them with the one on the note you sent me. They don't match."

Mrs. Maitland stared at the page for a long time. She leaned in and touched the screen, almost like she thought she could wipe away what she saw.

"Yes," she murmured. "Yes. Now, the question before us is whether this is Ellis's work, or Dorothy's."

Her calm was nothing short of astounding. I'd have been shouting and pacing. But then, I hadn't been raised in the house on the hill and trained since birth to be polite and perfect, no matter what the circumstances—even if I was trying to find out whether it was my son or my old friend who had betrayed me.

"I'm really . . ."

"Yes." Mrs. Maitland waved her hand. "You are sorry. You've said so. It is neither here nor there. My son has an office upstairs. I think if we go there, we will find what we need to clear this last question up fairly quickly." She stood, and I stood and followed her.

The main staircase was graceful, broad and curving. You could picture women in silken gowns sweeping down it, ready to climb into their waiting carriages for the harvest ball. Mrs. Maitland did not sweep. She climbed slowly, her back straight, her hand resting lightly on the railing. Even on her way to find out if her son had tried to frame her for murder, she was not going to sacrifice a single shred of dignity. There was a special kind of steel in that attitude, and I couldn't help admiring it.

Until I got to the top of the stair, and the Vibe hit.

Anger. Anger like a tidal wave. Like a wildfire. I staggered from the pain of it. From the fear of it, because there was fear, too, a tsunami's worth of panic.

"What is it, Anna?" asked Mrs. Maitland, but her voice seemed to be coming from a long, long way away. "Is something wrong?"

"Bad," I croaked. I was leaning against the wall. I

couldn't catch my breath. I couldn't focus my eyes. "Something bad happened here. Right here." *Sad, sick, sorry, angry, angry, angry.* My head was swimming. I was going to pass out. Hands. There were hands on my shoulders, pushing me . . . I was falling.

No. Not me. Somebody else. I tried to breathe. I couldn't breathe. I had no protection, no shelter, no friends to help.

"I thought so," Mrs. Maitland was saying. "Ellis. I am severely disappointed."

"When have you ever been anything else, Mother?"

I wheeled around and nearly toppled over. Strong hands caught me and held me steady, just like that other time, on the other staircase, where I'd felt Dorothy die.

Except that time I'd been held by a friend. Frank Hawthorne. But Frank wasn't here. This time, Ellis Maitland's tanned and perfect face swam in front of my vision.

"You better sit down, Anna," he said. "Here. Put your head between your knees." He pressed down on the back of my neck too hard, forcing me to double over. "Just breathe."

"I can't breathe . . . I can't . . ." He had doubled me over too sharply. I couldn't get enough air into my lungs. "I can't . . ."

He pressed down harder. "Yes, you can, and you just won't stop, will you? And that, Anna Britton, is your problem."

The world closed in around me and was gone.

I WOKE UP slowly and painfully. I was sprawled on my side on bare floorboards in a bare brick room. There was a skylight and some windows letting in just enough light for me to see. I pushed myself upright. My backpack was nowhere in sight, but my purse was on the floor beside me, half its contents scattered across the floor. I crawled over to it and in a fine display of priorities started scooping my stuff back in. It didn't take long to see that my phone was missing. The house keys were there, but my car keys weren't. Neither was the wand. Ellis might not be able to work magic, but he knew enough to take that away.

"Okay." I breathed deep. "Okay." Slowly, I pushed myself to my feet. I stayed steady. "Okay, that's something."

The windows were old and multipaned and not made to open. Wherever this was, it was right on the river. Instead of overlooking some conveniently busy sidewalk, I looked over the sparkling silver span of the Piscataqua.

I made myself turn around and get a better look at my surroundings. There was one door, splintered and old. I tried the handle, just for the heck of it. It was, of course, locked. I leaned my forehead against it. Now what? Break a window and shout for help? Somebody might hear.

"Merow?"

I looked down. Alistair was rubbing against my shins. "Merow?"

"Oh, my God. Alistair!" I swept him up in my arms and hugged him until he squirmed in protest. "I've never been so glad to see anybody in my life!"

Had I ever doubted the magic? I was done with that.

"Merow!" Alistair slid out of my arms and padded over to the door. "Mrp?" he inquired.

"It's locked. I can't get out. Can you open it?"

Alistair scrabbled at the wood for a minute and favored it with a particularly baleful cat glower, but nothing happened. He meowed again and circled around my ankles. I understood. I also bit my lip. This was beyond what my familiar could handle on his own. I had to do something. But what? Could I send Alistair to get Julia? The coven was all gathered in Midnight Reads, waiting to hear from me. I'd told Kenisha about the hidden account so she could use it if anything . . . went wrong.

She had not been happy. She'd wanted to come along. I'd thought it would be better if I went on my own, because if it turned out that Elizabeth wasn't involved, I wanted her to keep trusting me and to try to talk her into coming forward on her own. Kenisha agreed to my plan in the end, but it was a near thing.

But I hadn't counted on a kidnapping. It would take time for Alistair to get to the coven, and time for them to understand him, and more time for them to find me, even with Kenisha on the job. And . . . I swallowed hard. And there was no guarantee he'd get to them. It must have been Elizabeth who kept Alistair from finding Julia and the others the night Dorothy died. She had interfered to protect her son and her family name that night, just like she'd done when I went to the house tonight.

"Merow!" Alistair batted at my purse. "Meow!"

"The phone's not there," I told him. "Neither's the wand." I pressed my hand against my stomach and swallowed hard, suddenly more than a little bit seasick.

I rattled the doorknob again. When it didn't move, I squatted down until I was eye level with it. It was a match for the building, old and plain. It felt loose, but I knew nothing about picking this kind of lock. But maybe I could jigger the latch. Or . . . I glanced at the edge. The hinges were on my side. Maybe I could unscrew them somehow?

I wished my dad were here, or one of my brothers. They always had a Swiss Army knife or a multitool with them. Suddenly my nail file seemed a little pathetic.

"What's the point of being a witch if you can't blast a door down?" I muttered as I pulled the file out. "Or turn Ellis Maitland into a frog? He'd make a great frog. Or maybe a toad. Definite toad potential there. Julia said no toads, but maybe she just wasn't trying hard enough . . . Yeah, keep talking, Anna. That'll make it all better."

"Merow!" Alistair bounded around in a circle.

"What? You pick now to chase your tail?" Hysteria was bubbling way too close to the surface.

Alistair wasn't listening. He just turned in another circle. And another.

A circle. He was drawing a circle. He was reminding me I

was a witch. A baby witch, but a witch all the same. Maybe I couldn't blast the door down or turn anything into a toad, but I had magic. A plan formed, strange and slow, stacked together from ideas my brain was not used to considering possible.

I needed to cast a circle.

I upended my purse again, spilling the contents across the warped floorboards. I grabbed the pen and scratched a circle to stand in.

"Okay. Directions. Right, Alistair? I need directions. Where's south?"

"Merow." Alistair plumped down so his back was to the window.

Okay. I guess that was south. Which meant left was east and right was west, and the door faced north.

"Okay. Directions. Check. Now, elements. Right?"

"Merow," agreed Alistair.

I needed metal to represent earth. That was easy. I laid down my ring of house keys. What did I have for water? I picked up the miniature bottle of mouthwash I carried in case of garlic. It was at least liquid, and kind of blue. Fire next. There was an LED light in my key chain. I separated it from the key ring and put it on south. What about air? I grabbed the pen again and sketched a cloud with a set of puffed cheeks like a cartoon wind on the floor.

Hey, it said "air" to me, and I had limited options here.

I stood in the center of the circle, clutching my nail file instead of the wand, and tried not to feel stupid. I tried to focus. I dug deep. I began to breathe, slowly, in and out. Alistair rubbed against my shins, his purr rumbling steadily. My thoughts started to settle. I reached, down to my center, down to where my Vibe waited, down to where the magic waited.

"In need, I call," I whispered. "In hope, I ask. An' it harm none. An' it harm none. So mote it be."

I made myself picture an open door, as if I was getting ready to draw it in the air. In fact, that wasn't a bad idea. I lifted the nail file, and I moved my hand, sketching the lines, adding the shading. I tried to get my hand to feel not just the sketch, but the door itself. I imagined the knob turning, the click of the latch, the slow creak of the hinges as it swung open. I spoke my disjointed spell again. I made myself remember the other latches I'd jiggered with my nail file, at home, in college. Here, in Portsmouth.

I pictured the attic door in Dorothy's house, my house. I remembered how it felt when it swung open at my touch.

Open.

Open sesame.

Open all night.

Open 24/7.

Open.

"In need, I call. In hope, I ask. An' it harm none. So mote it be."

I felt myself moving. It was distant, strange. I'm not even sure I opened my eyes, but I knew exactly what I was doing. One hand held the doorknob. One hand slipped the nail file into the big old-fashioned keyhole. It wriggled, scraped and twisted.

Click.

I felt the knob turning.

"Meow!"

My eyes snapped open and all my breath left me in a rush. My knees shook, but I turned the knob and pulled, and the door swung back.

Ellis Maitland was waiting on the other side.

❧ 42 ❧

❧ ALISTAIR VANISHED. I felt him go. I was alone.

"Oh, good try, Anna," said Ellis. "You've really gone native, haven't you?"

I stumbled backward. I felt something snap against my back as I crossed the circle outline. Ellis stalked forward and scuffed at that same outline.

"Let me go, Ellis."

"Seriously?" He laughed. He actually laughed. "That's the best you can do? Well, we're all making this up as we go, I guess. Get your purse."

I didn't move. "You're not letting me go, are you?"

He sighed. "Oh, I'd like to. I really, really would. Maybe I'd do it, too, if there was some way I could believe you'd see sense. But then, I'd never know when you'd change your mind and go blabbing to your friend Officer Freeman. I can't risk it." He waved his hands helplessly. No. Not hands; hand. He kept one hand in his jacket pocket. I swallowed hard. I'd never seen a gun bulge in real life before, but I had the nasty suspicion I was seeing one now.

"You don't want to do this either," I said, surprised at how little my voice shook. I couldn't tear my eyes away from his pocket. "This isn't you. I know it isn't."

"So, you're saying no matter how far I've gone down the wrong road, I can still turn back? I've *killed* two people! I've got nowhere to turn back to!" The hand in the pocket twitched. "Get. Your. Purse. And get that junk into it. All of it."

I got my purse. I gathered up the stuff left from my broken working, taking my time. My hands shook. Where was Alistair? Had he gone to get the others? He must have. Should I call him back? I wasn't sure I could concentrate enough for that with Ellis pointing his gun at me. I considered trying to charge him with my nail file. If I couldn't hurt him, I could startle him enough to get through the door. I considered making a running jump for the window and screaming for all I was worth. Maybe breaking the window.

And then what? Try defying gravity? I didn't even have a broomstick. An involuntary giggle escaped me.

"Hurry up!" snapped Ellis. "I don't want your body found here, but if that's what has to happen, I can live with it."

He pulled the gun out. It was silver and sleek. Kenisha would have been able to tell me what kind it was. All I knew was it was the kind with a barrel leveled at my belly and a desperate man on the wrong end.

"Okay." I swallowed. I also slung my purse strap over my shoulder. "Okay. I'm done."

"Your Jeep's downstairs. You're going to drive us back to Dorothy's house."

I am? But I didn't argue. I just concentrated on keeping both my hands where Ellis could see them.

Ellis held the door open so I could walk in front of him down the creaking stairs and out into the driveway. Every nerve in my body buzzed with fear and adrenaline.

It was dark and the sodium lights turned the little gravel parking lot a sickly yellow. Ellis waited while I climbed into the driver's seat and buckled my seat belt. He climbed into the passenger seat. He didn't buckle up but he did hand me my keys.

"Drive," he said.

I drove. It must have been really late. We had the streets to ourselves. There was no other car I could signal to for help, not even when we had to stop for the red light on Route 1.

I gripped the steering wheel. Where was Alistair? Had he gotten to Julia yet? Had he been able to make her understand?

I had to buy him time. I had to think of something.

"You've been careful, Ellis," I made myself say as I shifted gears. "Dorothy and Brad could have died by accident. How are you going to explain m . . ." I couldn't say it. "This one?"

I don't think I've ever seen anything as awful as Ellis Maitland's smile at that moment. "I don't have to explain it. The good cops of Portsmouth, they'll do that, headed up by your friend Kenisha. They'll find fraudulent documents with my dear mother's signature all over them and they'll know exactly who's to blame for three tragic deaths." He leaned closer. "And I will finally be free!"

"She knows what you're doing."

"Oh, she knows, and she's not going to do a damn thing about it. See, this is her mistake." He laughed again. "This was always her mistake. She assumes I care about the family name. She doesn't want a scandal, and she thinks I don't either."

"But your reputation . . ."

"Oh, who gives a crap! I've got enough money now to start over anywhere I want."

"So why . . ."

"Why bother framing my mother?"

"Well . . . yes." We were almost home. Two more turns and we'd be there. There weren't even any more traffic lights, just stop signs.

"Because I want to see the look in her eye when they haul

her away," he said softly. "I want her to know that no matter what she tried to keep from me—my father, her magic—she never controlled me. I want to watch when the whole world she built so carefully comes crashing down, and for her to know it was me that finally beat her."

I pulled into the driveway. I turned the keys. I couldn't speak. What was it like to hate your family so badly? But I knew the answer. It was like insanity.

"Don't do this, Ellis. It'll come back on you. Dorothy's death came back on you, and you had to kill Brad. Who are you going to have to kill after me?"

"Probably that damn cat." Ellis laughed, a nasty hiccoughing giggle as he motioned for me to get out of the Jeep. "Probably should have started with him anyway."

I clenched my fists. *Keep calm,* I ordered myself. *You have to keep calm. Everything depends on it.*

Oh, Alistair, please hurry up.

I walked up the path. I could feel Ellis's breath on the back of my neck.

"Open the door and leave it open," he ordered.

"Okay. You're the boss." I turned the knob. It was unlocked. Had I left it open? I couldn't remember.

"Front room," said Ellis. "Go."

I went. And I all but screamed.

My living room was trashed. Everything was turned over; all the drawers were pulled out and tossed on the floor. One of the candlesticks was gone.

"What . . ." My hands and jaw dropped.

"You discovered a break-in," he said. "Surprised the perpetrator. The place has been ransacked before, hasn't it? They must have come back. So sad."

"This is what you did with Dorothy, isn't it? You killed her at your mother's house and you brought her here to be found?"

"She'd come over to try to convince me to turn myself in." He clicked his tongue at such naïveté. "For my mother's

sake. She actually said that! I pushed her, and she did fall.
I thought she was dead. I never would have moved her if I'd
thought she'd been alive, or . . . or it would have been somewhere different, something. I don't know. But I thought she
was dead. It couldn't be at the house. So, I brought her here.
I put her at the top of the stairs." He glanced sideways. "I'd
already pushed her down one flight. One more wasn't such
a big deal."

Which was why the police hadn't thought Dorothy's
death was murder. She'd been alive when she fell down her
basement stairs. Of course it looked like an accident.

"What about Brad? What did Brad do?"

"He listened to her." Ellis's hand was shaking. It was
almost too much for him. Almost, but not quite. I stood in
the dark ruin of my living room and faced the man with the
gun. I had to keep him talking. It was the only the hope I
had. "Like some kind of sad little mama's boy. He listened
to an old lady blathering on about honesty. In real estate!"
Ellis barked out another harsh laugh. "It's not like we were
hurting anybody! The only ones shelling out were the banks!
After all the money they stole during the boom, you'd think
I'd get a freakin' medal for getting some of it back!" His
gun wobbled again. My heart was going to explode. *Be calm,
be calm, be calm,* I told myself. *Just keep him talking. Help's
on the way. Believe it.*

"It was fraud."

"It was nothing! Stupid fed regulations. Can't buy this
property with that loan, can't buy that property with this
kind of name or that kind of credit. *Who the hell cares!*" he
screamed.

"So that's why you were using your mother's name?" I
asked him. "Because the purchasing regulations are different for individuals than they are for corporations? But she
refused to play along, so you forged her name?"

"Who was being hurt? Huh? The feds? The banks? You
tell me! *Who was I hurting?*"

Yourself. I felt a moment's pity and worked very hard to keep it off my face.

There was a gleam in the darkness. A blue spark. My eyes jerked sideways. Alistair, a faint round blur in the dark, hunched on the window seat.

"Was Brad was helping you?"

"I thought he was. After all the trouble he'd been through, you'd think he'd have been grateful, but oh, noooo . . . Along comes saintly Dorothy Hawthorne and he discovers he's got some kind of conscience left."

And there it was. The last piece. "Dorothy convinced Brad to help turn you in. He'd been passing her evidence. But when she died, he lost his nerve."

Ellis snickered. "He figured it out. Too late. See, he really had been helping me. He'd been selecting the properties, preparing the documents for deals he knew were fakes." He grinned. "I had at least as much on him as he had on me, and if it all came out, he was going to jail too. Then who would take care of his poor widdle family?"

Alistair flowed down off the seat, as silent as the shadows around him.

"And that's why he didn't just tell Frank," I said. "He was afraid Frank wouldn't believe he'd been helping Dorothy in the end, or that he'd just publish the whole thing as a scoop for the paper and Brad's name would be dragged through the mud."

Alistair slid forward, climbing carefully onto the over-turned chair.

"And Anna Britton gets a gold star on her forehead! You know, I really didn't want to have to kill you." His regret was genuine, and I felt very, very sick. "I was sure you were going to accuse Mother and hand over the evidence and I could be all shocked." His eyes went wide. "Oh, Mother, what have you done? Don't worry, Mother. We'll get you the best lawyer there is. Don't say anything else, Mother." He grinned again. "Whaddaya think? Oscar-worthy?"

Alistair perched on the chair. His eyes glittered silver and blue as he watched Ellis Maitland like he was a very big, very bad kind of bird.

I put my hands up. "This can end now, Ellis," I said. I meant it. I willed it. "Just put the gun down and . . ."

"Sorry." He raised the barrel and pointed it at me.

Alistair jumped. With a howl fit to wake the dead, he launched himself right at the back of Ellis Maitland's skull.

Ellis screamed, a sound I hope I never hear again.

I ducked low and ran for the front door. Next thing I knew I was grabbed and shoved out onto the porch into the arms of a couple of burly strangers in police uniforms who dragged me stumbling across the lawn.

"Police!" shouted Kenisha from inside the house. "Police! Ellis Maitland, drop your weapon! Now!"

Arms enfolded me. A big sphere pressed hard against my belly, and it took me a minute to realize I was being hugged by Valerie. And Julia. And barked at by the dachshunds. I buried my face in Valerie's shoulder, and I waited for the bang. There had to be a bang. A big one. Somebody was going to die. There had to be a bang. I clenched myself tight to hear it. It didn't come. Instead, it was Kenisha yelling again.

"Clear!"

I crumpled to my knees, and for the second time that day, the world went away.

❧ 43 ❧

🐾 IN THE END, Ellis Maitland was charged with the murders of Dorothy Hawthorne and Bradley Thompson. There were also charges of forgery, document fraud, mail fraud, and several different kinds of real estate fraud and intent to defraud yet more people and organizations fraudulently, or something like that. There was also assault, and kidnapping with intent.

Throughout the investigation and the trial, Elizabeth Maitland stuck to her story that she knew nothing about anything. I told Detective Simmons that she was there when Ellis kidnapped me. But she said Ellis had knocked her out after I fainted and she didn't wake up until after it was all over.

It might have been true, but I doubted it. It did get another assault charge added to Ellis's list.

I had to do a certain amount of editing when it came to my testimony, but Pete Simmons was more than ready to believe that the reason some of the details of the evening remained a little fuzzy was stress. The prosecuting attorney coached me expertly through the rough patches.

Subscriptions to the *Seacoast Times*, which carried the full story of Ellis's criminal doings and his trial, soared. I wished it had been for a happier reason and told Frank so. He agreed. He also banked the money and started paying down the paper's debts.

Alistair, as befitting his status as a noble hero, ate tuna for a week. I think we both regretted that decision, but not too much.

Didi, Shannon and Trisha, backed up by Julia, declared they would take turns sleeping on my couch until after the trial so I wouldn't be alone at night. Just in case. I didn't complain, too much.

Val and Roger brought breakfast over every morning. Martine insisted I show up at the Pale Ale for dinner every night so she'd know I was okay. I didn't complain at all.

Laurie Thompson sent four paintings to Nadia, and all of them sold. Colin worked out a deal with his high school so he could go part-time and take online classes part-time, which would let him keep working through the school year to help his mom make ends meet. He also apologized for yelling at me. I told him not to worry about it. It had been a very bad time for everybody.

Which really left only one major question.

"Why didn't you tell me it was Elizabeth's familiar who was following me when I first got to town?"

I was sitting in the kitchen with Julia and Val. Alistair was curled up on the windowsill, absorbing sun and purring like a motorboat. The dachshunds were doing the same, only in a sunbeam on the floor, and they were snoring rather than purring.

Julia sighed and looked into her cup. I had dried some mint from the garden and used it to make tea. The results were not bad, for a beginner. "I didn't tell you because, despite everything, Elizabeth was my friend," Julia said. "And even if she hadn't been, I didn't want to be the one to accuse a fellow practitioner in public, not while there was any chance at all she was innocent. Or that she might see reason."

I nodded, and so did Val, only a little reluctantly.

"And I didn't want to scare you," she added softly.

"Scare me? With murder and magic going on around me, you thought the bird was going to scare me?"

Julia smiled, just a little. "It was the family quarrels that made your grandmother leave town. I didn't want to reignite them." She paused. "I do still miss her, you know."

"Yeah, and I think she misses you, and Portsmouth."

"What about you?" asked Val. "Now that you're back and you've seen . . . all that you have seen. What do you think of us?"

"I think I don't know," I said honestly. "I'm going to need some time."

"Of course," said Julia. "Well, if you do decide to stay and continue your practice, I for one will be more than happy to welcome you into our coven." She held out her hand. "Thank you, Anna Britton, for all you have done."

I shook her hand and tried to think of something to say that wouldn't sound too awkward. Thankfully, I was saved by the bell, or at least the knock. Martine stood at the back door with a ceramic dish covered in aluminum foil in both hands.

"That smells great. What is it?" I said as I opened the door.

"Monday night casserole." She set it down on the table and peeled back the foil to reveal a steaming dish of au gratin potatoes and ham. "I figured since things have calmed down, we could finally get around to doing the neighbor and housewarming thing."

"How do you know I'm staying?" I opened the cabinets and brought out a couple of dishes. "I don't even know if I'm staying."

Martine looked at Val and shook her head. "Get used to it. She's a little slow like this."

"Hey!" I snapped. Alistair opened one lazy blue eye and huffed.

"I know you're staying," said Martine, "because this time things are different. Finally," she added.

I laughed. Two murders and a magical heritage waiting for me, not to mention a house and . . . Alistair.

"Maybe they're too different." I handed Martine a serving spoon so she could dish out layers of cheesy potato goodness. I inhaled the scent of too much Gruyère and just enough pepper. "Maybe I want normal."

"Have you ever wanted normal?" asked Val. "That's not what I've heard."

I frowned. Clearly, Val and Martine had been gossiping way too much. My glower, however, had no visible effect.

"Maybe I've always wanted normal," I mumbled around my mouthful. "Maybe I've just been lousy at finding it."

"You keep talking." Martine pointed her fork at me. "But all I hear is blah, blah, blah."

"Maybe it gets boring after this. Maybe I've used up all the mystery at once."

"You honestly think there's any chance of that?" She sliced open a layer of potatoes with the side of her fork and pushed them apart, critically examining cheese, onion and ham.

"Maybe you should join the coven, Martine," said Julia. "You seem to be very comfortable around magic and mystery."

"Not me." Martine waved her fork. "My grandmother did a divining for me back when I was a teenager. Said I should save my energies for other things. Always listen to your grandma."

"Thus endeth the lesson?"

"Not a chance, Anna Britton." Martine shook her head. "Your lessons are just getting started."

Alistair opened the other eye. "Meow," he agreed.

And who was I to argue with that kind of logic?

About the Author

Born in California and raised in Michigan, **Delia James** writes her tales of magic, cats and mystery from her hundred-year-old bungalow home in Ann Arbor. When not writing, she hikes, swims, gardens, cooks, reads and raises her rapidly growing son.

Ready to find
your next great read?

Let us help.

Visit prh.com/nextread